ANGEL IN BLUE JEANS

RICHARD L. COLES

PROMONTORY PRESS

Angel In Blue Jeans
Copyright ©2016 by Richard L. Coles

All rights reserved. No part of this book may be used or reproduced in any manner without prior written permission.

This is a work of fiction. The characters, incidents and dialogue are drawn from the author's imagination and are not to be construed as real. Any resemblance to actual events or persons, living or dead, is entirely coincidental.

Promontory Press
www.promontorypress.com

ISBN: 978-1-987857-47-4

Cover Design and Typeset by Edge of Water Designs, edgeofwater.com

Printed in Canada
987654321

DEDICATION

In memory of Ronald Coles, my Father,

who taught me to observe the world—the universe—around me.

ANGEL IN BLUE JEANS

ACKNOWLEDGEMENTS

Stories grow—characters grow—as one becomes more familiar with them; and they grow, too, as they are shared with others. I sincerely thank those who met this story and its characters in the early stages: thank you to Margaret Ann, to Aidan, to Kate, and to Ben, for your ideas and your comments. Especially, I thank Mary Rosenblum for her insightful critique and recommendations, which have greatly improved the flow and strength of the story and its characters.

I am extremely grateful to Bennett Coles, to Amy O'Hara, to Lauren Olson, to Stephanie Puckett, and to Louise Sundberg, all of Promontory Press, for their professionalism, help, and advice in the preparation and publication of the book. Thanks also go to Marla Thompson of Edge of Water Design for her artistic contribution.

I thank my wife Ann for her love and encouragement; for her patience over a very long time as I sat, maybe in my office, maybe on the other side of the room from her, pecking away with random fingers at a keyboard, endeavouring to tell the story of people I knew only in my mind.

ANGEL IN BLUE JEANS

PART 1

PART 2

ENVOI

PART 1

- 1 -

Dana clutched tightly at Tony's arm, her left foot slipping on the ice covering the ground, as they picked their way toward Brewster Gardens in the darkness along Millerby Lane from the bus stop on Otterbrook Road. The freezing rain had begun several hours ago throughout the Ottawa region; it was unusually early for Eastern Ontario, only mid-November. The roads were already treacherous.

I'm so glad, Dana thought, *that I convinced Tony to leave his car at home.* They had taken the bus downtown to the movie. She was still comfortable with using buses, but Tony had become accustomed to the so-called comforts of the car, his beloved old Malibu. Now he, too, agreed it had been the wise thing to do.

They had been an item for about two months now; Dana Munro, at sixteen, and Tony Ferruccio, at seventeen, had lived opposite one another since early childhood, but had only now become a couple.

As they turned into Brewster Gardens, a police car eased round the corner, slipping slightly on the ice. Gingerly, it rolled up the crescent. Dana saw the bright stoplights come on, glaring reflections in the ice coating everything.

"Hey, that's at my house. Come on." Tony lunged forward.

Dana followed, treading unsteadily on the ice, her lighter boots not having the grip that Tony's had.

A large policeman eased out of the car, adjusted his cap, and walked round onto the Ferruccio driveway. A policewoman appeared out of the other door and joined him.

By the time Dana and Tony reached the bottom of the driveway, Dana could see the officers entering the house.

"What the … Jeez, where's the Malibu?" Tony gasped.

Dana's heart skipped a beat. The driveway was slippery, but they were quickly at the door, Dana's pulse pounding. Inside, they caught up with the police, who were being shown into the living room.

The policeman spoke, looking at Mrs Ferruccio, Tony's mother, Carmella.

"We're very sorry to disturb you at this time, but we have a serious situation that may involve you." He looked around, and saw Dana and Tony coming in behind him. "I'm Constable Klein, and this is Constable Hunter," he continued, indicating his partner.

Carmella looked at her husband nervously.

"Please—sit down." Pino Ferruccio indicated two chairs. "This is my wife, and this is my oldest boy and his girlfriend."

Dana smiled nervously, sensing trouble.

"Is there anyone else at home?" asked Constable Hunter.

"My two girls are downstairs—should they come?"

"How old are they?" the policewoman asked.

"Sixteen and eleven."

"Perhaps the older one should stay there with the young one for the moment."

Dana hugged Tony more closely; she wondered what was coming.

Constable Klein leaned forward, looking at Pino Ferruccio. "Sir, do you own a blue Malibu?"

"Yes sir, I do, but it's Tony here who drives. It's in my name, but he pays for insurance."

"I see," said Klein. "Did you use it today?" He looked over at Tony, still standing.

"Sir, I drove it to school and back. That was about four o'clock. I haven't used it since. But I left it in the driveway. It's gone."

Dana snuck her arm around his and pulled closer.

Tony continued, "We just came back. We were coming down the road when you drove by."

"Yes, I noticed you. I have some disturbing information to relay," Klein continued. "Your car has been found, overturned, off the road, near Careby Corners."

Carmella gave a little cry, and Dana tensed again.

"Do you know where the keys are?" Klein asked Tony.

"Yes sir." Tony put his hand into his pocket and produced a bundle of keys, separating out two.

"Good," said Klein. "Is there a spare anywhere?"

"No, sir, I've been meaning to get one made."

"I see." Klein paused and looked over to the policewoman.

Constable Hunter spoke. "We have some rather more serious business to raise. Perhaps the young people would care to leave us?" She looked straight at Dana.

Why me? thought Dana.

"If it concerns the car, I would rather stay," said Tony firmly.

"I want to stay with Tony." Dana squeezed his hand, and gave the policewoman an *'I'm strong and in control'* look. The policewoman nodded.

"Very well," said Klein. "Please sit down, though."

Dana sat close to Tony on the couch. She was, however, really worried now.

Klein continued. "The car was badly damaged, and the two

occupants had been thrown from the car." He paused. "Neither survived the accident."

The silence was intense; it was cutting. Pino cleared his throat. Klein fingered his lapel. "Neither person carried any identification. They were both teenage boys."

Carmella gasped. Pino moved to her, placing his arm around her shoulders.

Dana shivered; she could feel her heart pounding as she moved closer in to Tony.

"One of the youths was wearing a jacket with a large six-zero on the back—"

Dana screamed, "That's Bryce!" She turned into Tony, clutching at him as tears welled in her eyes. She felt his firm hold, and sensed that the policewoman had moved to comfort her on the other side.

Dana could hear Carmella shrieking hysterically. "Poppa, where's Vincent? Where's Angelo? What have they done? Poppa, find them!"

Dana pulled away from Tony and looked up.

Pino's face had become ashen white. "Wh-what was the other boy wearing?" he asked.

Klein, the policeman, looked at Pino and said quietly, "He was wearing a purple and blue jack—"

A piercing wail came from Carmella. "My Vince, my poor baby." Her wail turned to sobbing as she threw herself to the floor, pounding the carpet. Pino, tears streaming down his face, knelt down beside her, trying to console her.

Dana looked up at Tony; he was too shocked to move, his arm still holding Dana as she struggled to find a tissue. She could feel his heart pounding as she leaned against him, the magnitude of what had happened freezing all tears now, all emotion.

Dana watched as the constables looked at each other and grimaced; Klein nodded that Hunter should help Carmella. He moved over toward Tony, and laid his large hand on Tony's shoulder.

Tony looked up at him.

Klein whispered, "I'm sorry."

Tony nodded as Dana reached up to kiss his cheek. She squeezed his hand.

Klein knelt down at Tony's side. He whispered again, looking at Dana. "Bryce your brother?"

Dana nodded.

"I'm sorry. Where do you live?"

"Across the street."

"And your name, please?"

"Dana Munro."

Klein patted them both on the shoulders again and stood up. He motioned to Hunter to join him at the far side of the room.

Dana had dried her eyes, and now turned to embrace Tony. She felt cold and empty. *My poor mother,* she thought. *She'll be devastated.*

Constable Jane Hunter stepped out onto the icy driveway. She enjoyed police work most of the time, but tonight was not one of the enjoyable times. She'd been on the force five years now, and had come across most types of incidents. She'd even been shot at last year. But conveying bad news like this was not easy, not easy at all.

She gingerly crossed the slippery road and walked up to the door, pressing the brightly lit bell-push. Sounds of latches sliding came through the screen door. The inner door opened slightly, then more fully as a light went on and the man saw her uniform.

She opened the screen door. "Mr Munro?"

"Aye?"

"Constable Jane Hunter. May I come in, please?"

Bob Munro hesitatingly indicated that she should enter, and closed the door after her.

"I'm sorry to trouble you at this time, but I have some important

7

information. Is your wife at home?"

Bob Munro nodded. "Please," he said, indicating the entrance to the living room.

Jane stood at the doorway. It was quite a large room. A fireplace with a glowing gas fire and flanking bookcases occupied the far wall. The television in the corner was on, the sound down low.

Across the centre of the room was a couch, facing the fire, its back to Jane. A woman's head projected above the couch back.

In the corner to the right was a table with a lamp. A young man was sitting at the table, reading a magazine. He looked up as Jane entered.

"This is ma elder son, Iain. Cal, we have a visitor."

Caroline Munro turned and stood up.

"This is ma wife, Caroline." Jane sensed a Scottish brogue.

"Sorry to disturb you all. I'm Constable Jane Hunter. I'm sorry to say I have some serious news to bring to you. Is there anyone else at home?"

"No?" said Caroline, with a questioning look. "Our other two kids are out with their friends. They should be home soon, though. Do sit down, please."

As she moved to a chair, Jane noticed that heavy drapes covered what she presumed was the window facing the street side. *I guess they're not aware of our car arriving across the street*, she thought.

She looked at the three of them, waiting expectantly. She shuddered inwardly, and felt cold in spite of the warmth of the room. "I have to tell you that we have reason to believe that your son has been involved in a serious car accident." She paused. "He did not survive."

The words were ice. Everything froze. The silence was eternity. No one moved. Nothing. Then, as if in slow motion, Caroline stood up, her hands clutching her head.

"No—no—no, it can't be, it can't. Are you sure? Where? Who

was he with? Oh, Bob ..." Bob caught her as she fell into his arms.

Iain sat, deathly pale, staring into Jane's eyes. She moved to him, placing her hand on his shoulder. "I'm sorry, I really am."

Caroline was sobbing in Bob's arms. Bob was valiantly trying to suppress tears, as Jane moved to comfort them both.

In a breaking voice, he asked, "D'ye know what happened?"

"Not in detail. The car overturned on failing to negotiate a bend, probably on ice. Both occupants were thrown out of the vehicle, but did not survive."

"D'ye ken who the ither person was?" The tension was strengthening his Scottish accent.

"Yes, we believe we do," said Jane quietly.

She let the three of them absorb some of the shock. Iain came round to place his arm on his mother's shoulder. Caroline responded and pulled him in tighter.

Suddenly, Caroline straightened herself up and sniffed heavily. "I need a tissue."

Jane looked around. There was a box on the end-table. She reached for it and passed it to Caroline.

"Thanks." Caroline raised her head. "I'm sorry."

Jane smiled at her. "I'm sorry to have to bring such news."

Caroline glanced at the clock on the bookshelves. "Dana will be home any minute. She'll be devastated."

Jane adjusted her position. "Mrs Munro, Dana already knows."

Caroline gasped, and Bob drew back in surprise. "How?"

"The other person in the car was, we understand, Vincent Ferruccio."

"Oh no! Oh dear, not that poor family too." Caroline was in tears again.

"But who was driving, whose car was it?"

"The car, a blue Malibu, belongs to Mr Ferruccio, but is usually driven, we've been told, by his son Tony."

"Oh," gasped Caroline, tensing again. "But where are Tony and Dana? Are they all right?"

"Yes," continued Jane, reassuringly, "yes, they are safe across the street with the Ferruccios and my partner. They didn't use the car this evening, and were walking back down the street as my partner and I arrived at the Ferruccio home some minutes ago."

"But how were Bryce and Vincent in the car?" Bob asked.

"That, sir, we don't know yet, but we have to try to find out. It seems the car was taken from the driveway by someone without permission. Who and how, we don't know."

Caroline was regaining control of herself and the situation. "This is awful. I should be with Dana. How are the Ferruccios? Do you think we should join them at this time? How are they coping?"

Jane could only tackle the last question first. "With great difficulty," she said. "If you would excuse me, I'll contact my partner; he's with them right now."

Jane called Klein on her cell-phone. "Karl, got a question for you. Mrs Munro is asking whether the Ferruccios would like the Munros to join them at this difficult time, or not."

"Let me see."

"Okay, I'll hold while you ask." A pause.

"They'll be welcome."

"They would? Okay, they'll be over shortly. Thanks."

Jane closed her phone. "You're welcome to join the Ferruccios and your daughter. I'll leave you now. Come over when you feel ready."

Bob nodded in acknowledgement.

Jane let herself out of the front door, into the icy cold. The sky had cleared, and the temperature was dropping fast.

She crossed the street and entered the other house. There were more people now. She saw another teenage girl, dark-haired and strikingly pretty in spite of her tear-streaked face. She thought this must be the sixteen-year-old daughter. And there was a young girl, small and thin, on her mother's lap, her arms round her mother's neck, face resting on Carmella's bosom.

The blonde teenage girl, Dana, was crouched at their side, smoothing the young girl's hair.

Dana rose as Jane entered, and came over to her. "Are they coming?" she asked.

"Yes," said Jane. "They just wanted a few moments in private."

"Is my mom okay?"

"She cried, and is very upset, of course, but she says she's okay now." Jane smiled at Dana, and grasped her arm in support. She liked this young girl; there was just something about her—a presence, an awareness.

As the Munros entered the Ferruccio home, Dana embraced her mother, who broke into tears. Dana held her tight as her father came to them, putting his arms around them both. Iain joined them.

"Mom, whatever happened, it must have been quick. The policeman said he must have died instantly." Dana hugged her dad, and pulled Iain close. "We've all gotta be strong now," she said, her voice breaking.

Caroline gave a weak smile, catching Dana's eyes, and looked about the room. She moved over to Carmella, and they embraced.

As they released their embrace, Carmella spoke, tearfully. "But we don't know where my Angelo is. He is not home."

"Oh my God, was he with Bryce and Vince?"

"We don't know—we just don't know. This is terrible."

Dana suddenly felt herself in a heightened state of awareness. Something was tugging at her inside—what, she didn't understand, but she just felt she was being called to a new role, a new direction. She looked over to the two police constables.

"We're going to have to do something soon," the policewoman

was saying to her partner. "Until the other son is found, there'll be no rest here. We also need to arrange for positive IDs. With all of them together here, do you think the two fathers would be prepared to come with us?"

"We'll ask," Klein replied. "But we should also call the station to see if they've found out anything more from the accident." He moved over to Pino. "May I use your phone, sir?"

Pino nodded.

Klein was about to pick up the phone when it rang. He answered it. All eyes were on him. "Ferruccio residence?"

Dana could not hear the other side of the conversation. She let Klein's own words slip by her until …

"Yes, I'll tell them—just hold a minute."

Klein lowered the phone and spoke to the roomful. "Your son Angelo is safe. He and a friend Peter are at the police station now."

He returned to the phone call. "Have the parents of the other boy been contacted?"

Dana sat down by Tony again and held him tight.

After a few minutes, Klein ended the call and put the phone down, confirming to everyone, "Peter Baxter and Angelo are safe at the station."

Dana sensed the communal sigh of relief. She looked around; her mother was now looking pale, but more composed. Carmella was still agitated.

"Will they bring them home?" Carmella asked.

"Ma'am, I was told that they'll have to stay there for some time. They're helping us sort out what has happened tonight." Klein paused and then continued, "Now, I have to ask Mr Ferruccio and Mr Munro if they would come with us to the station as well, to help sort out the situation. I am truly sorry, gentlemen, ladies, but this has to be done. Constable Hunter here and I do extend our sincere sympathies to you all. If you will please excuse us … gentlemen?"

As the fathers left with the police, Dana realized that she had to take charge; both mothers were too distraught to act. She moved over to Gina, the older Ferruccio daughter.

"Gina, come help me make some warm drinks. We need to get some kind of comfort and warmth into them. Are you okay?"

Gina nodded as they went to the Ferruccio kitchen.

Dana looked back. "Tony," she called, "could you help us too, please?" Dana felt empowered.

❊❊❊

It had been a long, emotionally draining day. The apartment door closed behind Jane, and she slid the deadbolts across. As she crossed the floor, she took off her jacket and dropped it over a chair's back. Constable Hunter was changing, for a few hours, she hoped, into plain Jane Hunter. She kicked off her boots.

By the time she had reached the bedroom, her pants were at half-mast. She stepped out of them, bending to toss them onto the bedside chair. As she unbuttoned her blouse, she glanced in the mirror. *Yes, it did show.* She had shed some tears as she drove home. It had been very hard to restrain herself at several times during the evening, but once off duty, well … The blouse slid off her shoulders.

She walked into the kitchen, reached up for a glass, and poured orange juice from the carton she took from the fridge. She opened the box on the counter and lifted out four crackers. She smiled to herself. *What a diet for a working girl!*

She carried the crackers and juice to the coffee table, picked up the remote, and turned on the television. She sat down on the couch, unhooked her bra, and relaxed, breathing deeply.

The commercial finished. The program restarted: a police car slid into the palm-tree-lined avenue. That image alternated with one of a convertible carrying two well-tanned men, obviously crooks, careening down San Francisco hills.

Jane pointed the remote. The channel changed. The jungle. Heavily armed soldiers in fatigues were stalking through the undergrowth. A blast, flames, sounds of a chopper.

She changed the channel. Conan O'Brien. Channel change, quick. Weather channel; floods in the States somewhere, ten years ago. Channel change. Old movie, gangsters in Chicago. Click. The screen went dark. *Why bother? I don't need any of that. What time is it anyway? Two-thirty a.m. Jeez, I'm on again at six tonight.*

She finished her juice and crackers, and went into the bathroom. Through the partly open window, she heard a police siren. *Wonder who that is?*

Entering the bedroom, she dropped her bra and pantyhose to the floor and reached over for the nightshirt that Graham had given her. She slipped it over her head. She liked this shirt, especially since Graham had chosen it for her himself, without her prompting or input.

She lay on the bed, on top of the covers. The bedside lamp gave just enough light for now, as she went into her final relax-down phase. Usually, five minutes were enough. Then she would turn off the light. After another five minutes or so she would creep under the covers, and pretty soon she would be asleep.

She turned onto her side and looked at the bedside clock. The green digits stared back at her—04:30. No way could she drop off. The images would not go away.

The two mothers sat there, pale and distraught, their remaining children spread around the room, as she had left them, some five hours ago. Those two young teens, shiveringly drunk, hunched on the bench in the police station. But they had been able to tell their part of the story.

Apparently, the lad called Vincent had learned how to hot-wire a car to start it. Bryce was doing the driving. But the bad part about it all was that they had liquor with them.

At some point, the younger pair had decided to get out, and went their own way on foot. Another cruiser had picked them up by a park down on Otterbrook Road, drunk as coots. And the other two went on a joyride till they hit the ice on that bend.

And the fathers—the tragedy of it all, as each silently identified his dead son. *Why,* she thought, *why does it have to go on like this?*

Jane had done all the courses when she was on training. She'd handled drunks galore in the backstreets of downtown. She'd been on the early RIDE detachments. She'd been along on countless drunken domestic abuse calls. But this time it was different. Somehow, she couldn't get those boys out of her mind.

Try thinking of other things. Graham, wonder if he got to Montreal okay? It'll be nice to be together at Christmas. Be nice to go down to Windsor again; it'll surely be warmer. Wonder if Mum and Dad will like Graham? He's sure to get on with Dad, but Mum might not latch on to him so quickly.

But the image of that overturned car would not go away, and the half-empty bottle of scotch that she and Klein had found inside the car told the story so clearly.

Get out of bed. Walk about, do something. Like what? Read a book; watch TV. Have a drink. Can't do that; it'll wake me up.

She walked round the lounge twice, and sprawled out on the couch. Click: the screen came to life. An insect reared its head and scuttled into a burrow. The camera panned over the desert scene as a voice monotoned on. More insects—click. The rock music channel. *No, not now.* Click. *This looks better: sailboats racing. No commentary? No, just music.* She adjusted her head on the cushion. The sails in her mind filled with the wind, her eyes glazed, and at last she was asleep.

※※※

Dana sat close to Tony in the front, right-hand pew of the Funeral Home Chapel. To Tony's right sat Mrs Ferruccio, then Mr Ferruccio and the other Ferruccio family members, all in their best dark suits and black dresses. Carmella, Gina, and little Roberta wore black net scarves on their heads. Behind them sat other Ferruccios and Callonis, Carmella's family.

Dana glanced over to the other front pew, where her family sat, looking straight ahead. Dana and Tony would join them partway through the service.

She turned and looked behind. The chapel was nearly full, and she could see people still crowding in at the door. So many faces. She shuddered involuntarily. She felt Tony's hand on hers. So many faces, so many people. And then everyone, as a wave, began to stand. Dana turned and stood too, as the two ministers entered.

Dana's mother went quite regularly to the Anglican Church down on Otterbrook Road. Dana couldn't remember when her father had last been, nor Bryce and Iain. She had been a few times with her mother, when she was younger.

Tony's mother went to Mass at St James the Apostle quite often, but Dana didn't think the rest of the Ferruccio family were regular attendees.

So, the two grieving families had decided that the proper thing to do was to ask the Anglican minister and the Catholic priest to conduct a short service for Bryce and Vincent in the Chapel.

Dana thought the first prayers, some of them sounding vaguely familiar and carried by the sonorous voice of the minister, set the right atmosphere. Then came the contrast of the higher-voiced priest as he spoke to them about losing a son, a brother. She sniffed and fumbled for a tissue.

The priest and the minister stepped back. Dana and Tony stood, and, reaching forward over the front of the pew, each lifted up a wreath of flowers. They moved out into the open space, where the two black caskets rested. Gently, Tony laid his wreath on the right-hand casket, Vince's, and bowed his head.

Dana placed hers on Bryce's casket. She could hold back the tears no longer. Tony put his arm round her, and helped her back to the other pew. They sat down with the Munro family.

Caroline laid her hand on Dana's. Their tear-filled eyes met. "Thank you," mouthed Caroline.

Dana managed a glimmer of a smile in return.

Dana and Tony had agonized together for hours over the events of that terrible Friday night. They had thought long and hard about how they could do something together during this service.

In spite of this tragedy, and the immensity of the present situation, they were in love; they wanted to be together. They wanted, they needed, each other's support. If Tony had sat with his family, and Dana with hers, they would have been separated. So at last, they had thought of the wreaths and the changeover, and had talked to the minister and the priest. It was agreed.

Dana had a nagging fear, and she knew Tony had too. That time just a few weeks ago, when they had come across Bryce and Vince, and Peter too, in the old brewery grounds, drinking—what if she and Tony had squealed on the boys? Would it have prevented all this—would it?

She and Tony were so caught up in their own secret trysts at the time, that perhaps they hadn't realized the magnitude of what was happening. She remembered Tony saying he was worried about what the boys would get up to next as they left the trio in the brewery yard that night. Was there anything they could have done, should have done? Or was it already too late, even then?

Constable Jane Hunter had managed to squeeze into the Chapel at the last minute, and was wedged between two local residents of Brewster Gardens: Dwayne Hampden, a grey-haired fellow in his sixties, and David Adkins, a balding mid-forties guy, based on her brief interaction with them as she arrived. The service had now come to a close, and the families filed out into the private rooms.

Jane moved outside as the friends and neighbours began to disperse. She zipped up her uniform parka, pulled on her gloves, and moved toward the sidewalk. The funeral limousines were at the front, clouds of condensed exhaust vapours rising from them in the unusually cold air.

Jane watched as the Munro family members came out to their car. She saw Dana, helping her mother along the path.

Suddenly, Dana looked up and turned in Jane's direction. There was recognition. Dana raised her hand, and mouthed, "Hi, thank you."

Jane raised her hand in return. To her surprise, Dana came running over to her.

Dana was puffing in the cold air. "Ma'am," she began, "could I meet with you? We need some help, guidance—badly."

"Come on, Dana, we're leaving," came a shout from the limousine.

Jane, momentarily taken aback, pulled a business card from a top zippered pocket. "Er … here, Dana. Call me at this number, and we'll arrange something—I hope I can help."

"Thanks." Dana gave a half-smile and turned. "Gotta go now." Dana dashed back to her family.

With a downcast face, Jane turned abruptly, about to walk to her car.

"Nice young lady. You know the family, then?" came a voice in

Jane's ear. She stopped and looked up; Dwayne Hampden had spoken.

"Er—well, not really. I was one of the officers who broke the news to the families. Not an easy task."

"I can imagine. You know, some of us here in the community are a bit concerned about the antics of some of the young folk," Dwayne continued.

"Darn right," another voice joined in. Jane saw that it was the other local she had met earlier, David Adkins.

"You see," Dwayne said, "there's this set of old brewery buildings between the old railroad track-bed and the far end of Brewster Gardens. They've been there for decades, and generations of kids have played in and around them. But just lately, people have noticed a few teenagers going in there, as if looking for trouble. One neighbour is sure he saw them lugging in a six-pack of beer one day."

This struck a chord with Jane, and her mind went back to some of her training courses on youth issues. Right from the start of this tragedy, on that Friday, she had had a strange sense, a sense that she somehow would become involved in this whole affair; that this would be something more than a routine, underage drunken-driving tragedy. Somehow, she knew not how, these events were telling her something.

"Can anything be done about the old property?" asked Jane.

"I think the city should pull it down," said David. "It's an eyesore and a hazard."

"Trouble is," countered Dwayne, "if they do that, it will become prime building land, and the community doesn't want more housing around here."

"Thanks for telling me all this," said Jane. "I'll let my super know. We do have an on-going watch on youth activities around the city."

- 2 -

It was two weeks after the tragic crash and the deaths of the two boys. Dave Adkins was strolling round Brewster Gardens with Brutus, his wife Barbara's Malamute. Ahead, Dwayne Hampden appeared from the side of his house to tend his flowerbeds.

Dwayne looked up. "Oh hi, Dave. Did you get any more signatures for your brewery petition?"

"No, we didn't. Barbara went round this afternoon, and saw Mrs Abraham and Jenny Lindsay; the Thompsons were out. I called at the Munros, but only the daughter, Dana, was home. Jill Benson said to come back when Keith was at home, though she understood our concern.

"I don't know, Dwayne, people just don't want to sign. Maybe we've gone about this the wrong way? But I don't see why. Kids have been getting hurt or into trouble round those old buildings for years.

"Ann Baxter did tell me that her son had cut his hand badly the other week, on glass apparently, but that he wouldn't say how—and he was one of the boys that survived the disaster. I've made it as clear as I can to my boy Cody that I don't want him in there.

"It's time the city did something. They oughta pull the place down and close it off, or put the land to some good use."

"But Dave, that's what's bothering people. Most of them say that if the buildings were torn down, then it wouldn't be long before some builder would move in and fill the place with townhouses or something worse."

"Damned if we do and damned if we don't. We only have six signed up, out of twenty households. It's not enough. Damn it, we've gotta do something about that place before more kids get killed. Maybe even a proper gate at the entrance would be enough."

"I don't know, Dave," said Dwayne, as his forehead wrinkled and his lips puckered. "I don't know. If we could track down the owner of the place, we'd stand a better chance; somehow I doubt we could do it without his go-ahead—and anyway, why shouldn't we get him to foot the bill for it all?"

"Well, I was thinking that if we all chipped in, the job would get done sooner, and we'd get a gate on the place that would do the trick."

"David," chuckled Dwayne, "you're being a bit naïve. If there's something in there to attract the kids, they'll find a way in, gate or no gate. But, I grant you, a high gate is a good deterrent. Look, tell you what, I'll call the city tomorrow and ask them to track down the owner for us."

❄❄❄

It was a raw December wind that whistled round the buildings on the midtown Ottawa side-street. Dried leaves scudded across the road, dying in eddies in corners, partly covering the patches of early snow.

After searching city records, writing letters, and waiting, Dave and Dwayne were keen to take this next step in their efforts to deal with the old brewery issue.

They quickly mounted the six steps of the building that had, in its day, been a well-to-do townhouse for some Ottawa valley landowner, or maybe an MP, but now sported an ubiquitous, engraved brass plate at the side of the outer door: Simpson Stocker Wyatt Pimms—Barristers and Solicitors.

Dwayne grasped the large brass doorknob and eased into the vestibule; Dave followed quickly, huddling against the wind. He was surprised, given the weather, to find the inner door open, revealing a narrow hallway going back into the depths of the building.

On the right, parallel to the hallway, a grand staircase ascended, bannistered in rich, dark wood and covered in a luxuriant red and brown carpet.

To the left, Dave saw a reception room, with three austere chairs, a table mounted with a rack of small pigeonholes, a fireplace with an ornate mantel—clearly not used for many years—and, at her desk, a receptionist: pert, attractive, brunette, and paging Mr Stocker.

Dave and Dwayne stood at the entrance to the room. The young woman looked up, flashing a smile at them as she juggled a couple of phone calls, motioning to them to be seated. Dwayne sat; Dave remained standing, but moved into the room.

"Good morning, gentlemen, how may I help you?"

"We have an appointment with Mr Simpson; Hampden's the name, and Adkins," said Dwayne, his right hand motioning toward Dave.

"Oh, yes. Mr Simpson is still with another client at the moment, but he won't be long. If you don't mind waiting for a few moments?"

"Not at all," Dwayne assured her.

Dave sat down, watching the receptionist as she busied herself with the two incoming lines, the intercom, and a keyboard. She looked up and, momentarily catching Dave's eye, flashed another smile.

Cute, Dave thought, fascinated by the skill with which she handled the multi-tasking. He watched her closely. She looked up, caught his eye again, smiled coyly, and looked back at her screen.

The sound of voices coming down the staircase destroyed Dave's dream. With his eyes still fixed on the receptionist, he half-heard some words of parting as the outside door opened and someone left.

A tall, heavily built man stood at the doorway of the reception room. Dave and Dwayne stood as the receptionist introduced them.

"Good morning, gentlemen—George Simpson. Do come this way"—he turned back—"Kelly, if Mr Jackson calls, tell him I'll be free tomorrow afternoon."

"Yes, Mr Simpson," replied Kelly as the phone rang again. Dave reluctantly dragged his eyes away again.

As they climbed the stairs, Dave observed that George Simpson's head only just cleared the overhang in the ceiling as they reached the landing. George Simpson was indeed large, six-foot-five Dave guessed, thickset, with a commanding presence.

As they were ushered into one of the two front rooms on the second floor, Dave felt at a distinct disadvantage. At work and in the community, he had no problems with confidence, but around lawyers, he was ill at ease—and this time was no exception. He sensed that Dwayne felt the same.

"Please be seated." Simpson indicated two leather armchairs as he rounded a dark, highly polished desk. He settled himself in his own leather chair, silhouetted against the large window, and picked up a small pile of papers and spread them on his blotter. He separated out one of them, and looked up at Dave and Dwayne.

"Gentlemen, I appreciate your taking the time to come in to see me. It is Mr Hennigan's wish that we deal personally, and not just by exchange of letters. As you may already know, Mr Hennigan is ninety-four now, but still very alert and—shall we say—'with it'?" Simpson smiled.

Dave relaxed a little; he no longer felt his pulse racing. He knew he was not on comfortable ground.

"Mr Hennigan," Simpson continued, "now lives in Kingston, has done so for many years in fact, but we, that is, my father and I, have continued to represent his legal interests.

"When Mr Hennigan received your letter expressing your community's concerns about the old brewery, he immediately telephoned me. He, too, was most concerned, and expressed regret that the matter had not been raised many years before."

Simpson smiled again. "In spite of his years, Mr Hennigan is well aware of what young people can get up to!"

Dave smiled back, and nodded his head.

"So," continued Simpson, "Mr Hennigan has instructed me to work with you and your community to make the situation safe." Dave felt a great load off his mind, sensing that Dwayne had relaxed too, evidently so noticeably that Simpson added, "I'm sure that's a great relief to you. I can imagine that you quite expected that an opposite course could have been set."

"Well, yes," said Dave. "To be honest, we really had no idea of what, or rather who, we might be up against. We are relieved."

Dwayne nodded in agreement.

"Let me give you a little background," continued Simpson. "You see, the brewery was first established in the late 1880s by Inge Hennigan, the grandfather of our Mr Hennigan. On Inge's death, it was bequeathed to his son, Emil, on condition that it was never to be sold out of the family, nor be torn down. Given the demand for beer in the first two decades of the twentieth century, that was not an unreasonable wish. Emil wrote the same condition into his will.

"Sadly, Emil did not survive his father by many years, and so it passed into the hands of Kurt, the last Mr Hennigan. Kurt revered his father and grandfather, having grown up in the brewery business, and was determined to continue a successful operation."

Simpson moved back in his chair, swivelling a little to cast his profile in silhouette. "But the winds of change were blowing across the country," he continued. "Temperance and prohibition were killing the breweries, slowly but surely; and then the Depression came. Kurt had no option left but to close down the Hennigan Brewery. Twenty people lost their jobs.

"Kurt could not do anything with the buildings or the site by way of disposal. In no way would he break the conditions of the wills. For years, the buildings were deserted, but in those days it was not a concern, being so far out from the city, with only a poor road as access, and the trains just steamed on past. During the war, a need for temporary barracks arose, and Kurt gave permission for the Army to upgrade the road and use the buildings."

Simpson swung round to face Dave and Dwayne. "After the war, the Army used the buildings for storage for a few years, and then turned them back, empty, to Kurt. I say empty, because back in 1934, Kurt had had the foresight to remove any machinery, and the vats and yeast tanks. So, there it stands, gentlemen."

"Very interesting," said Dwayne. "Now I understand why it wasn't pulled down long ago."

"Yes," responded Simpson. "Let me give you Mr Hennigan's, Kurt's, proposal. He would like you, and others in your community as appropriate, to define what needs to be done, and to present me with the plan and its cost for his approval. He will then pay for the work and the materials; however, he asks whether there is someone in the community who is competent to contract and supervise the work. He has also asked me to work closely with you."

Dave looked at Dwayne.

"Well," began Dwayne, "that is a very acceptable proposal, and I'm sure the community will be pleased to work along. As far as a general contractor—do you agree, Dave—I think I can recommend Joseph—Pino—Ferruccio; he's in that business, and he lives in Brewster Gardens. However, he has just lost his son in that tragic accident we noted in our letter to Mr Hennigan. I don't know if he would be willing to take on the task at this time."

Dave nodded, and looked at Simpson, who had taken on a concerned expression.

"Yes, Kurt and I were both greatly saddened to learn about the loss of the two boys. Kurt has asked me to find out the details of the two families; he wants to contact them to express his condolences. Would you be willing to approach your neighbour—Pino, was it—to ask if he would take on the contractor role, for the community?"

"That we will try," Dwayne replied.

"Good," said Simpson. "I'll have my secretary put all this down in writing and send it to you. I'd appreciate a written response from you, for the record, so that I can keep Mr Hennigan properly informed. Here's my card. Please don't hesitate to give me a call if you have any queries or concerns."

Simpson stood up and shook their hands. "Dwayne—Dave—do please call me George. We'll work together on this project. I'll come downstairs with you. My, I don't like the sound of that wind out there. Do you think we'll have some of this job done before the deep winter?"

"We'll certainly see what we can do," replied Dave, feeling much more confident and positive than when they had entered.

- 3 -

Tony stood at the east side of the school's metalwork shop, checking on the chart for the correct drill size for the thread he was about to tap. His mind wandered as he gazed at the lists of numbers; he and Dana were meeting after school to go to a movie, and that was more attractive to think about than last class of the day in Metalwork TIN4.01.

Actually, he enjoyed this class normally; it was one of his favourite courses. He was much happier with hands-on work than the more academic courses. But today was dragging, and thoughts of Dana tugged at him.

There were only eight in the class. The teacher, Old Marky, as they called him, was checking out Sean's lathe work over the far side of the room. Other students busied themselves at various tasks.

Suddenly, Tony was startled by a loud shout and a yell. He turned. A fight had broken out. Lucasz Woslewski and Andre Gagne were going at each other. The next thing he knew, Lucasz had a knife in his hand.

Marky buzzed the office. Johnny and Steve tried to hold off Lucasz and Andre, but Steve nearly got knifed himself.

Then, Pete managed to knock the knife out of Lucasz' hand with a steel bar. But Lucasz went berserk; he started throwing anything he could get his hands on.

Tony ducked down behind the nearest work bench, and others did likewise. It seemed like an eternity as Lucasz raved on, swearing and cursing, throwing steel rods, tools, and anything else he could reach.

At last, Vice-principal Lebrun arrived, followed quickly by the police. They soon had Woslewski tied down.

Tony and the others came out of hiding, relieved and shaken.

"Take it easy, lads, relax," said Mr Lebrun. "I'm sure this has shaken you. Sorry, but we're going to have to ask you all to come along to the office, because the police will need to take statements from you—I really don't know how long it will take."

Tony groaned inwardly. *What about my date with Dana? She'll wonder where I am.*

While the police went into the inner office with Woslewski, Lebrun, and Old Marky, the rest of them had to stay in the outer office.

Tony couldn't sit for long; he stood up and started pacing. This wasn't good; he and Dana were really becoming a firm item, but he was still conscious of the risks of letting her down, or of putting doubts into her mind.

The time dragged on and on. At last, one of the police officers came out and took statements. Tony was third in line. He told what he had heard and seen, and was then free to go.

He ran to the bus stop, hoping a bus would come soon.

―

Tony stepped off the bus and saw Dana waiting across the street, as planned. He marvelled at her, a shapely figure in a heavy white sweater and blue jeans, an angelic face under blonde hair. But she looked cold.

He ran up to her, lifted her hand and kissed it. Surprised, she jumped. Quickly, he explained about the fight and delay.

"'T's okay," she said, squeezing his hand. "Let's go eat, I'm starving."

"Me too. Where? Harvey's?"

"Sure."

They set out to walk the two blocks to Harvey's.

"What made Woslewski do that?"

"Don't know. He's had it in for Andre for weeks about something. But Johnny says Lucasz was drunk; he said you could smell it on his breath. Don't know if the police did any tests; they took him into Lebrun's office as soon as they'd got him tied down. We had to stay in the outer office."

"You know, a few days before the accident, Bryce said something at dinner that seemed strange at the time, but now I wonder …"

"What'd he say?"

"Something about polishing things off."

"Wonder what Bryce meant?"

"Do'know. Er … Tone, I was talking with some of the other cheerleaders this morning, an' we'd really like to do a cheer for your student council rally on Tuesday. The rest of the girls are really keen to support you—I'm getting quite jealous, you know!" Dana nudged him in the midriff.

"Thanks, Dan. But I'm still a bit unsure I want to go through with it."

"Oh Tone, you can't back down now, after all the work we've done with posters and campaigning for you. You're by far the best. Everyone in my class says they'll vote for you. Look, when we get home, I'll give you a private showing of our cheer, okay?"

"Okay, okay." Tony knew in his heart that he couldn't back out, but he was worried that he wouldn't be strong enough to represent Grade Eleven adequately on the student council. He just didn't seem to have the self-confidence that Dana showed. *Change the topic,* he thought.

"Say, how did your meet with that cop lady go?"

"With Jane? Great, she's a really cool person. I like her. See, I thought she might be able to help with, like, how to cope with, er, grieving. Mum and Dad have hardly spoken since the accident except for, like, essential things. Iain just does his own thing, says nothing. My house is, like, dead. And, Tone, your house is no better. Your folks are, like, zombies. It's a misery there."

"You're right there. So could she help?"

"Yeah, she had lots of suggestions, and gave me some leaflets to give to Mum and Dad. Maybe your folks should see them too. She even offered to spend more time with me, if I wished, to talk about new ideas for young people."

"Cool. You game?"

"Yeah, I'll have to think about it. Like, what kinds of things would we talk about? But she also told me that the police have a watch on some kind of youth gang that's been doing break-ins in Ottawa, and across the river, too. She's real cool: sharp, but nice about it."

"Yeah, she seemed okay, what I saw of her."

"You know, Tone, I really feel I want to do something for Bryce and Vince, like, I dunno, some kind of memorial, maybe. I know Bryce was often a pain in the ass, but he was my brother, an' I really did love him, deep down. I can kinda understand how Mum and Dad must feel. It isn't the same without him and Vince around."

"Yeah, the place is too quiet." *Dan's right,* thought Tony. *Yeah, I do miss having Vince forever asking me questions, bugging me. But he was my brother.* "Yeah, mebbe you're right, Dan, some way to remember them."

"You know, Tone," said Dana. "Another idea came to me after I'd talked with Jane. Maybe I could think of a career as a policewoman?"

"Meh," grunted Tony. "Not too keen on that, Dan." *Too risky,* he thought.

- 4 -

Dave Adkins slumped down in his chair and stared at the carpet. How could this happen at this point? One day, the world is proceeding in an orderly fashion: you know your place in it, and you are secure, confident—then, bam, sideswiped, you're out of a job.

He knew the overall situation, or so he'd thought he did. He'd felt that he was safe for another year or so—that was what he'd inferred from the Director-General's 'chat with staff' back in July. But he knew that deep cuts in the Federal Public Service were not far away, and now they had hit home.

But why did it have to be me? After all that I've contributed to the unit; why, I came up with the new inventory system, even won an award for it. And then there was the info-chat idea I put to the Director—it resulted in those very successful Wednesday sessions—everybody thought they were great. Sheesh! It's really knocked the wind out of my sails.

"Hi, you're home early! Are you okay?" came his wife Barbara's voice from the kitchen. She walked through to the hall closet. "John has asked me if I would work full days for the next six months instead of just mornings."

She entered the room. Dave did not move.

"Is something wrong, dear?" she knelt by his side.

"Everything's wrong." His voice choked. "I'm being laid-off at the end of January."

"Oh, David." She kissed his forehead and put her arms around him. "How could that be? That's awful. Just a few weeks' notice. How could they do that to you?"

"Quite easily. They have to cut, and some have to go."

"But you thought you would be okay till next year or the year after?"

"Well, I was wrong."

"Who told you?"

"Thompson. He called me into his office and gave me an envelope; then he sat there and watched me read the letter. He made some platitudes about my work, and about regretting having to do this—all part of Government downsizing, and all that—told me about my options, and wished me well in the future. That was it—five minutes!"

"David." Barbara repositioned herself. "You mustn't give up. You have to go out there and fight. You've got a lot of skill and experience that somebody else will want to use. Come on. Buck up! It's not the end of the world. I'm going to have a scotch, you want one?"

He nodded. Barbara set about pouring two drinks.

"Has anyone else been given notice today?"

"Not that I know of. I know Fred's on the block, but that's been common knowledge for a while. I think Sue and Janet might be surplused before long. Come to think of it, Thompson did have a long meeting with Sue yesterday. I don't know." David sighed. "I really don't care about the place anymore. I've put a lot of effort into the job, and look what I get."

"Let's look on the bright side, dear. Did you hear what I said when I came in—about me going full time? I think that's just what we need right now. It'll give you time to get back on your feet."

"I guess you're right. But can you handle it?"

"Of course I can! I did before I had Cody, now, didn't I?"

"Yes, but that was quite a while ago."

"Don't worry so. It'll be all right." She sipped at her scotch. "Guess we will have to reduce on a few things though." She looked at her glass ruefully.

They sat in silence, sipping their drinks, gazing into space.

Dave spoke first. "I'd really like to do something different. I'm fed up with this rat-race, and all the uncertainty, and reorganizations, and budget cuts. Something right away from government."

"Now that's talking," Barbara sat forward brightly. "Let's think about what you're good at."

"I don't really know. You tell me."

"Well, for a start, you like dealing with people—"

"We-ell," Dave interrupted. "That depends."

"You know what I mean. Look at all your Scouting experience, and the Navy Reserves before that."

"Yes, but that was a long time ago."

"I know, but you get on well with people, and they seem to get on well with you, especially the young people. What else?"

"Outdoors, I suppose."

"Yes, and you're a good administrator. Think of the stuff you did way back, before I met you."

That last point brought a twinge of anguish to Dave. It brought back the rocky times with Helen, when he was so over-committed with scouting and church activities. But he and Barbara had always got on well, ever since they first met at the Shakespeare Festival in Prescott, a few weeks after Helen had left him.

Nonetheless, Barbara was right. He had done a lot of things that he could perhaps do again, so long as there was a paycheck attached. *Yes, I really did enjoy working with all those bright, energetic young people, full of ideas, full of energy. Wonder what they're all doing now.* "I just need a change."

"Don't fret, there's Christmas on the horizon. There'll be Cody's Christmas concert with the Scouts, and you did promise him that you would help them out this year. There's a lot going on. Just do what you have to do at work and don't worry about it. It'll be somebody else's problem soon."

Dave sighed and finished his drink. Barbara stood up, walked over to him, patted his hand, and continued on into the kitchen.

Time passed. *I wonder if there are any jobs going in the Scouts head office? Or even in the Reserves? It'd be a desk job, but that's what I do, I guess. Or a park ranger, yeah, outdoors, that would be cool.*

He heard the back door, and the sounds of his son Cody galumphing into the house: the fridge door slamming, sounds of voices, and Cody crashing downstairs, presumably to watch videos or play computer games.

He didn't really care—he really didn't care about anything right now. He'd helped in the fights against the cuts, and it hadn't worked. That's all there was to it.

He looked at his empty glass. He needed to act. He walked over to the cabinet, refilled his glass, and stood watching the streetscape through the window. This was a habit. He sipped his drink. He enjoyed good scotch, often. *Some say it's not good for you, a bad habit. Humph!*

There was a swirl of fallen leaves blown by the wind gathering on the street at the end of the driveway. Two teenagers ran through the pile as they moved along the street. *Angelo and Peter,* thought Dave. *Yeah, I guess scotch wasn't good for them, but they're still kids, and we're blocking off the brewery so they won't be into that gig again.*

He continued to sip his drink. *Damn government bureaucrats,* he thought, *screw you.*

- 5 -

Dana snuggled her head against Tony's shoulder, curling her feet up onto the couch. Tony stroked her hair. The only light in the Ferruccio basement rec room came from the television, a vivid light in ever-changing colours, staccato-like images, freeze-framing any movements Dana and Tony made.

They watched as if entranced, yet not absorbing. Heavy rock wasn't really their thing, but there was nothing else to watch, and at least they were on their own. The others were scattered about the house.

Since the accident, Carmella spent most of her time fussing in the kitchen or tending to Roberta, who seemed to be chronically ill these days. Angelo was grounded; he was on probation. He had taken to heart the loss of Vincent—they had been very close—and spent his evenings in the room they had shared. Gina was very quiet about the whole business; she said little, and kept mainly to herself.

Pino had taken it very badly; night after night he sat in silence in the front room, in a subdued light. Often, he was still there the next morning. He went to work as usual, but did not enter into conversations at home. He usually ate his meals alone, separate from the others. A month had passed since that fateful night.

Tony adjusted his position, causing Dana to sit up. She kissed him.

"Lucasz Woslewski's been suspended again," said Tony.

"Why?"

"He and Jake were found drinking round the back of Keeler's portable. An' Pete says Woslewski's been charged by the police."

"What for?"

"Seems he's been doing some trading in liquor. He bought stuff from some gang that did a heist across the river in Gatineau. Then he's been selling it to kids. Been doing it for months."

"Tony, I bet that's where Bryce and Vince got their stuff."

"Probably."

Dana shifted her position, and sat facing him.

"Tony, does your dad know this?"

"Don't think so; I've not told him. Why?"

"Don't you see? Just look at your poor dad. He's going through hell. He thinks it was his liquor they got into. You know he's locked everything away. We have to help him out of this horrible mess."

"Yeah, I see what you mean. I could check with Angelo if he knows; I think he's been shocked enough to give me a straight answer. I mean, he and Peter were with Vince and Bryce in the car till they jumped out. Then I'll talk with Momma first, before I say anything to Pop."

Dana kissed him again. "Do it quickly; your dad needs help."

They embraced.

Suddenly, light appeared from the stairwell. Dana and Tony unlocked and watched the doorway.

Gina came into view, and stood silhouetted. "Hey, you guys, can I come in?"

"Sure. Wassup?"

Gina came into the room and sat cross-legged on the carpet in front of them. "Turn that sound down, Tone." Gina winced.

Tony picked up the remote and silenced the television.

"Momma's crying again," Gina continued. "We gotta to do something. She and Poppa are hardly speaking to each other these days. They're so miserable. It's awful living here with them."

"Okay. Dana's just had an idea, but we need to check it out. We need to find out how Vince and Bryce got the liquor, and if that really is what's eating at Pop and Momma, then we might have the answer."

"Listen up, guys." Dana was in charge. "Look, all our parents, yours and mine, are in a mess. They don't know how to handle what's happened, and how to handle themselves. It's goin' to be up to us, we three, to help them. Like, we're old enough, we know what's going on in the world. An', like, I really did get some good ideas from Jane, the policewoman; I think we need to try some of them, like, now."

"Hi, dear." Caroline Munro called out as Dana slid into the house.

Not as quiet as I thought I was, realized Dana. "Hi, Mom. Is there anything to eat? I'm starved!"

"Look in the fridge; there's some stew, or there's still some rice and stir-fry."

"Nah, I'll just have some cheese and a yogurt."

The fridge door slammed, and cutlery clattered in the kitchen, as Dana found sustenance. The noise gave way to the normal quietness of the Munro household as Dana moved into the living room, balancing a hunk of cheese on a yogurt tub in one hand, a glass of milk in the other, and a spoon in her mouth.

She dumped herself onto the couch, placed the milk and cheese on the side-table, and proceeded to fiddle with the top of the yogurt tub.

"How's Tony?" her mother began.

"Mm-okay," the response emerged through a mouthful of yogurt. Dana swallowed two more mouthfuls, and paused. "Mom. We've found out how they got the liquor."

Dana realized too late that she had hit a tender point too directly. She watched her mother tense up immediately, and her breathing become rapid.

Dana knew that Caroline was willing herself to be strong, but it was a fragile state that she had been living in, this past month. Her mother and father rarely spoke to each other these days, except for essential day-to-day things.

It was not that they had any disagreement, or anger, between them—they had both separately assured her of that. It was just—well, just that the spark had gone. Neither could pinpoint any one thing, except the one enormous gap: for all his faults, all his troubles, Bryce was their son—but no longer.

Images flashed into Dana's mind: the little baby, the toddler, the Cub Scout, the day he knocked the paint can all over his head, the time …

Dana, stop. Your mother needs you. "Mom, are you all right?" Dana moved and knelt at her mother's side.

"Huh? Oh, yes, dear. I'm sorry."

Dana put her hand on her mother's arm.

"Sorry, Dana, what did you say?"

"You sure you're okay?"

Caroline smiled, and nodded.

"Tony and I've been checking a few things out. One of the guys in Tony's homeroom's been charged with selling stolen liquor. Apparently, he's been doing it for months. Anyway, I wondered if that was how the boys had got theirs. So Tony talked to Angelo tonight, and Angelo says that, yes, they did get it from Lucasz Woslewski."

"I see. Well—that will be some relief for your father. He's been wondering all along where they got it from."

"We think Tony's dad thinks they stole it from his bar in the basement—and that's why he's so miserable. Tony's going to try to talk to him later."

"Is he?"

"Mo-om?" Dana had recognized that her mother was still struggling.

"Uh-huh?"

"Mom, is everything really okay with you and Dad?"

"Yes, dear, of course," replied Caroline, unconvincingly. "Don't forget your yogurt."

Dana returned to the couch and continued her snack. Her mother picked up her book and began to read.

Dana noticed that one of the leaflets on grieving that Jane had given her for her parents was lying on the side-table. *At least Mom or Dad must have looked at it,* she thought. *I gave them to Mom in the kitchen.*

They sat in silence for several minutes. Dana emptied her glass, and stood up. "Night, Mom."

"Night, dear."

- 6 -

Often when he needed to think, Dave took the dog for a walk. These days, he was desperately trying to think of a new career, a new direction. Brutus was, perhaps, one of the fittest dogs in town.

This morning, Dave kicked off his boots angrily in the back entrance, having brought Brutus back from his constitutional, given him fresh water, and put him into the run at the back of the house.

"Cold out, hon?" Barbara called from inside the house.

"Damn cold for the second week in December." Dave was blowing on his hands and rubbing them together. "There's a signboard gone up on the wasteland along Millerby Lane. We've all feared the worst—now it's going to happen."

"Oh dear, I don't like the sound of that."

"You sure won't when I tell you what's on the sign," replied Dave. "It says this: J. Albez Builder—Fine Townhouses—Ready by Spring. Brewery Mews: Prices starting at—"

"Oh my God, not that," gasped Barbara. "Just what no one

wants around here."

Dave was still shocked cold. *How could they?* he thought. There had been no notices in the paper—at least, he hadn't seen any. *They couldn't just do that, like this, surely?*

"That's awful," Barbara mused.

"I'll say it is. They oughta do something about it. I mean …" Dave fell silent, lost for words.

At that moment, the phone rang in the Adkins' kitchen; Dave picked it up.

"Hello, Dwayne." Dave saw the name on the display.

"Hi, Dave—you've seen the sign?"

"Hell, you can't miss it."

"Look, Dave, I'm calling to ask if you would draft up a petition to the city against this construction."

"Dwayne, I have to say I'm not keen, really."

"Don't underestimate yourself, Dave. I feel you just have a way with words for a good petition—far better than me, and anyone else I can think of right now. The Johnsons and the Baxters have already agreed to help take it round the community.

"Please, Dave, for the community. We've gotta do our best to stop this guy from building, and it ain't going to be easy."

Dave sighed. "Oh well, okay. I guess I could—should. I still don't feel it's really my bag. I mean, the last one about the brewery fizzled and came to nothing."

"Good man. Thanks, Dave." Dwayne rang off.

✻✻✻

Dave mulled over the wording of the petition for several days. His heart was not really in it, and he wondered whether the community would be.

He knew the mood in Brewster Gardens was sombre. Usually by this time in the year, most homes sported strings of Christmas lights along their eaves, or on trees in their yards. But not this year; not a special light was to be seen, anywhere. And even those families who tended to leave drapes open, so that house lights spilled their glow out onto the snow, had drawn their drapes or muted their lights.

The kids were nowhere to be seen: no street hockey, no noise, no chatter. The commuters and the shoppers seemed to come and go invisibly. The whole crescent was still in mourning for those two boys.

And yet, life must go on. Dave knew that if they didn't do something quickly, the builder would be on the wasteland, and there would be no hope of stopping the townhouse project.

But he really was finding it hard to be enthused; somehow, losing his job had destroyed his own self-confidence. He felt unsure of anything he started to do. This was unlike him, and he knew it, but he could do nothing about it; he couldn't muscle up the power to get motivated for anything.

Dwayne and a couple of others had pressed him hard, and he finally agreed to help with actually taking the petition round. Hesitantly, he decided to start at the brewery end.

Petition in hand, he set off round the Gardens. The Donnellys gladly signed. They would be directly affected. Being the first house on that end, the view from their windows would change drastically, and they would be greatly affected by increased traffic and general activity. The Donnellys were in their eighties, and valued a quiet life.

Feeling encouraged at last, Dave moved on to the Hampdens next door. He knew he was welcome here.

Elizabeth Hampden came to the door. "Good evening, Dave. Do come in, and sit yourself down. Dwayne's down in the basement; I'll fetch him."

Dave sat in the easy chair by the fireplace. The room breathed confident comfort. He knew Dwayne had a good job, and he knew that both Dwayne and Elizabeth had an artistic bent that meant that their choice of furnishings and decor was always in keeping with a theme. He wished that he and Barbara could have half of these skills to use in their home.

Dwayne came clumping up the basement steps in his slippers. "Hi, Dave, what's up then?"

"I've brought the petition about the townhouses. I hope you and Elizabeth will sign it."

"Let me just have another look at it." Dwayne's hand reached across, and Dave offered the clipboard to him. Dwayne studied it for a moment.

"Well, Dave, I can't think of better words; I knew you would do a good job. Let's hope it will do the trick, and we get enough signatures. Liz?" Dwayne called, leaning toward the back room, where Elizabeth was sewing, "Liz, do you have a pen out there?"

Elizabeth came fussing in with three pens. "I don't know why you couldn't have come out and found one yourself. You knew I was busy."

"Now then, 'mother hen'. I wanted you to come and see this petition Dave's brought. It's about the townhouses."

"Oh yes, I certainly don't want any of those round here. Three or four new single-family homes on that site would be nice, but not townhouses. Just think what it will do to house values."

Dwayne chose a pen and signed his name on the next line. "There you are then. Liz, you're next."

Elizabeth signed below Dwayne's name. "There, Dave," she said. "I do hope this will be more successful than that last petition about the brewery buildings."

Dave thanked her and turned to Dwayne. "I guess Pino will have the new gates on the brewery yard in a day or two, now?"

"If the weather holds. And he told me that George Simpson has agreed to hold one key, Pino will have one, and they want you to have one," explained Dwayne.

"I guess I'm around here more than most until I find a new job," commented Dave, glumly.

"I feel so sorry for those two families that lost their sons in that accident." Elizabeth pulled up a straight-back chair and sat down next to Dwayne in his La-Z-Boy rocker. "And they're such nice people, the Munros and the Ferruccios, I really don't know how those boys could have got into so much trouble so quickly."

"I know one thing," said Dave. "Gord Johnson told me he'd given his kids a good talking-to. And I did the same with Cody. It has shaken them all. All the kids seem to be very quiet."

"I hope it's been a lesson they will learn," added Dwayne.

- 7 -

Never had she expected to find herself in such a turmoil, and certainly not at this stage. Jane walked back into her apartment, closed the door and leaned back against it. She folded her arms and closed her eyes, basking in the warm feeling that had engulfed her.

"Jane Hunter? Jane Stennings," she rehearsed to herself. "Jane Stennings—I like it."

She opened her eyes, and bounced across the room to sprawl out on the couch. She felt her cheek. Boy, was she ever warm. But what was that knot in her stomach? She felt so excited, she might burst. "Oh, stop it, Jane," she told herself, "you're on duty in two hours. Pull yourself together. But I can't, I've gotta tell somebody."

She dialled the digits on the phone at her side. "Hi, Angie. It's Jane."

"*Hi, Jane, you okay?*"

"I'm fine. Guess what?"

"*You got a raise.*"

"No." She laughed. "No, better than that. We're getting married!"
"Yay! This year?"
"Yessss! Soon!"
"Have you set the date then?"
"We don't know yet. Before summer …"
"Wowee! A spring bride!"
"Yessss!"
"I have to be there."
"Of course! I'll tell you soon as we know!"
"Did he actually, like, propose?"
"Yes, he did. Not on his knees, though." She laughed. "No! He said it all formally. 'Dear Miss Jane, will you …'" Jane burst into a fit of giggles. She gulped in a deep breath. "No, seriously, Graham was sweet. He'd got it all prepared in his mind what he was going to do. I just let him take the lead."
"So was this all planned, or did he sweep you off your feet?"
"Well yes, we'd sort of decided we would when he got his promotion."
"I didn't know he got his promotion."
"Yes, he did! Oh yes, you were out when I called you on Tuesday. Anyway, he's Captain Stennings now."
"You moving in with him or he with you?"
"Well, no. Neither apartment is really big enough. We're sort of thinking about a townhouse, or something like that."
"Sounds cool. There's quite a lot being built now."
"Yep. Anyway, better let you go. I'm on in less than two hours."
"Bet the guys will give you a tough time!"
"Yeah, I bet they will too!"
"Bye then, Jane, great news. See ya."
"Bye Angie." Jane put down the phone, paused for a moment, then bounced up and into the bathroom to prepare for work.

She could just imagine the ribbing she was in for, as soon as she let word out. Most of the guys at the station knew Graham, though; he'd been out and joined in their softball games last summer, before he'd gone to the Middle East.

She shivered in excitement, and found that her eye shadow just would not go on right the first time.

- 8 -

Dave Adkins stood gazing out of his front window. He had lost track of the hours he had spent in this activity in the past several months. It was now early May. "Meditating on the scene," was his reply when challenged, usually by his son Cody.

Barbara, his wife, was more understanding, and rarely commented openly when others were there. Since his lay-off at the end of December, Dave had changed in many ways, some subtle, others more blatant.

Dave and Barbara had a great relationship—they talked. They talked with each other about their problems—Barbara had shared her concerns with him again only last night.

She could see the subtler changes in him. She saw listlessness, an unwillingness to venture into new fields, a loss in self-confidence, more grey hairs increasing among the sparse coverage on his head, and, most disturbing to her, she had told him, the bitterness eating into him along with his increasing consumption of scotch.

I know all this. I can see it all happening, almost as if I'm hovering above myself, watching. But somehow I just don't have the desire to do anything about it—well, not yet, not now. Maybe someday.

As he stood there at the window, watching the light breeze stirring the twigs on the trees behind the houses opposite, he felt a slight tickle in his throat. Instinctively, he looked down at the glass in his hand. It was empty.

He shrugged his shoulders and turned away from the window. Well did he know the next step—toward the cabinet in the corner. He took that step, and another—and then stopped.

Goddammit, man. What the hell's up with you? Pull yourself together. He turned sharply and began to pace, back and forth, up and down the room. *I've gotta snap out of this. It's driving me crazy.*

He set the glass on the mantel over the fireplace, and turned to face the window again. From that position, he could see the new townhouses, most of them now completed.

All that bloody effort with the petition for nothing. Jeez. I wonder what kind of people will move in? His gaze settled on the flags fluttering over the recently opened townhouse show-home. *If I only knew what to do with my life: what course to move on, what direction to take.*

A flash of colour and sudden movement outside caught his attention. His son was home.

Wait for it, he thought, expecting the usual crashing sounds as Cody entered the house. Sure enough, there they were—sounds of the door slamming and of the heavy sports bag that seemed essential gear for all teenage boys thudding to the floor and sliding against the wall.

And then, an unexpected contrast ... Silently, Cody appeared at the entrance to the room. He was just fourteen, at that gangly stage. "Hi, Dad. Whatcha doing?" he said quietly.

"Hi, Cody. Oh, nothing much, just meditating on the scene."

"That's what you always say! Why do you do it?"

Dave sighed. He knew it was a cop-out. "We-ell. You know I

was in the Navy for a while."

"Yeah, in the Reserves."

"Each summer, I would go to sea on a ship. I spent a lot of time working on the ship's bridge, the command centre. I was one of the Officers of the Watch. We each took turns on duty for a watch; that's like a shift.

"I would spend a lot of time standing, surveying out across the sea ahead, out to the horizon. Sometimes, it was pretty hectic, with lots of other ships around; other times, it was very quiet, and it could get quite boring. And so I guess I acquired this habit."

"Were you, like, a captain then?"

"No way!" Dave chuckled. "I was just a lieutenant—naval, that is. Hmm—come to think of it, though, that's equivalent to an army captain, I guess." He laughed at his own little inside-joke.

"Da-ad?"

"Uh-huh."

"Scouter Ray was asking if you would be interested in helping out at the camp, on the May long weekend."

"We-ell—would you like me to?"

"Sure thing, Dad. Remember in Cubs, when we found that nest of snakes in the rocks, and Tommy nearly shi— had to go to the bathroom in a hurry?"

"Course I do. That was a great weekend. An' do you remember the wasp nest under the eave of the old barn?"

"Yeah, an' Baloo tried poking it with that pole and got stung."

"So, what's the plan for the camp?"

"Do'know yet. We're s'posed to meet in patrols next week to plan food an' stuff."

"Where's it going to be at?"

"Killarney Farm. You know, where we went two years ago, when you an' Mom came to pick us up, an' Mom got mad 'cause our boots were all muddy."

"Hope it's going to be drier this time. Anyway, does Scouter Ray want me to call him back?"

"Yeah, sure. Thanks, Dad."

Cody left, and Dave heard the fridge being raided. He smiled. He felt uplifted, somehow. He had always enjoyed camping, and especially working with young people. It was some years now since he had been active in Scouting, and he was pleased that Ray had asked him—and that Cody seemed to want him to go too.

Something good to look forward to now. Those were the days. I can almost smell the wood-smoke now. Trouble is, I can see the old faces, but the names are gone.

Reassured, he picked up his glass from the mantel, refilled it from the bottle in the cabinet, and resumed his position at the window. He sipped slowly at his scotch. He felt good.

He thought back to his ship-borne summers. And, it suddenly dawned on him: it was during that ship-time when he had acquired another habit. The ward-room was only a short distance from the bridge and, off-duty, he and his fellow junior officers, mostly young unattached guys, found the pleasures of alcohol—scotch especially—extremely attractive.

What else was there to do? Granted, you paid for it with a heavy head when your next watch came up, always too soon. But we were young then ... and foolish.

His reverie came abruptly to an end as Barbara's car came into the Gardens and swung into the driveway. Almost as a reflex action, he had moved his hand holding the glass behind his back as he edged away from the window.

As the front part of the car went out of sight close up to the house, he swallowed the remaining half glass of scotch, and placed the glass in an inconspicuous spot in the corner of the room.

He sat down in his chair, relishing the warmth from the rapid intake of the liquor, and picked up the magazine lying on the coffee table, flicking it open. He heard the sounds of his wife entering the house.

"Hi, dear, how are you?" she called out, as she stepped into the room.

"Oh, not bad. How was your day?"

"The pits, but not to worry. John lost a case, and you know when John loses a case the whole court house is at fault, not to mention his own staff." Barbara flopped into her chair, her arms hanging limp over its sides, her legs spread out in front. She kicked off her shoes.

"I'm sorry, love. You could do with a drink." Dave was on his feet, making toward the cabinet.

"Thanks, Dave, but no. No!" Dave stopped abruptly. "Yes," Barbara continued, "I would love one, but no, I'm not going to have one. We have to stop this habit. Come and sit down, please. Give me a kiss—that'll do me far more good."

Dave had caught himself in mid-stride. He turned back to her chair. Kneeling down, he gave her a kiss.

She squeezed his hand. "I feel so much better now," she said, smiling. "Seriously, love, we do have to cut right down on our scotch. It's doing bad things for us, for you."

"Hunh." Dave's grunt was a reluctant acknowledgement.

"So, how was your day?" Barbara's tone was cheery and upbeat again.

"Me? Oh, well—I did the laundry, cleaned out the closet in the basement …"

"That's good; it needed it. I had a call from Maggie this afternoon; she said to say hi to you. We didn't get to talk long, 'cause that was when John came back from court. Was he ever black. But give him his due, give him a day to get over it, and he'll be his normal, friendly self again."

"Big case?"

"No, not really. I think that was why he was so mad. If it had been a big one, he would have taken it as part of the game, but if he loses a small one, he kinda takes it personally."

"Mmm."

"Cody home?"

"Yep. He's got a Scout camp coming up, and he's asked me to help out."

"Oh Dave, that's nice. Did you say yes?"

"Of course."

"I'm glad, love. It's what you need. Something to take you out of yourself, doing what you like doing. Where will it be?"

"Killarney Farm, Cody says. You know, where he went a couple of years ago?"

"Yes, that muddy, mucky place. I hope it's drier this year."

❄❄❄

After a couple of days of showers, the bright sunny afternoon in Brewster Gardens was much warmer than normal for mid-May, in the high twenties in fact, and Dave felt no need for a jacket as he and Brutus stepped out for their walk.

The new townhouses had really upset their route, but they turned to go along the pathway alongside the little newly fenced yards, a shortcut to the remaining wasteland by the old brewery.

Suddenly, there was a scuffle and a snarling bark as Brutus stopped and backed up. Dave was shaken out of his daydream. Attacking Brutus was a small white terrier, on a leash already tangling around Brutus' legs. The leash ran upward to, *wow*, a sharp-looking young woman.

"Hamish, stop it. I'm so sorry. He just doesn't like big dogs," she said.

With some effort, Dave and the young woman eventually calmed the terrier and untangled the mess. Brutus took it all with little fuss.

"I really am sorry. Hi, I'm Kelly. We've only just moved in here, and Hamish is trying to stake his territory."

"That's okay. I'm Dave, and this is Brutus. And we're just getting used to these new houses being here."

"Let me get the dogs some water. It's so warm today. Come into the yard—I've a couple of dishes down here by the steps."

Dave found himself following Kelly into the yard. She motioned him to sit at a picnic table as she put water from the outside faucet into the dishes.

He watched her, and liked what he saw. She was wearing short shorts, with a form-fitting tee shirt. She had a pretty face framed with a pert hairstyle. All in all, very attractive. She sat down opposite him at the table. Somehow, she seemed vaguely familiar, but he couldn't place her.

"So is Brutus a husky?" she asked.

"Actually, he's a Malamute," Dave replied. "And yours is a Highland …"

"West Highland White," Kelly filled in. "He's a nice little dog, is Hamish, except when he meets big dogs for the first time. Just look at them now." She laughed. The dogs were lying contentedly on the new sod in the yard. "It's so warm today. Let me get us some juice." Without waiting for a response, she went into the house.

Dave, not really at his best after two scotches for lunch, watched as she quickly returned, carrying two plastic cups and a container of liquid. She poured juice into the cups. Just watching her movements was starting to arouse his own juices.

"My parents used to breed West Highlands," she continued. "But I lost Mum and Dad in a car crash five years ago."

"I'm sorry."

"Thanks. It was a difficult time. Ted and I had just got engaged, and we had all gone out for a celebration. Their car was hit by a drunk driver."

"That's awful."

"But we got married just after my twenty-fifth birthday."

Dave found himself fascinated by this young lady. It was just her manner, her bubbling personality. It was as though she really wanted to talk with him.

He sipped at the juice in the cup. He already had those two scotches inside him, and his groin was reacting on its own.

"So you've all moved in here now." Dave smiled, assuming a family of Kelly, her husband, and the dog.

"Just Hamish and me," Kelly smiled ruefully. "I lost Ted while he was diving. Something went wrong with his scuba, and he drowned."

"That's terrible. You've really had a run of tragedies."

"Yeah, it's been so hard these past two years, with only Hamish as company. We stayed in the apartment that Ted and I had, until I could buy this place. I just hope I can make a new life out here."

Dave looked at this attractive, vulnerable young woman, her face showing sadness, yet beauty. He felt drawn to her, but the picnic table saved him. Reality kicked in.

"Kelly, I feel really sorry for you. Let's hope that a new house, a new area can work for you. Er ... I guess Brutus really needs his walk. We'd better get going. Thanks for the juice."

They stood.

"No problem. I've really enjoyed meeting you and chatting. We'll see you around." A broad warm smile flashed across her face.

"You bet."

Brutus and Dave left the yard to continue their walk. Dave adjusted his groin, feeling aroused, refreshed, but strangely puzzled by his own reactions.

- 9 -

Dana reached her hand across the table and clasped Tony's hand. Their eyes met. She smiled coyly and looked down at the table. Tony slid round on the booth's curved bench seat until they were together. They kissed lightly, then sprang apart as the waitress sped past on her way to another booth.

Tony reached into a pocket in his jacket, which lay on the outer end of the bench. He laid a wrapped package on the table in front of Dana. She looked at him with wide eyes.

"Happy birthday," he said.

Dana quickly unwrapped the package, and held up the bracelet. "Tony, it's lovely." She turned toward him. "Thanks."

They leaned together and shared a long kiss. Tony helped her fit the bracelet on her wrist, as they gently caressed each other.

This was her seventeenth birthday, the twentieth of May, the first one she had not spent at the family table with her mother fussing over a birthday cake and some special food dishes.

Not that she hadn't enjoyed those other birthdays, but this one was different. She had her special someone to share it with. Tony had asked her parents if he could take her out for the occasion, and they had agreed immediately. She was so relieved; she had thought they might object.

"Are you ready to order now?" The waitress was standing at the table.

Dana felt quite bubbly as they waited for the food to arrive. "Did you see that crowd hanging around in the gym this aft?"

"No, what were they doing?"

"Trying to practice for a rally for Julie Henderson."

"D'you think she's gonna win?"

"Course not, Tone, Andrea's the best candidate for Student Co-President. Everyone knows that."

"I'm not so sure. I'm really not too keen on how she gets some votes."

"Come on." She snuggled up to him. "You know I'm going to vote for you next year." They kissed.

The food arrived, which was fortunate, as they were both hungry.

"You want ketchup?" came the call from the waitress.

"Please," replied Tony, and he proceeded to hide his fries under a red ooze.

"I don't know how you can do that," said Dana, reaching over and dipping one of her fries in Tony's red ketchup carpet.

"'Cause I like it!" He grinned.

Dana and Tony got off the bus down at the far end of Millerby Lane. They strolled hand-in-hand along the Lane, past the little warehouses and the lock-up units that several small businesses worked out of. It was always deserted along there in the evening.

The sun had set some time ago, and its twilight afterglow was almost gone. Dana and Tony fell into silence. Nothing need be said.

It was so difficult for them to be truly alone together, without someone likely to burst in on them at any moment. At Tony's house, they could go down to the rec room, but that wasn't private. Any other Ferruccio could appear there without warning, and had done a couple of times when Dana and Tony had had to do a quick cover-up.

At Dana's place, it was even harder, not having a real rec room, and the atmosphere being different. Her mother and father always seemed to need to know what was happening in every room of the house.

Granted, there was the Saturday when her parents had gone on a visit to her uncle in Montreal, and Iain had had an all-day training session; Dana and Tony had spent that afternoon in her bedroom. But that was so long ago, all of two months.

They walked around the side of Dino's Auto-Body Shop, past the ghostly hulks of derelict car bodies, and onto the straight, flat ridge that was all that remained of the old railroad track-bed.

They turned along it, walking away from the Gardens, the old brewery with its now-padlocked gates on their right, its high brick wall looming in the darkness. Bushes and small trees clustered up against the wall.

They continued on, past the section where the wall was broken down, to the stream, where the piers of the long-ago-removed bridge still stood on guard at each side of the water. Dana felt a warm flush pass through her.

Tony stepped off the flat trail and, helping Dana down over the grassy tussocks, guided her toward the darkness by the brewery wall. They found a secluded grassy bank, backed by the wall and shrouded by bushes, whose new leaves now provided a partial screen.

They settled into a comfy hollow on the bank and embraced. Dana eased up her sweater. She could feel Tony's weight as his arm pressed across her midriff. He felt so good and warm. Suddenly she tensed and raised her head, peering into the darkness. Tony pushed himself up and rolled away.

"Wassup?" he whispered.

"Do'know. There's something out there."

They both heard the sound: chink, chink—like a chain. It came from the railroad trail.

Dana reached down and, arching her back, smoothed down her sweater. Tony struggled to recover his composure.

There was the sound again, closer.

"There's somebody coming along," Dana whispered.

"Just lie still. Don't make a sound," hushed Tony, sliding his left arm under her neck and cradling her breast with his right hand.

In the light of the moon, Dana could see the source of the sound. One large dog on a leash, held by a man, and a smaller dog led by a woman.

She and Tony lay still and close.

The quartet came along the track-bed, right up to the bridge pier, and stopped. They were no more than fifteen metres away. The larger dog sat down as the small one snuffled in the grass.

The man and woman turned to each other and continued their conversation, the man pointing to various features around them, including the wall and the old bridge piers.

Suddenly, the woman leaned forward and kissed the man on the cheek. Somewhat taken aback, the man hesitated for a moment; then, he put his arms around the woman and they embraced, her head against his shoulder.

Dana gasped, then struggled to contain herself as her foot dislodged a small twig.

The dogs stirred and the big one stood up, looking toward the wall. Unaware of being watched, the couple unlocked, turned, and began to walk back along the track-bed from where they had come. The dogs led the way.

"Did you see who it was?" gasped Dana, once the group was

out of earshot.

"Yeah," muttered Tony, disparagingly. "I'm almost sure it was Mr Adkins."

"Yeah, I know, but it wasn't Mrs Adkins—did you see who it was?"

"No, I didn't get a good look at her face."

"It looked like a woman I've seen going into one of the townhouses. She had a little dog, too."

"She only looked to be in her twenties."

"Yeah. Sexy old man."

Tony's hand slid across Dana's front. Gently, she stopped him. "No, Tony. Not now."

"Can't we?"

"It's too late." She smiled at him. "Help me up."

He obliged. She kissed him and gently stroked his hair.

It was evening, a short while after sunset. Dave and Brutus reached the end of Millerby Lane, to find Kelly standing there as Hamish watered a thistle plant.

"Oh hi, Dave."

"Hi, Kelly, how are you today?"

"I'm great. Dave, what's down that old trail over there?"

Dave, flushed with the warmth of the two scotches he'd taken, as a custom, before he and Brutus had set out, did not hesitate. "Let's go down there, I'll show you."

They set off along the old railroad track-bed, Brutus stoically plodding along, Hamish snuffling at every upstanding plant.

"This used to be one of the railroads that came into the Ottawa area from the south. Steam trains used to come chuffing through here long before all the houses were built. I think the tracks were actually still in place when the first folks moved in."

"That's fascinating. I've always loved steam engines. I liked it when my Dad would take me to one of the train museums. What was this brick wall for?"

"Yes, these old buildings over here were once a thriving brewery. The wasteland back there was a rail yard with sidings, with freight cars bringing in supplies and taking full barrels of beer away."

"How do you know all this, Dave?"

"I love learning about the history of an area, and if railroads are involved, that's a double interest."

"Just like Dad was. If he wasn't at dog shows or seeking out breeding matches for his West Highland Whites, he was searching out old railroads and digging in museums."

Kelly was silent for a while as they strolled along, the only sound really being the chinking of Brutus' chain and the rattle of the clip on Hamish's leash. Dave felt strangely at ease in her company.

"I noticed what looked like new gates in the brewery wall back there," Kelly suddenly broke the silence. "That seems odd, if it's not used now?"

"Oh, yeah, they are very recent. There was a bit of trouble in there last fall, with teens drinking. We contacted the old owner and he paid to have us put the gates on."

"Old owner?"

"Yeah, lives in Kingston, in his nineties."

"Cool."

They had reached the old bridge pier, the end of the trail. Dave waved his arm out toward the water.

"So this is the Otter Brook."

"As in the street name?"

"Yep. You know, they used to soak the new barrels in this stream—"

Suddenly, Kelly turned and kissed Dave on the cheek.

Dave looked at her, standing there in the half-light, and hugged her closely. *Her boobs feel so good,* he thought. Her head rested against his shoulder. He sensed a stirring in his groin, a hardening.

63

How long they stood there, he had no idea. He caught the sound of a twig snapping; the dogs stirred, and he eased back from the hug. Without a word, they all turned and slowly made their way back to the Millerby Lane.

Dave was in turmoil. *What the hell is happening?*

"That was great, Dave, thanks." She flashed him a smile, turned, and, with Hamish trotting alongside, headed toward the townhouses.

Dave's mind was in a real mess now; his whole body was churning. *Kelly, Kelly, oh, jeez, what do I do now?*

He made his way home, dealt with Brutus' needs, headed to the basement, and drank half a glass of scotch before flopping into a chair. His head sagged; he heaved himself back up in his chair and took another swig of his scotch.

Bloody hell. How could I have fallen into this mess? he agonized. *More to the point, how can I get out of it? What next? I can't just avoid her; we're bound to meet in the street. I can't just have an affair with her—that's wrong. I don't want to hurt Barb. Jeez, but just thinking about Kelly now makes me ache. Oh, shit! An' this on top of everything else—oh, man!*

- 10 -

Six months can see a lot of changes, thought Dwayne Hampden as he pottered in his front yard, cutting off the winterkill from his roses. He raised his eyes as he straightened his back and caught the view of the townhouses across the roadway. *It's amazing how they almost look as if they've been there for years,* he said to himself.

Albez, the builder, had made an effort to blend the new construction with the existing landscape, and had planted a few trees that looked as if they were going to survive. They had bright new leaves now, a good sign.

Most of the townhouses were sold. They had been snapped up in less than two months. Dwayne had heard that some fellow had bought up four of them and was renting them out, but most were occupied by their owners.

Better that way, he thought. *People likely will have more respect—don't want the area going downhill.*

Dwayne liked things the way they had been. He was not one for rapid changes, if he could avoid them. 'Slow and easy' was one of his favourite sayings. He went back to tending his roses.

The sound of a car engine starting made him look up again. Two houses down, Roger DeLaunais was backing his car off his driveway.

Dwayne straightened his back and gave a wave as Roger drove slowly past, acknowledging with a return wave. Dwayne had plenty of time for Roger: a good steady fellow, he was a master plumber.

Suddenly, the peace was shattered by a squealing of tires, and then shouting. Dwayne turned sharply, and looked up to see people running out of the townhouse parking area into the Gardens roadway.

Roger's car was stopped in the middle of the road, and a young girl was lying on the road, a few paces in front of the car. A ball was rolling loose.

A crowd of children was gathering as Dwayne started toward the scene. Roger had got out of his car and was squatting down by the girl. A young woman with a little white dog was running over to them, and he could see Barbara Adkins coming along the sidewalk as fast as she could.

A woman came rushing from the townhouses. She took one look at the girl lying on the roadway and started screaming and yelling at Roger, who was clearly taken aback.

As Dwayne reached the scene, the young woman with the dog was stooping over the girl, and at the same time trying to intervene in the confrontation occurring above her.

"Let me take the dog," offered Dwayne.

The young woman smiled up at him and passed over the leash. "I know First Aid," she said, gently caressing the girl. "You're going to be okay, little girl. I'm Kelly, and we're going to help you feel better." She was carefully checking the girl.

Barbara had joined the group, and Dwayne gave his attention to the confrontation between the yelling woman and Roger. It was evident that she was the child's mother, and assumed that Roger had knocked her daughter down with the car. Roger was protesting that he had not.

Dwayne took charge, and moved them a few steps away from the still-unconscious child. "For Pete's sake, have some common sense. Your child is hurt—deal with that problem before worrying about anything else. Has anyone gone to phone for the police and ambulance?" He had raised his voice for everyone to hear.

"No, but I'm calling on my cell right now," came an anonymous voice from the gathered crowd.

"Is she going to be okay?" The mother was now showing concern about her child.

"We can't tell yet," Kelly said. "She's breathing okay. Does someone have a coat or a blanket to put over her?"

"Here, take my jacket." Barbara slipped off her jacket and passed it over. "You know, I saw the whole thing as I was coming round the corner there. Roger here didn't run into the little girl. She ran out in front of the car and tripped—it's lucky he could stop before he did run over her."

"Huh." The mother was not convinced.

"That is what happened," confirmed Kelly, as she tried to make the child comfortable without moving her. "I saw everything."

"Huh, we'll wait till the police come, and see what they have to say." The mother lit a cigarette and turned her back on the group.

What a silly woman, thought Dwayne as he unwound the dog's leash from his legs. *Full of accusation, and barely any concern for her child.*

Gradually, the gathering of children and other adults was dispersing. A couple of girls about the same age as the injured one hung on, sheepishly waiting on the sidewalk.

Kelly was again tending to the girl, who was stirring. "It's okay, you're going to be all right. I'm Kelly, and I'm looking after you right now. Don't worry, little one." She looked up toward the mother. "What's her name?"

"Jeannine."

"Okay, Jeannine, try not to move. Does anything hurt?"

The sounds of a police car, followed by an ambulance, drowned out any response, as everyone changed stance. The ambulance crew immediately went to tend to the girl, with Kelly briefing them on status. The policeman came over to the others, to be set upon immediately by the mother.

"I'm Connie Weston, officer. This idiot here hit my daughter with his car."

Roger and the others protested loudly.

"Hold on, now. One at a time. I'll have to take statements in an orderly fashion. You, sir," he said, looking at Roger. "Were you driving this car?"

"Yes, I was."

"Please come with me to my vehicle. I'll need to …" The sounds were lost as they went from earshot.

Barbara took Dwayne aside and whispered, "He definitely didn't hit her—I could see it all. The poor thing ran out into the road and tripped. Must've hit her head on the pavement."

"Must say, I don't think much of her mother, Barb."

"Me neither."

They stood and waited. The mother was standing some distance away, smoking and looking pained. One of the ambulance crew walked toward her.

Kelly joined Dwayne and Barbara.

"You did a good job there," said Dwayne, as he handed back the dog's leash.

"Thanks, she must have hit her head hard on the road as she fell. I'm Kelly McDowell," she held out her hand. Dwayne shook it.

"Dwayne Hampden. Say, have I seen you somewhere before?" Kelly looked puzzled.

"Barbara Adkins. You're new around here, Kelly?"

"Oh, er—hi, Barbara. Yes, I moved into the Mews a few weeks ago."

"Nice little Highland White."

"Hamish. Yes, he's lovable. Aren't you?" said Kelly, as she stooped and scroffled the dog's head.

"We have a Malamute, Brutus. You've probably seen him around with my husband, Dave."

"Er, yes. I—er—met Brutus and Dave the other day."

Roger was coming from the police car, looking shaken. The policeman had gone over to the mother, who was still talking with the paramedic. She returned to the police car with the policeman.

"You okay, Roger?"

"Not really, Dwayne. He grilled me through and through, like I'd hit the kid. I don't think he believes me."

"Well I know you didn't, an' I'll tell him straight," said Barbara vehemently.

"And I saw it all as well," added Kelly, "and I'll tell him that too. By the way, I'm Kelly McDowell."

"Thanks. Roger DeLaunais."

Dwayne looked about him. The two girls were still on the sidewalk.

Suddenly the door of the police car opened. The mother got out quickly, slamming the door shut, and strode over to the ambulance. One of the crew helped her inside, and in seconds the ambulance was gone.

The policeman came over to the group, pushing his cap back and scratching the top of his head.

"Did any of you others actually witness the incident?"

Barbara raised her hand. "I did."

"And so did I," said Kelly.

"Good. Could I talk with you first, please, and then you?" He motioned first to Barbara and then to Kelly. Barbara went with him to his car.

Time was beginning to drag now. Dwayne had not actually seen the accident, and so was not a witness, but he felt an integral part of the whole incident.

Clearly, the mother was convinced that Roger had hit the child, but Dwayne had known Roger for so long that if Roger said he had not done so, Dwayne believed him. He felt he needed to stay around to support Roger. Anyway, both Barbara and this Kelly said that Roger was in the clear.

Come to think of it, I didn't actually see the girl fall, and as the mother arrived only moments before I reached the spot, how on earth could she know what actually happened?

Barbara returned. Now it was Kelly's turn. Dwayne took the leash again; not that he normally looked after dogs, but it seemed to have become his automatic responsibility as Kelly's deputy. He smiled to himself at the thought.

"Seems a nice young lady," he said, once Kelly was in the police car.

"Yes, seemed to know what she was doing with the little girl," agreed Barbara.

"Pretty, too," commented Roger.

Barbara stooped to fuss the dog. "There's a good boy. She'll be back in a minute or two."

Soon, Kelly returned. As she rejoined the group, the policeman walked past them to the two girls, still hovering on the sidewalk. He squatted down in front of them, bringing his face to the level of theirs.

Dwayne watched as the policeman talked with the girls. They were obviously very self-conscious.

Suddenly the policeman stood up, patted them both on the shoulder, and walked over to the group. "Sorry for all the trouble, folks. I do have to get all the facts and talk to the witnesses. Mr DeLaunais, you are quite free to go. You clearly were not the cause of the child's misfortune. Thank you all for your patience. Good day."

"Thanks."

"Bye."

They watched the police car depart. Roger shook his head.

"Just take it very gently now, Roger. You sure you're okay?"

"I'll be okay, thanks, Dwayne. Just sets you back a bit, though." He climbed into his car and started the engine.

Kelly gathered her dog. "Bye, then."

"Bye, Kelly, see you around."

"Bye."

Dwayne and Barbara wandered slowly across to the sidewalk. "Well, I guess we've got younger kids in the area again. They need somewhere to play, I s'pose."

"But not in the roadway, Dwayne, eh?"

Dwayne nodded.

Thwack—zing—thwack.

Taken by surprise, Dwayne turned toward the sounds, coming from the same area as the accident. He could see a youth with a baseball glove now standing in the middle of the roadway.

Zing—thwack. A ball appeared from deep in the parking area, straight into the waiting gloved hand. The youth took the ball into his other hand and wound up for the return throw. *Zing*—a quieter thwack, out of sight. And so it continued, back and forth.

Dwayne shook his head. Well did he know the pleasures of playing catch; he'd played it often enough when his kids were young. But in those days the road was much safer, he thought. Now, with the extra traffic, somebody's going to be hurt.

"See you, Dwayne."

"Bye, Barbara." He turned and walked back up to his rose bushes, wondering what the next disturbing event might be.

- 11 -

The Trans-Am rounded the corner from Millerby Lane and eased into the Mews parking area, coming to rest in the third parking spot. The driver quickly jumped out and, handing himself off the trunk lid, leapt round to open the passenger door with a mock salute.

Jane Stennings, with a decorous smile and a nod of acknowledgement, stepped out and promptly gave her husband Graham a friendly punch in the stomach.

He grinned. "What was that for?" he protested.

"'Cause I love you."

"Oh!"

At that instant, a movement out in the Gardens' roadway caught Jane's attention. She puzzled for a second, followed by recognition. Someone was waving to her—yes, it was Dana, the young girl whose brother had been killed back in the fall, that awful tragedy.

Dana hadn't said much that icy night but she had a presence, Jane remembered, and then Dana had asked for Jane's help for her family.

Yes, Jane remembered, *Dana and I had a good chat when we met later. I'd be happy to do more with her.*

Jane smiled and waved back. "Hi, Dana," she called as Dana approached.

"Hi, er, Jane ... I didn't know you lived here."

Jane laughed, taking the lead. "Well, we've only been here two weeks. Nice to see you again, Dana. Yes, do call me Jane, please. This is my husband, Graham. Graham, Dana. Graham's in the Army."

"Pleased to meet you, Dana."

"Hi."

Jane sensed Dana's slight embarrassment after this initial contact with the imposing figure of Graham.

"Actually, Dana, we've only been married a month—since May nineteenth."

"Congratulations—that's great." Dana seemed impressed. "Look, I've gotta go now, but ..."

"Come and visit with us, Dana," said Jane, earnestly.

"Thanks, I'd love to. Bye for now." Dana jogged away.

"Bye," said Jane. Turning to Graham, she added quietly, "That's the girl I told you about after that tragedy, when the two boys were killed. She's the sister of one of them. The family lives just down the road."

"Seems a nice girl."

"Yes, I agree."

They entered the townhouse. It still had that new smell to it—paint, plaster, an indefinable aroma. It was still sparsely furnished—they simply hadn't had time to shop for much furniture yet.

In spite of their careful planning leading up to the wedding, they hadn't bargained for that two-week trip that Graham had had to make back to the Middle East—that had really given them problems, with so much falling at the last minute on Jane's shoulders. But the guys on the Police Force had been really helpful.

The actual wedding had been down in Windsor, because Jane's mother was not strong enough to travel. Graham's family had gone down from Sudbury, and Jane's brother and his wife had joined them from Niagara. In all, a quiet affair. But because most of Jane's and Graham's friends and workmates were up in the Ottawa area, they had held a bigger reception for them here.

It had been a bit of a rush—Windsor one weekend, then half a honeymoon, then back to Ottawa for the reception, then off for another week together. They were glad to be in their own home, at last.

Graham was finding his new Army duties rather more demanding than they had both expected. Being a liaison officer meant just that—to liaise, to go-between, and there had been rather a lot of going. *But,* Jane thought to herself, *the coming-backs are great.*

"I have to go downstairs and see to those pants," said Graham, standing at the top of the basement stairs.

"Go on then, you can do mine while you're at it." Jane grinned. "You could do my boots too."

"Yeah, sure." Graham grimaced as he went downstairs.

The basements of the townhouses had been rough-finished by the builder—rough-taped drywall and electrical outlets. Graham and Jane had set up one corner as their uniform storage: a simple movable armoire, some pegs on the wall, a chest of drawers, a cupboard to contain cleaning and repair materials, and, of course, an ironing board.

Jane snuggled down in her leather chair in the living room and flicked the remote to turn on the stereo. *Must have one of his CDs in,* she thought as sound filled the room, *I don't recognize it.* Their music tastes differed, but there were overlaps. Graham was mostly into late-nineteenth to mid-twentieth-century classical music. Jane preferred musicals. But they both got a kick, literally, out of country and western.

The music drifted past Jane. Her mind was on the brief encounter they'd had with Dana. She recalled the feeling she'd had when she'd got back to her apartment that tragic night last November. How she'd felt that she was involved in some way beyond her role as a police officer. Again she felt an urge to help Dana in some, as yet undefined, way.

She heard Graham bounding up the stairs. "Ta-dah," he exclaimed, waving her shining boots in front of her.

"Gee, thanks, hon." She smiled. "I didn't really expect you to."

"That's okay. You can do mine when I get back from the Petawawa range next weekend."

"What a deal. Come on," she said, standing up and slipping her arm round his waist. "Let's get some supper on the way—oh, that reminds me, we left a bag in the car trunk. I'll go get it."

Jane was just closing the trunk lid when she noticed a car coming round the corner from Millerby Lane into the Gardens. It was weaving a bit, and hit the curb on the turn.

Jane automatically flipped into work mode, and watched as the car pulled into a driveway farther along the street.

Dave Adkins was stepping out of his car as he caught sight of a woman running up the road toward him. "Excuse me, sir ... sir," she was calling.

He stood still. *What's going on?* he thought.

"I watched as you drove round the corner and along the road here," the woman started as she reached the driveway. "I am a cop, but I'm off-duty, and I have no means of testing you. As a neighbour, though, I do have the duty to warn you that driving under the influence of alcohol or anything else is illegal, and dangerous. What I just saw with your erratic driving prompted me to speak to you." The woman stood back, looking hard at Dave.

Dave was surprised, and a bit confused; he didn't know what to say.

Jane continued. "Sir, your face is familiar. We've met before. Weren't you at the funeral of those two young boys last year?"

Dave was now in a befuddled mess. Slowly his mind caught up with Jane's questioning. "Er, yeah, I was," he replied.

"Then, sir, I beg of you, think of the possible consequences of your actions." Jane turned and jogged back to the Mews.

Dave picked up the bag of items he'd just bought at the 7-Eleven store by the new traffic lights at Otterbrook and Millerby and went into the house.

Sheesh! All I did was drive half a kilometre to the store and back, he thought. He put the carton of milk into the fridge, and left the rest of the items on the counter. *I need a drink.* He wandered into the living room, poured out a scotch, and slumped into his usual chair.

Out of the corner of his eye, he saw the flash of red, and then the loud bang as the front door opened. Cody and two friends barged into the house, crashing sports bags on the floor, kicking runners off their feet, and yelling at one another in loud voices.

"What the hell are you doing?" Dave blazed. He was furious.

"Just, er, coming home ..." said Cody, weakly.

"Then for God's sake, get out and come in again properly. Out, out, the damn lot of you."

Cody looked at his friends, shrugged his shoulders, and they gathered up their stuff, slinking quietly out of the door.

Dave was now in a real mess. He walked unsteadily through the house to the rec room downstairs.

Dave woke to a shaking feeling.

"Come on, Dave, wake up, it's seven-thirty in the morning; you slept all night down here."

He could hear the voice, and gradually realized that Barbara was shaking him, hard. "Er, wha—?" was all he could muster.

"Come on, David, this is enough. We've had enough of this nonsense. You've got to take hold of yourself and stop this drinking, for your sake and for the rest of us."

Gradually, he came into a semblance of consciousness. His head pounded, he felt queasy; in fact, he felt like shit. Barb was on her knees in front of him, staring hard at him, straight into his eyes. He couldn't face her, his eyes turned away.

"Look at me, David, look at me. Do you want to destroy this family? Do you? Look at me, will you?"

Dave met her eyes for a moment. "I'm sorry. I'm sorry."

"Just being sorry isn't good enough anymore, David. I love you, we all love you, but something has to change—you have got to change, right now. We can't—you can't go on like this anymore. You are going to get up, have some breakfast if you want, and then we'll talk. I've called in to work and taken the morning off. We've got to get you sorted out—that's priority number one."

Late that afternoon, with the sun low in the sky, Dave and Brutus reached the bottom of their driveway and turned right along the street. At least, Dave did. Brutus was still not used to this change in tack; they had always turned to the left, for years. Why the change now?

These last few days, Dave, in his torment, had taken to walking the dog on a different route, round the Gardens the opposite way, out onto Millerby, down to the traffic lights at Otterbrook, and over beyond the 7-Eleven. He dared not pass by Kelly's place—he just did not know how to handle the situation, if they were to meet.

The dog quickly recovered from the mis-turn, and they set off for their evening walk.

Dave's mind was in turmoil again. He was struggling with the incident with that cop-lady—that was not nice. He had essentially been given an ultimatum by his wife over alcohol and what it was doing to him and the family.

And there was this. What would happen if Barbara did invite Kelly round for a visit? And she was likely to do so. What was really going on? Was he imagining things—was he reading things into that stroll, that kiss, that embrace, that just weren't there?

But I can't go on like this, I would be bloody stupid. Sure she's real pretty, a breath of fresh air. But it's got to stop there—whatever was in that evening can't go on. But what will she do? What will she think? How will she react? How did she react when she met Barbara at that accident?

He had to find out; he had to know. He just had to know, so he would know how to react, how to handle himself when this visit happened. He knew Barbara; when she had an idea like that, it always came to pass. Kelly would be visiting them. But he couldn't face an encounter just yet.

All went well with the walk until they were coming back up past the side of the 7-Eleven to the traffic lights. Coming along Otterbrook were Kelly and the terrier. No escape—there was nothing he could do to escape. They met at the lights.

"Hi, Dave."

"Hi, Kelly."

Kelly had a pained look on her face. "Look, Dave, we need to talk."

Dave nodded, uneasily.

"Dave, I want to say I'm sorry."

"Sorry? You?" Now this really threw Dave. He had no idea what might come next.

"Yes, I truly am. I didn't realize what I was doing to you."

Dave was becoming more uncomfortable. *What's next?* he thought.

"I was giving you wrong signals when we talked, when we went for that walk, without knowing what I was doing."

Now Dave was really puzzled.

Kelly continued. "Dave, I found myself desperately wanting to talk with you, to be with you, to listen to what you were saying, so much it hurt at times. I really was attracted to you."

Dave was sweating. He was so tense he could sense his pulse throbbing in his neck.

"I so wanted to be with you, to not let you go. When you hugged me, it felt so good," she continued.

Dave could feel a tightness building in his groin. He looked at her standing there, so attractive, so vulnerable. He was lost for words, what could he say?

"Kel—" he began.

"Dave," she continued, "you are so like my father was, your balding hair, wisps falling over your forehead, your love of the outdoors, just how you were telling me all about the history of the railroad, and everything. Oh, it was just as if …" Tears welled in her eyes. "Oh, Dave, I am so sorry."

Dave was stunned. So he was a father figure, not a lover. Deflating in one sense, but a profound relief in another.

"Kelly, I'm sorry too. Sorry if I embarrassed you that evening."

"But I've embarrassed you far more, dear Dave. I'm alone, but you, you have your wife to think of. Please, can we put this behind us and be normal, neighbourly friends? I really do enjoy your company. You will always remind me of my father—except he would have been quite a few years older!" She chuckled. "And, truly, I'd like to be a friend of your wife, too. I met her the other day—there was an accident …"

"I know. Barb told me you'd met …"

"I—I was a bit taken aback when she introduced herself, 'cause I was so worried about what I'd done to you, and how you might have taken it. But Barbara was so pleasant …"

"Kelly, Barb has said she would like to invite you round to visit. I must say, I've been more than a bit uptight about it, to say the least."

Kelly put her hand on his arm. "Dear Dave, please—let me see my father through you, but let me get to know the real Dave, and Barbara too." She flashed him a smile so warm that her teary eyes seemed to sparkle. Dave looked at her in a new light.

"Kelly, you're on." He looked up at the lights. "Let's cross while the lights are green for us."

They walked on up toward the townhouses.

"Where do you work, then?" This was a topic they hadn't touched on before. Dave was feeling so relieved now; his world had been imploding in on him. He could handle the alcohol, he felt; he could cope with the all-pervading feeling of depression; he could resolve all the stress he had wrought in his family, he was sure; but he had had no idea how to fix this Kelly affair. Now, it was solved.

"Oh, just outside of the downtown core. I'm a receptionist at a law firm, Simpson Stocker Wyatt Pimms. I answer the phones and do some of the typing for the two junior partners."

"Hey! Now it all comes together. I felt when we first met that I'd seen you somewhere before. Last December, two of us came to see George Simpson—now I remember your eyes and your smile as you worked the phones."

"Yes—and I remember now thinking that that man reminds me so much of Dad."

Dave and Brutus turned into their driveway, Brutus automatically heading to the gate of his pen.

After checking the dog's food and water, Dave stood there, in the light of the setting sun. The air was still; overhead, the evening star was beginning to shine through the last remnants of daylight in the sky. The evening sounds of the community were subdued. But there was a strange clarity in the air.

It suddenly hit him: what a bloody stupid idiot he had been these past months. A cold shudder rippled through him, as he stood in the warm air.

What stupidity, what an idiot! Poor Barbara, and Cody, what have I put them through—hell, that's what. And why? Why? Because of my own blindness, my own weakness, my own self-centredness.

He felt his legs crumpling; he grasped at the fence and edged himself over to the wooden bench at the side of the house. His head in his hands, tears fell down his cheeks.

Everything came crumbling down: the events, the actions, the inactions of the past months paraded through his mind. *What an idiot!* And Barbara, dear Barbara, she had tried so often to get through to him—but he couldn't see, he couldn't understand what was happening to him. And his reaction had been to become even crabbier, more cantankerous, uncooperative—and to drink more.

Another cold shudder rocked his body. *I could have lost Barb—I could still lose her. Shit!* He sat bolt upright. In a flash, he was heading down to the basement, two stairs at a time.

———

"Hi, love," Barbara called out as she descended the basement stairs. "What are you up to?"

Dave looked up. "Doing what I should have done long ago, getting rid of this stuff."

He was pouring the contents of a bottle of scotch down the bar-sink. Several empty bottles stood on one side of the sink, with other full bottles of various liquors lined on the other side.

"Oh, Dave." She rushed over to him and hugged him. He hugged her hard, then held her back at arm's length.

"I love you," he said, tears streaming down his face.

"And I love you." Barbara pulled him close again.

After all the bottles of liquor and beer and wine had been emptied, they sat close together on one of the sofas in the semi-light of the rec room. Dave felt he owed it to Barbara to open up on all his issues, including the Kelly business.

"Love, no matter what," Barbara said quietly as he ended, "we've come through all this together. It's history. Let's go up to bed now, and I'll show you how much I love you."

- 12 -

The sun hung in the hazy July sky, with not a breath of wind to stir the leaves on the trees. The Gardens were quiet. Everyone, it seemed, was too hot to do anything energetic.

The large linden tree between the Johnson house and the Ferruccio's cast a wide area of shade on the grass, and there had gathered most of the Gardens' older teenagers. In fact, Dana realized, this was rather a rare event, because normally they mostly went their own separate ways—there was no unifying force among them. They went to at least three different schools, some had part-time jobs now, and somehow they did not normally 'gel' as a group. But the heat today seemed to have melded them together in the shade.

Dana and Tony sat there, Tony with his back up against the tree, Dana leaning against him. Jason Johnson sat cross-legged to his side of the tree. Fiona Stacey, usually a loner, had wandered over and was sprawled out on her front near Jason. Gina Ferruccio was lying on the grass, a little down the slope toward the roadway from Dana. Her brother Angelo sat on the edge of the group.

Dana's brother, Iain, had just joined them, flumping down in an overheated heap near the kerb. "Sup?" he asked nobody in particular.

"Nothing much."

"Whatcha doing?"

"Just sitting."

"Hunmh." Iain joined the demanding silence.

It was true; they were doing nothing much. Barely twenty words had been passed among them all afternoon, and few had risen above the level of the eight just exchanged. It was just too damned hot to bother to think, let alone speak. Silence reigned.

Then suddenly, Dana spoke. "What we need is a Youth Centre."

"Hunh?"

"Eh?"

Those first words had shattered perhaps the longest of the afternoon's silences. Dana had raised herself to an upright position as she had spoken them.

"Whadya mean, Dan?" asked Iain.

"Like the Y?" quizzed Gina.

"Well, kind of. What I think is, like, we've all grown up here with nothing close by where we could go and do things together. Like, if we wanted a dance, or just to hang out, or do things, crafts or whatever. Play ball or something. Like, we don't even have a softball diamond."

"We've used the one down Otterbrook," noted Jason.

"Yeah, I know, but that's not here," responded Dana. "I was just thinking. This afternoon's the first time I can remember us all being together like this."

"Yeah, well, so what? Okay, we need a Youth Centre. Where and how do we get one?" Jason was a demander.

"I think we've got one waiting for us, if we ask the right people," said Dana, coyly.

"Come on, Dan, give it to us," said Tony, a little impatiently.

"Listen up," began Dana. "Lookit, we've got the buildings, and the land, all waiting. We've just got to convince the right people to help us make it all work …"

"Come off it, Dana, whatcha talking about?" Jason too was not clued in yet.

"The old brewery, you jerks," said Dana, smiling and shaking her head. "Look, if we can convince the old guy that owns it, and get people round here to help us, I'm sure we can do it. Whatcha think?"

"Yeah, sure, whatever."

"Sounds good to me."

"Cool."

"Yeah, we'd need air conditioning!"

They laughed. Dana stood up and smoothed the seat of her shorts.

"Hey, you guys! You want to cool off?" came a voice from the Johnson driveway.

They turned to be greeted by Mr Johnson, carrying a box of popsicles.

"Hey man, that's great."

"Gee thanks, Dad."

"Thanks, Mr Johnson."

They all stood in the shade, licking and scrunching their popsicles.

"You guys been setting the world to rights, then?" Mr Johnson inquired.

"Not exactly, too hot."

"Yeah, but Dana's come up with a great idea, if it'll work."

"What's that then, Dana?"

"Well, I think the kids around here need a Youth Centre. Like, to do things together, games, dances, crafts, just hanging out. Better than the young kids playing in the street or in the parking by the townhouses. An' we wouldn't have to drag off into town if we just wanted to do anything beyond sitting in somebody's basement."

"That sounds like a great idea," said Mr Johnson, but his

expression became quizzical. "But what do you have in mind? Where and how?"

"The old brewery, Dad." Jason filled him in.

"Hmm! That *is* a good idea, if it could work. You'd have to get the owner to agree. And then there's the whole business of fixing up the place. That'd cost a lot of money. And who would run the place? It wouldn't look after itself. And there's the security aspect, too. And the city would have to approve—there'd be a lot of work involved."

"I know," said Dana. "I know. But I've had this idea going through my mind for a while now. I've thought of all those problems. But if it's something we all think should be done, I think we can make it happen."

"Good for you, Dana," said Mr Johnson.

"Maybe we could apply for a grant or something," suggested Fiona.

"Yeah, an' maybe we could get people around here to help out, to get the place fixed up," added Gina.

"Yeah, why not?"

Mr Johnson stood taller than the rest of them. He was used to coaching teams, and he began to slip into that role.

"Look," he started, "first, you need to find out what the old fellow that owns the place thinks about the idea. Maybe, Dana, you could contact him or, better yet, his lawyer—what's his name now? Er—Simpson, yes, George Simpson. Mr Hampden and Mr Adkins dealt through him—oh, and so did Tony's dad."

"Do you think people around here would go for the idea?" Dana looked straight at Mr Johnson. He looked back at her. She felt a hint of uncertainty.

"Hmmm, you've got a point there." He paused, and stroked his chin. "I don't know, to be honest, Dana. There's a few people who might not like the idea. But the only way to find out is to ask them."

"I guess we'd have to check with the owner first. If he's not for it, it's dead."

"Surely."

Dana turned to Tony. "We'll go talk to your dad when he gets home, and see how to get hold of Mr Simpson."

The group began to break up. "Thanks for the popsicles, Mr Johnson!"

"No problem. My pleasure!"

Dana and Tony wandered across the grass to Tony's driveway. She caught his hand.

"How long you been thinking about that, then?" he said.

"Dunno, it kind of grew on me."

"D'you think it'll fly?" Tony's look was sceptical. He had said very little.

"If we all want it to, it'll fly, yeah."

Tony squeezed her hand and they kissed lightly. Dana danced over the street to her house, a little puzzled by Tony's reaction—he seemed a bit doubtful about her idea.

- 13 -

Mike was in a bad mood. He'd just received yet another cannonading letter from his ex-wife's lawyer; matters were deteriorating still further. Once inside the 7-Eleven, he stormed down the first aisle. He reached into the cooler and lifted out a carton of milk. He was closing the door, when …

"Mike Carson! What brings you here?"

Mike turned, startled, still black in mood. An older man was standing there grinning at him. Mike frowned for a moment, and then recognition lit up his face.

"Dave Adkins! How are you? Gee, haven't seen you since that Jamboree in Guelph. Man, you're looking great. How's life?"

"Not so bad, not so good, Mike. Got laid off at Christmas—been out of work since, but …"

"Gee, that's too bad. Say, how's Jackson doing? He must be out of school now."

"Yep, he's in college, doing Commerce. How about you?"

"Not so bad. Working out in the east-end with Ferrier; you

know, air conditioners and so on."

"So, you living around here, then?"

"Yeah, I'm renting a room from a couple of friends who just bought one of the new townhouses. Elaine and I split last year. You?"

"We're in the Gardens, third house in. That's great, Mike, you must come over and visit with Barbara and me."

"Barbara? I thought …" Mike bit his lip.

"Er—I guess you didn't know Helen left me and Jackson."

"No, Dave, I didn't. I'm sorry."

"That's okay. Anyway, I met Barbara sometime later, and we're fine. We've produced another young Scout, Cody."

"Great. So are you still into Scouting, then?"

"No, not really. I had to give it up; too much pressure from work. But I've helped out with Cody's troop this year."

"That's good. They'll have you back in uniform before long." Mike chuckled.

"So are you still doing Venturers?"

"Not really. I keep contact with some of the old companies, but they all change as new kids come through. No, I've been doing more with Rovers lately. Though these last two years, I've found it heavy going. Too many other pressures."

"Ah, you're getting old, Mike. What are you? Thirty-five?"

"Not quite, thirty-four next January."

"Mike, now that you're single again, we'll have to find someone new for you!"

"Like heck! I'm still fighting the last one!"

"Hah. Say, look, I've gotta go. It's great to see you again. What's your number? I'll give you a call, and we'll get together."

"Six-two-five, seven-three-one-one."

"Got it." David wrote the number on the packet he was carrying. "Okay, Mike, see ya."

"Bye, Dave."

David Adkins paid for his packet and left the store. Mike wandered round the aisles, looking for the rack of Kleenex boxes. He thought back to those great scouting days when he was a young Venturer Advisor, to the jamborees, to those days when Dave Adkins was the Area Coordinator, back in the heyday, when they were all younger, and fun seemed to come so much more easily.

Boy, I could use some fun right now; that bitch Elaine has raised yet another obstacle. Let my lawyer sort it out, he thought, *that's what I'm paying him for.*

He picked up two boxes of Kleenex and walked over to the cash, glancing out through the glass doors to see Dave standing there, chatting with a very sharp-looking and pretty young woman. He kept one eye on the doorway as he dealt with his purchases. She entered, flashing him a smile on the way.

Hmmm, he thought, *nice,* as he punched in his PIN; he glanced up again, but she was gone into the depths of the store.

- 14 -

Tony sank back into the luxury of the backseat of the Lincoln Town Car and watched distractedly as the scenes along the roadside flashed by. He had given up trying to be a part of the conversation in the car.

In spite of the quietness of the ride, he often did not catch what Dana and Mr Simpson were saying. Sometimes, Dana would turn and throw a query back to Tony, seeking confirmation of something she had just said. But somehow, he felt out of his depth.

This was bothering him. He was used to being in the lead. Right from the start, when Dana had first aired her idea for the old brewery, he had felt on the defensive, searching for a role.

He had found their first visit to Mr Simpson the lawyer quite daunting, and had barely spoken at first. But he had found it easier when Mr Simpson told them that he had been a keen sports car buff in his youth. He and Tony did have a common interest.

But now, he felt out of it. He was seeing another side of Dana that he had not really recognized before. Sure, she had led him sometimes when they were alone, like when deciding what to do or where to go. But this was different. She had a determined tone in her voice. She sounded more mature—yeah, that's it, he realized. He had heard that tone before—Dana's mother. But this was Dana speaking, and she clearly meant what she was saying.

The sun shone through the car window at a different angle as they rounded a bend, and caught the edge of Dana's hair, highlighting her face as she turned to speak to Mr Simpson. *She really is cute,* thought Tony, letting his concerns fall away, watching her eyes as they sparkled, her lips as they formed the words he no longer heard or cared about.

At last, they reached the junction with Highway 2, and turned westward down the hill into the valley of the Cataraqui, between the rock faces blasted out for the roadway.

"Soon be there now," George Simpson turned his head to speak to both Dana and Tony.

"This is Kingston already?" Dana queried.

"Yes," Mr Simpson replied.

"I've never been before."

"I came once with the PeeWee Hockey Team," supplied Tony. "But it was winter and dark, so we didn't see much."

"What's that place over there?" asked Dana, pointing to a collection of stone and concrete buildings, highlighted with trees, with several playing fields around it.

"Oh, that's RMC, the Military College. It's like a university, only the students are training to be officers in the Armed Forces as well," Mr Simpson explained. "Actually, I did a stint of training there myself, right after World War Two. Great place."

"So that's where RMC is," said Dana. "I can remember when my Uncle Alex used to visit us; I must have been about five or six. He used to tell us about all kinds of tricks he used to do at RMC. I remember how short his hair was, and how bristly it felt when I rubbed my hand over it. One time, he brought his uniform, and my head was only as high as his white belt. And that funny little hat he had to wear. But we don't see him much, now. He lives in Halifax."

The car swung down the road, past an impressive archway leading into the college, across a massive girder bridge over the Cataraqui River, and round into the centre of Kingston.

George Simpson seems to know his route pretty well, Tony thought, he's probably known the place for over fifty years.

They passed the lower ends of streets full of shops, on past the city hall and an old railroad locomotive on its stubs of track, past high-rises of luxury apartments and hotels overlooking a marina and yacht basin. They turned right, up into streets lined with large, mature trees and imposing, gracious houses. Tony had that feeling again, small and unsure of himself.

Mr Simpson turned the car into the small forecourt of a greystone house, whose contrasting, lighter stone bay windows stood like sentries on both sides of an imposing front door recessed under a stone arch.

"Here we are," said Mr Simpson, pulling the keys from the ignition with a flourish. "Right on time."

As the three visitors approached the front door, it opened to present a middle-aged lady dressed in an ageless light grey suit, the skirt hanging decorously to slightly below her knees. Tony hung back behind Dana.

"Sheila, how are you?" greeted Mr Simpson.

"Very well, thank you, Mr Simpson. It's good to see you. Are you keeping well?"

"Couldn't be better. Sheila, I'd like you to meet Dana Munro and Tony Ferruccio." Turning to Dana and Tony, he added, "This is Mrs Tovey, Mr Hennigan's housekeeper."

"Oh, don't be formal, my dears. Call me Sheila," she added, as Dana and then Tony shook her hand.

She closed the door behind them. "Mr Hennigan is in the West

Room," she continued as she led them along the hallway to a door on the left.

Tony's attention was drawn to the pictures that lined the walls, pictures of ships, some ancient, some just old.

They were ushered into the West Room. Tony was taken aback by its apparent size. At the far end, light shone in through the tall window, obviously the left-hand bay on sentry duty outside. A second window on the wall opposite the door added to the openness. But what made the room seem so vast was the height of the ceiling and the sparseness of the furnishings.

By each window was an antique-looking couch. Opposite the bay window, the wall was taken up with a fireplace and ornate mantel surround. Two high-back antique chairs and two low-back chairs formed a rough semicircle in front of the fireplace. A small table stood in the centre of the room, behind the chairs.

In the far corner, between the two windows, was a writing desk, and sitting at it on a straight-back chair was a very old, white-haired man. He turned and stood, smiling, as they moved into the room.

"George, how are you, young fellow?" The voice was old, but it still had power.

"Kurt, I'm fine. My, you're looking well."

"I'm feeling well, too." A gleam in the eyes joined the smile on the old face.

"Kurt, I'd like to present Dana Munro and Tony Ferruccio."

Tony was again taken aback, this time by Kurt Hennigan's greeting. "I'm honoured to meet you both." Mr Hennigan first took Dana's hand by the fingers, raised it a little, bowed his head slightly, and brought his heels together sharply. He then moved to take Tony's hand, grasping it firmly as he shook it once with a nod of his head.

Mr Hennigan gestured them to be seated around the fireplace. "George tells me that you have a proposal to make," he said, looking at Dana.

"Yes, sir, we have." Tony noticed that Dana seemed a little nervous at this point, in the rather daunting surroundings.

"Tell me about it then, dear, I'm very interested."

"You see, sir, our community has never had a place, a hall, or a schoolyard, like, where the young people could play safely, or do things together, or just …"

"Hang out?" interjected Mr Hennigan, smiling.

Dana was put off her stride again, but soon regained her confidence. Tony sensed that Mr Hennigan was with her in what she was trying to say.

"Yes—or to have a dance, or just to get to know each other better. Like, if we ever want to play softball, or football, or catch a movie, we have to go out of the area, an' that. It's not so bad as we get older, but the young ones need to get rides with parents all the time."

Mr Hennigan nodded, knowingly, and looked at her expectantly.

"So I thought, like, the old brewery, it's been standing there for so long, and all the kids used it to play in at some time or another, but it's not right, like it is, all overgrown and dangerous, but it would be great if it could be done up and used properly as a Youth Centre." Confident though she was, Dana had said it all in almost one breath. It was her key point; it had to come out fast.

"Dana," began Mr Hennigan, "I think that is a marvellous idea, and I want to thank you for bringing it to me. But I do want to ask you both a few questions about the idea, to dig a bit more deeply."

Dana swallowed and crossed her legs. Tony adjusted his position in the chair.

"You see," continued Mr Hennigan, "those buildings are very old, and will need a lot of work and materials to put them into usable condition. Had you given any thought about how to do that?"

"Uh-huh, yes, I have," replied Dana, confidently. "I think that if the people, particularly the kids, really believe this is worth doing, then people will volunteer to help as much as they can; and we could also try applying for a grant from the city, or from the provincial government."

Tony cleared his throat. "There's lots of skilled people in the Gardens. Like my dad, he's in construction, and Mr DeLaunais, he's a plumber, and that."

"Good. Now, have you asked the people: first, do they want a Youth Centre in the community, and second, will they help?"

Dana responded. "Well, no, we haven't asked everybody, just some, but they thought it was a good idea. We thought it would be better if we talked to you first, because if you didn't like the idea, then that would be the end of it, like."

"Good thinking. Now, let's put that first step firmly behind us. When I first heard of your idea, I must say that my reaction was negative—I just could not see how it could possibly be done. For many years now, I have been concerned about how to dispose of that property. You see, it was willed to me by my father, on condition that it not be sold out of the family."

Mr Hennigan paused, and Tony followed his gaze toward two paintings on the wall, of a young man in an army uniform and of a young woman in a nurse's uniform.

Mr Hennigan turned back into the group. "But I have no surviving family," he said quietly.

Tony did not know how to respond, and he could see that Dana was at a loss for words. They were not accustomed to offering sympathy in such situations. Both their faces must have shown disappointment at Mr Hennigan's response so far.

The awkward silence was broken by a quiet knock at the door as Mrs Tovey entered with a tray.

"Oh, thank you, Sheila, that's just right." Mr Hennigan brightened quickly. "Just put the tray on the table here, and we'll look after ourselves."

Mr Simpson passed out refreshments.

"Now," said Mr Hennigan, "back to business. As I said, at first I was negative—all I could think of were the problems that would have to be faced. And there are many things that would have to be done. But, my dear, the more I thought about it, the more I liked your idea; I realized that it could be the solution I've been seeking for so long. I've already asked Mr Simpson to start exploring the legal side of the matter, and how we proceed with the city about rezoning the land. So, to come back to your plan, yes, I am on side, and I will support you fully."

Tony watched Dana's widened eyes expressing relief. He was surprised that things were already happening.

"Yes," Mr Hennigan continued, "as soon as I realized the value and strength of your idea, I didn't want to waste time. But I did want to meet you personally."

"By the way," Mr Simpson looked toward Mr Hennigan, "I've talked to the city people. In principle, it can be done; but they insist on going through all the paperwork and informing the local residents in writing, with all the delays in giving due notice and setting up a hearing."

"Of course. I expected they would. Now," Mr Hennigan looked at Dana and Tony, "it's up to us to make sure that we have everyone in your community on our side."

Tony liked the sound of that. He was warming to Mr Hennigan, and losing his feelings of awe and insecurity.

"We could write a letter explaining the idea and send it to every house," Tony suggested.

"Maybe," Dana opened, turning to glance at Tony. "Maybe we could take the letters round ourselves and actually talk to people, an' then leave the letters with them."

"Yeah," agreed Tony, feeling encouraged. "Then we could try to explain things if people had questions."

"Good thinking." Mr Hennigan looked over to Mr Simpson,

who nodded his head.

"Would you do all that yourselves, or would other young people help?" asked Mr Simpson.

"We-ell," began Dana, "I know it might seem a bit pig-headed, but, I'd kind of like to be able to talk to everyone—with Tony of course," she glanced at Tony, "'cause that way, everyone would get the same story, and we'd get all the reactions back. It would make it easier, don't you think?"

"Mmm, yes—it would in a way, but would you be prepared to accept quite a lot of negative reactions, at least at first?"

Tony realized Mr Simpson was right; there could be some people against Dana's idea.

"I think that's something we'll have to learn to do," Dana turned and looked into Tony's eyes. He nodded.

"Dana, you mentioned the idea of applying for a grant," said Mr Hennigan, shifting the topic. "Do you know how to set about doing that?"

"Yes, I've already gone to the city hall to ask about applying for city grants, and Mr Johnson—he's Tony's neighbour—he told us he knows how to apply for a provincial grant."

"You have certainly done your homework." Mr Hennigan beamed.

The conversation stalled for a moment. Dana broke the silence.

"Er—there is—another part to my idea," she said, rather hesitatingly. Surprised and querying looks converged on her. Tony wondered what was coming next.

"Do tell us then, Dana," Mr Hennigan said softly, responding to her uncertain opening.

"Sir, these buildings were once a brewery," the formal address tripped off her tongue as she launched into her piece, "and were an important part of life in olden times. Nowadays, there seems to be such a lot more trouble that alcohol causes …" She bit her lip and put out her hand sideways, groping for Tony's.

He grasped her hand as a reflex, but then, as the significance of what she was saying began to sink in, he felt tears well up in his eyes.

Dana sniffed and continued. "Tony and I lost our brothers because of alcohol." She swallowed hard. "What I'm trying to say is, it would be good if we could make part of the buildings into a sort of museum or display, to tell the story of brewing, the good parts and the not-so-good parts. We seem to see so much more of the bad side these days, but I know there's a better side as well."

Mr Hennigan smiled generously. "Dana, that's another wonderful idea. I agree entirely with you, and I will give you all the backing you need to achieve what you've set out to do. And, to both of you, my deepest sympathies on the loss of your brothers. I remember that now." He turned to Mr Simpson. "George, you didn't tell me the museum part—and I hadn't made the connection between Tony and his father Pino."

"That's because Dana hadn't told me either. I agree. It would be a good way to bring home a balanced message to our young people—to the whole community. Kurt, if it's all right with you, I think we should be heading homeward soon."

"Of course. Dana and Tony, I am truly grateful for your inspiration, and I admire your energy and initiative. I wish you good luck in this venture, and I want to reassure you that I am with you all the way."

They all stood. Mr Hennigan led the way into the hallway, turning to Mr Simpson. "George, work closely with these young people. They deserve our strong support. I have another idea that will help us, but I want to consider the consequences a little more. Will you be available tomorrow afternoon, if I phone you then?"

"Yes, certainly. I'll make a point of keeping it clear."

"Good." Mr Hennigan noticed Tony's interest in the pictures of the ships. "Yes, that one was one of the first cargo steamers to work Lake Ontario. I had the privilege of sailing on her once, not long before she was finally broken up."

They reached the front door. Mr. Hennigan shook hands with them all, again in his formal way, but warmly. "Have a safe journey home, my friends."

As the car turned out of the driveway, Mr Hennigan waved from the steps, a tall white-haired figure framed by the stone arch.

So old, thought Tony as he returned the wave, *but is he ever with it—wow.*

The first part of the journey home was quiet. No one had much to say. Dana sat in the front again, and Tony sat in the middle of the backseat, to catch the bits of conversation that did take place—none of which were of any consequence.

As they approached a small village, Mr Simpson turned his head to address both Dana and Tony. "How about a little refreshment? I know a neat little spot here."

They pulled off the highway into a small parking area. An ice-cream stand was open for business.

They sat at a picnic table, consuming their ice-creams.

After a few moments of silence, Mr Simpson shifted his position on the bench, and spoke. "Well, what did you make of Kurt Hennigan, then?"

Dana jolted, as if from a daydream. "Er—he's a marvellous old gentleman," she replied, her eyes brightening again.

"Yeah," added Tony, "I was amazed how he seemed to have everything all sorted out in his mind, like, no hesitation."

"Yes," Mr Simpson continued, "he still has a very sharp mind. And, of course, his body too. He's in excellent health for a man his age, you know. He goes for a walk every day, summer or winter."

"Wow, that's more than most people less than a quarter his age."

"Say, Mr Simpson, I liked those pictures of ships on his walls. Was he into shipping or something?"

"He most certainly was, Tony. That's how he made most of his money. You see, as I told you the other day, he inherited the old brewery from his father, while it was a profitable going concern. But he was smart, he could see the writing on the wall, and knew prosperity couldn't last for the brewery. It had to be closed. He'd invested in other breweries in the Kingston region, in Toronto and the Waterloo area, and had also started to invest in shipping. Kurt was able to buy land before the stock-market crash of 1929. Being a smart fellow, he bought up a lot of land on the outskirts of the cities, anticipating that eventually cities would grow, and the land values would skyrocket. And of course, they did."

Mr Simpson paused to deal with his melting ice-cream.

"And," he continued, "just at the start of the depression, he had had the foresight to buy up for next to nothing an almost defunct shipping line that worked both the Great Lakes and ocean trade. He was able to hang on to it until trade picked up again. During the war and afterward, the Hennigan Line became one of the premier lines on the Lakes and on the trans-Atlantic runs. As a result of that success, and of his land sales in the growing Toronto suburbs and in other cities, he became very comfortably wealthy."

"That's really something," said Dana, in a tone of admiration. "To survive the Depression, and make money like that—sheesh … We were doing the Depression this last term. It was really hard for so many people back then."

They finished the ice-creams and set off again. Tony realized that it had been a long time since the hurried lunch the two of them had eaten at Harvey's on their way to Mr Simpson's office that noontime.

That reminded him of the receptionist at Mr Simpson's office— she looked familiar, kind of like that woman they'd seen with Dave Adkins that night on the old trail.

It was a little past the usual supper hour when the car rolled into Brewster Gardens. Almost as a reflex, all three, Mr Simpson, Dana, and Tony, glanced over to the old brewery as the car made the turn.

Since the building of the townhouses, the view of the brewery from that point was more obscured, but it was still there, as it had been for over a century.

Mr Simpson stopped the car by their two homes. "Well guys, you made a good impression on Kurt. He's with you all the way. Keep up the good work. We'll keep in contact. What's next, Dana?"

"I think we should try to write a letter to all the people explaining what we have in mind."

"Good. If you want, I'll be happy to help you with it. Why don't you two write out a draft letter, and then let's talk about it. Give me a call when you're ready."

"Thanks, Mr Simpson. Thanks for taking us to see Mr Hennigan."

"Yeah, thanks very much," added Tony.

"My pleasure. Bye for now."

Dana and Tony waited at the roadside as Mr Simpson drove away.

"That was great, Tony, don't you think?"

"Yeah, it was."

"Let's hope there's some supper left." Dana kissed him lightly on the cheek. "I'll be over at nine, okay?" And she danced up her driveway to the house.

"Sure."

Tony watched her enter the house, her white sweater and blue jeans almost glowing in the evening sunlight. He turned and crossed the road to his house. Somehow he felt agitated, uneasy.

Something's different, he thought, *something has changed. Dana isn't the same. What's happening?*

- 15 -

Mike Carson closed the front door behind him and followed Dave Adkins through the house to the backyard patio. "Barb, Mike's here."

Mike had met Barbara a week or so ago, when Dave had first invited him over. He and Dave had slipped back easily into their old friendship, and had enjoyed reminiscing over old times. Quietly, Dave had also filled Mike in on the past few months, and the brighter future he hoped for.

Mike appreciated knowing all that, and understood why the Adkins household now only carried soft drinks. He would stand by Dave, if needed.

"Hi, Mike. Good to see you. Glad you could come." Barb was arranging the table.

"Can I help with anything?"

"No thanks, not right now. Just help yourself to a drink, they're in the kitchen."

"So, Mike, how was today?" Dave inquired.

"Oh, not bad I guess, put an AC window unit into a fifth floor apartment, down on Creswall St. Jeez, you can't have vertigo in this business. Nearly lost the whole unit out the window once. One of the screws stripped out its hole just before I got the thing secured. Just caught it in time. An' all the time this old lady was hovering, watching every move—'shouldn't you do this, shouldn't you do that, let me hold it for you'—jeez, I nearly called it quits at one point. But, you know, you have to feel sorry for them. It was probably the highlight of her week. Sure as hell, it was hot in that place before I got the unit turned on."

"I bet."

Dave busied himself with the barbecue, carefully scraping and oiling the grill bars, tweaking the burners, organizing and re-organizing the utensils. Mike sat and watched absent-mindedly. Barb came out with fixings and set them on the picnic table.

Suddenly, a new female voice broke the local silence. "Oh, hi there, am I too early?"

Barbara, momentarily startled, looked up. Dave turned. Mike raised his eyes.

"Hi, Kelly. No, of course not, come on through," Barbara replied, reaching over to open the gate. At this time of day, the sun was over on the other side of the house, placing the yard in comfortable shade. Mike stood, bringing his eyes to bear on the owner of the voice. He liked what he saw, recognizing the view from the 7-Eleven store a few days back.

"Kelly," Barbara continued, "you know Dave, of course. I'd like you to meet Mike. Mike, Kelly."

"Nice to meet you, Mike."

"Pleased to meet you too, Kelly."

Barbara continued the lead. "Kelly's a new neighbour living in the Mews. She and I met the other day, so I thought we could get to know one another over a barbecue."

"That was a lovely idea, Barbara, thank you for inviting me. I haven't got to know many people round here yet."

Mike moved his glass along the table. "Care for a seat?" he offered to Kelly.

"Thanks."

"Can I get you something to drink?" Mike continued. "Some juice, Coke, Sprite?"

"Oh, a juice would be fine, please."

"Orange, grapefruit, or apple?"

"Orange, please." She flashed him a smile.

Mike walked back through to the kitchen. *Wowee,* he thought. Quickly he poured the juice, and returned to the table. Kelly flashed him another smile.

Mike moved over to the barbecue, absently watching Dave as he seared the steaks. Kelly and Barbara had engaged in women-talk, he realized, but his eyes kept returning to Kelly.

After a couple of minutes, Barbara stood up. "Dave," she said, "would you come and help me with the dishwasher stuff for a minute?"

"Sure, no problem. Mike, just keep one eye on the steaks, will you?" Dave handed Mike the tongs, and he and Barbara stepped inside the house.

Mike poked at the steaks for a few moments, aware that Kelly was watching him. "You like it here, in the outer 'burbs?" he opened.

Kelly stood up and moved to the other side of the barbecue. "I didn't at first, but every day I feel more at home."

"You on your own?"

"Yes—well, me and my dog."

"You have a dog? What kind?"

"A little Highland terrier. My parents used to breed them."

Mike was captivated by her face, but sensed a sudden change in its expression as she said those last words. "They live locally?" He regretted saying it as soon as he saw the sadness in her eyes as they turned downward.

After a pause she said, "I lost them both five years ago."

Mike felt terrible, wishing he had never broached the subject. "I'm sorry, Kelly, I really am."

"Thanks." Kelly looked up at him, and forced a smile.

"I guess these are about ready for turning." Mike busied himself with the steaks and the flare-ups as their juices dripped onto the hot rocks below, knowing Kelly was watching him.

Suddenly, she let out a little cry and stepped back quickly.

Mike looked over to her, questioningly. "What's wrong?"

"Oh, it's nothing. I was standing too close. A little sprink of fat just spat at me. It's okay." She rubbed at a slightly darker spot on her shirt above her left breast.

Mike took in the whole picture. "Sorry, I wasn't thinking as I turned that one," he felt obliged to say.

Kelly reached out and touched his arm. "'T's okay. It'll wash out; I'm fine." She flashed him that smile again.

A sound at the patio door made them both turn.

"How are those steaks, Mike?" Dave called.

"Should be about done, for those that like rare."

"That's good for me," called Barbara as she came out, carrying a pile of plates.

"How about you, Kelly?" Mike asked, as he pulled off one for Barbara.

"Medium rare, please."

"Oookay." Mike pulled off one for himself, and poked at the remaining two.

"I suppose, then, you want yours burnt, as I remember, Dave?" he called.

"'Course, what else?"

"I thought you might have come out of the stone-age by now."

Dave ignored the dig.

Mike pulled off Kelly's steak, placing it carefully on a plate and presenting it to her.

"Thanks, Mike."

"Say, Mike, you get started on yours, I'll tend mine for another coupla minutes."

"Okay, you want me to get the fire extinguisher ready?"

Barbara and Kelly chuckled. Dave was silent as he pursued his task.

The meal was good, and the conversation ranged over the usual topics of weather, the new townhouses, traffic in the city, and so on.

After clearing away the debris of the meal, they all sat around the picnic table, sipping at their drinks.

"I guess we'll have a good sunset, by the look of those clouds," offered Dave.

"Yes," Kelly said, "I like sunsets, always brings back happy memories. When I was a kid, we had a cottage at Dayton Lake. Used to spend most of the summer up there. Had some wonderful sunsets, with the sun going down behind the trees on the hill across the lake."

"Mmmm," Barbara murmured.

"Did you go out on the lake much, then?" asked Mike, recalling that he had canoed up there a couple of times way back.

"Oh yes, they used to call me a 'water baby' when I was really small. I love canoeing. Had my own canoe when I was fourteen."

"I've tended to prefer to look at the water rather than be in it or on it," said Barbara. "I don't know, I always feel uneasy when I'm too close to water."

"I think you get that from your mother, Barb," Dave said gently. "You know she's terrified of water if it's more than a bathtub-full."

"Maybe so."

The sun was dipping behind the clouds, and rays of sunlight shot out across the sky. Kelly finished her drink and stood up.

"Well guys, I really do appreciate you asking me over; I enjoyed it, thanks. But Hamish is probably getting desperate. I'll have to give him his walk."

"You're very welcome, Kelly, any time. We'll talk to you soon." Barbara gave the response, with smiles and nods from the men.

Mike had stood up as Kelly rose, noticing a special glance between Kelly and Dave. "I have to go along to the store for a couple of things. Thank you too, for inviting me over. It's been great," he said to Dave and Barbara.

"See you soon," replied Barb, as Dave nodded with a wink.

Mike followed Kelly out of the gate. "Mind if I join you and Hamish for his walk?"

She flashed him that smile again. "Not at all, Mike." They quickly reached her house. "Won't be a minute." She opened her patio door and greeted Hamish, who had been scrabbling at the glass from the inside. Hamish scurried after her as she disappeared into the house.

It suddenly dawned on Mike. Had this evening all been a set-up? Was that why Barbara had asked Dave to go help her with the dishwasher things, which seemed an odd request?

He smiled. So what? He was hooked, and happy so far.

Kelly soon emerged, with Hamish on his leash. "You wanted to go to the store?" she asked.

"Nah, it can wait, I'll stop by in the morning on the way to work. Which way does Hamish want to go?"

"He likes going down that trail by that old wall, toward the stream."

"Let's follow him then. Did you say stream? I hadn't noticed one."

They began their stroll, Hamish in front, snuffling at the grass tufts.

"Oh yes, it's called Otter Brook. That's where the name Otterbrook Road comes from."

"I see."

After slowly following the old railroad track-bed, they reached the stream and stood looking out at the water swirling around the rocks from the vantage of the old pier of the long-gone bridge.

Mike was intrigued by the information that Kelly gave him about the history of the place, the railroad, the brewery, and so on, wondering how she knew so much.

"Because I like learning about new places," she told him. The more they talked, the more Mike wanted to know about her.

They turned and strolled back along the trail, the last decaying rays of the sun striking chords across the darkening sky.

As they came to Kelly's gate, Mike knew he couldn't let things drop. "Kelly, one of the guys at work gave me a couple of tickets for a ball game on Saturday. Would you be interested in going with me?"

"Sure, Mike. I'd love to. What time?"

"Game starts at two-thirty. What-say we leave here around one-fifteen? Should be time to get parked and seated okay."

"It's a date, Mike. See you then. G'night."

"Night, Kelly."

Mike bounced along to his gate, and entered the house where he lodged. He dialled the Adkins' number on his cell.

Dave answered. *"Hi, Mike, good stroll?"*

"You bet, you scheming devil," Mike responded, grinning to himself. "Did you plan the whole evening?"

"No? It seemed to me you took over halfway through!"

"You know what I mean. You invited her over to get me interested, didn't you, eh?"

"Kelly's a very nice person, and she's gone through a rough time. So have you, Mike. Barb and I just thought it was a neighbourly thing to do, as she is so lonely, and if something else came of it, all well and good."

"I see. Dave, you said she's gone through a rough time. I found out she'd lost both her parents. Is there more?"

"Uh-huh. She lost her husband in a diving accident. The scuba tank valve failed, or something. They'd only been married a year."

"Oh my God, Dave. I wish I'd known." Mike felt guilty, and figuratively kicked himself for some of the things he had said that evening—nothing bad, but had he known, he would not have said them.

Dave continued, *"She and Barb and I have talked a bit, the few times we've seen her. I think she's over the worst, but, Mike, she's desperately lonely. And Mike,"* Dave changed his tone, *"I thought you two might be able to help each other."*

Mike swallowed hard. "Thanks, Dave, you're great."

- 16 -

Fortunately, the weather was cooperating. Dana stood at the edge of the wooden deck, leaning slightly on the handrail, surveying the growing crowd of people gathering before her in the backyard of the Johnson home. Everyone in the community, from the older homes and the townhouses, had been invited, and it seemed to Dana that almost everyone was turning out. Lawn chairs were everywhere.

The Johnsons had generously provided their yard for the meeting. Being on the outside of the Gardens' street, they had one of the largest lots, shaped like a sector of a circle with the pointy bit cut off. There were several large trees at the back of the lot, serving to convert the sun's rays into dancing fragments of sunlight as the leaves fluttered in the slight breeze.

Perfect, thought Dana, *it couldn't have been better.*

She scanned the gathering, a friendly crowd, it seemed. People were turning to chat with neighbours; scarcely a single tongue appeared to be still.

Here and there, she saw her 'allies', the people who had wholeheartedly pledged their support when she and Tony had visited every home with the initial explanatory letter. And too, there were the surprises, those who unexpectedly had shown resistance to her idea. But one face she was depending on had not yet appeared.

"Hey, Dan." Tony had jumped up the steps to her side. "Guess we should get started, eh?"

"Not for a few minutes. Mr Simpson isn't here, and I do really need his support, Tone."

"Don't worry." Tony put his arm round her shoulders. "He'll be here soon, I'm sure."

Dana thought back to only a month or so ago, when they had sat under the shade tree that hot July afternoon, where she first unleashed her idea. It had had its beginnings long before that, having gradually taken shape in her own mind. What had started it she really didn't know, but she was determined to see it through. It was tied, in a way, to her feeling of wanting to remember Bryce and Vincent.

That visit with Mr Hennigan had been a critical step; it had given her the confidence she needed. She realized, as she saw the expectant faces spread before her, the conversations having suddenly stopped and eyes now focussing on her, that she was in charge; she had the power.

A slight movement over to the right by the side of the house caught her attention. Tony stepped back from her as she saw George Simpson squeezing to a spot partway down the yard, by the cedar hedge. Mr Simpson looked at her and raised his hand in greeting. He had been most generous with his time and help over the past few weeks.

Time to begin now, she said to herself, straightening up, and pulling back from the handrail.

She chose her first words, and hoped that they would come out right. "I'd like to thank all of you for giving up your time by coming this evening."

She paused to clear her throat. "And I do want to thank Mr and Mrs Johnson for volunteering their yard for this meeting. And," she grinned, pointing upward, "I want to thank the person who booked the weather for us."

A light ripple of chuckles passed through the gathering.

Dana felt the exhilaration that you get when talking to a large crowd on something that you feel very strongly about. "Over the past few weeks, Tony and I have visited pretty well all of you—at least we've talked to someone at every house about our proposal."

She had come to refer to it as 'our proposal', even though it was truly her idea; Tony had only supported her, and had added nothing new or original. Yet she felt it was right to include him.

"But, as we went round, we sort of realized that some of you are on side all the way, others are not in favour, and others are somewhere in between. So we thought, like, the best way to explain, and hopefully convince the ones who were against, would be to meet like this."

Dana paused to collect her thoughts, some of them being jotted down on the piece of paper in her hand. She glanced over to her mother, sitting down to the left near the front, smiling back at her. Mentally, she thanked her mother for her guidance and advice.

Caroline Munro had not at any point really said what she felt about the idea, but she had been an enormous help in building up Dana's confidence for speaking before a large group. Caroline, being a teacher herself, had coached Dana during several evenings.

"Know your material," Dana recalled her mom's words. *"Believe in what you are saying."*

"First," Dana continued, "I want to take a few minutes to recap on the proposal, bringing in some of the problems that some of you raised when we came to talk with you. Then, I think it's your turn to stand up and say what you think about it. I'd like to think that by the end, everybody will be in favour of the idea.

"It's basically like this. The young people in this area have had nowhere nearby to do things they like doing for relaxation, or exercise, or," she paused, then smiled, "even learning new stuff. If we want to play sports, we've had to go off to Otterburn Arena, and that's always crowded, an' some of us don't like the kinds of kids that hang out down there. And, like, if we want to do something more creative, like, for instance, Fiona and her Highland dancing, there's nothing round here.

"And it seems to me that, like, when you're at a loose end, with nothing much to do and nowhere to go, that's when you can get into big trouble, like ..." And here Dana paused, because she had not said this at any of the homes they had visited, and it was going to be hard, though she had rehearsed it in her mind over and over again. "Like Bry—" Her voice broke. "Like Bryce and Vince."

She was through it. She paused, in relief.

"We have to do something, so we'll never have a repeat of that horrible night." She had regained her stride. "We owe it to those boys, our brothers, sons, friends—we can't just assume that everything will be okay, 'cause it won't be if we don't do something.

"And just look at all the little kids that there are round here now, with the new families that have come to the townhouses—where can they play safely?

"But it dawned on me that we could have a place for all of this, if we're willing to put a lot of effort into it. And you know that I'm talking about the old brewery. And as you all know, Mr Hennigan, the owner, has really been wonderful. He's told us that he supports the idea fully, and has already done some digging into details to check that it is feasible. I think that's really great. And I'd like to thank another person that most of you haven't met yet, and that's Mr Simpson, who is Mr Hennigan's lawyer. He's standing over there by the hedge." She indicated George Simpson over to her right.

Mr Simpson acknowledged with a raised right hand.

Angel in Blue Jeans

Dana continued, "Mr Simpson has helped us and advised us, I mean, me and Tony, a tremendous amount in these last few weeks, and we really appreciate it. Thank you."

George Simpson bowed his head in acknowledgement.

"But now," Dana went on, "now we come to some of the problems that some of you raised when we visited you. First off, the place can't run itself. Somebody has to be responsible for the day-to-day running. Somebody has to actually pay the bills, and make sure the place is safe and secure. Like, we would need a sort of administrator. And, like, that could turn out to be a pretty demanding job, depending on how much the place would be open and used. Now, Mr Hennigan has a proposal about that, but I'm going to let Mr Simpson tell us about it a bit later on."

Dana turned and whispered to Tony, who was standing in the shadows at the back of the deck. "Tone, get me a glass of water, please; I'm parched." She turned back to her audience.

"The second point is there needs to be some kind of program of things going on, 'cause even though kids like to have free time to do their own thing, they do like to have some organized stuff. Some might like one thing, others something different. So that means there needs to be somebody, or maybe several people, who would organize activities, and keep things on some kind of track.

"A couple of people have said to us that there should be a committee of adults to make sure the place doesn't get out of hand. But don't you think that's a bit of a putdown on our youths' abilities? Yeah, I kinda see what they're at, but I think a much better way is to have a young peoples' council, say, five or six kids of different ages, and give them the responsibility to make sure the place works properly. To help them, I suggest there be two adults, a woman and a man, who would be advisors. I really think that's the way to go for young people to learn about being responsible.

"A lot of you said it would be too big a job to fix up the old brewery, and cost too much, an' when we were visiting you, we really didn't have an answer for that. But we were sure then, and even more sure now, that with your help, it can be done. See, Mr Simpson told me a few days ago that Mr Hennigan had asked him to have an engineer check the buildings out, and the engineer had reported that they are still structurally sound, but would need to be brought up to today's standards."

Tony nudged her elbow and offered the glass of water. She turned, took it from him, took a long sip, and set the glass on the handrail. "Thanks, Tone," she whispered.

She turned back to the crowd. "So you see, that eases the job a great deal. Also, Mr Ferruccio has volunteered his company to do all the construction work needed, like drywall, floors, and so on. And Mr DeLaunais has volunteered to do all the electrical and plumbing stuff. I think that's a fantastic start, and I think if we all did a bit, the whole job would soon be done. Okay. I've probably said enough to start with. Now it's your turn."

To her complete surprise, her audience gave her a round of applause as she drank the rest of the water Tony had brought. She smiled and raised her left hand in acknowledgement.

There was a pause. Who would be the first to speak? Dana glanced across the gathering. Were things going well or not? Her pulse was deepening; she could feel her heart thumping.

Slowly, Dwayne Hampden rose to his feet. She felt her heart quiver; Mr Hampden had been one of the surprises during their visits.

"Dana," he began, "first of all, I really want to compliment you on having the courage to stand up and say what you have said to all of us here tonight. It's not an easy thing to do, and we admire you for your initiative."

He paused, and Dana was not at all sure what was coming next; Mr Hampden had been quite negative when they had talked with him.

Mr Hampden continued, "Now, when you and Tony talked

with me and Mrs Hampden the other day, I brought up some points that you haven't touched on—maybe you just haven't got to them yet. But one of the things that concerns me greatly is this: how is all this going to be funded? Not just the fixing up of the buildings, but the costs to run the place, things like electricity, water, taxes—who's going to pay the administrator you talked of? This small community isn't able to come up with that kind of money. And you probably know that the city is cutting back on its support for similar programs elsewhere. You know, the Otterburn Arena has had to cut back its hockey schedules for the winter, and next year the softball leagues are going to have their equipment grants cut in half."

He paused. Dana was just about to cut in when he started again. Dana smiled meekly, and let him continue.

"Well, that's my first point. I'll make my second and third points, if I may, and then I'll sit down.

"The second problem is that with all the new townhouses, there's just too much going on round here for comfort, what with all these new people with loads of kids, and all their cars. We don't need another big attraction like a youth centre to bring in even more.

"The third problem I see kind of follows on from the second. It's not from the kids of this community, but it's from others that would come into the area, maybe friends, or friends of friends. Sort of gate-crashers, you might say. That sort of thing often causes a lot of trouble, especially in some parts of the city, with gangs—and then there's the whole business of drugs. We don't want that kind of trouble here, no thank you Bob. Now, Dana, if you've come up with some solutions, I'll be glad to hear them, but I have to say, at the moment I'm not convinced that what you want will work. In fact, I should say here that I am against it." He sat down.

The intensity of the silence that followed was heightened by the slight fluttering of the leaves in the trees. Dana was tense. She liked Mr Hampden, although he often seemed stern, and some kids held him in awe. He had always seemed kindly to her as she grew up. Somehow, tonight he seemed cold, almost as an enemy.

The silence was finally broken by George Simpson. "Dana, if I may, I think I can set our friend's mind at rest on his first point."

He turned so that he was able to alternately face Dana and Dwayne Hampden simply by turning his head slightly. "Dana said in her opening remarks that Mr Hennigan—to use her words—has 'really been wonderful'. I can confirm that. As you know, Dwayne, from our previous work related to the brewery, I look after Mr Hennigan's legal interests. And as Dana and Tony may well have told you, I took them to meet Mr Hennigan. A few days after the visit, he asked me to work with his accountants to begin the necessary paperwork to set up a trust fund for the purpose of providing a continuing source of funds for the long-term operation of the proposed centre. To use his words, this would be to 'preserve something of our heritage, to protect the well-being and nurturing of our young people, our future.'"

He paused to let those words sink in.

"I should explain," he continued, "for the benefit of many of you, that Mr Hennigan, the owner of the brewery site, is a very wealthy man, and has no surviving family. It is his hope that your community will accept this proposal; it will please him immensely. I should also note that Mr Hennigan is now almost ninety-six years of age, but very alert and clear in his decisions. Separate from the trust fund, he will pay for the cost of all the materials that will be required to bring the buildings up to current standards, if you in the community will accept the tasks of providing the labour. And I am very gratified that Mr Ferruccio, Pino, with whom I have already had the pleasure of working, and Mr DeLaunais have volunteered their valuable services."

He turned to Dana. "Thank you, Dana."

Dana scanned the faces; who could follow that? When Mr Simpson had told her yesterday about the trust fund, she was overwhelmed, both by the generosity of Mr Hennigan and by the fact that this issue of money had been one of the weakest spots in her idea.

There was a rustle over to the right, not far from Mr Simpson. Jane Stennings was coming to her feet. Jane was one of her 'allies'; Dana and Tony had had a great visit with Jane and her husband Graham.

"Dana, if I could take up a few moments?"

Dana held out her hand, palm up, indicating the 'floor' was Jane's.

"Let me introduce myself first," Jane began. "I'm Jane Stennings, I live at number six in the Mews. I'm a Police Officer with the city. On a daily basis, I'm confronted with situations involving young people in trouble, whether it be alcohol, drugs, prostitution, theft, assault, and so on. And I see common threads running through many of these cases. One of them is a lack of direction, a lack of focus, no aim in life. And this can have many root causes, such as a broken family, an unloved childhood, low esteem, difficulties in learning, lack of challenge, lack of recognition. Young people in such a state can become the targets of more serious crime, where they get into trouble big-time, or may even become the victims of crime.

"From what I've seen and heard from Dana, and Tony, what is being discussed here tonight is one of the best ways of counteracting youth delinquency—a good organized program, a good assembly place, designed by young people for young people. I've discussed this proposed centre with my inspector, and he agrees with me. If it goes ahead, he's authorized me to take on, as part of my regular duties, the nurturing of this youth centre. I'll be happy to do so, and I'll say here too, I'm willing to volunteer my own time in whatever way I can help."

Jane sat down. Dana saw Graham take his wife's hand, as a light buzz of talk flitted across the gathering.

"Thank you, Jane," said Dana, still not used to being on first name terms.

Jane smiled back at her.

The sound of a throat-clearing drew Dana's attention over to the left at the back. In the shadows, she recognized the shape rising to stand. "Yes, Mr Donnelly," she said.

"I just have one concern in all this," he began in a wavering voice. "My wife and I have lived here since the beginning. The Gardens has always been a quiet place, until very recently when all the new houses have sprung up—not that I want to leave people here with the impression that we're against newcomers—but it's just that more people make the place noisier and more crowded. Edith and I chose our house in this street all those years ago just because it was quiet."

He paused to cough and clear his throat. Dana remembered that when she had visited the Donnellys' house, Mr Donnelly seemed to be continually clearing his throat.

"Now, we chose our house at the end of the Gardens so that we only had neighbours on one side. And we've been fortunate, I can say, in having such good neighbours as Dwayne and Elizabeth Hampden. I'll get to the point—but, young lady, I do want to say before I get there that I do admire your efforts. Now, the thing that Edith and I are concerned about is the cars that young folk seem to be able to buy these days—we couldn't afford such things when we were young—but where are they going to leave their cars when they come to this centre of yours? Eh? That's my concern. I don't want rambunctious kids running all over my front yard and parking their cars in front of my house—because it's the closest house to your centre. Edith and I are both getting on in years, and we don't stay up late, so there's no way we're going to put up with noise and car doors slamming half the night …"

He stopped to clear his throat again. This time it took longer. Dana was itching to get her response out, but she felt sorry for him; he must have something wrong with him to be coughing and clearing his throat like that, she thought.

"So," he continued, "have you given that any thought?"

He sat down. Dana took a couple of breaths. "Mr Donnelly, this centre is first of all intended for the local kids—from the Gardens and the Mews. They can walk, they don't need to drive cars. And not many have cars—in fact, nobody that I can think of has a car right now, among the young people. So I don't really see it being a really big problem. But the other day, when Mr Simpson and Tony and I were sketching out some plans, we did include a parking area that would turn off Millerby Lane, next to Dino's Auto-Body. Actually, we planned that that would be the way into the centre, so there'd be as little effect on the Gardens as possible. Does that answer your question?"

Mr Donnelly stood up again, clearing his throat. "Thank you." As he sat back down, somebody—Dana couldn't make out who—patted Mr Donnelly on the shoulder.

A woman was now standing, over by the big tree in the back right-hand corner.

Dana looked hard, and recognized her as one of the more difficult ones from the Mews. "Yes?"

"I'm Connie Weston. It's sending the wrong message to our children to have an old brewery turned into a youth centre. It'll always be thought of as a brewery. It's not going to help reduce the death toll on our roads. I wouldn't want my two little ones going to play in a brewery. Put up a new building on the site, but not an old brewery, no way. I am definitely against your idea, and I expect there's a lot of people here that think the same way."

Dana felt hurt. This woman was aggressive, as she had been during the visit to her house. Dana realized the time had come to open the wound she knew had been so hard on her family and on the Ferruccios.

She was collecting her thoughts and was about speak, when suddenly she realized her mother was standing. Dana motioned to her mother to speak.

"I'm Caroline Munro, Dana's mother. Ten months ago, two families in this community suffered a tragic loss …" Caroline was struggling, her voice was breaking up; Dana watched as her father took her mother's hand and steadied her.

Caroline continued, with tears streaming down her face, "Two families lost young sons—Dana and Tony both lost brothers—because of alcohol and a lack of organized, safe activities. Two families are changed forever …" Caroline choked back a sob. "I am proud of my daughter. She alone thought this through, and came up with her idea. She is thinking ahead, to making this new centre tell the whole story, the good and the bad. Yes, it can be a positive factor in our community, if we make it so. And I would say to you, Mrs Weston, that if you make it a positive learning experience for your young children, the new centre will be good for them, too."

Connie Weston, who had remained standing while Caroline spoke, sat down abruptly.

Dana watched her mother sit down and bury her head in her father's shoulder. People around tried to console her.

Dana's heart went out to her mother and father. It had been so hard for them. Dana had realized long ago that Bryce's death had almost split them apart. Her father had become so reclusive for months, and her mother had lost herself in her school work.

Dana felt proud of her mother; on reflection, she doubted she could have handled the situation brought about by Connie Weston's remarks.

But the meeting must go on. Dana looked around. A youngish man was now standing. She turned to face him, recognizing another ally.

"I'm Mike Carson, I live in the Mews. I'd like to support this idea of a youth centre. I think it's an excellent idea, and I'm volunteering my services right here and now. I've worked with young people for a number of years in the Scouting movement, from Cub age to late teens and young adults. And, because she asked me to, I'd like to speak on behalf of my friend here, Kelly McDowell." He jestingly put his hand on the top of the head of the woman sitting next to him. "Kelly has done the same sort of things with the Girl Guides plus she has some other skills that would be useful. So she's volunteering as well." Kelly and Mike exchanged grins.

Mike was still standing. *There's more?* wondered Dana.

"Now," continued Mike, "if I could touch on another issue that somebody raised earlier, I think we have sitting here tonight the ideal man to run this centre. He has wide experience in working with youth, he's a top-rate administrator, he has excellent credentials, and I feel sure that if we asked him, he would jump at the opportunity ..."

Mike had stopped. Another light, questioning buzz wafted around the yard. *Who's he talking about?* Dana didn't quite know how to handle this one. She watched and waited.

She saw Mike nodding his head and catching Mr Adkins' eye, then Mr Adkins shaking his head firmly, and Mike nodding his head again very emphatically.

Mike spoke. "Ladies and gentlemen, he's being very modest, but I am, of course, referring to Dave Adkins. I believe he's just the man for the job. He's held a senior position in the Region's Scouting movement, which involved both program and administration, and, as I said before, he's had a working career as an administrator."

Mike sat down. Dave Adkins remained in his seat, clearly embarrassed. Dana did, however, know that he was a strong ally.

"I really don't know what to say in response to that," Mr Adkins began. Then, he stood up. "First off, somebody would have to draw up a job description. I'd have to think about it. In any case, there may be others who could do the job better than I could. And, anyway, whose say is it? That needs to be defined. But anyhow, putting that aside, I do want to say that I endorse Dana's idea wholeheartedly.

It's an excellent initiative, and I think we as a community would benefit greatly from it in the years to come. What we should realize is that we have the opportunity here to create a place not just for the young, but for the young-at-heart too—and I would hope that includes all of us."

"Thank you, Mr Adkins." As her eyes moved from Dave Adkins, she noticed another man standing. "Yes, Mr Benson."

"I want to speak on behalf of the residents in this community who do not have children, at least not here. This idea of yours puts great demands on the whole community, and there are some of us that don't appreciate being put upon. We have no need of a youth centre; we have our own adult interests and activities. And we don't intend to be 'voluntold' what to do with our time. In short, I and others are against the idea."

Dana remembered their visit with the Bensons. Keith Benson was a nasty piece of work, it seemed. She and Tony were glad to be out that house.

However, tonight she had to respond to his remarks. She took a deep breath. "Mr Benson, no one has told you or anyone else here that you 'must' do anything. Any involvement is entirely voluntary, and as you can see, a great deal of voluntary help has already been offered." She paused, thinking fast. "And if I could use a term that Mr Adkins just used, which I really like, because it greatly broadens the concept, this can be a centre for the 'young-at-heart', a place that can benefit everyone, whether or not they have children."

Dana wondered how long this meeting should go on. At some point, she had to bring it to a conclusion, a conclusion that cleared the way forward, she hoped. How to proceed right now?

Fortunately, someone solved that one for her.

"May I suggest," Mr Stacey, Fiona's dad and a Carleton University professor, was standing, "that we take a short break, ten minutes say. I think enough new bits of information have come out so far tonight. It might help if people can discuss among themselves for a few moments."

There was a general bustle and buzz. Clearly that was the thing to do.

"Okay," Dana shouted above the noise, "let's start again at eight-fifteen."

It was dusk by now. Mr Johnson had had the foresight to rig up a few lights. He moved over to the house to plug the cable into the power outlet. The lights, some white, some green, some red, lent a festive air to the gathering.

Dana turned as Mr Simpson came up the steps onto the deck.

He smiled at Dana and Tony. "You're doing a grand job, guys. I sense that there are more positives than negatives, but we need to be sure that there'll be enough positives at the hearing on Tuesday."

"Yeah," replied Dana. "I know, but how can we guarantee that?"

"We can't. But I suggest we work on the people who have expressed concerns. If they've felt strongly enough to stand up here and voice them, they are serious. But I think they—"

Mr Simpson turned, as Dwayne Hampden parted from a cluster of people and came up the steps. He held out his hand to Mr Simpson. "Good to see you again, George," he said.

"Good evening, Dwayne. Dana, Tony, and I were just discussing how we might proceed."

Mr Hampden addressed Dana. "Dana, I'm impressed. You and your team have really done a good job. I came to this meeting in a very negative frame of mind—I just could not see how your proposal could really work. I intended to try to convince the community to pan it. But I want you to know, after what I've seen and learned this evening, I've no reason to hold you back. In other words, I will support you, and if there's any way I can help, I will." He reached out and lightly grasped Dana's upper arm; Dana interpreted it as an 'I'm with you' action.

"That's really wonderful, Mr Hampden," she exclaimed, a broad smile spreading over her face as she looked first at Simpson and then Tony. "That's great."

"Thanks, Dwayne." Mr Simpson was smiling too. "That's just what we wanted to hear. Now, there is something you could do right now to help us."

"Go ahead."

"Dwayne, when this break's over, would you let the whole gathering know what you've just said to us?"

"No problem."

"Thanks, Mr Hampden." Dana felt elated. She knew that Mr Hampden was well respected in the community, and if he was an ally, that counted for a lot.

"Shall we get back to business then?" Mr Simpson was moving toward the steps.

Dana raised her voice as she faced the several clusters of people. "Can we start again, please?" Her voice only caught the attention of the nearest clusters.

Suddenly, a piercing whistle cut the air by her side. She turned to see Tony grinning at her.

"Well, it's working, look."

She pushed him, playfully.

Order having been restored, Dana asked for further comments or questions. For a few moments there was an awkward silence.

Then, Dwayne Hampden stood up. He had positioned himself so that he could address the whole gathering. "When I came here this evening, I must say I was really negative about this project. But thanks to our benefactor, Mr Hennigan, the financial issues have been resolved now. And I'm very pleasantly surprised—in fact, I am very impressed—at the generosity of the people who have volunteered their help, and significant help it is, too. I have no reason to oppose the project now, and I'll go further than that to say I will help Dana and her team however I can."

Dwayne paused momentarily. "And I urge you all to support the application for re-zoning and for approval to proceed, next Tuesday at City Hall."

"Thank you, Mr Hampden. Are there any others who want to speak?" Dana watched Graham stand up.

"I'm Graham Stennings. I live in the Mews with my wife Jane here. I'm in the Army. I—er—don't have any construction skills to offer, Dana, but I do have much work experience in writing texts and documents. I would like to offer to work with Mr Hennigan and others to write the history of this place, particularly of the brewery itself—it's part of our heritage, as Mr Simpson said earlier—and to help to put into perspective a warning of the dangers of alcohol."

"Thanks very much, Graham."

Dana had just realized that the woman next to Mr Carson, who had introduced her as Kelly McDowell, was the same woman she and Tony had seen with Mr Adkins that night in May down along the old railroad trail.

Her mind flitted over the associations. What was, or had been, going on then? Mike Carson and Kelly McDowell seemed to be an item, at least now, from her observations tonight. And Mr and Mrs Adkins were both there, seemingly on good terms.

Oh well, one of those sweet mysteries, she thought.

That cough again. Mr Donnelly began standing up. "Young lady," he began.

Why does he keep on calling me that? Dana wondered.

"You obviously have a lot of support for your plan, and my wife and I wouldn't want to be seen as a pair of stick-in-the-muds or wet blankets. I've made my point earlier; you've given your answer. All I ask now is that you and all the people that come to use the place respect other people who live nearby. That said, I can assure you that we won't object to your plan next Tuesday."

"That's wonderful." Dana felt the adrenaline pumping. *Dare we risk asking for a show of hands?* she thought.

Someone else was already giving the answer. "I propose," Mike Carson was on his feet, "that we give Dana a real demonstration of our support by a show of hands. All those in favour of Dana's project, please raise your hands."

Dana saw a mass of hands waving, most at full height, others up but perhaps a bit hesitant.

"Thank you," continued Mike. "Against?"

Silence. Dana scanned the scene. Connie Weston's hand was stridently waving, and there were Mr and Mrs Benson's hands, and near them another but she couldn't see whose it was.

"Thank you." Mike turned to face Dana. "Dana, I think that should give you all you need to proceed."

Dana felt a lump in her throat, and tears formed in the corners of her eyes. "Thank you all for coming out this evening; it's been a really great—"

A burst of applause drowned the remainder of her sentence. The tears welled in her eyes. Emotion was gaining the upper hand. She tried hard to fight it down. She had felt the stress growing these past few weeks as she and Tony had visited all the homes. The difficult ones had really taken a lot out of her, especially when she couldn't give a firm response or a clear resolution of their concerns.

Tony had now put his arm around her shoulders and was proffering a Kleenex. She took it, dabbed her eyes, and wiped her nose. She sniffed.

"Thanks, Tone."

"Great job, Dan."

"Thanks, Tone, but I couldn't have done it without you." She gave him a reassuring smile.

Mr Simpson was there. "Well done. That was good, very good. You're going to have some very good helpers out there. Oh, by the way, that lady who was volunteered by her companion, Kelly McDowell, she is one of my receptionists. I didn't know she was living out here; it's a small world. But she will be a good asset, she's a very nice person; get to know her. Well, I don't think anything more is needed now before Tuesday next, except … Yes, it would be a good idea, Dana, if you could give me a call on Monday, just to touch base."

"Sure, Mr Simpson, I have spares Periods Six and Seven, after lunch. That okay?"

"That's fine. Bye for now."

"Bye, and thanks again."

Mr Simpson had gone.

Sounds of buzzing conversations and the folding up of lawn chairs filled the air as Dana and Tony stepped down onto the grass. Dana felt a slight tug at her sleeve. She turned to see Connie Weston.

"I didn't know your families had lost two boys—I'm sorry for you. But I still think that your idea is wrong. We lost my brother an' his girl last year because of a drunken driver. I'm going to talk with the chief of police, and meet with our local councillor and the mayor tomorrow—I've already made the appointments."

And she was gone, into the milling crowd.

Dana looked at Tony. "We'd better let Mr Simpson know about that right away. I'll call him first thing in the morning."

"Yeah. Er, Dan, I—er, I don't think I can be with you at the council meeting on Tuesday night. I've got to drive Momma to her art class; Pop says he can't do it that night. Gotta go and finish that essay now." He gave Dana a peck on the cheek, and left.

"Er, Tone, wait—" *Strange*, thought Dana. *What's up with him now?*

- 17 -

Jane was curled up in her leather high-back chair. This was her relax time, an essential part of her survival routine. The pressures of her work were so great, so demanding, that she had learned years ago to program in a definite time for relaxation each day.

Almost without fail, she was able to find an hour for herself every day. Even Graham respected that. At the moment, he was somewhere down in the basement, doing his own thing. What he was doing didn't matter. If it was his relax time—fine. If not—if he was studying some new bulletin on training, say—fine.

She read a few more pages and came to the end of the chapter. She gently closed her book, letting it rest on her thigh. Relax time was now over.

The quietness of the room was broken by the sound of the doorbell. Dana, she thought, and heard the sounds of Graham bounding up from the basement to open the front door. The voices connected up with faces as Dana and Graham came into the room.

"Hey, Dana, good to see you. Make yourself comfortable."

Dana sat in a leather beanbag.

Graham settled into a broad-armed easy chair. "That was a pretty good meeting you had the other night," said Graham. "You handled it well."

"Thanks, but I couldn't have carried it through without people like you two backing me."

"We're happy to be involved," responded Graham.

They sat silent for a few moments.

"So what's up then, Dana?" Jane asked, knowing that Dana had asked Graham last week if she could come over to discuss something with them—nothing to do with the brewery plan.

"It's like this. See, I'm going into Grade Twelve now, and I've got to be thinking about what I want to do with my life. Like, we've got to apply to university—if that's what we want to do—pretty soon."

"I see," said Graham. "Is that what you want to do? Do you have good marks?"

"Uh-huh, I've had an eighty-five, eighty-six average the last two years. But I don't know for sure if university is what I want."

"Have you thought of anything else?" asked Jane.

"We-ell, kind of. That's why I wanted to come and talk with you both. See, the more I think about it, the more I want to do something that isn't, like, selfish. Like, if I just went to work in an office, just earning money so I could eat and live and do things, it doesn't grab me. I kind of want to do something more exciting, something that can really help people, like you both do."

"Mmm," said Jane. "You mean you want to know about police work—and the military?"

"Yes, if you don't mind."

"Not at all. I can tell you for a start, though, that police work is pretty demanding, and very stressful, all of the time. There's very little let-up. To be honest, Dana, I came into policing with ideas similar to yours. I wanted to help people. I wanted to be doing something I felt to be constructive. Now, some parts of my job can be considered constructive, but there's a great deal that isn't."

"Yeah, I realize that."

"Along quite another line, though, for a moment," Jane continued. "Have you considered teaching? Your mother's a teacher."

"Yeah, she is. But I've talked to her, and I've watched her, too. That doesn't seem to be a good career to get into now. Mom's all stressed out, and comes home exhausted most days. And I see the teachers at school. Some of the kids make it hell for them, but the rest of us can't seem to do anything about it."

Jane could see Dana's point. She had become quite friendly with Caroline Munro, and knew a lot about the troubles caused by some students.

"You're interested in the military, too?" Graham asked.

"Well, yes. I think it might be what I'm looking for. The more I've thought about it, the more I like the idea of the discipline that seems to go with the military or policing. I look at kids that go to regular college or university, and a lot of them don't get decent jobs, they just seem to be hanging around, picking up any kind of work where they can. What's the point? I want to feel that I'm really contributing. And I don't want to hang around here all my life, either."

"I see," said Graham. "You know what might be a good idea for you? I'll see if I can arrange a tour of the Base up at Petawawa for you; I have to go up there next weekend. I have good friends who live there, and I'll talk to one of my wingers, Captain Ellis. I think she'll enjoy showing you around."

"Wow, that would be great. I'd love that."

"Dana ..." Jane's thoughts had gone back over the times she had seen Dana, not many times, really. But on each occasion, there had been something about her that made her stand out in Jane's memory. "Dana, have you thought about going to university through the military?"

"No, I haven't seriously, but now you mention it, the thought did cross my mind when Mr Simpson took us down to visit Mr Hennigan in Kingston. We went past that military college, RMC? I did wonder what it would be like to go there."

"If you're at all interested in going into the military, I'd suggest you find out all you can about RMC." Graham stroked his chin. "I'm just trying to think who I know down there now. No, Jeff Albrecht has gone to other things. Mmmm, I think all the people I used to know have gone, now. But the college does sometimes have tours set up for high school students—you might ask your careers people, they should know."

"Yeah, I'll talk to my guidance counsellor."

"You know, Dana," Jane was taking a different tack, "in spite of my dire warnings earlier, if you do want to have an inside view of what policing is like, we do have a program where students ride along with someone on patrol. We avoid dangerous situations, of course, but you would see something of the range of problems we have to deal with."

"I'd love to try that, too, if you could, please, Jane. I'm really torn here. I know I've got to make a decision sometime in the next few months that will affect my whole life, and, to be honest, I'm a teeny bit scared. It's a bit like going into a pitch-black room where you've no idea what's ahead of you."

"Maybe so." Graham's voice was reassuring. "But you have a lot going for you already, Dana. You're looking out ahead for yourself, which is a lot more than many others your age do."

"What does Tony think of these ideas of yours?" Jane was grinning with a quizzical smile.

"Er, well, I haven't talked with him about any of them, really. Well, not in any specifics." Dana shrugged her shoulders. "I guess—he might not like it. Then again, maybe he could choose to do something

I didn't like ... I really don't know. I know he wasn't keen when I mentioned once that I might join the police force. But it's my life, my career—not his."

"Do you like sports?" Jane was off on another tack again.

"Hmm. I like tennis, but I don't often get the chance to play. There's no courts near here, and it's always a pain to travel across town. You know, that's one thing we could set up in the old brewery; there's enough space for one court, at least."

"Good idea." Graham nodded his head.

"I like cheerleading. I've been in the squad about a couple of years now, though I did drop out for a while after the accident. We do quite a bit of aerobics as well in the cheerleading practices; helps to keep us slim, I guess."

"I'll get some drinks," Jane said. She twisted her body to let her feet come to the ground. "We've juice, Diet Coke ... "

"Diet Coke would be fine, please," Dana replied.

"Do you want me to get them?" Graham had a note of concern in his voice.

"No thanks, I'm okay." But as she said it, she wished she had taken up his offer. There was that nauseous feeling again. It had been around for the past week. She couldn't be, could she?

She was glad to get into the kitchen, to sit down for a few moments. So Graham had noticed, then. She hadn't said anything to him, because she wasn't sure herself. What had gone wrong? This wasn't part of their plan, at least not right now. But if she was, it would have to become part of their plan. It would change a lot of things.

That settles it, she thought, *I'll get checked out tomorrow.*

Carefully, she stood up and poured the drinks. She paused, to be sure she was okay, and returned to the others.

Graham was describing army life to Dana. Jane placed the drinks by each of them, and sat back in her chair. She watched as Dana sat enthralled, listening to Graham's tales. He recounted his days at college, first at Royal Roads in Victoria, which closed the year after he was there, and then at RMC, Kingston. He went back over his early days as a green, newly commissioned officer, and had all three of them in fits of laughter over a couple of gaffes he made.

He went on to tell of his experiences in the Balkans, and later in Afghanistan. Some of those were pretty harrowing experiences. Jane could see that Dana was captivated.

"… So there you are, Dana. That's a quick run-down on the side of the military I know."

"Thanks so much, Graham, that was great, it really was. You've given me such a lot to think about. I'm really interested in finding out more."

"Well, as I said, I'll set something up for Petawawa, and you see what you can find out at school. And you could also go off to the Recruiting Office downtown. They're pretty helpful, and can give you up-to-date info on what kinds of MOCs are in demand at the moment."

"Yeah, I will. Gee, it's time I was going. Thanks again for having me."

"It's a pleasure, Dana." Jane stood up—okay this time, she reassured herself. "I'll also look into the student patrol program, if you want me to."

"Please do, Jane. I don't want to cut off options at this stage. I might get stuck in something I can't stand if I jump too quickly."

"Very true." Graham held the door as Dana stepped out into the night.

"Thanks again. G'night."

"Night, Dana, talk to you soon."

Graham closed the door and turned toward Jane, who had sat down again. Jane watched as he crossed the room and crouched in front of her, looking into her eyes. "Are you okay?" he asked, furrowing his brow.

"Yes, I'm okay."
"Is it what I think it is?"
"It might be. I don't know."
"If it is, I'm happy." He leaned forward and kissed her.

She put her arms round him and hugged him tight. "If it is, I'm happy too."

- 18 -

"Hey, you there."

Dwayne Hampden straightened up abruptly at the sudden sound of a woman's voice. He lowered the bag of fertilizer back into the car trunk, and turned around. Standing at the end of his driveway was a woman, dressed in jeans and a T-shirt, smoking a cigarette.

"You mean me?" Dwayne was not used to this form of address.

"Yes, you. The guy who started off on the right track at that meeting about that damn youth centre, and then screwed everything up when you changed your mind."

"I beg your pardon ..." began Dwayne, now quite angry at the woman's accusatory tone.

"Forget begging," the woman went on. "If it hadn't been for your speechifying, I'm sure there were enough of us there that didn't want the damn thing to go ahead that we would have stopped it right then."

"Lady—I don't know your name—for goodness sake, calm

down. And if you want to have a discussion about that business, fine. But I tell you, I don't take kindly to being shouted at and accused of whatever." Dwayne was regaining control. "Now, I'm Dwayne Hampden, and you are?"

"Me? Connie Weston, and I live—"

"In the Mews. Yes, I remember you now, from that incident some weeks ago in the street with your little girl."

"That's another thing. I know that idiot in the car hit her, but the cop listened to all you others and he got off free. Fricking police—can't trust them with anything."

Dwayne shuddered inside. *What a woman,* he thought. "Mrs Weston …" he began.

"Mizz," she almost hissed.

"Look, I don't know what your reasons might be for not wanting that new centre, but anyone is entitled to change his opinion based on new information. My first negative opinion was based on finances—there wasn't enough money to support the idea, but it soon became clear that the money issue was solved. And the response from the people around here as volunteers to build and run it was amazing."

"But it's still an old brewery, stinking of alcohol. Even if it gets cleaned up, it'll always be a brewery. That girl said something about a display on the history of the place—even worse. Did anyone think about hurting people who've lost someone through drink? I don't get it—that girl lost her own brother, and still she wants to go ahead."

"I'm sorry you see it that way, *Mizz* Weston. That girl, Dana's her name, has a very good idea, a good initiative, and now that the money issues and volunteer issues are settled, I can see the immense value of it. Dana's brother and the other lad had got into trouble because there was no safe place for them to hang out. This set of old buildings can form the base of an excellent centre, not only for young kids, but for the whole community. Dana intends to use the fact that it was a brewery to try to teach about the dangers of alcohol."

"I lost my brother an' his girlfriend because of a drunken driver. Tear the place down."

"I am truly sorry, Ms Weston, I am. But Dana is right. She wants to turn tragic events and a heritage structure into a means to move onward, positively."

"You all make me sick—the whole frigging lot of you. Even the mayor wouldn't buy my arguments—said it was up to the community—he wouldn't interfere. And the councillor, he's just a rat—just wants to get re-elected. Even the police chief, even when I told him about my brother, wouldn't see my point—said he was in favour of any project to benefit youth and reduce delinquency, even when I told him it was an old brewery."

"Ms Weston—please. You're entitled to your opinion. But I really must go; I have things I must do. And I hope that, when the centre is built and working, you'll see things differently."

She threw her cigarette butt on the driveway, stamping her foot on it as she turned and stormed off toward the Mews.

Dwayne shook his head and walked back up to his house. *Are there any others like that hidden in the Mews?* he thought. Now that he understood what Dana and the others were doing, he was all for the project.

- 19 -

"Come on in, both of you," said Jane as she opened her front door. "Dana, let me take your jacket. No, Jason, don't worry about your runners, it's dry out. Graham's in the living room. Just go on through."

Graham stood as Dana and Jason Johnson entered the room. "Hey guys."

"Hey, Mr—Captain Stennings."

"Hey, now, that's enough of that, Jason. Look, we're working together. Call me Graham, please."

"And call me Jane, too."

"Thanks, Cap—Graham."

Everyone laughed at Jason's stumble. Dana was comfortable now with first names for the Stennings, but she realized that this was maybe a first for Jason.

"Come and sit down; make yourselves comfy," said Graham, spreading his arms to indicate the easy chairs and sofa in front of the fireplace. Dana sat in a chair, and Jason spread onto the sofa.

Graham sat down in the other chair.

"Okay, I'll leave you to work, then," said Jane, as she went down to the basement.

Graham nodded, and then turned inward to the fireside grouping. "So, where shall we start?" he asked, looking at Dana.

"Well, maybe you could tell us how you got on with Mr Hennigan, first?"

"Sure," responded Graham. He settled back in his chair, picking up some notes from a side table. "I had a really good chat with Mr Hennigan on the phone; he was very helpful, and seemed to be bubbling over with ideas."

"I know," interjected Dana. "He's a wonderful old man. I think he has been lonely for so long, he's happy to meet new people. He seemed to enjoy talking to us."

"So, we talked about the old days," Graham continued, "when the brewery was first built, when the Hennigan family lived close by. He said he has some old photographs that we can use. I said we would have copies made of the originals, and perhaps enlarge them for a display. He told me a lot about the problems in the brewing industry with the coming of prohibition, and about his family's move to Kingston. We must have talked for over an hour on the phone. I was taking these notes, so I think I probably have the bones of what we might do for a history of the place."

"That's a good start, then," said Jason, adjusting his position and leaning forward.

"Yes. Now, I guess the question is, how do we want to tackle the problem side of alcohol?"

Dana took over. "Jane has already given me some good stuff on the RIDE program that she used to work on. She'd brought it from the station. I've got it here."

Dana pulled out a pile of leaflets and papers from her bag, and spread them on the coffee table in front of the fireplace.

"There's some advertising leaflets, and here's a couple of reports with statistics an' that. And Jane gave me a few photographs of accidents that we can use to show the kind of damage that can happen."

"Quite a haul you have there," Graham complimented Dana.

"I spent some time over at the library on Saturday," said Jason, pulling out a sheaf of papers. "I found a couple of good books that had sections about beer, and wine, and liquor. Like, how they were made in olden times, like, the middle ages an' that. Did you know everybody drank beer then? It was safer than the water to drink. An', like, I didn't know that in some countries in Europe, kids drink wine with their meals. It's weird, like, the laws are so different in different countries. There's even places in Britain, Wales I think, where in some towns you can't buy beer on Sundays, but in the next town two miles away, you can, so everybody just goes to the next town. It's stupid."

"Yes." Graham smiled. "There's quite a lot of confused thinking about alcohol."

"Yeah." Jason grinned. "Anyway, I copied some pages here. P'raps we can use some of the stuff in them."

Dana made as if to speak, then sat back. Graham looked at her quizzically. She smiled. "I was going to say something, but I couldn't think of how to start," she said, apologetically.

"Try another approach," suggested Graham supportively.

Dana was having difficulties formulating her point. Graham and Jason waited.

"I guess what I'm trying to get at is how do we get the message across that beer an' stuff are not bad in themselves, but that it's the way we misuse, abuse them, that's wrong?"

"Yes, that's going to be hard. It's one of the big problems in society; it can strike at any place, in any family."

Dana caught that allusion, not intended, she was sure; it still brought up images from the back of her mind.

Jason spoke. "Like, we've got to decide who we're trying to get the message to. Who's going to see what we put together in the Centre? We're not going to get through to guys like that Lucasz Woslewski, no way."

"I think we need to aim it at the young kids, and at our local teenagers; they're probably the most easily influenced, for good or bad," said Dana pensively.

"One of the major factors in alcoholism seems to be stress," said Graham, shifting the topic slightly. "We haven't considered talking to Alcoholics Anonymous yet."

"Of course." Dana brightened. "We should, and there's a teenager offshoot of AA, what's it called? Alateen, or something. Yeah, that's right. Angelo and Peter had to go to a few meetings after the accident. Why didn't I think of it before?"

"Not to worry," reassured Graham, tilting his head at the sounds of Jane busy in the basement.

"So, where do we go from here?" Jason spread his hands over the piles of paper.

Dana was the one who responded. "I suggest we each tackle one aspect, try writing up something on just one topic; not too long, otherwise it gets unreadable. Maybe, we each work on the stuff we've found out, and then we try putting it all together." Dana was taking control.

"Good idea, Dana," said Graham. "When do you suggest we reconvene?"

"Mmm, how about two weeks' time? I've got a book report due next Wednesday, but after that I'm clear, at the moment."

"Yeah, that's okay," agreed Jason. "We've got a Math test Tuesday, and a term paper for Lit, but that's not due till the end of the month. Yeah, no problem; two weeks today?"

"Sure."

They all stood, gathering up their papers.

"I'll contact George Simpson and ask him if he would bring back the old photos when he next visits Mr Hennigan," added Graham as they walked toward the door. "By the way, Dana, I spoke with Captain Ellis at Petawawa. How about the weekend after next, are you free? She could give you the whole weekend—I'd take you up Friday eve and bring you back Sunday late. Check with your parents—we'd need their written permission."

"Sounds great, I'll get back to you. Thanks."

Jane had come upstairs. "Busy day tomorrow?"

"Yeah, I have a cheerleader squad practice before school tomorrow." Dana made a mock grimace.

"We've come a long way since our first chat," explained Graham. "We're at the first draft stage now. Next meeting should take us a lot longer. We'll be getting down to details then."

"It's good to see all this happening," said Jane as she helped Dana with her jacket.

"Yep, people working together," agreed Graham. "G'night Dana, Jason."

"Yeah, thanks. Bye Graham. Bye Jane."

"See you again soon."

As the door closed behind them, Jason whispered to Dana, "They're a really cool couple, like, normal people."

Dana chuckled. "Of course, whadya expect—zombies?"

At that, she suddenly jumped aside as another person appeared abruptly. "Tony!" gasped Dana. "What're you doing? You scared me."

"Huh? Sorry, Dan, didn't mean to, just walking along. More to the point, what're you two up to?"

"We've just been meeting with Cap—er, Graham, about words for the museum at the Centre," put in Jason.

"Thought you said you had too much work to go out tonight." Tony addressed Dana in a disbelieving tone.

"Come on, Tone, don't be like that. I knew I had this meeting tonight and a mid-term test tomorrow morning. I have to study for the test now. I'll see you tomorrow."

"'Kay. Bye." And Tony walked off.

Sheesh, thought Dana, *what's got into him, again?*

- 20 -

David Adkins sat back in his chair, staring at the brass and glass doors that enclosed the hearth of their stone fireplace. His thoughts were far away, racing back through his life, dashing into one old scene, jumping to another, and another. Images crowded into his inner eye.

"What are you thinking about?"

His thought line snapped. "Uh, what?"

"I said, what are you thinking about?" repeated his wife Barbara.

"Do'know, really," responded Dave. "I was just wandering, I guess."

"Well, do you want the job?" Barbara came straight to the point.

"Uh? Oh, that."

"Come on, Dave, love, it's a wonderful offer, right up your street."

"I know, it's just …"

"Just that you don't like the idea of it being handed to you on a plate."

"Yeah, I guess."

"Look, Mike was a bit forward, putting you on the spot at that meeting, but he was only thinking of what you could do to help Dana's project succeed. And George Simpson was very gracious when he came round to see you. I s'pose it was a kind of interview he gave you. Oh, and the other day, John called me into his inner office. He told me he'd had lunch at the courthouse with George the day before, and George had been telling him about the old brewery project. John said that George had spoken highly of a Dave Adkins, who had been offered the job of administrator. John told me he had put in a good supporting word for you. So you see, sweetheart, it's just made for you."

"I guess you're right. I suppose any other job I've had, I've had to apply for, I've had to compete for. That's what's so different here."

"Well, deep down, do you want it?"

"Yes, but—"

"But no but. Go pick up the phone and call George. Tell him you accept, and ask when you start. Go on!"

Dave sighed. "The job starts at the beginning of next month. Hennigan wants the administrator to be involved right from the start. But …"

"But what, love? What's holding you back?"

"I guess it's because it's so close to home. I'll be working with all our neighbours. I'll be paid a salary, but they'll be volunteering their time. And I've always gone out of the neighbourhood to go to work before. I don't know if I can match neighbours' expectations."

Dave knew he was in a much better state than he had been several months ago, thank goodness, but he also felt that he had a way to go to regain his full self-confidence.

"Of course you can, and you will. Dave, come on, this whole community is behind you. Young Dana has done a great job, starting the ball rolling the right way. We all need you to pick it up now and run with it."

"I guess you're right," said Dave with a deep sigh. "I guess you're right."

Barbara stood up from her armchair, walked over to him, and kissed him. "Go and do it now," she said softly.

Dave sat still in his chair for thirty seconds, mustering all his strength. He knew the job was not going to be an easy one; there would be many pitfalls, many challenges. It would be different, and yet so similar to all his past experiences; it was just that it would combine all of his past work and volunteer experience into one single job, so close to home.

Slowly, he rose and walked to the kitchen phone. Cody and a friend were in the family room beyond the kitchen, watching television—loud.

Dave turned, opening the door to the basement. He turned on the light and slowly descended the stairs. He walked over to the telephone at the far end of the bar counter.

His eye caught the glint of the glasses on the shelves at the back of the bar—no longer any bottles of scotch, or anything else alcoholic. He knew in his heart that he had conquered that problem. It had only started to take control of him after he had lost the job last Christmas-time. There had been a point where he was really on the edge. Looking back, he now realized how close he had been to sliding down the wrong side of that slippery alcoholic slope.

And then there was the incident with the policewoman, and the mess with Kelly. But Barbara had been a tower of strength. God, he knew now how hard she had worked on him during those dark days, when he was so down, when he seemed unable to last no more than a couple of hours without another shot of alcohol. Without it, he became a trembling wreck, but with it, he was not much better.

He could see the kids' faces: the older two disgusted, Cody fearful. No visitors came into the house in those days through May and June, and he and Barbara had no outside social life, either.

Dear Barbara, she gave so much. She had worked steadily on him, coaxing, reassuring, supporting, rebuilding his confidence. That, he now realized, was probably the root cause of it all. His confidence in himself, his self-esteem, had been shot away, and all he could find to try to bolster it had been scotch—the smooth, warm, engulfing sensation of good scotch sliding down the throat.

But it was oh so temporary, for so short a time, that soon he had felt the need for more, before the demons, the tremors took over.

He suddenly felt a shiver run through him, and came back to the present. Now he had a real purpose in life again, he had no need, no excuse, for crutches. He had no need for false support. His confidence was back. He had made up his mind.

Carefully, systematically, he dialled Simpson's number.

- 21 -

Dana lay on her bed, her head propped up on her two pillows, gazing up at the pink lampshade her mother had given her for her twelfth birthday—how twee. The late afternoon light was fading fast, but it was enough to light her room.

Her mind was far away, out on the range, following the platoon, crouched low, skulking through the underbrush, laden with gear, weapons at the ready—*switch*—riding the armoured personnel carrier, head out of the hatch, windswept hair flying behind, breath in gasps, radio crackling, down into the hollow, mud splashed everywhere, gunfire—*switch*—now in the Ops Room, tense, markers on the map table, blues are failing fast, radio crackle, blues kayoed—but what if it were real?—*switch*—riding in the patrol car, dispatcher's voice, siren wailing, red lights flashing, store window reflections, traffic lights on red, must go through, traffic peels away, tearing through streets, multiple collision, there are casualties, note the plates, blood, dead—*switch*—parade square, music, rhythm, precision, marching boots, flags, cannon-fire, solemn, quiet—*switch*—dispatcher calling,

"B and E", into the 'burbs, look at the mess, broken glass, hysterical mother, wailing child—*switch*—officers' mess, guest, what a place, four stripes—what's that? challenge cups, order—*switch*—in the market, in the doorways, on the sidewalk, cruising, watch that john, okay they've got him, was she a cop? yeah—*switch*—*thumpa, thumpa, thumpa, thumpa,* louder, *thumpa,* louder, *thumpa,* cover your ears, watch the helo, hovering, watch that rope, here they come, *zip,* down the rope one, *zip* two, *zip* three, watch the injured, two cover, weapons ready, one clears the injured, up he goes, up goes one, up goes two, up goes three, *thumpa, thumpa, thumpa, thumpa,* fainter, *thumpa,* fainter, *thumpa,* mission accomplished, sir.

She rolled onto her left side and reached over to pick up the booklet from the side table. She toyed with it, idly gazing at the front cover and then the back, upside down—in French—before opening it.

The booklet opened quite naturally now, the crease at its spine having been bent back many times in the past few days. Her eyes were drawn again to the aerial view of the college at Kingston. Kingston would be fine; at least she'd visited it now.

She leafed through the pages yet again. The more she thought about it, the more attractive the whole thing seemed. But everything seemed so rosy, and yet there had to be another side to it all.

She held the open booklet in front of her for a long time, not really seeing it. Gradually, she focussed: the upbeat words, the photos of typical activities; the whole tone was encouraging, positive. But the other side wasn't there—if she chose this as a career, her commitment would be to obey, whatever the cost—so Captain Ellis had stressed.

Could she do that? Could she really, really imagine herself in that kind of situation? Could she steel herself to take what she had actually seen some of the people up at Petawawa being put through—and that was only training? Could she really?

A shiver passed through her; her hands were tingling, her heart racing. *Yesss, I can*, she thought. *That has to be for me.* She had made the choice. She must succeed.

She closed the booklet, set it down beside her, and rolled onto her back again. She closed her eyes.

Now came the doubts. She could see the stress in the faces of the soldiers going out on the range. Could she really stand the discipline? Could she stand the putdowns, the crap that would be thrown at her?

Captain Ellis had pulled no punches when she took her round Petawawa and the range. It's no camping holiday, no ma'am. She would be pushed into the dirt, climb out, and be ordered to do it again, and again …

She shuddered. *I can do it, I must do it. Why must I do it? Yeah, why?*

Because that's what I'm made for. I want to know I can take all the crap and still do my job, whatever the job might be. I want a job with a real challenge. Yeah, that's it; I need challenge.

Her mind went back to the meeting in the Johnsons' backyard. She had had the whole of the Gardens and the Mews in her charge. She recalled the feeling of exhilaration it had given her, the feeling of power. And yet, with that feeling of power, of control, was the sense of concern, the knowing that she wanted them to accept and believe in what she believed in.

Tony. What would he say? What about Tony? She liked Tony a lot, a real big lot. But … but what? Somehow, she couldn't put her finger on it, but … it wasn't she didn't love him, 'cause she did.

Or did she? Was it real love, was it what everybody says 'you know for sure when it's for real'? But she wasn't sure …

So, it wasn't real love, then. But what did Tony think it was? Did he think the same way as she did? *Probably not, he's a guy. Guys just don't.*

And she and Tony had not been seeing each other quite so frequently in recent weeks—not that she didn't feel the same, or anything like that. Dana was just finding that she had to spend so much more time on schoolwork in Grade Twelve, whereas Tony, being in a different program, didn't seem to need the time.

He was, though, spending more time with some friends who often went over to the Quebec side, where the minimum drinking-age was only eighteen. Tony was eighteen now, and she knew he was drinking when he was with that crowd.

Yeah, she knew lots of kids did the same, and it was legal, but considering what had happened to Vince and Bryce, she worried about him sometimes.

What would he think if she joined the Armed Forces? He hadn't been keen when she'd mentioned being a policewoman, ages ago.

And she couldn't understand why he seemed to be less involved in the conversion of the old brewery buildings. That was the other thing that was taking up so much of her time. Mr Simpson often called on her to join this meeting or that, with architects or with Tony's dad's workmen. She found that exciting, but Tony seemed to be making excuses all the time and avoiding helping. She just didn't get it, and she felt hurt.

What would her Mom and Dad say? She didn't know; she really didn't know what their reactions would be. They knew, of course, that she'd been to Petawawa; Mom and Dad had met Graham. They knew Jane from the accident; in fact, Jane and her mother had become quite friendly, now that Jane lived nearby. And they knew that she had been out with Jane and a couple of other police officers on patrol.

She presumed her mom and dad had just taken all this as valuable hunting out of information on possible careers, and they had kept away from seeming overbearing and prying.

In fact, Dana had been out on a number of tours of businesses, organized by the school's careers counsellor.

When she would get to tell them about her decision, her dad

wouldn't say much; he rarely did, especially these days. Her mom would probably be all logical-like, and list all the reasons for—then list all the reasons against.

How should she tell them? Together? Or one at a time? Maybe one at a time, then she'd more likely get straight reactions; her mom wouldn't be 'tut-tutting' her dad.

Maybe her dad would talk to her more openly if it was just him and her; he'd been in the Air Force when he was young—but he never talked with her about it. Yep, she would talk with him first.

She began to see that she needed some reassurance that she was going to do the right thing. But why? She already knew in her heart that it was decided; she just had to do it.

Somewhere, she heard a voice, faintly—or was she imagining?

She was startled into the present by a light tap at her door, and a voice: "Dana, it's time for dinner. Are you okay?" The room was in darkness now, but she hadn't noticed.

"Coming," she called back.

The mealtime was a usual Munro ritual. Not much conversation, beyond the necessary words to conduct the ceremony of the meal. Her mother made the usual attempts at kick-starting conversations, but they always ran out of fuel before they got anywhere. Her mother's standard opener was: 'What did you (do/think/say) …?'

Oftentimes, her brother Iain wasn't there, because of some sports practice or other, so with her father's general reluctance to say much at any time, she was mostly on her own to contend with her mother's openers.

It wasn't that she didn't like conversing with her mother—to be honest, she did, at other times. But at mealtimes, her mother's style always seemed to be prying.

She felt sorry for her mother, though, especially this past year. Her mom always seemed so tired and drawn, exhausted in fact; she couldn't be enjoying her job. Maybe her mom wanted something new to talk about at mealtimes, separate from her school troubles. She knew her mom had a tough time with some of the kids.

After the meal, Dana helped her mother with the dishes; no real conversation, except to comment on rejects and to watch those greasy pans against her jeans.

Chores finished, she went off to find her father, down in the little den he had built in the basement when Dana was still a little girl. It was so long ago that Dana had only vague recollections of the upheaval of building it, when her toys and Iain's toys had to be uprooted to make way for the big pieces of wood and stuff. And this was because their new little baby brother, Bryce, was in need of a room upstairs.

And there he was, her dad, watching some program on sports. "Hi Dan, my sweet," he smiled. He always gave her a smile. For all his quietness, she loved her dad.

She sat down at his feet, spreading her arms up over his knees and resting her chin on her hands.

"Something on your mind, love?"

Dana loved listening to his soft, Scottish accent. "Yeah, there is."

"Wanna talk?"

"You mind?" Dana tilted her head toward the television.

"Och, not at all." He turned the television off with the remote. "It was only a rerun of the game last weekend—Ah've seen all the good bits."

He shifted his position slightly, causing Dana to re-adjust her position while retaining the basic arrangement.

"Fire away."

Dana was quick to hear the unwitting pun only she could catch at the moment. *Quite an appropriate remark,* she thought to herself.

"Dad?" She paused. "Dad, why did you join the Air Force?"

He thought for a moment. "Well, Dan, ye see, it was a good way to get a job in those days, and to get trained for a job when you came out."

"Did you enjoy it?"

"We-ell, I canna say I didn't enjoy it, but then again, I canna say I did enjoy it. Ye see, it was a lot of both. There were some good times, some real good fun, but there were some god-awful times, and a lot of them. Why are you asking, love?"

"Dad, I want to join the Army and go to military college."

Her father didn't speak for what seemed to Dana like an eternity. She watched his face, his eyes half-closed, his breathing steady but light, his head leant back to touch the high back of the chair.

"Ma dear Dana," he spoke at last, quietly, and obviously with feeling. "Dana, if that is what you truly want to do, if that is your choice, if you're really sure in your heart, then go to it. Ah'm proud of you." He leaned forward and kissed her on the forehead.

Dana reached upward and hugged him. "Thanks, Dad, I love you."

"And Ah love you, too." He reached out and gripped her arm. "Dan, Ah want to tell you I'm really proud of you, the way you've come up with this idea for the old brewery, and especially the way you handled that crowd over at the Johnsons' that night."

"Thanks, Dad, thanks a million."

Dana was pleased to hear her father's compliment—he rarely gave them, so to receive one really meant something.

"Have ye told your mother about your Army plan?"

"No, not yet. I wanted to talk to you first."

"Thank you, love. Wait to tell your mom till she's rested and relaxed. Give her an hour or two to unwind from the horrors at school. Ah won't say a word till ye come and tell me you've told her. You know she worries."

"Yeah, I know."

Dana had gone back to her room after talking with her father. She knew it was too soon to broach the subject with her mother, but it had to be tonight.

She had lain on her bed, letting her mind find its own direction. It had retraced all the steps that had brought her to this day, and this decision. That rainy day when she and Tony first noticed each other in a new light; the discovery of Bryce and Vince and Peter in the old brewery, drinking; the accident, how it hurt so much in her heart, but how she somehow gained the strength to try to comfort others, as they all came together; the encounter with Jane, as the policewoman, and somehow there seemed to be an indefinable bond between them; that Lucasz Woslewski, who sold the boys the alcohol; the gradual realization that she had the power to do something that could help others avoid the fate of Bryce and Vince; the journey to Kingston; seeing RMC for the first time; the meeting with Mr Hennigan; the support from Mr Simpson; the tension of visiting people's homes to tell them about her plan for the old brewery; the rally in the Johnsons' yard; her talks with Graham and Jane; the police patrols; the CFB Petawawa visit; the visits to the Recruiting Office; the tour round RMC last week. It all pointed her to where she was, right there, on her bed, wondering how to open up with her mother.

She left her room and softly walked into the living room. Her mother was there, as usual, but instead of watching the TV or listening to a CD as she normally spent her unwinding time, Dana saw she was reading a book.

"Whatcha reading, Mom?"

Her mother looked up, taken by surprise by the soft-footed Dana. "Oh hi, dear." She looked down at the book. "I was just starting a book about a woman whose lover has gone off to battle with the Duke of Wellington against Napoleon. It's a kind of historical romance, I s'pose. I don't know if there's much in it, but somebody at school said they'd enjoyed it, so I thought I might as well try it."

Dana sat down on the sofa next to her mother.

"Something bothering you, dear? You've spent a lot of time in your room today."

Dana knew that her mother had near-psychic powers of detection about things that were bothering her daughter. It was certainly not the first time her mother had known something was up.

"Mom?" Dana began. "I want to talk with you about something I feel very strongly about."

Her mother's eyes had widened, and her brow was creased, as if to say 'go on'.

"Mom, I've decided I want to join the Army, and go to RMC at Kingston."

Her mother sat stock-still, staring at Dana with those widened eyes, unblinking. Gradually, her expression changed, and her eyes shifted slightly, looking past Dana into the distance. Her features hardened, saddened. At last she turned away, and set her book on the end-table. "I thought you might. You haven't been exactly secretive about it …"

"Mo-om!" Dana exclaimed. "I haven't said a word about it until right now."

"But think of what you've been doing these past few weeks—yes, I grant you, you've been exploring police work with Jane, fine. And you've been off to tour some of the businesses in the region, fine too. You've been to Petawawa with Graham, nothing wrong in that. You've been on a tour of RMC with the school. You've been down to the Recruiting Office twice, that I know of."

"Come on, Mom, what's wrong with that? Other girls are doing the same sort of thing, and some of the guys are too."

"Yes, but you've done far more concerning the Army than any of the others."

"But that's just because I had the chance. Mom, be real. Look,

Neil Miller went up to Petawawa a couple of weeks ago; somebody his dad knows took him. Neil was on the trip to RMC. There were about half a dozen from school, and others from other schools. I told you when we got back."

Her mother put her hands up in a T, to call a stop. "Dana, dear, I'm not criticizing you. I'm just saying that, even without uttering a word, it was clear to me from your actions, your moods, and so on, that you were most interested in the military option."

"Huhnm." Dana was suddenly deflated. How was it that her mother could see everything, even before she did herself, it seemed? Scary.

"Look, dear, let's look at it rationally."

I knew it, thought Dana.

Her mother continued, "If you get accepted into the military, one, if you are accepted into RMC, two, then you will have to learn what real discipline is all about."

"I know that, Mom, I know that."

Her mother rolled on. "And you will be a girl in a dominantly male organization."

"So? Captain Ellis at Petawawa is doing pretty well, and she told me if I work hard, and don't pull the 'weak female' stunt, I could do very well."

"You will have to keep up your studies, if you intend to graduate."

"Sure, why else would I want to go to RMC, if I didn't intend to graduate?"

"I just wanted to make the point. And when you have graduated, you would become an officer; you would have a tough job of work to do, with people under you, and people ranking above you. And that could take you anywhere, into real danger even."

"I know that, Mom." Dana was becoming more than a little rattled now. "That's the whole point of having an army. Not to play toy soldiers on a parade ground. I want to go places, I want to have the challenge; I want to do something for real, where there are risks involved. That's why I talked with Jane, and looked at the police option. But that didn't give me what I think I want. The army does."

"Okay," her mother relaxed, and changed her tone. "Now what would be good about it? You would get a good education academically, and on top of that you would get a military training, discipline training, health, fitness, sports. You would make a good network of friends. You would travel to exciting places, and to some not so exciting. When you left the army, or retired from it, you would have good skills to put you into a good job, if that is what you want."

"So you see, Mom, I really do think it is the career for me."

"Mmmm. Have you told Tony about this?"

"No, I haven't, yet." Dana looked down at her hands, with their backs together, trapped between her knees. She pulled them out, realizing once again that she did that when she was excited.

"Don't you think you should?"

"Mom, I'm not sure. I'll tell him, all in good time, okay?"

Dana knew her mother wouldn't press after that; she knew she couldn't tell Tony if their relationship was on muddy ground, as it seemed to be heading. If it got bogged down completely, and fell apart, there'd be no need to tell him. If it was going to struggle out onto solid ground again, she certainly didn't want to tell him now; it might blow the whole thing apart. And her mother probably knew all that as well, she thought.

"Dana, dear, it's your choice, it's your life. If that is what you want to do, do everything that's necessary to make sure you get there. And do it well. It wouldn't have been my choice for you, but it's not my choice to make. Have you told your father?"

"Yes, I did after supper."

"I thought so; I saw you go down to his den. What did he say?"

"He said he was proud of me, and told me to go to it."

"Yes. You know, Dana, your dad thinks a lot of you, even if he doesn't say it very often."

Dana felt herself blushing.

"And I do too," her mother added, leaning forward to hug her. "What you might do is phone your Uncle Alex, and ask him about military college. It's probably better to leave it for tonight though, it'll be past eleven o'clock in Halifax now."

"Yeah, thanks, Mom. I'll try calling him tomorrow after supper."

"Alex is a good sort. Pity he's so far away. He's such a contrast to your father, he's outgoing, and always fun to be with."

"I haven't seen him since we all went to Halifax that time when I was thirteen. He seemed so much younger than Dad."

"Not surprising; he's ten years younger. There was another brother between them, Andrew, but he died as a young boy. That was while your dad's family still lived in Scotland."

- 22 -

It was a gala atmosphere, on that April day when the new Centre opened. Noise, bustle, balloons, coloured lights, the sounds of voices young and old, all mingled together in a smorgasbord of excitement.

Jane was impressed; she knew how much effort had gone into achieving all of this. She felt buoyant, honoured to be part of Dana's idea, her creation.

The old brewery building had never seen anything like it, the culmination of countless hours of planning and work. And now it was ready to take on a new role, a new lease on life, a giver of life to the people gathered there that day.

Most of the residents, adult or child, from the Gardens and the Mews were there, crowded into the main hall, where the big brewers' tanks had sat a century ago. The sounds lofted upward, high into the upper reaches of the hall to the great oak beams that held the roof, beams that strutted out from the bare brickwork standing firmly above the smooth lower reaches of the walls, now covered in plaster and wallboard.

At one end, a raised platform held several seats arranged in an arc. In front of them, a microphone on its stand waited. Behind, a bare stone wall framed a square of blue drapes.

A door at the side of the platform opened, and a man's face peered out. The crowd fell silent, expectant.

Dana felt nervous. This was it; this was her dream, her idea, come to fruition. She still found it hard to believe that all the people who had been involved had come together when needed.

She stood in the hallway, with the rest of the platform party, waiting for Mr Simpson to give the word. She watched as he opened the door. A wave of sound burst through. As he leaned into the open doorway, the sound died; she could feel her heart thumping.

At the signal from Mr Simpson, they filed out onto the stage and took their seats, Dana, Mr Hennigan, and Mr Adkins, leaving one more for Mr Simpson, who had walked over to the microphone.

Dana was overwhelmed by the sight spread in front of her. Her mind flashed back over the past few months. What a whirlwind of events had crowded into such a short time: the City Council meeting at which the project was formally approved; the planning meetings with the architect—she had been amazed by the generosity of the architect and the engineers—all their work was done at no charge; the formation of a young peoples' council and beginning to work with the volunteer advisors; watching, as Mr Ferruccio and his men, along with Mr DeLaunais, began the challenging task of changing the old Hennigan Brewery into the new Hennigan Centre; the several visits down to Kingston with Mr Simpson, and various others on occasion, to consult with Mr Hennigan; the discussions on the ceremony about to begin; the dedications (she had been greatly saddened by what she learned from Mr Hennigan); and then, to cap it all, only yesterday she had received the news that she had been accepted by RMC at Kingston. She was on Cloud Ten.

Mr Simpson was speaking, she realized. "… and so, I would like to call first on Dana Munro. Dana?"

She walked to the microphone. Mr Simpson helped her adjust the height, to the amusement of the audience—Mr Simpson being six foot five, and Dana a mere five foot six.

"Mr Hennigan, friends," she began. "I really do feel it's a privilege to be standing up here in front of you. You've all been wonderful in your support, and I can't thank you enough. This has been my dream, and you have made it come true.

"This Centre's going to be a place where people, young and old, will enjoy being together, playing together, working together, learning together. It'll be a constant reminder of good times, but also of sad times—sad times that can teach us all lessons.

"I can't thank all of you by name, it would take far too long, but you know what you have contributed, and I thank you for it. But I would like to give special thanks to a few people, who have given me, personally, special encouragement.

"First, I want to thank Mr Hennigan." She turned to him, nodded her head, and then returned to the microphone. "He had the faith to take my idea and let it grow into this wonderful place."

The audience burst into applause.

As it died down, Dana continued. "I would also like to thank Mr Simpson." She let her left arm move back to include George Simpson in its sweep. "Mr Simpson has given countless hours to helping me and guiding me—and transporting me. I really do appreciate all that he has done for me."

The audience applauded.

"I want to thank someone who came into my life at a tragic time, and who has been an example for me to try to follow. Jane Stennings. Jane, thank you. Thank you for being there when we needed help, and thank you for being an inspiration for me."

Again, the gathering applauded.

"And I must thank one more special person, who has been my sounding board for so many of my thoughts on this project, who has been my supporter and my companion as we dragged the idea around to meet with all of you. Tony, thank you."

And with that, Dana returned to her seat.

The audience, however, rose to its feet, applauding loud and long, so long in fact, that Dana, exhilarated though she was, began to feel embarrassed.

She turned to Mr Hennigan, who indicated that she should stand again. She did so, and bowed her head, opening her arms to the crowd.

At last, she sat down, as the audience resettled into its various spots on the floor and the seats.

Mr Simpson returned to the microphone.

"I would like to say a few words at this point in the proceedings," he began. "My association with this building began way back, just after the Second World War, when I was billeted here as an army lieutenant. It was a cold and drafty place then, a far cry from this fine structure we see now. There were no houses here, way back then.

"I am proud to say that now I count many of you as good friends. This whole project, and the events that led to its conception, have been very enlightening. It has certainly given me a new view of people, of what people can do together.

"I will now call upon Dave Adkins, our administrator." He sat down, to more applause.

Dave approached the microphone. "Mr Hennigan, and friends. I feel a bit out of place up here. The three people up here with me have far more claim to be here than I do. They have done wonders. I have only just begun to play my part in this whole business.

"And I, too, want to thank people for their confidence in me.

When I was first 'volunteered'," he made quote signs with his fingers, "by my good friend, Mike Carson, I was at first embarrassed, and then honoured by the support you gave me. And I am indebted to Mr Hennigan and the Youth Council, who took me on as the only person on the Centre's payroll. I am truly grateful for this opportunity; it's a wonderful experience already, and I can assure you that I will do my level best to serve you well.

"And I want to thank particularly those volunteer assistants who have already been working hard with the Youth Council to put together an exciting and challenging program of activities; activities, I should add, that are for all young-at-hearts. That is the role of this place: it is a youth centre—for the young at heart. Youth is not an age; it's an attitude. I thank you all."

Dave returned to his seat to the audience's applause.

Mr Simpson moved to the microphone and readjusted it again, to Mr Hennigan's height. "I now have the pleasure of introducing our honoured guest, Mr Kurt Hennigan."

Mr Hennigan moved to the microphone, to loud applause. "Ladies and gentlemen, friends—I hope I may call you all friends. It is a great honour for me to be with you today. It is one of the greatest occasions in my life. And, may I add, that I'm going to be ninety-seven in a few months—"

Thunderous applause cut him off for a full minute.

He continued, in his old but strong voice, "This place has many memories for me. It was built by my grandfather. When he died, he left it to my father. I knew this place when I was a young boy. I remember the horse-drawn wagons that brought the barley, and others that carried the great barrels of dark beer and lager to the town. And the coming of the railway, and the old steam locomotives that shook their rattling freight cars laden with our barrels over the bridge that once carried the tracks over the Otter Brook. And as the influence of the Depression took effect and the brewing businesses faltered, I moved my family away to Kingston, sadly leaving this brewery with just a dozen men left working it and driving the two-horse drays, or driving the three motor-trucks we had by then. My son and my daughter, little more than babies, were sorry to leave this place.

"The brewery struggled on, but finally it had to close, and the men were out of work. This was a most difficult and sad time for me. I knew each one of the men and their families. Eventually, they all found new work, but many had to move far away.

"This property had been left to me by my father, with the same conditions under which his father left it to him. I could not sell the property outside the family. And so, I hoped that in time I would be able to find a use for the place, and eventually leave it to my children."

Here he paused, and turned toward Mr Simpson, who realized at once that Mr Hennigan needed to sit. His chair was brought forward, and the microphone lowered.

"My old legs are faltering a bit these days," he continued, smiling. "I work them a bit too much sometimes."

The audience chuckled.

He continued, "After six years of World War, peace was again close at hand, but there were still conflicts, erupting in the Korean peninsula. My son had joined the army at age eighteen. Shortly afterward, my daughter volunteered as an army nurse. She had already begun her training before the conflict erupted. They both went to Korea ..."

A deep stillness filled the hall, as Mr Hennigan's voice grew softer.

"... but they did not return."

Dana felt the tears well up in her eyes again. She had been deeply moved when she had learned the details the day before from Mr Hennigan. He had told her more at that time, looking at her with deep, sad eyes. His daughter had been killed, not by the enemy, but when an army truck, driven by a drunken soldier, had collided with the truck carrying her and several nursing friends, all returning from

167

a dance. His son had been killed at the Battle of Kapyong.

Mr Hennigan continued, softly. "I have no surviving family. My dear wife died forty-two years ago." But here his voice picked up. "So when I received a phone call from my good friend George here, about a young lady who had a proposal for this old brewery, I was interested to meet her and hear her ideas. When I met her, I was impressed at once."

He stood up from his seat and beckoned to Dana. Surprised, she rose and came to him. He grasped her hand and raised it to head height.

"In Dana, I see my dear lost daughter. God bless you, my dear."

Dana struggled to form a smile through the tears that were brimming in her eyes.

He released her hand. "Now, my friends," Mr Hennigan was in firm control now, "we will move to the most important part of our ceremony today. And please, I ask that Mr and Mrs Munro, and Mr and Mrs Ferruccio, join us on the platform."

This was all pre-arranged, Dana knew, though it had been difficult. Both mothers had been reluctant, fearful of their own emotions, but Mr Hennigan had taken each one aside during the small reception he had given last evening at his hotel, and in his gentle but persuasive way had urged them to take part. Part of the grieving process, he had said to them.

The four parents joined them on the platform. Dana stood on the left of the blue drapes at the back, with her mother and father next to her. Mr Hennigan stood on the right of the drapes, with Mrs and Mr Ferruccio beside him. Mr Simpson had moved the microphone over to the side to not obscure the group. Dave Adkins had moved away to the far side of the platform, taking the chairs with him.

Mr Simpson began, "Would everyone please stand."

A general bustle and noise erupted momentarily, with a cough or two, and sounds of Kleenex being used, as the audience came to its feet and readjusted to obtain a clear view.

Mr Simpson continued. "We are gathered here today to rename these buildings and their grounds as the Hennigan Centre, and to dedicate them to the memory of four young people, lost forever from our world."

Dana and Mr Hennigan pulled at the cords and the blue drapes parted, revealing a bronze plaque.

"I shall read the words inscribed on this memorial." Mr Simpson adjusted his reading glasses. "This Hennigan Centre is dedicated to the memory of Richard Hennigan, Lorna Hennigan, Bryce Munro, Vincent Ferruccio, for enjoyment by the Young-at-Heart."

Dana and Mr Hennigan walked together to the front of the platform. They took their cues from each other, and together pronounced, "We declare this Hennigan Centre open."

- 23 -

The snowfall had been heavier than forecast. Jane was glad Graham had suggested he stay home with the baby, instead of them all coming out in the cold to trek over to the Centre. It was the Children's Christmas Party, the first ever held that included the whole 'Brewster' community, and the first in the Hennigan Centre.

Jane felt excited as she trudged through the snow on the sidewalk, not plowed now as a cost-cutting measure by the city. She liked the Christmas season, and this one was made all the more special by her own little baby.

Most of the townhouses had put up lights, making the place bright and cheery, and as she looked across the snow-covered playfield to the walls of the Centre, she could see the coloured lights arranged in the form of a star, high on the end wall. Dave Adkins and Pino Ferruccio had been up a tall ladder back in November setting that up.

As she stepped into the entrance hall, Jane pulled off her boots and slipped on a pair of flat, soft shoes. There was the sound of high-pitched children's voices coming through the inner doors.

She quietly entered the main hall to find Fiona Stacey in the middle of the hall with a crowd of small kids chasing balloons in some form of game. Jane smiled, thinking it didn't really matter what the game had started out as, the kids were having fun anyway. Some older children were helping Fiona as best they could.

Jane glanced over to the counter that opened from the kitchen to see several of the mothers busily preparing the food and drinks that would be served up later. Spread around the benches along the walls of the hall, fathers sat in groups. Occasionally, a father would swoop in like a hawk and pick off a child from the crowd, and mildly chastise or gently comfort the child, depending on the circumstances.

Jason Johnson had a group of young teens over by the platform at the other end, deeply involved in some kind of guessing game. Everything seemed to be moving along well.

"Hi Jane, where's the babe?"

Jane turned to see Kelly McDowell coming toward her from the kitchen. "Hi, Kelly. Graham suggested, as it's colder and snowier than expected, that he stay home and look after Trishy. He sent me to represent the family."

"Oh, and I was looking forward to seeing her. But you're right, it is a bit on the cool side."

"While I think of it, Kel, would you and Mike care to come over tomorrow night, say, around eight?"

"Sure, that would be nice. I'll check with Mike, but it sounds good."

"Great. Is Dana here yet?"

"No, not yet. She only got home from Kingston last night. I expect there's a lot of catching up going on with her family."

"I bet. She's been away from them basically since, when, beginning of July, wasn't it?"

"Mmm, I guess so, but I think her parents did go down a couple of times in early September. But I don't think she's been allowed any leave from RMC before this. I expect we'll see some big changes in her. She'll have had a tough time."

"Yes, but I'm confident she can take it." Jane knew much of what was involved at RMC from what Graham had told her, and she had had to go through some similar kinds of training herself, in the police force.

She had been deeply moved by Dana's comment back at the opening of the Centre, of how Dana had looked on Jane as a role model. Jane had not appreciated that she was, though she had felt the bond with Dana since the time of the accident.

At that point, the doors from the entrance opened, and in stepped Dana, dressed in her full scarlets. The children took one look at her and ran to surround her, clamouring to touch her, to feel her uniform, quizzing her about what this was for, what that was for.

Gently, Dana tried to calm them down, only to be caught by the onslaught of the teens and surrounded by an even bigger and louder mob.

Laughing happily, she carefully walked across the hall, sweeping the horde along with her, waving to Jane and Kelly, and to the fathers, most of them having stood up by now, all of them laughing. Dana brought the clinging mass to the centre of the hall, and stopped.

Suddenly she flung her arms high and in a firm voice shouted, "Freeze."

It had the desired effect. Silence fell upon the horde.

Dana spoke quietly, "Sit down, all of you, please, right where you are." She lowered her hands slowly.

The children obeyed.

Methodically, Dana proceeded to tell the children, and most of the fathers who had wandered over from the benches, about the several parts of her uniform, and how she had to keep them clean, polished, and pressed. Gradually, the children began asking questions again, but now in an orderly fashion, and even some of the dads added theirs. Dana was clearly in her element.

She moved on to telling the cluster around her about how strict things were at the college, and how little time they had to prepare for drills and inspections; about how clean and tidy they had to keep their rooms, and she gave a little, light-hearted lecture to the teenagers on that issue.

Jane and Kelly had held back, watching the action from afar, not wanting to distract anyone from Dana's control.

"You know," began Kelly, "even in the five months or so since I saw her last, she's matured a lot."

"Yes," agreed Jane, "and she was mature even then. She's going to do very well."

The sound of tinkling bells was heard by all, and attentions diverted toward the double doors, where the sound was coming from.

"Ho, ho, ho! Me-erry Christmas, everyone; Mee-eerry Chri-istmas. Ho, ho, ho!" In waddled Santa Claus, carrying his sack.

The little kids squealed in delight, rushing over to surround him as he made his way over to a big chair that had been placed up on the platform near the big Christmas tree. Several fathers acted as shepherds, collecting the children into a noisy but orderly group. Mothers and helpers came out of the kitchen as the strains of Christmas carols wafted out from a portable stereo resting on the end of the serving counter.

Dana took charge of the line of fidgety children waiting to talk with Santa. The little ones were first, then older ones. Each child came back from Santa clutching a small present, which was quickly unwrapped.

While all this was happening, Jane went over to the teenagers, who, as usual, were hovering on the edge of the gathering of fathers, mothers, and their smaller offspring. Jane and Kelly had been working with the teens for several weeks, helping and giving encouragement to them in developing and practising 'Christmas Carols with a Twist'.

There were, Jane had found, several good musicians in the group, and what had evolved was quite spectacular.

While the smaller kids played with their new toys, the teens quietly set up their gear on the platform, in readiness. Kelly had walked back to turn off the Christmas music.

At a sign from Jane, Jeremy Johnson walked over to the microphone at the side of the stage. "And no-ow we have grrre-eat pleasure in pree-senting … Thee Bre-ewster Pla-ayers. Take it away, Jase!"

A blast of discordant, whole spectrum sound from the synthesizer shook everyone into rapt attention, as three disguised teens moonwalked onto centre stage. The beat started, and the middle moonwalker began a rap version of "Rudolph the Red-Nosed Reindeer", backed up by the others, to the great amusement of the adults, and vigorous applause at the end.

As the moonwalkers departed, six girls in cowgirl boots, short-shorts, Western shirts, and hats, bounced onto the stage to line-dance a Country and Western version of "God Rest Ye Merry, Gentlemen". Thunderous applause helped them execute some pretty fancy footwork.

As a finale, the rappers, the cowgirls, and the whole troupe combined forces, with Jason Johnson on synthesizer and brother Jeremy on triangle, urging their audience to join them as they sang the conventional version of "Silent Night".

Jane was proud of them. It had all been the teens' ideas. She and Kelly had suggested, led when they seemed to be faltering, had offered resources where needed, but it was all the kids' efforts.

It was time for refreshments after all that effort. The kids were organized down by the counter as parents and helpers handed out juices and cookies.

Kelly carefully handed a tray with a tumbler of juice and three cookies to a little five-year-old girl, who timidly carried them across the hall to Santa, who had stayed to watch the performances. Dana had waited by Santa, and helped the girl offer him his treat.

Santa thanked the girl and patted her on the head. She ducked timidly and ran quickly back to the others, turning to watch Santa from afar. He quickly consumed the cookies and juice. Standing up, he gathered up his sack, and waved to everyone.

"Ho, ho, ho, Mee-rry Christmas to all!" he called.

"Merry Christmas," was the reply, as Santa left by the double doors. Dana followed him.

Jane and Kelly quickly ran after three of the know-it-all twelve-year-old boys, who were intent on blowing Santa's disguise, and prevented them from reaching the doors.

Outside, Tony stopped for a breather, pulling down the hairy beard and moustache that he had caught in his mouth as he ate the cookies. Dana caught up with him.

"You were very good with the kids," she said.

"Thanks, Dan. I really thought that big fat kid was going to tug the beard down when he leaned forward to say thank you."

"Oh, Joey Lister? Yeah, I remember him from softball last spring. He's too pushy."

"So, how've you been?"

"Okay. Nice to be home for a while. Not having to get up early, do all the inspection routine, drill, before even eating breakfast; it feels good."

"So, do you like it, really?"

"Yeah, it's tough, but I can see why they make it like that. It really does make you organize your time, and learn self-discipline. The courses are pretty good; there's a couple I'm having a bit of trouble with, but I think I'm okay. So how about you?"

"Aw, not bad. Think I took on too many courses. Though they said that was what I had to do to be full-time. Got one instructor who's a jerk though, he and I don't see eye-to-eye on much. Think he's got it in for me. He even told me I couldn't go into class one day."

"Why ever not?"

"Said I'd been drinking."

"Well, had you?"

"Just had a beer with my lunch in the pub. Nothing wrong in that."

"Just one?"

"Er … maybe two."

By now they had reached Tony's car.

"Jeez, where did I put the key?" he said, frowning as he struggled to pass his hand through the Santa suit to his own pocket. "Damn. Oh yeah, it's in the other one."

As he struggled, Dana smiled at his discomfort. "Got anyone special?" she enquired.

"No, not really, there's a gang of us hang out in the pub at breaks. Girls and guys. I've dated a couple of the girls, they're friends, good fun, but nothing serious. You?"

"You kidding? I don't have time! No, there's this one guy, he's a hulking six foot two. Thinks he's God's gift to women. But he's gross; none of the girls has any time for him; wouldn't want him if we had time!"

Tony had found his key at last. He opened the car door. "See you around before you go back?"

"Yeah, sure. Merry Christmas, Tone."

"Merry Christmas."

Dana watched as Tony drove away. They had ended their close relationship before she went to RMC. It was a mutual, amicable break-up; it just seemed to be the sensible thing to do.

It had been Tony's suggestion, and at first Dana felt hurt. But trying to maintain a long-distance relationship, with both of them embarking on new ventures, would have been difficult, and Dana knew in her heart that it wouldn't have worked. The old days, when they were still in high school, were long gone now. And to be honest, the last few months of that era were not as much fun as the earlier times.

The change, Dana suddenly realized, had set in just after they had first gone with Mr Simpson to visit Mr Hennigan in Kingston; after that visit, Tony had often seemed a little more distant, and as time went on, they had gradually spent less time together.

Granted, Dana thought, *I really did spend a lot of time working on getting the Centre up and running, plus all the extra schoolwork I had to do.*

But as she walked back toward the Centre, she realized that, although they were no longer an item, she still had strong feelings for Tony; she really was interested in how he was doing at college; she did want to know about his girlfriends, and she knew there were little niggling seeds of jealousy lurking in there. And she worried about his mention of hanging out in the college pub—after all that had happened with Bryce and Vince.

Yeah, she thought, *and that instructor banning him from class—was that an isolated incident, or is it more than that? Is Tony into the habit of drinking and skipping, or missing, classes?*

She shrugged her shoulders as the wind whistled past her, and she hurried back to the warmth. She had four more years at RMC to concern her; that had to be her number one priority.

PART 2

- 24 -

"It was a nice funeral yesterday for Arthur Donnelly, if you could use that term to describe a funeral." Dwayne Hampden closed his car trunk lid as Dave Adkins was walking past with Brutus the dog.

"Was it? Good. I'm sorry I wasn't able to be there. I had a youth workers' workshop in Toronto yesterday and the day before."

"Sad really, but he'd had a good life. You know, Arthur and Edith Donnelly were about the first to buy a house in this area, sort of had a wide-open choice of lot at the time.

"Anyway, he's gone now, bless him. He's done well. An old friend gave a short eulogy. I hadn't known that Arthur fought in the Second World War—he was wounded and was a POW."

"He'd been ill for quite a while, hadn't he?"

"Yes. He'd not been in the best of health. It was cancer of the lung in the end. He'd had that nasty cough for a long time, but then it flared up quite quickly."

"Is his wife staying in the house?"

"Uh-huh, she will, at least for a while. Edith is a very quiet person. I don't know how she'll get on without him. I gather there's a son somewhere out west—he didn't come to the funeral, so I don't suppose there's much hope of him looking after his mother. Elizabeth and I will keep a good eye on her, but we're getting on in years ourselves."

"Aren't we all, eh, Dwayne?"

"Yes, I guess we all are. There was quite a turnout, though, at the funeral. I was quite surprised really, particularly at the number of younger folk there from the community—you know, the late teens and early twenties. To tell you the truth, though I was against it at the beginning, I really think that your new Centre has a lot to do with it. I say new, but it's been around now for, what, three years or so? The way it's run by you and your council, it's done a lot to give the young folk a sense of—of—community, if you like. You have a lot of support and help from some good people, too. You can be proud."

"Thanks, Dwayne, I appreciate that. Er, you know, I don't usually pry into other folks' business, but I was rather concerned the other night as the dog and I were on our walk."

Dwayne looked up quizzically from the rosebush he had been checking.

Dave continued, "There was an awful row going on at the Ferruccios' place. It seemed that Pino was raging at young Tony about something, and throwing stuff out onto the driveway. I couldn't hear much of what was being said, but what I did hear was not pleasant. Never heard Pino in that state before; Tony must have screwed up really bad."

"Haven't seen Tony about for many months," said Dwayne. "I've heard that he isn't too welcome at home. Apparently, he's got in with a crowd of not-so-goods somehow, lots of drinking and such."

"I thought he was going to Algonquin College."

"He was, but Elizabeth told me he'd failed a lot of courses and had to quit."

"That's too bad, he's always seemed a good kid. What happened with him and Dana? I guess they split when she went into the military? Dana has never mentioned it when we've talked."

"Probably. They wouldn't have seen much of each other, with her being away."

"Guess so. Maybe that's what sent him off on a bad track."

"You never know …"

- 25 -

As she turned the corner onto Millerby Lane, Dana felt the cool wind on her cheeks. *There's certainly a nip in the air now,* she thought, as she picked up her stride again after skipping over the broken sidewalk.

It was early October, Thanksgiving Saturday morning, and she was home for three days. Her three years at RMC had given her the routine of taking her morning run usually very early in the morning, but at home it was a little later. She had found a route that was long enough and quiet, so that she wasn't interrupted by traffic.

Back in Kingston, she enjoyed being able to run around the perimeter of the college and up around the Old Fort Henry. The hill up to the old fort was quite a challenge, and gave her legs and lungs a good workout. She found the view at the top quite exhilarating, out across the college to the town and, to the left, out over Lake Ontario.

At home, there was nothing so uplifting. She would set out over to the intersection of Millerby Lane and Otterbrook Road. At that early hour, there was usually no traffic to delay her crossing over to the old railroad track-bed as it stretched away from the Gardens. It followed a ridge through a lightly wooded region for about a kilometre, until it crossed Axelford Road. She would leave the track there, and return along Axelford Road to meet Otterbrook Road down in the hollow, near the little white church her mother sometimes went to.

Back along Otterbrook, she would pass over the Millerby-Otterbrook intersection and on for another couple of kilometres until the bottom end of the winding Millerby Lane came back to meet Otterbrook.

Years ago, Millerby Lane had been the main road in this area, until Otterbrook was built to cope with the increased commuter traffic from out beyond the Greenbelt. The lane was showing its age, with many derelict buildings, their businesses long since removed to better sites—or bankrupted. Parking lots full of weeds, rusting signs, and other debris gave an air of despair to this end of the lane, in stark contrast to the new townhouses and the Hennigan Centre at the other end. The old sidewalk was crumbled and potholed, and Dana usually skipped out onto the roadway itself at this point, rarely seeing any vehicles this early in the day.

Her rhythm was steady, her breathing came regularly and naturally, her legs moved smoothly and evenly; she was in great shape.

Over the years, Dana had learned to use this time during her run to off-load all the petty issues that could clutter up her days. She was now able to bring each nagging thorn up into her consciousness, deal with it, and cast it out of her mind, or, if necessary, decide on an action or strategy. Once dealt with, it could give no further stress. On her return to college, or home, she was refreshed, bright, and ready for the day.

She felt sorry for some of her classmates, who seemed to be at their peaks just as each day's activities were closing down. How could they ever survive?

She reached the section of Millerby where a few businesses still struggled to survive: a couple of auto-collision repair shops, a welder, a home renovator, and a floor tile place that looked as if it had gone bust since she was home last time.

"Heyunh."

She heard the cry, more of a grunt maybe. Not sure of what or where it came from, she stumbled in her stride.

"Hunh, Danh."

She stopped. She looked around her.

"Herenh. Upv herenhh."

She turned toward the sound. Under the sagging awning of Carlo's Collision, she saw a body sitting slumped against the wall, raising its arm sluggishly. She hesitated, not from fear—her training had taught her how to deal with one-on-one combat—no, not from fear, but from revulsion.

"Danh, zh mee."

Slowly, she walked over to the body, slumped against the wall, its feet in mud-stained runners, its legs clad in torn jeans, the torso wearing a shirt that probably had colours in it if it were washed, topped by a grisly unshaven head of long, unkempt hair. Streaks of vomit splattered down its front to a pool between its legs.

Dana gave an involuntary shudder. She had seen some pretty disgusting, gut-wrenching sights during her training, but this was too close, this hit home too hard. She stood, arms akimbo, three paces from the mess.

The face lifted slowly. "Danh, helv muh."

"Tony, how could you? How could you get into this state?" Dana approached closer, torn between revulsion and concern. Was this really Tony, her Tony she had spent so many good times with before they parted?

A wave of nausea came over her as she caught the stench of stale alcohol, vomit, and body. Steeling herself, she went down on her haunches, gazing at the horror, searching for an answer.

"Danh, helv muh uv. Ah godha gedh homevh."

Dana held her stance. "Tony, I don't think your mom and dad are going to let you in like that."

"Ah godha gedh homevh. Danh ..." His voice trailed off as he slumped further.

Dana stood up smartly, and took charge. "Okay, guy, you boozed up once too many. On your feet, come on, come on. Make it snappy, I don't have all day."

Tony gave a token effort to rise, but slipped into the pool of vomit.

Dana grabbed his arm, on the cleaner side, and pulled him into a shaky standing position. She gagged at the stench. "Okay, you're coming on your own legs. I'll guide you, but no nonsense."

Slowly, they wended their way past Dino's Auto-Body Shop, past the Hennigan Centre parking area. Tony stopped.

"Come on, come on," Dana pressed.

"Godha leekh."

Tony fumbled with his jeans, half-turned his back on Dana, and urinated.

By this time, Dana felt nothing but disgust for him, but yet she couldn't just leave him, especially here, in front of the townhouses. Kids would be out playing soon.

Slowly, she manoeuvred him along, into the Gardens, past the neighbours' houses, and onto the Ferruccios' driveway.

"You're on your own now."

"Nonh, Danh, helv muh."

She relented, and heaved him up to the door. She rang the bell.

After a few moments, the door opened. Carmella Ferruccio appeared in a housecoat. She saw the mess and let out a loud shriek, promptly slamming the door.

"I'm outta here." Dana turned, but before she had gone ten steps, she heard a great roar. She glanced back to see Pino, Tony's father, throwing Tony to the ground, grabbing the garden hose, and turning it on Tony as Tony crumpled on the driveway.

Pino was yelling and cursing in a mixture of English and Italian. Dana could take no more, turning and jogging over to her house, letting herself in through the side door.

The Munro house was quiet, early on that Saturday morning. Dana sat in the kitchen, still in her running gear, nursing a glass of milk, staring vacantly at the doorway into the dining room. The shock of the encounter with Tony was still with her.

Why did he do it? What has brought him to this? And Pino's reaction—phew!

She sensed a sound—there it was again—someone was tapping gently at the front door. Moving quickly to the front hallway, she softly cracked open the door.

It was Tony's sister, Gina. "Can I come in?"

Without a word, Dana pulled her inside. Gina embraced Dana, sobbing on her shoulder. At last, she broke away.

"Come in and sit down."

"Thanks," Gina forced a smile, and reached out to grasp Dana's hand. "Oh, Dana, it was awful. Mamma was screaming, Poppa was yelling, and he threw Tony out into the yard and turned the hose on him. Then he beat him with a broom. Tony just lay there on the grass—he's still there now. Oh Dana, what can we do?" Tears streaked down her face.

"Has he done this before?" Dana asked.

"Not like this, though. He's come home drunk before, but that's before he left home, and he was clean."

They sat in silence, neither sure what to say next.

Dana took the lead. "Gina, Mom told me some months ago that she thought Tony was having problems, but she didn't elaborate, and I just thought she meant with work. I didn't give it much thought, 'cause I was in the middle of exams at the time. Tell me what's happened to Tony."

"Oh Dana, I wish sometimes that it could be like the old days, like when you were still here, and you and Tony were together—we had great times, then. But—oh, Dan, please don't get me wrong, it's not your fault, that's not what I mean, it's just that, well, Tony's never been the same since you two broke up.

"You know he went to college—he did all right for a while. He was pulling good grades, but he got in with this crowd, see, an' they spent most of their time in the bar when they weren't in class. I got to know some of them; they were okay, most of them. I went out with one of the guys for a while, but then he wanted to get serious, an' I didn't.

"But then Tony began to slip, he was cutting classes; he got kicked out of one. And then he came home drunk, not very, but drunk enough. Poppa hit the roof; Mamma went to her room in tears. Poppa kept going on and on about losing Vincent, and how could he, Tony, dare to come home in that state.

"Eventually, everybody calmed down; it took days, and things were okay, for a while. Then it happened again, and Poppa took away Tony's key, an' said the doors were locked at ten-thirty, an' if Tony came home later and drunk, he was not coming in.

"Well, one night, Tone came back drunk, and broke in through the basement. That was it. Poppa threw Tony out, and threw all his clothes an' stuff out on the driveway, in the rain, and told him to find somewhere else to live. Poor Mamma was crying and pleading with them both.

"The clothes stayed there all that day and the next—they were soaked—Tony had gone. Eventually, one of his friends brought him in a van, and they took all the stuff away."

"Where did he go?"

"We don't know—we didn't hear from him for weeks. It was awful in the house—Mamma always crying again, Poppa crabby as hell. Angelo, Roberta, and I, we just kept low and did what we had to.

"Then Tone met me as I came out of work one day—he needed money, he said. 'Like, for what?' I asked him. 'For rent.' So I quizzed him a bit, an' he told me he was rooming in this place, like, but he wouldn't say where. So I asked if he was working, an' he said he was, but he'd just lost his job. But, Dan, he was so vague, he wasn't with it, somehow. So I gave him what I could, I don't know—sixty bucks, I think, that time. Well, he tried that again a few weeks later, but I wasn't going for that same story again, an' didn't give him anything.

"Then, sometime in the summer, my friend Hannah told me she'd seen somebody that looked like Tone picking through garbage cans down behind Turgat's Restaurant."

"No?"

"Yeah."

"Oh Gina, that's awful. Oh, I feel so bad for you all. And this morning, I brought it on you all again; I'm so sorry."

Gina put her hand out and rested it gently on Dana's arm. "No, Dana. You did what was right, you brought him home. That's where he needs to be. He needs our help, he needs our love. And that's why I had to come here now, to thank you, Dana, to thank you. Thank you for bringing my family to the point where we have to make a choice—either to solidify, and help when one of us is in desperate need—or to disintegrate forever. Because that's our choice now. Either our love for one another carries us through this crisis, or we're doomed as a family."

"Gina, is it really that serious?"

"You better believe it. I love Poppa, I love Mamma, but they're all wrong on this with Tone. He needed help months ago, but they rejected him. I'm sure they made him worse."

"Do you think they need help themselves?"

"I'm sure of it. They need lots of help, Dana, lots. Ever since we lost Vince, things have not been good between Mamma and Poppa, and this business with Tone has made it worse."

"Do you think Father Hennessey at your church could help?"

"Nah, he's too straight-laced and dogmatic—he doesn't understand. No, it's got to be someone Poppa respects, an' Mamma too, of course."

"Mmm. About Tony, have you thought of talking to Jane Stennings? I'm sure she could help, or know where you could get help. She was into that sort of thing in the police force."

"I haven't. Dan, I don't really know Jane that well—an' it's a hard thing to talk about when it's your own family. You know her much better."

"Yes, I do. But she and Graham and Trishy are away this weekend, and I have to go back to Kingston on Monday, before they get home." She paused. "But maybe if I gave Jane a call in the week and broached the subject with her, and then you go talk with her after?"

"Thanks, Dan."

They turned their heads as they heard a rustle of clothing and a floorboard creak. Caroline Munro appeared at the kitchen doorway in her house-robe. "I thought I'd heard voices!"

"Hi, Mrs Munro."

"Hi, Mom."

"Hi, Gina. Haven't seen you for a while. How's the job going?"

"Oh, fine, thanks, got a raise last week."

"That's nice. How is your mother? Anne Baxter told me she'd hurt her wrist."

"She's fine now, thanks. It gave her trouble for a couple of weeks, but she's okay now." Gina gave a quick smile. "I'd better be going, now. It's been good to talk, Dan, thanks. See you, Mrs Munro."

"Bye, Gina. Say 'hi' to your mom for me."

"Sure."

Dana walked with Gina to the front door.

"Thanks, Dan." Gina gave another smile.

"You be strong." Dana watched as Gina ran across to her house, then closed the door.

Her mother was sitting at the kitchen table. "Unusual for Gina to come over, especially this early?"

"Yes, Mom. They're having problems with Tony."

"I know, dear."

- 26 -

Dana slid her bag under the seat in front and wrapped her legs around it. She preferred to sit about halfway down the bus, on the right-hand side. It was usually dark when she made this journey, whether she was coming home from Kingston or on her way back. She made a point of being near the head of the line-up, so she could get a window seat.

This Thanksgiving Monday evening, her brother Iain and his girlfriend, Tracey, had dropped her at the bus terminal—they hadn't hung about—no need to; these days, the journey had become a routine.

The bus was starting to fill up. Sometimes it was half-empty, and Dana liked it when she had a double seat to herself. Not that she minded fellow passengers, but after a while it was a bit of a drag, trying to make polite conversation with an old lady, or a business man, or worse—having a young, fidgety kid in the next seat. Students, like herself, were the best, usually. But she did prefer, really, to be able to just watch the dark, shadowy scenery slip past, with occasional lights from farms or the villages—it gave her a chance to adjust from the home situation back to the military scene, or vice versa.

She certainly needed time to adjust during this journey. She just had to come to grips with the Ferruccio situation, with Tony's state.

Idly, she watched the end of the line-up as the bodies shuffled toward the bus door. Suddenly, one body, one face, caught her attention.

No, it couldn't be. She felt a wave of stifling emotion, body-steeling tension, rush through her.

It is. Oh God, it is. Woslewski. Lucasz Woslewski. No! Did he see me get on? Jeez, I hope not. What's he up to? Actually, he looks quite neat, decent clothes.

Her mind flew back to those dark days after the deaths of Bryce and Vince, of the discovery that Woslewski had been selling them liquor. She shuddered, and tried to close the images from her mind.

He was on the bus, coming down the aisle, with not many seats left. She kept her head turned to the window, hoping he would pass by.

He stopped. "Hi, er, do you mind if I sit here?"

Trapped. She turned her head, feigning surprise. "Er, no," she responded, weakly.

For a few moments, he fumbled with his bag, cramming it into the overhead rack. He sat down. "Lucasz Woslewski."

"I know." Her voice was soft, low, and uncertain. She was uncertain, barely controlling something; was it tears, or was it anger? She didn't know.

He took the lead. "Dana, this is quite a surprise." He paused. "Dana, I want you to know that this is not the same Woslewski, the scumbag you remember. And before we go any further, I want to apologize to you for all the hurt and harm that I caused you and your family."

Dana raised her head.

He continued. "I'm not asking you to forgive me. What I did

is unforgivable. But I am responsible, and I am truly sorry for what I did. I have paid for it in many ways, but never enough to make up for your loss."

Dana felt tears well up in her eyes, and sniffed. She nodded her head. This was almost too much for her to handle, coming so soon after realizing the trouble with Tony. What a reversal.

The images of those dark times after the accident were rushing in again; over the years, she had succeeded in pushing them so far back into the depths of memory. But not far enough.

"Dana, I'm sorry I've disturbed you again, but I had to tell you, as soon as I saw you at the head of the line. May I stay here and talk more with you, please?"

She turned and looked at his face, his eyes. They were bright, alive, alert—not the dull, murky eyes of the drunk, the asshole she remembered from school. "Yes."

"Thank you."

The bus was swinging out of the terminal and up onto the Queensway as it headed west. Dana was quiet as she let the flashes of light from the traffic distract her.

She was grappling with emotions. Here, sitting beside her, was the man who, through his actions, had indirectly caused the death of her brother. And he had just sat there and openly apologized—and it sounded genuine, for real.

And yes, to listen to him, to look at him, he wasn't the jerk, the half-drunken lummox that picked fights with anyone, given half a chance, those days in school. Could she bring herself to talk with him, to share a journey with him? Mind in turmoil, she agonized.

The bus had cleared the suburbs now, and the countryside was mostly dark. She turned her head toward him. "So what are you doing now?"

"I'm going back to Lifeline Lodge, the other side of Smith's Falls."

"Lifeline Lodge? What's that?"

"We-ell, before I tell you that, may I tell you more about what has happened to me since you last saw me?"

"Uh-huh." She nodded.

"I went to jail for what I did to your brother, and others. And that was what I needed, to start knocking some sense into me. I also needed to dry out. They put me through the detox centre. Did they ever lay it on the line. Tough? You better believe it. But I didn't get the point, it didn't really sink in, I was still hooked, see, and when I got out, I started drinking again.

"I didn't have a job, and one thing led to another, and I got caught breaking into some place. Before I knew it, I was back in the slammer. Dry again, and boy, did it ever start to get to me. Then the detox again. An' that time it started to sink in—I began to see what they were doing, what they were talking about. And they had this guy, a counsellor, great guy who knew just how to talk to you—he wasn't preaching, he'd got it just right—and he didn't pull any punches, either. And when he talked, you knew he knew what you were going through, what you'd been through.

"Well, it was through him I began to see the wrong, the damage, the hurt that I'd done to others, and to myself, and that I, me, myself, was responsible for all that—no one else, nothing else, not the system, but me, just me. An' then he talked about the ways I could take responsibility back to myself, to change, to take proper control.

"Dana, I did a lot of thinking during those days, and a lot of reading. I watched others and I watched myself—and I realized what a complete asshole I'd been, and how, through my actions, so many people's lives had been screwed up, destroyed. And I'd got to do something about it.

"Well, about then, I'd done my time, and I was a free man again. And that was when it really hit me, what this responsibility bit really meant. I'd been dry all the time I was inside, but that was artificial. Now I was on the outside—I could walk into a bar and buy a drink whenever I wanted. But I have not had a single alcoholic drink to this day. That first day outside, I watched a couple of guys roll out of a bar, get in a car, and weave away down the road, and it all became clear."

He turned to face Dana. "Now, that's not to say I've not been tempted—for a while there, I was a real social misfit—I didn't drink, and I'd been inside, twice. Hard to make conversation about what you do. An' I was out of work, anyway.

"So I joined an AA group, like the counsellor had suggested—and I'd found out later that he'd been an alky in a really bad way, and done a lot of damage, before he got himself straightened out—so I realized then why what he said seemed so straight and direct—he'd been through it all.

"Anyway, this AA group was a great help. It was through one of the guys there that I heard about Lifeline Lodge, and that they were looking for some help out there. So I came out to the lodge, and ended up with a job.

"It's a great place—we deal mainly with teens with alcohol and drug problems, but some older people come as well. It's in the backwoods, and everybody works to keep the place operating—it's live-in, of course. We grow much of our own food, not the meat of course, and we keep a few cows and hens for milk and eggs. We've got a wood-shop and a tin-shop, so the kids can actually make things and sell them to help support the Lodge.

"We have about a dozen counsellors, and probably about thirty residents at any one time. I've been there about two and a half years, now. I was appointed deputy director a month ago."

"Lucasz." Dana cleared her throat. "Lucasz, that really is a great story, and I'm very impressed with what you've told me. And, Lucasz, thank you for what you said at the beginning, for your apology. I know it must have been hard."

"Thank you for accepting me as I am now."

They fell silent, as the lights of a crossroads blinked past. The drone of the bus seemed to grow louder as it pounded through the night. Dana's thoughts wandered back over what she had just heard. How could she help Tony? She certainly didn't want him to go through the same route that had brought Lucasz here to his senses. But what? How?

"So, what are you doing these days?"

"Me? Oh, I'm in the Army. At least, I'm a cadet at RMC in Kingston."

"You are? That's great. I admire you. That's a really tough challenge. How long've you been there?"

"This is my fourth year, beginning last month."

"So you like it?"

"Oh yes. It's tough, but it's a really good atmosphere, and great people, and I feel I'm learning worthwhile skills."

"What, shooting and killing and guns and stuff?"

"Well, yeah, but that's only a part of what it's all about. It's all about people, discipline, how to control yourself and other people, how to take command, and how to follow commands."

"I understand. Because we have to know about that in our work at the Lodge, too. Are you specializing in anything?"

"Yeah, Psychology and History."

"Sounds great. Hey, I need to be getting off. We're nearly at my turnoff."

"So how far is the Lodge? Do you have to walk?"

Woslewski laughed. "No. It's about 10 K west. One of the guys will be there at the bus stop with the van—I hope! They know I'm on this bus."

He continued, "Look Dana, I am glad we met tonight, and that we could talk. It truly has helped me greatly." He pulled out his wallet, and slipped out a business card. "Look, please take my card. If ever there is anything I can do to help you, please, call me."

"Thanks, Lucasz. And thank you for all you've told me. Good luck."

"Bye."

He moved forward as the bus slowed to a halt for its brief station stop at the crossroads. Dana looked at the card in her hand. At the left was an open hand with its lifeline bolded; across the top was *Lifeline Lodge*, and below: "Lucasz Woslewski, Deputy Director", with a phone number and a rural route number address.

No new passengers came on board, and as the bus prepared to continue south toward Kingston, Dana could see Lucasz and his driver close the van doors and drive off to the west.

She sank lower in her seat and leaned her head against the window, unfocussed eyes gazing into the darkness.

- 27 -

"There you go," said Sheila Tovey, as she helped Dana edge Kurt Hennigan's wheelchair down the ramp that had been built at the side of the front steps of his Kingston house. "It's a bit breezy off the lake today, but not bad for mid-October."

"Not to worry," responded Mr Hennigan. "I need the fresh air, don't we, Dana?"

"Of course we do." Dana chuckled. "Bye, Sheila. We'll be back about four."

Sheila closed the door as Dana pushed the chair out of the driveway and onto the sidewalk.

They continued on along the streets, down to the small park alongside the shore, near the hospital. Mr Hennigan liked to come here. They could sit and look out over the lake. On a good day, there would be many sailboats. Occasionally, a lake freighter would put into Kingston, but usually only a small one.

"This harbour was such a busy place years ago," said Mr Hennigan, as Dana set the brake on the wheelchair and sat herself on the bench.

"And all we have today are three sailors out there."

"I would have expected more today, with a wind like this," commented Dana.

They sat and watched. Dana enjoyed these visits with Mr Hennigan. In her early days at RMC, he was still quite agile, and they had walked a great deal when she visited him. He told her much about the history of Kingston, of life as it was there in the '20s and '30s.

But gradually, as the months went by, his legs weakened—and then he suffered a fall in his house. Much to his frustration and annoyance, he became dependent on a wheelchair. At first, Dana had found it very hard work, pushing the wheelchair, but she was determined not to rob Mr Hennigan of his 'walks'.

"You're very quiet today, my dear. Something is troubling you."

"Actually, I do have a lot on my mind at the moment, and I really don't know what to make of much of it."

"The military do work you hard at the college, don't they?"

"It's not college stuff, Mr Hennigan, it's … it's … Oh, Mr Hennigan—Tony Ferruccio's got himself all tangled up with alcohol, he's in a terrible state … a disgusting state."

"No! Young Tony? After all his family went through with his brother's death, and your brother's, too! What's happened to cause all this? I see now why you're so troubled. He always seemed such a fine fellow when I talked with him."

"I don't know, Mr Hennigan, I really don't. I only discovered all this last weekend, when I was home."

"But you and Tony have not been 'seeing each other' for a long time now, have you?"

"No, you know we broke up, kind of when I came to RMC. But I was out running last Saturday morning and found him. Oh, he was in a terrible state. I took him to his home—his parents' home, that is, but his dad threw him out again."

"No? Pino did that? He seemed such a kind, gentle man. Such a generous family."

"He seems to have changed, at least so far as Tony and alcohol are concerned. I've had several long talks with Tony's sister, Gina. She seems to be the only one in the family who has any love left for Tony right now. But she's desperately in need of support, she can't help him alone."

"What is Tony doing now?"

"Staying with some friend or other—I don't know where. Mr Hennigan, I feel so awful about all this. I know Tony and I broke up, but we did it in a friendly way. We could still talk to each other, though I hadn't seen him since last year. But something Gina said this week has got me all uptight, kind of guilty, as if I'm to blame."

"Dana dear, whatever has happened with Tony and liquor, it's his own responsibility. You cannot take any blame."

"But Gina, although she said she didn't hold it against me, did say that he had never been the same since we split up. I do, sort of, feel—er—involved."

"Did he have other girlfriends after you?"

"I think so, but sort of, like, more casual? Not going steady?"

"But you don't know anything about them?"

"Nope."

"But you care for Tony?"

"I guess I'm realizing that I do, more than I thought. I mean, we meant a lot to each other when we were going out, when you first knew us. But then we started to drift apart. I guess I got caught up in the work of the Centre, and then coming to RMC. I had lots of things happening …"

"And Tony went to college, too."

"Yes, but he was still at home, in the same old scene. But from what Gina told me, he kind of drifted into a group that spent a lot of time in the college pub."

"That in itself needn't cause a problem. Many young men go through such a phase, none the worse for it."

"I know."

"Come now, my dear, don't take blame. Let's talk of how we can help Tony. Have you done anything so far?"

"Actually, yes. You remember Jane Stennings, my friend the policewoman?"

Mr Hennigan nodded.

"Well, I talked with her on the phone on Wednesday, and she suggested a number of things. She's going to talk with Gina first, to help her handle the family situation, and she's going to get some reading stuff, leaflets and so on. Sort of like some of the stuff we set up in the entrance at the Centre, only more specific. And she's going to give Gina the name of a doctor who can help."

"That's good. But you realize that the only person who can really get Tony out of this is himself?"

"I know." Dana was downcast. "And that brings up the other thing that's been bothering me."

Mr Hennigan turned in his chair to look straight at Dana, a concerned look on his face.

"When I was on the bus coming back from Ottawa last weekend, I met someone from the past, and he told me things that have really thrown me for a loop."

Mr Hennigan's eyebrows were raised in query.

"It was the guy who had sold the liquor to Bryce and Vince before the accident. He apologized for what he had done, just like that."

Mr Hennigan put his hand on her sleeve in reassurance.

"And then he told me his whole story, how he was sent to jail, twice, and then reformed, got off the alcohol, and is now working at a place helping young people to kick drug and alcohol habits."

Mr Hennigan was shaking his head in surprise.

Dana continued. "You see, all in one week, someone I guess I really do care for has slipped into alcoholism in a bad way, and then someone I had every reason to hate has reformed, recovered, and makes an open apology to me. It's kind of turned my world upside down, in a sense."

"Dana, look at it this way. If the man you met on the bus could do what he has done, then there's every reason for hope for Tony. You and others are already working for Tony. Can you find a way to let Tony know that you do care for him, as a friend, a dear friend? He needs something to grasp onto, something to help him pull himself out. But you must not feel guilty. Do it because you love him, as a friend in need."

Dana leaned over and kissed Mr Hennigan on the cheek. "Thanks, Mr Hennigan, you've really helped me. I do feel better." She glanced at her watch. "I guess we should be heading back."

"So we should. Sheila brought in some fresh scones this morning. Fancy some?"

"You bet."

"Come on then, let's go." Mr Hennigan swept his arm round, as if to wave forward his cohorts. Dana gave a great heave on the chair to set it in motion as they began the uphill journey home.

- 28 -

"Here's one for you."

Dave Adkins startled, and sat upright in his chair. His head had begun to nod as he had pretended to read his book. Barbara had closed her own book, and was looking across at him.

"Huh? What?" he grunted.

"Don't tell me you were just resting your eyes again!" Barbara chuckled.

Dave knew he was tending to slip into a mid-evening nap these days, given the chance. But then, he couldn't sleep properly at night, tossing and turning and, likely, keeping Barbara awake.

"Huh? What did you say?"

"I said—here's one for you."

"One what?" Dave played dumb.

"Who was Dogberry?"

"Oh, Dogberry. Yes. That's right. Mm. I know the name … Hang on, I'll get it in a minute."

Barbara smiled back at him and waited.

He chuckled inwardly. She had succeeded in her task; he was now awake and thinking, searching in the back of his mind for something he knew she knew he knew, from long ago.

Barb and Dave, both recently divorced at the time, had first met at the Shakespeare Festival at Prescott, down by the St Lawrence River.

"Yes, I've got it. Constable Dogberry, in *As You* ... No—wait a minute—no. *Much Ado About Nothing.*" He grinned broadly.

"Right. Now, what were his first words in the play?"

"Oh, come on, that's not fair. I don't know Shakespeare that well."

"Think what he was doing."

"He was with the night watch, wasn't he?"

"Uh-huh. So?"

"Halt—who goes there?"

Barbara laughed. "No, but you're close. Put it into Elizabethan time."

Dave stared at the ceiling, his mouth poised to speak. *I know I know it; come on, brain.*

Barbara waited.

"'Are you good men and true?'"

"Yesss. Well done."

"I was in *Much Ado* at school. I played one of the bad guys, what was his name now, the one that got the maid?"

"Borachio."

"Yes, that's it."

"What was she like?"

"Cold, and kept forgetting her lines." Dave turned as the doorbell rang.

"Wonder who that might be?" said Barbara with a frown.

Dave put on his slippers, which had fallen off, and walked through to the front door. "Hi, you two, come on in. What's new?"

Barbara turned as the couple walked into the room. "Oh, it's you. Hi, Kelly. Hi, Mike."

"Hi Barb. This is new, Dave!" Kelly thrust her left hand out toward Dave, showing the ring on her third finger.

Dave was a bit slow on the uptake, but Barbara was in there first. "Oh, congratulations, both of you." She rushed over to hug Kelly and then Mike.

Dave caught up with the action and gave Kelly a big hug, but shook hands with Mike. "Come and sit down. This warrants a little celebration," said Dave. "What will you have?"

"A Diet Coke would be fine, please." Kelly flashed a smile at him.

"And for me too, please," added Barbara.

"Root beer for me," came from Mike.

Barbara led the way back to the fireside and sat in her chair. Mike and Kelly sat together on the sofa. Dave could hear their conversation from the kitchen.

"So, have you set the date?"

"Yep, January ninth," said Kelly, with a bounce in her voice.

"My, it'll be cold then. Is there a special reason for that date?"

Kelly suddenly became reflective, and her voice lowered slightly. "Yes, it is special, Barb. It was my parents' anniversary."

"I understand. It's a nice way to commemorate them."

"Here we are." Dave passed around the drinks. "Now, a toast. Here's to you two, many years of happiness together."

"To Kelly and Mike," added Barbara, as they all sipped at their drinks.

"Brrr. You'll have to put in an order for a January thaw." Dave smiled.

"I guess so," said Mike. "As Kel was saying, it would have been her parents' anniversary, but it's about the earliest we could get anywhere booked that was half decent, what with Christmas and New Year's."

"Where are you having the ceremony?"

"At the courthouse, the registry office," explained Kelly. "And then we're having just a small reception, mainly our friends, because I have no family, and Mike has only a cousin in Montreal. And that brings us right to why we're here now. David, I have a request to make of you."

Dave put on a querying look.

"As we just said, January ninth would have been my mum and dad's anniversary, and like, well …" She glanced at Mike. "Dave, would you please escort me into the ceremony?" Her eyes were tearing as they met Dave's.

Dave gasped, and for a moment was tongue-tied. *Wow*, he thought, *really a substitute dad.* An emotional shudder ran through him. "Kelly," he began, then he cleared his throat. "Kelly, my dear, it will be an honour, a pleasure." He stood, reached over, and gave Kelly a hug.

"Thank you, Dave, it means a lot to me, as you know."

"Say, is it going to be dress-up?"

"Dave!" said Barbara disdainfully. "How could you?"

"Only kidding," Dave spluttered.

"That's all right." Kelly laughed. "Don't worry, David, it's not tuxes. We want to be comfortable, and we want all our guests to be comfortable, too. But Mikey is going to wear a suit, aren't you, dear?" She snuggled into his side.

Mike grimaced, changing it to a smile as she looked up at him.

Barbara laughed. "Well, we'll have to see whether Dave's suit has shrunk from hanging in the closet."

"Yes, it's terrible how they do that, you know," said Dave in mock seriousness.

"Talking of shrinking, let me get you a snack," offered Barbara, standing up and making toward the kitchen.

Kelly raised her hand. "Barb, you really don't need to go to any trouble for us, please."

"No problem. I have some things right here." Barbara walked

into the kitchen.

Mike took up the conversation. "You might wonder why we've decided to take the big step now."

"Well, I might, but you're big people now, and you're clearly made for each other," said Dave.

Kelly leaned forward. "We've known one another now for over four years, thanks to you and Barb, and we've proved to ourselves that we can live together—"

Dave chuckled.

"Yes, Dave." Kelly smiled. "*And* we want to!"

They all laughed.

"Here we are. Please, help yourselves." Barbara put down a tray with date slices and Nanaimo bars onto the coffee table. "Would you like some tea or coffee?" She asked.

"That would be nice, thanks. Tea, please. Let me help you." Kelly rose to her feet and followed Barbara to the kitchen.

"No thanks, not for me," Mike added, reaching for and consuming a Nanaimo bar.

Mike and Dave sat in silence for a few moments, then Dave stood and walked over toward a bookcase in the corner, behind Mike.

"I've been meaning to give you a book," he began, "but I—"

Mike was reaching for a date slice when he heard a strange moan behind him, followed by a crash. He jumped up and rushed over to find Dave slumped to the floor.

"What's wrong?" asked Mike. No response.

Barbara and Kelly had heard the noise and came running.

"What's he done now?" Barbara asked. Then she was close enough to see Dave on the floor. "What's wrong?" she gasped.

Dave was gasping, and his colour had drained from his face.

"Get the ambulance, quick, Kel." Mike was taking control.

"Now, Dave, it's Mike. Does it hurt anywhere?"

Dave did not answer, but his actions gave the answer, anyway. His hand had moved to his forehead, where there was a swelling graze. He had clearly hit his head as he fell, probably on the edge of the bookcase. But he wasn't verbalizing.

"Take it easy, Dave, don't move. You're gonna be okay."

Mike looked up at Barbara. She was now pale and trembling.

"Barb, can you get a blanket and pillows, please, to keep him warm?"

She hurried away, without a word.

Mike bent over Dave, loosening his shirt and his belt. He didn't like Dave's total lack of colour, and the blue tinge to his lips. He checked Dave's pulse—a bit erratic. Breathing: shallow.

Barbara returned with a blanket and a couple of pillows.

Mike carefully lifted Dave's head and shoulders, and helped Barbara position the pillows to prop him up, but not obstruct his breathing.

Suddenly, Dave's eyes opened, and he attempted to move.

"Hold on, Dave," said Mike, quickly. "You've had a fall, a bit of a turn. Lie still for a few moments to recover." Gently, he spread the blanket over Dave.

"They're on their way." Kelly had returned. "Is he okay?"

"I sure hope so," said Mike tersely.

The minutes ticked by. Barbara and Kelly stood back while Mike tended to Dave, checking his breathing and his pulse at intervals. Dave's colour had gone, replaced by a grey pallor with a bluish tinge. His breathing was still shallow, but regular. His pulse was stable now. Mike spoke softly to him, reassuringly.

Kelly put her arm round Barbara, who was now quite shaky. "Let's get you a seat, Barb." Kelly dragged over a chair.

"Thanks. Is there anything we should be doing?"

"Mike is checking him as best he can …"

The welcome sounds of an ambulance distracted them. Kelly rushed to the front door and flung it open, waiting for the crew. Quickly, they came up to the house with their equipment.

"In here to the left," Mike called from where he was bent beside Dave.

❈❈❈

The telephone rang at the bedside. Mike leaned over to pick it up. Kelly immediately tensed up, fearing the worst.

"Hello? Oh, hi Barb, how is he now?"

Mike cupped his hand over the mouthpiece and whispered to Kelly, "Dave's going to be okay." He lifted his left-hand thumb, and returned to the phone. Kelly relaxed a little.

"That's good. That's a relief. Are you able to go and get a break and some rest?"

As he spoke to Barbara, he nodded his head and smiled at Kelly.

"Now don't you worry about us. We're okay; I'm glad we were with you when it happened. Bye, Barb. Now, you get some rest. We'll call the hospital first thing in the morning. We can come in and bring you home when you're ready. You call us again tonight if there's any problem."

Mike put the phone down and turned over to Kelly. In the half-light of the room, he looked into her eyes. "He's going to be okay, but ... he's had a heart attack. The paramedics called ahead to the heart institute, and they had a team ready for him. They put two stents into his heart; one artery was ninety percent blocked, and the other seventy. Boy, was he ever lucky."

"Oh, Mike." Kelly reached over to hug Mike. "I'm so thankful. I'm so worried that the shock of asking him to take me down the aisle caused it."

"Love, we'll never know, but don't fret. The main thing is he's going to be okay, and we're going to help him recover. Look, unless he has a relapse, he'll be on his feet well before the wedding. He has to walk as part of his recovery program.

"I said we'd call Barb in the morning. Just as well it's a weekend, so we can go help her tomorrow. She'll need to get home, anyway."

"Sure we can. Am I ever glad we were there when it happened. The ambulance came quickly, though, didn't it?"

"Thank goodness. Anyway, what time is it now?"

"Oh, about two-thirty. Time for some sleep, maybe?"

"Yeah." Mike yawned.

"Oh, Mike, I do hope he's going to be okay." Kelly pulled closer to Mike. He put his arm round her and kissed her on the forehead.

"So do I. But he'll be fine, don't worry."

※※※

"Okay now, David, Barb said you only have to go to the end of the street today and tomorrow." Kelly was supervising Dave's rehabilitation walk, since Barb had to attend a meeting. Dave had been out of the hospital for a week.

"I know, but I really feel I could go further."

"All in good time, but you must pace yourself, and not overdo it."

They reached the street corner and turned back.

"I tell you one thing, so long as I can walk you down the aisle, however long it is, I'll be happy."

Kelly leaned over and gave him a peck on the cheek. "And I'll be happy too."

"How are your plans coming along? Is Mike getting jitters?" Dave chuckled.

"No." Kelly laughed. "But he does have to get a new suit. His old one is actually too big, believe it or not. He's lost a lot of weight in the past year, with that new fitness kick he's on."

"And you?" Dave cast his eyes up and down Kelly, grinning.

"Me? No way, haven't changed a bit, sort of. I got measured up last week. Have a fitting the week before Christmas, but won't pick up the dress till a couple of days before the wedding."

"Barb made me try my suit on the other day. And it does still fit me!"

"That's good. Now, Dave, I know you've been fretting about the Centre, and wanting to come into the office. Look, it's far too soon for you to be taking on that kind of stress; you know what the doctor said. And Mike and I agree. I'm coping with the bills and mail, and Mike is coming to check the building operations. Jane has stepped up, and taken on any scheduling needs that crop up. Even Dana Munro called me and offered to come up from Kingston on her free weekends to help. So you can relax. We haven't taken your job away; it'll be there for you when you are healed. Okay, Boss?" Kelly grinned and nudged him in the side.

"Okay, if you say so, Deputy."

- 29 -

The late November night air was damp and cold as Tony turned into the narrow alley. The pervading stench of stale garbage drifted to his nostrils as he stumbled over a burst bag, kicking it sullenly to the side.

He fell in a heap onto a broken chair, discarded from the restaurant long ago. The chair sagged backward, and Tony lurched with it, breaking his fall against the wall. "Fucking piece o' junk," he muttered.

"Sit on the fucking floor like anybody else," came a response from the shadows.

Tony did not respond. He had no reserves left to think with. He sat where the chair had tilted him, legs splayed out to keep himself marginally stable. This was as far as he was going—for now.

The shadows moved, and a body fumbled to unscrew a bottle. It took a gulp, and handed the bottle to Tony. Tony grabbed it and swigged from it, wiping his mouth and the bottle with his sleeve, handing it back. The first body passed it on to another body in the shadows.

Suddenly, a door opened and a shaft of light flashed across the alley. A man tossed a cardboard box out onto a pile of garbage cans. As the light vanished, the shadows moved, and grasping hands sought the discarded bread and buns. Sounds of munching filled the stale air as the day-old food was consumed. Soon it was gone, and the quiet was broken only by the sounds of traffic in the street.

Time meant nothing now for Tony. He lived only for the moment. He ached perpetually; his head throbbed; his stomach was twisted and tortured; he was developing sores that would not heal; he craved for the next drink.

He had a small world now: the alley; two city blocks; a vacant lot for daytime and a toilet, when he remembered; a patch of grass; a couple of litter bins; and something resembling sleep—the state he occupied most of the time.

Others shared the alley, the source of food. Drew was the entrepreneur, the one who got the real stuff; he had no hang-ups about sharing—share it round till it was gone. Sleep it off, then go find some more—get a few coins on the street. Rejean was dark, surly, said little, did little, and stank. Albert was different; he seemed to look out for Tony.

The night grew quieter as the traffic dwindled. The door from the restaurant was locked and shuttered. The damp was turning into a slight drizzle.

"Fucking rain," grumbled Tony as he slid ungainly off the broken chair onto the ground, pulling his meagre jacket up over his ears.

Albert was stumbling to his feet, grabbing the cardboard box from the bread delivery. "Put this on your bloody head," he said, tossing the box at Tony and returning to the more sheltered corner of the alley.

The rain had stopped by dawn. Traffic began to move along the street. Gradually, wakefulness of sorts came to the alley. Slowly, one by one, the four ambled, stumbled really, out onto the street to daytime quarters—the vacant lot, for Tony. The garbage collectors would come to the alley some days, but Tony had no recollection of which days or how often. He just learned quickly not to be in the alley when they did come, which meant: be out every day.

He reached the vacant lot, and stumbled across to the back against a fence, shielded from the street by a few scrawny bushes. Albert sometimes shared the lot, but his spot was over on the other side, usually. Occasionally, they would sit together, rarely speaking.

Today, Albert had shuffled over and sat a few paces away. They sat in silence. The hours passed.

"Why you doing this?" Albert broke the silence at last.

The silence began again, but not so long.

"Why you here?"

"Do'know," muttered Tony, his face vacantly staring.

"You're wasting life."

"Fuck it, so are you."

"I'm old, worn out. You're young."

"So what?" Tony wanted no more of this.

A long silence.

"You lose job, eh?"

"Uh-huh."

"You drink too much. Eh?"

"Mebbe."

"You lose girl, no?"

Tony turned sharply. "Fuck it, man. Lay off, willya!"

Albert was quiet. Time passed them by, but they were not counting.

"We had some good times, that we did." Albert spoke suddenly.

"Unh?" Tony grunted.

"Then the bad times came …"

"Wha?"

"The guns, the fuckin' guns—we didn't stand a chance."

"What fucking guns?"

"In Cyprus—bloody peacekeepin', 'cep' there was no fuckin' peace to keep."

"You in the army?" Tony's mind was stimulated above its base level.

"Wasn't in the boy scouts." Albert spat on the ground.

"You survived."

"Lost me best buddy—right beside me, he was. Fuckin' snipers—thought we was the enemy. Got a rifle bullet in me shoulder. Can't do a fuckin' thing 'cause o' that."

"Sucks."

"You got life ahead, kid. Get outta here."

Traffic ebbed and flowed with the rhythms of the day. As the light began to fade, Albert stood and shuffled off on his rounds, maybe to call at one of the shelters.

Tony watched him go. Little had gone through his mind all day, but the last few exchanges had remained, lingering on his enfeebled memory: 'you're wasting life'; 'you lose job'; 'you drink too much'; 'you lose girl'; 'you got life ahead'.

Images of Dana drifted through his mind, his cloudy mind. He tried to suppress them, but he had no strength to think on other lines. They would not go away. Dana would not go away.

He found his hand fumbling in a pocket. He found a quarter and a dime, and another quarter in his other pocket. It had been days now, he had no idea of how many, since he'd collected coins by just sitting on Rideau Street, enough to buy a drink. He fingered the coins.

Suddenly, a new thought, a light, entered his mind, through a crack. The crack widened, brighter light entered. It was positively brilliant.

He was being pulled, up, up, upward. He was standing, walking, walking, onto the sidewalk … Phone booth, fumbling for the quarters. Fuck, dropped one. Got it. Get the phone. Put the coins in. Dial. Six ... two ... one ... fuck, what is it? ... Three ... four ... seven ... eight. Ringing.

Hi, this is Gina. I can't take your call right now, but please leave ...

Fuck. He waited for the tone. "'S Tony. Need help. Rideau ... pleease."

He was sitting at his usual spot the next day. Albert was somewhere else this time. Somehow, he felt different—lousy, but different. Everything ached still, his head throbbed, stomach squirmed, nothing new—yet his mind seemed clearer. Not that he had anything much to think about, his world had shrunk to so little—but there was light. He knew he had made the break—he just hoped that Gina would respond.

He sat there, his eyes half-closed, in that semi-sleep state he had grown into these days, the sunlight so bright today that he just couldn't leave his eyes fully open anyway ...

He saw her coming, blonde, shining hair bouncing around her head, her face radiant, like an angel—an angel in blue jeans.

And there she was, Dana, standing in front of him, arms outstretched toward him. He was drawn up, upward, now standing too. And now another one, dark-haired, joined them.

"I'm glad we've found you, Tone," Gina spoke first. "We've been so worried about you. It's taken us ages to find you. I called Dana as soon as I got your message."

"Yeah, it's lucky I'm home this weekend. Tony, you said you need help. What did you mean?"

Tony was struggling now. He had not conversed sensibly with anyone for weeks now. He was losing the ability to formulate points in his muddy mind. "Er—I—need help. Um—to—er—get better."

"You mean you want to be cured, dried out?" Dana's head tilted as she asked.

"Uh-huh."

"You really mean it?" Gina now.

"Uh-huh."

"Come on then, let's get started." Dana grasped his arm. "First off, you've gotta get cleaned up—you're filthy."

Dana and Gina guided him across the vacant lot to a spot near the sidewalk.

"You two stay here while I go fetch the car," Gina said, as she reached the sidewalk. She started off along the street.

Tony slumped down to the ground; he had no strength to stand for any length of time.

Dana squatted on her haunches beside Tony. They were close enough to the street for passers-by to sometimes turn and look at them both, obviously wondering why such a good-looking, well-dressed girl was hanging out with a bum like that.

Dana took no notice; she was only concerned whether Tony could really go through with what was ahead for him. It would not be easy. She prayed that he could.

- 30 -

Tears ran down Gina's face as she finished putting away the leftover food that had been sitting out on the kitchen counter since supper-time. How could he? How could Tony do this to her, after all she had done for him?

She was exhausted, at the end of her tether. Only one more day to go now to Christmas, and then a break. The store would still be busy on Boxing Day and the days after, but nowhere near as bad as it had been these past few weeks.

And on top of all that, now she had to cope with this. She slammed the fridge door shut after putting away the last bowl. Sighing, she wandered into the living room and flung herself down on the sofa.

An hour ago, Tony had come home drunk. *Yes.* She sighed. *Yes, I should have expected it.* Every temptation was put in his way—invitations to this party and that. It wasn't surprising, considering.

After Tony had been pulled off the street by Gina and Dana in November, he had responded well to their help and attention. Gina had agreed to let him live with her in her newly acquired apartment, on condition that he stay dry at all times, and that he get a job within a reasonable time.

With a bit of help from Gina, he had succeeded in getting a part-time job at the local 'Quickie' convenience store three weeks ago; not much, and not much pay, but it had given him a focus. And to give him his due, he had remained dry—until now.

Gina reached over for a tissue, wiping her eyes. She was devastated—she was angry. She was angry with herself, for not thinking ahead; for not realizing, with all the stress she had been under at work, all the temptations out there for Tony.

She was angry with his so-called friends, two of the other guys that did shifts at the Quickie. They knew the problems Tony was having—she'd explained it to them when he was first getting the job. Were they thick, or something? Or did they think it a joke—to let him get drunk?

She was angry ... no, she couldn't be angry with Tony, no—she couldn't.

Tony is sick; he needs me. No one else can help him right now—no one else around here cares for him. Tears welled up in her eyes again. What a depressing Christmas prospect ahead. There would be no Ferruccio family celebration, nothing like the old days.

Her brother Angelo had left home as soon as he turned eighteen, earlier in the year. She didn't know where he had gone. He couldn't stand the stifling, cold, depressing atmosphere at home anymore, with their mother and father barely speaking to each other.

Her little sister, poor Roberta, was the only one left, and she would not be there for long; she would be eighteen soon, and had no desire to stay longer than she had to.

Her mother and father refused to see Tony, to let him visit, and because Gina was sheltering him, she was out of favour too.

Gina just couldn't understand her parents, she really couldn't. They had all been such a happy, loving family until ... well, until

Vince was killed, and then things started to fall apart, slowly, but she realized, looking back on those times, the signs were there long ago. But then Tony's clash with the alcohol fiend, and everything that had followed, just seemed to be destroying the family.

In spite of all that, Gina had planned to call round at her parents' house on Christmas Day, just to drop off a couple of small gifts for them and one for Roberta, but not to stay … but now she didn't know what she could do. What would she do with Tony?

She saw in her mind the image of him, as she and Dana had brought him back to her apartment back in November—a dirty, drained, dreg of a man, with dull eyes and an expressionless face, who couldn't look either of them in the eyes, but looked away instead.

She thought how she and Dana had got him cleaned up, had gone out and bought some basic clothes, underwear, jeans, shirt, socks, runners, to get him started. They had thrown all his old stinking rags into the garbage.

She thought back on how he had become so docile, so—well, so dull, no spark—no longer the old Tony. But he had kept his promise—she knew, because she kept him on a very tight rein, even with all the pressures on her at work. She checked, and double-checked, his every move.

And he was okay, no false moves—until tonight. And all because her guard was down; she had not made her point well enough with those guys at the Quickie—and that was all it took. A whole month's progress … gone in a couple of hours.

And now he was sleeping it off. Gina sat up straight on the sofa. *Right,* she thought, *first thing in the morning, I'll tell him straight. A deal's a deal—stay dry and you can stay here, else you're out—that was the deal. You got drunk, so you should be out. But it's Christmas. I won't kick you out on Christmas Eve, though I probably should.*

The plan was evolving in her mind. She was committing herself to care for and supervise him to prevent a repeat. She had to make her point stick in the morning. She had to go to work, no option, but he was to be here when she arrived home. He could only go to the Quickie to work, nowhere else.

If he was not at home, sober, when she arrived home, he was out, right out—Christmas Eve or not. She had to play it that way, she knew, as a deterrent, but she wasn't sure she could go through with it, if it came to that.

Then, she would spend the whole of the Christmas holiday with him. There would be no more opportunity for temptation, no liquor of any kind. She would give up on any visiting with friends that she was planning to do, and going to their parents, all to help him survive the temptations of the holiday—and to give herself some breathing space to consider how she could deal with the longer term solution.

She stood up, resolved; that's what she would do in the morning.

❄❄❄

Thank goodness he's home, Gina thought to herself as she hung up her coat that next evening. Christmas Eve at the store had verged on a nightmare. The crowds had been awful; she'd had to go without her lunch break, and all the time she had been worrying about whether Tony would keep his word. He had been very sullen, yet sheepish, that morning when she had confronted him with her ultimatum, but he had volunteered a promise. That was her only hope.

"Hi, Tony, I'm home," she called out, as brightly as she could muster.

"Huh," came the reply.

She could see the back of his head as he sat in the easy chair, watching TV. Gina couldn't stand his current taste in TV shows—abysmally low, but she was just grateful and relieved that he was there. She joined him and sat down on the sofa.

"You okay?" she asked.

"Meh."

She was used to these 'meaningful' conversations by now.

"You eaten?"

"Nope."

"I'm having pizza. You want some too? There's a large all-dressed in the freezer."

"Whadever."

"You wanna put the stove on while I get changed, please? Four twenty-five, I think. Check the package."

"Uh-huh."

Gina went into her bedroom to change into more comfortable clothes. As she pulled her dress over her head, the phone rang. Reaching out, she picked up the phone by her bed.

"Hello?"

"Hi Gina, it's Dana. How are you?"

"Oh, hi, Dan. Where are you? Are you at home?"

"Yes, I got back from Kingston last night. Thought I'd call and see how—"

"Just a sec. Let me close the door." Gina reached out with her foot and pushed the door closed. "There, Tony's just in the kitchen, seeing to a pizza. Oh, Dan, he came home drunk last night …"

"No? Oh, that's too bad. What happened?"

"He went out with a couple of the guys from the Quickie, you know, where he's got the job at? An' they let him get drunk."

"So, what did he do? Did he come home?"

"Yeah, and I agonized all night about what to do with him. So this morning I gave him an ultimatum—I told him he had to be at home, sober, when I got back from work tonight, or else he was out."

"And was he?"

"Yes, thank goodness. 'Cause Dana, I don't know if I could have gone through with my threat if he hadn't, or if he'd been drunk. I've told him he goes nowhere without me this holiday. That basically means we stay here. It's the only way to be sure he doesn't get tempted again."

"But Gina, what about your Christmas? Isn't that going to upset your plans?"

"I didn't really have much in the way of plans. I was going to call in at Mamma's and Poppa's to drop off some gifts—I wasn't going to stop. But I can't anyway, with Tony. And Uncle Bruno had said to drop by sometime, if I got the chance, but that's all. Dan, I just want to keep Tony dry."

"But you can't let it ruin your Christmas. Tell you what, why don't I come over and Tony-sit tomorrow afternoon, and you can go out for a while?"

"But what about your family? They'll want to spend time with you."

"I know they will, but I'm sure they'll understand. What-say I come about one o'clock? Mom said she wanted us to have a late Christmas dinner about six. Have you got in anything special for food?"

"No, not really. To be honest, Dan, I really don't feel very Christmassy. I guess I'm all Christmassed-out from work, and then all this with Tony on top."

"You hang in there tonight. I hope you get a good rest. And I'll come earlier, say about noon. You'll be up?"

"Sure. At least I will. I'll tell Tony you're coming—maybe that'll get him up early."

"Okay. See you then. Bye."

"Bye, Dan, and thanks." Gina put the phone down and finished changing. She walked back out to the living room, where Tony had returned to his chair.

"That was Dana. She's coming over tomorrow."

Gina watched a noticeable change come over Tony. There was a distinct brightening. He adjusted his position in the chair, to a tidier pose, less slummocked. "Oh, is she?"

"Yes, around noon."

Tony nodded his head as he changed the channel on the TV. "The oven should be hot enough now," he volunteered, and went into the kitchen to put the pizza in.

Gina wondered at the abrupt change in his manner. This was the first time he had voluntarily done anything like that in all the weeks he had been staying with her.

※※※

It was Christmas Day. Tony sat back in his chair and turned on the television with the remote. He felt good, for once. He could hear Gina and Dana chatting in the background as he searched for the channel with the game on.

When the doorbell had rung an hour or so ago, he had gone to the door, knowing it would be Dana. There she stood, like a Christmas angel, her bouncy, blonde hair framing her face, with a broad smile and sparkling eyes. He had been speechless and overwhelmed.

Dana had brought a large box that he helped carry to the table. Out of it came Christmas candies, desserts, cakes, and a little gift each for him and Gina.

He knew Gina was surprised and touched by the way she thanked and embraced Dana. And he appreciated the warm hug he shared with Dana; it felt so good. They'd had a good time together, consuming some of the food and chatting about things, nothing difficult, nothing to cause tension.

Now, it seemed, some kind of arrangement had been set up between Gina and Dana. Dana was going to stay with him while Gina went visiting. That was fine by him. He had nobody he wanted to visit—probably nobody wanted him to visit, anyway—and he was quite content to have Dana's company.

Gina called out as she left the apartment and closed the door behind her. Tony raised his hand in a form of acknowledgement. He turned as Dana came and sat on the sofa, tucking her legs up on the cushion.

"You found the game yet?"

"No, maybe it hasn't started."

"Maybe not. Anything else on?"

"Do'know." Tony absently surfed the channels, round once, round twice.

"Leave it on forty-three till the game starts," suggested Dana.

"Okay." Tony flicked to the Country Music Channel. The music wafted through the room—a Prairie Oyster video.

He glanced at Dana. She was watching the screen. He turned his gaze back to the screen also. *She really does look great,* he thought. How could he talk to her? What could he say? She had done so much. He had done so little, had screwed up so badly.

He knew he had nearly blown it the other night; he knew Gina could have kicked him out, and he deserved it. He felt bad about letting her down, he really did. But Marc and Alain had insisted he go out with them, he couldn't help it. He knew he'd done the wrong thing as soon as he had the first sip, but it was too late then. He did so want to straighten his life out, but every time he tried, he slipped down again. If only …

Carrie Underwood's latest video was on now—he watched closely.

"You like her?"

He glanced at Dana. She was grinning at him.

"Yeah, she's good." He felt his colour come up.

"Good-looking too, eh?" Dana chuckled.

"Uh-huh," Tony nodded, smiling sheepishly.

"I like some of her songs, too. And she's got quite a following at RMC."

"I guess."

The song finished. Tony surfed the channels again. No game. He returned to the Country Music Channel.

"How's your job, Tone?"

"Uh? Oh, okay I guess." He wasn't really up to talking about it.

"You go in every day?"

"Yeah, except Sundays. Just for four hours, though."

"But it does give you something to do, and some money."

"Yeah, but nearly all of it goes to Gina for rent." Tony's voice was down-turning.

"I know, but that's only fair—you do have a nice place to live in. It's lucky, in a way, that when you called Gina for help, her roommate had just left to get herself married. So Gina had a room for you. You know, Tone, your sister really has done a lot to help you."

"I know, Dan, and so have you. And I am grateful … it's just that …"

"That you have a problem?"

Tony looked down at the floor. "Yeah, I have a problem."

They sat as the music played on.

"But there is real help out there, if you want it," said Dana at last.

Tony watched the screen, not really seeing the images. He knew in his mind, in his heart, that he wanted help, but … it had felt so good for a couple of hours the other night, once again.

But then he saw Gina's face in his mind, her gasp of horror as he barfed all over the kitchen floor. He felt a shudder pass through his body as he turned to Dana. "Dan … please, I do need help."

Dana stood up and walked over to him. Bending, she lifted his head and kissed his upturned forehead.

"Then we'll find the right help for you, this week. But, Tone, you realize, it's all up to you. You have to make it work."

Tony nodded. "Yeah, I know."

"Okay, let's see if the game is on now."

Gina turned her car onto the Ferruccio driveway. No matter how much snow was lying around the streets, the Ferruccio driveway was always clear. Her father, Pino, always had at least one company truck equipped in the winter with a snowplow, with an assigned driver, to clear all his staff's driveways—it saved the company time and money in the long run, he argued.

Gina picked up the gifts from the passenger seat and stepped out of the car. It was the family home, but she felt unsure, nervous. With some trepidation, she walked up to the door and rang the bell.

The door opened, and she saw her mother.

"Merry Christmas, Mamma. I've brought you some little gifts. May I come in?"

Carmella burst into tears, hugging her daughter, pulling her into the house without a word.

A sound of footsteps, then an explosion of sound. "What you doing here?" shouted Pino. "You not welcome in this house. Go."

Gina stood her ground. "Poppa, no. You are being totally unreasonable, and unkind. You are hurting everybody around you, and yourself. This is Christmas, the time for families and giving, and forgiving. I've brought you and Mamma and Roberta some small gifts."

"So long as you are with that tramp, you are not my family."

"Poppa, Tony needs our love, your love. He needs all the help he can get to carry him through and get out of his mess."

"He got himself into the mess; he can get out by himself. He disgraced this family; you disgrace this family when you help him. I do not want to see him or you again. Ferruccio name is a good name. Go."

Gina looked at her mother. She saw a sad, downcast face, but to her dismay, Carmella nodded, as in agreement with Pino. Gina realized that her younger sister had joined them at some point—she was crying.

There's nothing more I can do here, thought Gina. She turned and left the house.

"Gina, wait."

Gina turned as she reached her car. Roberta was coming down the driveway in her slippers. "Wait, please."

They embraced.

"Gina, it's like a prison and a morgue combined in there. It's awful. There's no happiness, no joy, no smiles. I can't wait till I can leave. I'm trapped—if I were to come visit with you, Poppa would kick me out. I just don't understand him. I daren't stay out here any longer, either."

Gina was lost for words; she didn't know how to respond to this cry for help. She hugged her sister again, and their eyes met.

"Be strong," she said, and they parted.

- 31 -

What a start to January! Kelly struggled to push the key into the door-lock, which was already covered with a glaze of ice. Her hair was wet. Her boots were slipping on the ice on the step as she at last managed to open the door.

Hamish the terrier was waiting for her on the inside, eager to go outside. Kelly dumped her bag on the floor, reached for the leash, and put it on the dog, who was already pulling hard.

Gingerly, she stepped back out onto the ice, but by that time, Hamish's feet had already slipped out of control down the two steps, to leave him at the bottom, shaking his head in bewilderment. The freezing rain had started in the late morning, about five hours ago, and according to the report Kelly had heard on the car-radio, it was pretty widespread.

She carefully let herself down the steps, hanging onto the handrail at the side, smiling at the antics of Hamish, whose feet were sliding out from under him at every step he made on the sheer ice that covered the sidewalk. She burst out laughing at the poor dog when he tried to balance on three legs to relieve himself. Miraculously, he eventually managed to do so, and they carefully made their way back into the house.

Kelly hung up her coat, and tidied her hair in the mirror in the hallway. *What a journey. Thank goodness I don't have to go into the office now for two weeks.* This was the week she and Mike were to be married. She was so excited.

There were so many last minute things to be done in the next three days before the big day, Friday the 9th, her parents' anniversary. How she wished they were still alive to be here. She wished Mike could have taken the days off too, but his boss had said the workload at this time of year was too much. He had reluctantly agreed to Mike having Friday off for the wedding, and the following week, too, for a honeymoon.

She walked into the kitchen. The red light on the phone was blinking. She picked it up, punched in the codes, and listened. Mike had left a message. He was going to be late. He had been called out on an emergency; somebody's furnace had stopped working.

What a night for that to happen. Poor Mike. But at least this place is warm and snug, she thought as she started to prepare supper. Hamish was snuffling around his dishes.

"You'll have to wait, Hamish. Let me put mine on first, then I'll get you yours."

Hamish stood with his head tilted to one side, and gave one small bark.

"Yes, I knew you'd understand. It won't be long."

Mike didn't arrive home until nearly ten-thirty, exhausted, and quickly they went to bed. He fell asleep almost at once, but it was a long time before Kelly could subside, listening all the while to the freezing rain pellets lashing against the bedroom window.

She awoke, yet again. She was so wound up now. *What time is it now?* She lifted herself up to look at the clock. Nothing. Darkness. *Shoot, must be a power failure.*

She got out of bed and felt her way through to the bathroom, flicking the switch as a reflex. Nothing. *Ah well, no problem.* She ventured over to the window. *What a sight! No lights in the parking area. No lights in any of the houses.*

In the faint glow of the night, she could see glistening ice everywhere, with tree branches bowed down unnaturally with loads of ice. Suddenly in the distance, she saw a blue flash. *What was that?* she thought, suddenly shuddering as the coldness of the room struck her. Quickly, she climbed back into bed and snuggled up to the sleeping Mike.

She awoke to dim, early morning daylight. As she opened her eyes, there was Mike, half-dressed. "Power's out."

"I know. I was up in the night. It was out then."

"Temperature's dropped a bit in the house. Looks as if the power's been off about five hours, from the clock in the kitchen."

"Ugh. So no coffee, no hot water?"

"Well, you might get enough warm water from the tank for a quick wash, but not much more. As for coffee, forget it."

"Have you looked out? I did in the night, and it looked fantastic. And I saw a blue flash somewhere, don't know what."

"Probably power lines touching and arcing over. Look out now, it's a real fantasy world, but it's breaking trees like crazy—branches cracking off over in the Gardens—some of those big, old trees are not looking good. There's ice coating everything."

"Do you have to go to work in this?"

"You know I do, my love. I'll probably have to work like crazy today. All kinds of problems will have come up. I'm sure glad that George was kind enough to let you have these next few days off. At least you won't have to go out in this today."

"But I've so much to do." Kelly was out of bed and standing now. Mike came over and held her against him. They kissed. Mike brushed her hair back from her forehead. "I'm supposed to pick up my dress and the accessories today," she sobbed.

"But nothing is so important that you have to go out in this. We have everything that is absolutely essential for Friday, just you and me."

She pressed against him. "I know, but I don't want this to spoil our plans."

"It won't. It'll all be gone in a day or so, don't you worry."

It was a strange light that dimly illuminated the house by noontime. Kelly was becoming increasingly despondent. All her carefully laid plans were unravelling. The spot where Mike's truck had been parked was almost iced over already. There was still no power, and the house was becoming decidedly cold now. The telephone line was dead, too.

She ran upstairs to put on a heavier sweater. Walking out of the bedroom, she wandered across into the spare room, whose window faced out to Millerby Lane. She looked out. At least some traffic was moving slowly out on Otterbrook, where they must have salted heavily. A few vehicles had ventured along Millerby, but there were several fallen tree branches partially blocking the lane.

As she surveyed the scene of destruction from the window, she remembered the little portable radio down in the basement.

The reports on the radio gave her the broader picture of the extent of the ice storm, as it was now being called. She began to realize how lucky she was, compared to many people out in rural areas.

Suddenly, a humming sound made Kelly look up. The hall light was on. Yes, the fridge was running again. She jumped up and tried the kitchen light. *Yes, we have power back. Great.* She felt quite upbeat again. She jumped as the telephone rang.

"Hello?"

"Hi Kelly, it's Jane."

"Hi, Jane, how long has the phone been up, then? It wasn't working when I tried it earlier."

"About half an hour."

"How are you and Trishy coping?"

"Tucked up in our sleeping bags. But we're good. How about you?"

"Mike had to work late last night. I haven't heard from him today. And the cell-phones might not be working either. I guess we got our power back because some of our lines are underground."

"All the houses in the Gardens are still without power, though."

"Are they? Gee. Not surprising, I guess, with all the trees—and their power lines are still on poles."

"Reason I called was that I figured we might be able to use the Centre as an emergency shelter. I know there's power there, I can see an outside light on."

"That's a great idea. I'm game to help, if we can get over there without breaking a leg on the ice. Do you think people in need would go there? Have you called Dave?"

"Yes. He agreed, and said he'll try to get over there. I cautioned him, knowing he's still recovering from his heart attack, but he said this is the kind of public service he feels he was made for."

"He said that? Wow, some guy. He's a good man, and true. Look, if you'll do the phoning around to people, I'll make my way over to the Centre to help Dave. Gotta find some boots with decent tread first."

"Okay. Bye. See you later."

Well, thought Kelly, *not what I'd planned to do today, but given the situation, I'm more use helping others than sitting here sulking.*

Kelly soon found her good boots, and throwing on her jacket, she gingerly tried her first few steps on the ice outside. It wasn't too bad, provided she avoided the areas where ice-melt had dripped, or where the ice had gone smooth. There was enough surface graininess in most places that she had enough traction to walk almost normally, if only slowly. It took her a good fifteen minutes to do the usual three-minute walk to the Hennigan Centre.

Dave Adkins was already there, desperately trying to chip ice away from the doorway so that they could get inside.

"Hi, Dave, isn't this awful?"

"Oh, hi there, Kelly. Yes, it's the pits. Thanks for coming over. Did Jane call you?"

"Yes, she did. I think it's a great idea—that is, if we can get inside!"

Dave chuckled. "If you'd like to try cracking off the ice from around the door jamb and the lock, I'll keep on chipping away at the step here."

"Okay. Dave, are you sure you're okay doing this? You're not putting too much stress on your body?"

"Look, Kel, there's no way I could sit at home, in the cold, knowing that elderly and sick neighbours were suffering, when I had the means to help them. It would be criminal. Yes, I will be careful."

Kelly began to thump and chip at the thin ice around the doorframe. Luckily, it was in a relatively sheltered spot under the porch overhang, and she got most of it off quite quickly using the metal spatula she had brought from her kitchen.

Fortunately, the lock was the type with a cap over the keyhole, so she concentrated on chipping the ice away so the cap could slide aside.

"Do you have the key, Dave, please?"

"Sure. You've got it free? Good for you. Let's see."

Dave put the key in the lock, and turned it. He smiled as the door swung open and they entered the building.

The Hennigan Centre was heated by natural gas but, of course, all the pumps and controls needed electricity. But its power came underground, like the power to the Mews, so Kelly presumed it came back on at the same time as for the Mews. The building was still very cool.

"It'll soon warm up," said Dave, checking the thermostat and raising it to occupancy setting.

"Okay. So what should we do first?"

"Well, first I'll call Jane and let her know we're in okay. She should have contacted the emergency people by now, and hopefully got a plow of sorts to come and clear the parking lot. Once that's done, we can start bringing people in, and having bedding and supplies brought in."

"Okay. I'll go check on the status in the kitchen, and start preparing hot drinks."

❄︎❄︎❄︎

Mike sat down wearily on a stool in the Hennigan Centre kitchen. *What a week!* It was now Thursday, and still the freezing rain was coming down in places. There was still no power in the houses in the Gardens. He had been working up to sixteen hours nearly every day so far that week. No sooner did he get one job fixed than another emergency erupted. And he was getting frustrated, too—some of the emergencies need not have happened if people had followed instructions and precautions with portable generators. He was glad to sit down and do nothing for a few minutes.

Poor Kelly, he thought, *she was so looking forward to this week, preparing for the wedding—so was I. And look what she's doing: she's been over here at the Centre every hour of the day, helping and looking after people.* Some of the families seemed quite organized and resilient, and helping others too, but other folk seemed disoriented, lost. *Strange how it affects people differently.*

"Hi, my love, glad you're back. How was it today?"

Mike slipped his arm around Kelly's waist as they kissed. "Could've been worse, I guess. How about you?"

"Busy, busy, busy. But fun, really. Most people are taking it in their stride, and there's lots of help now. I'm a bit worried about old Mrs Donnelly, Edith, though. She's finding it all a bit bewildering. Jane's trying to find a home with power that has space for her. Have you eaten?"

"No, I'm past food just now. Maybe later."

They stood in silence, arms around each other.

"Mike, what are we going to do? Everything's closing down for tomorrow. First the reception place cancelled, then the hairdresser lost power, now the courthouse will close. Oh, Mike …" The tears began to flow. "Why did it have to come this week, of all weeks?"

Mike held her close, putting his hand at the back of her head as she leaned on his shoulder. His eyes watered too.

"When I heard on the radio that places were being asked to close on Friday," he began, "I called George Simpson. He said he would see what he could arrange, and not to worry. He'll call this evening, or early in the morning."

Kelly lifted her head; her eyes were red as she wiped them. "What is he going to do?"

"Not exactly sure, but he sounded reassuring, and kept saying not to worry."

Kelly was not at all content with this, but she could do no more but wait.

※※※

"My congratulations and best wishes to you both, for a long and happy life together."

Judge Armitage stepped around the table and led Kelly and

Mike forward a couple of steps, announcing, "I present to you all, Mr and Mrs Carson."

Loud cheers and applause filled the Hennigan Centre. Kelly felt so happy and exhilarated; this was so wonderful, after all the stress of the past week.

She and Mike kissed, and then shook hands with or hugged everyone around. Kelly had a special hug for George Simpson, for it was he who had managed to arrange with his good friend, Judge Armitage, for this ceremony at the Centre. It had all been very much a last minute go-ahead, because it was not at all clear whether the Judge would be able to get there, given the ice conditions.

Kelly had been promoted to become George's personal secretary a couple of years ago, and she really enjoyed working with him. He was so kind and thoughtful, but this topped it all.

To their amazement, when they had arrived at the Centre earlier that Friday afternoon, Kelly and Mike had found that the whole place had been transformed overnight from the emergency shelter they had left fifteen hours before into a highly decorated wedding reception hall. They were overwhelmed by it all, and very happy.

They moved out into the crowd, for not only were their original invited guests in attendance—except for Mike's cousin, who was trapped by the ice storm in Montreal—but all the families who had come for shelter were there, also.

"Where's Dave gone?" called out Kelly, as she looked about her.

"He's coming over now," someone was pointing to him.

"Dave, this is wonderful. Thank you so much. Thank you for escorting me, it really meant so much to me." Kelly gave him a big hug and a kiss, planting lipstick on his cheek.

"You are very welcome, both of you," replied Dave as he shook Mike's hand. "You both deserved the best we could do to help you on your way. You've put out your best to the community in so many ways. And Kelly, escorting you meant a lot for me, too. It really has made my heart recover quickly." His and Kelly's eyes met.

"Thanks, Dave," said Mike. "But when did you plan all this, and pull it together?"

"Well, several of us got together as soon as you came in to say the reception place had cancelled, but we had to wait until we knew what was happening about the ceremony. We'd got everything ready to roll as soon as you went home last night, assuming that you got the good word from George.

"You see, things do go on behind your backs sometimes—George called me as soon as he'd finished talking to you, Mike, yesterday afternoon—to see what we could do. I told him we were already half-prepared, so he said to be ready to roll, and we were!"

"And you did a great job. Who all helped?"

"Just about everyone here, to be honest. They all knew what it meant to you. Elizabeth Hampden quickly made up a wedding cake, with a few bits from Barb; and we pooled all the other food from what we could gather."

"Bless you, Dave." Kelly grabbed and squeezed his arm. "And Elizabeth, there you are. What a great cake—thank you so much."

"You are so welcome, both of you. Congratulations."

Dwayne Hampden joined with his wife, shaking Mike's hand and hugging Kelly.

- 32 -

Jane set down the coffee pot and picked up the phone. "Hello?"
"Er—Jane? It's me—er—Tony, Tony Ferruccio ..."
"Well hi, Tony. Good to hear you. How are you?" Jane was upbeat in her voice, knowing something of Tony's situation and wanting to present a positive image.
"Er—not so good. I—er—need to talk. I—I need some help?"
Jane's mind was racing, now. She knew the general happenings in Tony's past few months—Dana had kept her in the picture. But what had prompted Tony himself to call her?
"Where are you, Tony?"
"At Gina's place, but she's at work till late."
"Can you tell me what kind of help you need? Is something wrong?"
"Albert's died ..."
Who on earth is Albert? thought Jane—*but keep going.* "Was Albert a friend, Tony?"
"Yeah, kind of."

"Okay, now you stay right there. Don't worry. I know where the apartment is. I just need to make a few arrangements, and then I'll be on my way. It'll take me maybe half-an-hour. Will you be all right till then?"

"*I think so.*"

"Good. I'll see you soon."

Now, act fast, Jane, she thought, *before he slips back—he clearly recognizes he's in difficulties.* She picked up the phone again and dialled.

"Hi, Kelly. Sorry to bother you, but could you possibly pop round and sit with Trish for an hour or two? An emergency has just come up, and I need to go right away … You will? Thanks a bunch, Kel. See you in a couple … Bye."

She walked over to her daughter, who was happily playing with her toys on the carpet. Trishy looked up at her with her blue eyes, holding up a stuffed bear toward her. Jane crouched down, and drew Trishy to her. "Mummy has to go out for a while, sweetheart. Aunty Kelly is going to come and play with you, and maybe she'll give you your bedtime snack. Will you be a good girl for her, please?"

"Ah-hah."

The doorbell rang, and Trishy's eyes lit up as she headed toward the door. Jane let Kelly in.

"Where's my big girl? Ah, there she is!" Kelly swept her up into her arms. "Don't worry, Mummy, we'll be good."

"Thanks Kel. I hope I won't be more than a couple of hours, but I'll have to see—I'll tell you about it later."

"No problem, Jane. Off you go."

"Bye."

Jane shivered as she entered the building and walked up the stairs to the second-floor apartment. It had been such a bitterly cold week, and her car heater wasn't working properly, so she was now quite chilled. The lobby was not well heated. She had never visited the apartment before, but she knew this area well from her early days with the Force, and had no problem recognizing it when Dana first told her of its location around the time that Tony had come to live with Gina.

She knocked on the door. After a moment, it opened. Tony was standing there, looking somewhat dishevelled, his shirt loose over his pants, and barefoot.

"Hi, Tony. Can I come in?"

Tony motioned to her to enter. They walked through to the living room as Jane slid off her jacket. *At least this place is warm*, she thought. Tony took the jacket and laid it on a chair.

He was not in good shape. Jane realized that she was going to have to lead. She sat down.

"Would you like to tell me about what has happened?"

"Yeah." Tony reached over to the newspaper lying on the coffee table. He found a page and passed it over to Jane, pointing to a headline. In spite of the warmth of the room, Jane felt an icy chill pass through her as she saw the words.

Homeless Succumb to Winter

She read the first few lines …

Two bodies, found yesterday in an alley off Rideau Street, appear to have been there for several days, according to Sergeant Guy, who is heading the investigation. Foul-play is not suspected. The two men, recognized as street people, may have died as a result of the intense cold last week. One of them was known as Albert, but nothing is known about the second man. Anyone able to supply further information about these men is asked to contact the Ottawa Police …

Jane lifted her eyes to look at Tony. Her heart went out to him. Clearly this sad event had affected him deeply. "You knew these men?"

Tony nodded. "I knew Albert. Don't know who the other one was." His eyes were still downcast. Jane knew he probably still had difficulty making eye contact—he still had a long way to go in his recovery.

"I'm sorry, Tony, I really am. Did you know him well?"

"Not really. He … he was good to me when … when I was on the street …"

Jane watched as he broke down and tears rolled down his face.

He sniffed. "He said things …" He sniffed again. "He said things that made me ask for help …"

Jane put her hand on his arm. "He was your friend," she said gently.

"Uh-huh." Tony lifted his eyes to look at Jane, but could not hold them there. "If I hadn't come here, I … I could have been dead as well."

Jane had seen some sights in her time as a policewoman, but she found this situation deeply moving. She knew something of Tony's time on the street, based on what Dana and Gina had gleaned from Tony's fragmented memories of those days. But this was something deeper. In spite of the conditions in which they had existed, there clearly had been some sort of a bond between Tony and Albert. She sensed gratitude in Tony for what Albert must have said to him—a realization by Tony that, if he had not acted on what was said, he could likely have suffered the same fate. And so she shared Tony's sadness that Albert was no more.

Although she had known Tony now for several years, she had not known him closely. There was nothing like the relationship she had developed with Dana, for instance, or some of the other people in the Gardens and Mews. She felt good that, in spite of all his troubles, Tony had thought to call on her, of all people, for help at this time. She wished that she could do more for him right now, but she had to come back to practicalities.

"I know you are very upset, Tony, and it is sad to lose someone you have known, especially someone who has helped you. But take comfort in knowing that Albert isn't cold and suffering anymore."

Tony nodded.

"When do you expect Gina home?"

"'Bout eleven."

Jane realized she could not stay with him that long, but neither did she feel she could leave him in this state. He was too fragile, and therefore vulnerable, and likely to go to the bottle. What should she do? She paused for a few moments. Tony was vacantly staring at the floor.

"Could I use your phone for a moment, please?"

"Sure." Tony absently waved toward the phone.

Jane moved across the room, picked up the phone, and dialled. "Hi Dave, it's Jane. I wonder if you could help me out. I'm not at home, but I have someone here who needs help and counselling right now. Could you possibly meet us at the Centre in, say, half-an-hour?"

"Is it going to take very long?"

"It probably will. Are you able to give an evening?"

"I guess so. Can you tell me more?"

"You'll understand when we get there. Thanks, Dave. See you there."

Jane felt a moment of relief. She knew Dave could talk with Tony on the level. She turned to Tony.

"I'm glad you called me and asked for help. I hope I've been some help, some comfort, to you. But I can't be with you much longer. If you'll come with me, though, there's someone else who is willing to talk with you, and help you through the evening. I've just called Dave Adkins, and he'll meet us at the Centre. Then one of us will get you back here for when Gina gets home. Would that be okay?"

Tony looked up and nodded. "Yeah." He sighed. "That's okay."

"We'd better leave a note for Gina, telling her where you are, in case she's back early."

Jane wrote a short note as Tony dressed for the outdoors.

Little was spoken as Jane drove Tony back to the Hennigan Centre.

Jane knew that Dave had come to grips with his own demons and alcohol, partly through that occasion when Jane had challenged his driving. They had developed a strong friendship through their work together in building the Centre's program.

Dave was waiting for them inside the Centre. Jane quickly explained the basic situation, and Dave agreed to get Tony back to the apartment.

"I'm sorry I have to leave you like this, Tony, but I have to get back to my little girl. Graham's away again. I'm glad you called me. And I'm truly sorry to hear about Albert."

Tony managed a wry smile. "Thanks, Jane, thanks for coming."

Jane let herself out into the darkness.

"Let's go into the lounge and make ourselves a bit more comfortable," said Dave brightly. "There's some instant coffee in the kitchen. Fancy a cup?"

"Not really, thanks."

They sat down in two of the easy chairs in the lounge.

"Jane tells me a friend of yours has died …"

Dave did not have the background knowledge on Tony that Jane had, but he skilfully, gently, learned of Tony's story, as best Tony could recall it and tell it—the story of Tony's time on the street, and of the significance of Albert.

Dave had not seen much of Tony since the early days of the Centre. He knew he had left home, under something of a cloud, but that was all. So as he learned of Tony's problems with alcohol, he felt compelled to do what he could to help Tony in his struggle.

Learning about Tony's descent into the pit took a long time, as Dave led the conversation very gently, very slowly, with many long pauses. Now Dave felt that it was time for him to share his experiences, in the hope that they might help Tony.

"You know, Tony," Dave began again, after a long pause. "You know, I've been down much the same road as you. I lost my job back a few years. I found out a few weeks before Christmas. I think you may know that, because it was well known around the Gardens at the time."

Tony nodded, but he continued to gaze intently at the table in front of him. Dave focussed his eyes on Tony's face, hoping he would look up and connect, if only momentarily.

"In the months following, when I was out of work, I became very bitter. I had nothing to do, and I felt so depressed and miserable. Barb and I had always had a habit of relaxing with a glass of scotch when I got home from work, before dinner.

"Well, without realizing at first, I began to drink more glasses of scotch, during the day, anytime, just for something to do. Each one gave me a kick, anyway, which helped me feel better, and helped me cope with the feelings of despair that I kept having.

"But what I didn't know at the time was that each drink, each kick, had a downer afterward, which, after a while, left me feeling the need for yet another kick, another drink. After several months, I was in bad shape. I just couldn't see what was happening. But thank goodness, Barb *could* see it, and she worked with me, bless her, and pulled me through. She told me straight what would happen if I didn't get my act together.

"Boy, it was hard, real hard at first. I was miserable, bitter, crabby with my family. I'd go on frantic searches around the house, to see if Barb had missed any bottles when we'd cleared the house of alcohol—but she hadn't. Gradually, with Barb's encouragement, I started to do things, little things that gave me some confidence back, things around the house. And things had improved so much, thank goodness, that when that meeting of Dana's came up—you know, about this place—I was there, and could hold my head up high."

To Dave's relief, Tony lifted his head and their eyes met, for a moment.

"I—I just don't feel good enough for anything, anybody."

"You know, Tony," Dave continued, looking firmly at Tony, "this job is the best thing that could have happened to me. It has made a new man of me. It's given me back the confidence I had lost; it's given me a purpose. I know breaking the drinking cycle was all up to me in the end—but I could never have done it without Barb's help. And this job, working with people, great people, has made it all worthwhile."

Tony shifted his position.

"D'you have someone helping you?" Dave wondered if he would get much out of Tony at this stage.

"Uh-huh." A pause. "Dana and Gina." Tony's voice trailed off.

"That's good," said Dave brightly. "How do you feel about that? What are they doing?"

"Gina doesn't let me do much at all, 'cept work." Tony was rather disparaging in tone, but then he brightened. "But Dana comes when she can …"

"Does—" Dave began, but Tony was still working through what he wanted to say.

"… she's got me going to this guy, a counsellor, once a week."

"Did you choose to go?"

"Yeah, I guess. But Dana set it up."

"D'you think the counsellor is helping you?"

"Not really. Don't like him."

"Does Dana know this?"

"No, not yet. Haven't told her." Tony's head sagged. "I just feel I'm not good enough for her to be doing all this for me."

"If he's not helping, p'raps you should go to someone else,"

Dave mused. "Look, Tony, I'd like to help you. Would you mind if I talked with Dana and Gina, to see what we can come up with?"

"Sure. Whatever."

Dave was hoping for a more positive response, but he acknowledged that it was probably the best he would get.

- 33 -

Dana rang the doorbell and waited. She was anxious. All that the message had said was that Gina needed help, and asked for Dana to come over as soon as possible. Dana instinctively knew why. But she could have done without this right now, right in the thick of preparing for RMC Grad. All the parade-ground practices, the drills, all the paperwork, it was never-ending—and now, this.

She'd come home for this one Saturday in April as a last breather before the final two weeks of college life. It was four months since she had set up that first counsellor for Tony—the one that hadn't worked out.

But then Dave Adkins and Jane had got more involved. They'd arranged for him to go into a detox unit for a few weeks, to which he had willingly gone. That had taken some of the stress off Gina. And they'd found another counsellor, who seemed to relate better to Tony. Things seemed to be going well. Last time she had seen him, a month or so ago, Tony had seemed much better, more like his old self. But all through final exams, he was on her mind; she worried about him.

Gina opened the door.

"Come on in, Dan. Thanks for coming over."

"'T's okay. Is he here?"

Gina put her finger to her lips. "Shh. He's watching TV, can't you hear it—loud, eh? Come into my room, quick."

The two slid into the bedroom, and Gina gently pushed the door shut.

"So, what happened?" asked Dana.

"We'd been invited to this barbecue, see, 'cause the weather's been so great all through April. One of the girls at work. She knew Tone was with me, so she invited him along, too. I didn't see anything wrong with that; he's been dry since Christmas—that's over four months."

"That's really good—so what then?"

"Well, we went. There was a good crowd there already when we arrived. We got to be introduced—well Tony did, I already knew quite a lot of them. Anyway, I got talking to this couple, when I suddenly saw Tony lifting a beer bottle to his mouth. I just screamed at him. Everybody stopped and stared—I guess I really didn't care. I just stormed over to Tone, grabbed the bottle, and threw it on the ground. That was the limit—I just grabbed his arm and dragged him away from the party. The amazing thing was, he didn't resist, he just came along. If he'd pulled back, I couldn't have stopped him."

"So what did you do then?"

"We just came home. He didn't say a word, just came in, sat in the chair, spent the rest of the day there. I managed to get up enough courage to phone Susan the next day to apologize and explain. She was very kind and understanding, thank goodness."

"He's been going to this second counsellor, hasn't he?"

"Yeah, but I don't think he likes him very much anymore—I don't think there's much of a rapport, now?"

"But Tony probably doesn't want to hear what the guy is telling him."

"Maybe not—but I don't think it's getting anywhere."

"How long is it since he came out of the detox unit?"

"That was early March—about eight weeks now, I guess."

"But do you think he actually went for the beer?"

"No. That's just it, you see. Actually, Susan was apologetic when I explained about Tone—it seems her husband had just done the, like, friendly thing and tossed a beer over to Tony without waiting for Tony's response—not that I can be sure what Tony's answer would have been."

"Hmm. Seems to me the message hasn't sunk in deep enough yet. Let's go talk with him."

They left the bedroom and walked into the living room.

"Dana's here, Tone."

Tony jumped out of the chair. "Hi Dan, I didn't hear you come in."

"No, you have the TV on so loud," said Gina. "Please turn it off now."

"Okay." Tony complied. He sat down again as Dana sat on the sofa, and Gina sat on the floor.

Tony looked from one to the other, but avoided their steady gazes. "Okay, okay. I get it. You've come to talk about me. Right?"

"Yes, we have, Tone," Gina acknowledged.

"Lookit, Tony, you've done pretty well these past few months, but we know, and you must know, that your problem hasn't gone away, has it?"

Tony looked down at the floor. "No. Look guys, I really do want to get sorted out, I really do. But it's times like the other day—that barbecue—give a guy a break. What do you do when the host tosses you a beer? Toss it back?"

"Yesss," said Dana and Gina in chorus.

"Aw, come off it. You can't do that."

"You certainly can," emphasized Dana. "That's the whole point. *You* have to understand that alcohol is like a poison to *you*, you alone. Avoid it. Refuse it. A proper host won't be offended. Like, there's some people that are deathly allergic to peanuts—they just have to check and refuse, no matter what."

"But beer is different."

"Good God, man, it's not different if it ends up killing you, is it?" Dana was raising her voice now.

Tony remained silent, eyes downcast.

Dana glanced at Gina. "Look, Tony, we all want you to pull through this. Do you want to go through with it?"

"Uh-huh."

"Look at me, Tone. Look at me. Do you?" Dana was determined to see this one through.

Tony raised his eyes, and for a moment they caught Dana's. "Yes."

The Munro house was quiet when Dana arrived home. She was alone. *Good,* she thought, *just what I need.* She searched through her purse and found the card. Lucasz Woslewski—and there was his number. She lifted the phone, paused for a moment, and then dialled.

"Hello, Lifeline Lodge?"

"I'd like to speak to Lucasz Woslewski, if he's around, please."

"Just a minute."

The minute seemed like five.

"Hello, Lucasz Woslewski?"

"Hello, Lucasz. This is Dana Munro."

"Dana, this is a surprise. How are you?"

"I'm fine, thanks. I'm—er—calling about some help, some advice, for a friend."

"Now, Dana, you don't mean—you don't mean you? That's the usual

opener that people with a problem use."

Dana gave a little chuckle, realizing what she had unintentionally said.

"No, Lucasz, that's not what I meant—it truly is not for me. It's—it's for Tony, Tony Ferruccio."

There was a moment of silence on the phone. Then—

"No. Not Tony?"

"'Fraid so. He's in a bad way. Gina, his sister, and I, and others, have worked with him for months now, and he's been to two counsellors and a detox unit. He's been good at times, but he can't be relied on. He doesn't really realize what it'll do to him in the end."

"I see. But how do you think I could help? You know, when we met on that bus, you were gracious enough to accept me as I believe I am now, but I couldn't expect Tony in his current state to understand and take advice from me, of all people."

"No, I realize that. What I had in mind was the counsellor you told me about—you know, the one that convinced you."

"Yes, Jim Broderick. Great guy."

"Do you know where he is now? Would it be possible for Tony to go to him?"

"Mmmm—I'd have to do a bit of digging. I mean, when I saw him last, I wasn't exactly what you would call high and dry, I still had a way to go along the road. But he certainly set me on the right road.

"Tell you what, Dana, give me a few days—I'll see if I can track him down, and see what he's up to. With luck, he'll be in a position where he can talk to Tony. How can I get in touch with you?"

"Why don't I call you next Saturday? That way you won't have to leave any messages that might cause a puzzle."

"I understand—wise. Yes, leave it till after eight in the evening, the place tends to be busy around suppertime."

"Thanks, Lucasz."

"I'm only too happy to help—please understand that."

Angel in Blue Jeans

"Thanks."

"Bye then, talk to you Saturday."

Dana slowly put the phone down. *The twists and turns of fate,* she thought, *how they make life so challenging.*

※※※

Dana, Gina, and Tony stood on the sidewalk outside Gina's apartment block. Dana's car door was open. She had just thrown her bag and the books into the backseat. She turned back to the other two.

"So you will phone when you get a chance?" Gina had a worried look on her face.

"Yes, but at this stage, I really don't know what sort of a schedule I'll be on. Don't worry, I *will* keep in touch."

"You take care, please, Dan." Tony had a drawn expression on his face.

Dana smiled. "Of course, Tone. And you, too, please?"

The past month had been hectic. Having graduated from RMC and received her commission at the beginning of May, Dana was now a Second Lieutenant in the army. She was about to depart on an extended training exercise, and would be away now for several months. No longer would she be no more than a two-hour drive from home, no longer ready to come to Gina's aid if Tony got himself into trouble.

But the events of the past month were encouraging. Lucasz Woslewski had indeed found his old counsellor, Jim Broderick, and Jim was available. And what's more, he was not far away, having set up a practice in Carleton Place, half-an-hour's drive away. Tony had been to visit Jim three times already, and was quite a different man as a result. Dana could already see cause for hope.

She had explained to Gina, carefully, all about Woslewski, and they had agreed that Tony should not be told, at least not now. Tony had even gone so far as to join an AA group, as suggested by Broderick. Things were looking up.

Dana reached out to Gina and they embraced. No words—they understood.

Dana turned to Tony. They looked at one another for a moment, and then embraced.

"Good luck, Dan, and—thanks."

"You take care."

Dana climbed into the car, and closed the door. The engine started, and she pulled away with a wave.

- 34 -

The lights changed to green as Tony approached the intersection. Easing the wheel over, he turned the car left onto the road home to Ottawa. The lights of the businesses and restaurants slipped by, as he noticed two police cars six-nining on the forecourt of a gas station.

Better watch my speed, he thought, as the road ahead narrowed into the darkness of the night. There was heavy construction in the area since twinning of the highway was underway, but traffic was still using the old road.

He had come to know this stretch of road quite well over the past few weeks as he had visited Jim Broderick. He had taken to Jim; he realized Jim understood what was going on—Tony had just not been able to see eye-to-eye with those other counsellors.

But Dana, dear Dana, had been convinced that this one, Jim, was different, and she was right. How she knew, he couldn't tell, and now he couldn't really ask her easily, she was so far away. But he felt good; he felt he understood what Jim was saying. It would be hard, but he could, he would, do it.

The lights of the oncoming traffic grew from pinpoints and flared as they passed him by. He glanced in the mirror: a set of lights not too far behind—and looked like a rig way beyond that. His eyes returned to the front. Ahead of him, lights approached the highway from a side road to the right. *That's the Ashton Road,* he thought.

Suddenly, he tensed—that vehicle did not stop as it came to the highway. It careened onto the main road heading toward him, lights glaring, brights full on.

Tony's pulse was racing. He gripped the wheel—the lights were coming straight at him. *The idiot's on the wrong side of the road.* Closer—and closer.

A split-second for action—Tony wrenched the wheel over, and at once felt the drag of the shoulder on the wheels. His foot went for the brake, but before he could act, he bounced upward, out of his seat. His belt pulled him down, as his head hit …

"Hey guy, you okay?"

"He's out …"

Tony could vaguely hear voices as he awoke. It was dark, but lights were flashing.

Dazed, he looked up. *Fucking hell, what's happened, where am I?*

There was a hammering at his side; he turned, realizing he was in his car. There were men trying to open the car door. Suddenly, it swung open. Tony's pulse shot up. "What the f—"

"You okay, guy? Take it easy, you're off the road. You've had an accident."

Tony felt a hand on his shoulder, and another hand took his other arm as he tried to get out. A flashlight was dancing around in front of him. Flashing lights everywhere. He straightened up as he stepped out of the car—but his legs gave way beneath him. He felt himself being borne up by strong hands.

"Don't worry, we've got you," came the voice again.

He felt himself being carried along, all the time aware of lights flashing around him. His head was hurting.

"Here, we'll set you down on this blanket. Wrap it around yourself if you start to feel chilled."

The voice was now in front of him. Tony looked up.

"Hi, I'm Serge. You were very lucky to get out of that. Do you feel okay now? Does anything hurt?"

"Er—my head's sore," responded Tony, unsurely, raising his hand to his head. He sensed the flashlight moving to allow Serge to check his head.

"No blood. You probably bumped it as you went off the road, probably a slight concussion. You were out when we got to you."

Tony had come to his senses now, and was beginning to take in his surroundings. He was sitting on a blanket at the roadside. There were lights everywhere; vehicles were parked at the side of the road.

There was a big rig, with all its marker lights on and a brilliant spotlight shining on the scene. Flashing lights appeared to be coming from several police cars. He could hear sirens. More flashing lights. He realized that fire-trucks were arriving. He shivered and pulled the blanket up around him.

"What happened?" he asked, vaguely remembering the brilliant lights coming straight at him.

"Some idiot came straight out of that side road, and lost control of his car in the turn. He must have been heading straight for you, but you managed to get off the road, out of his way. But the car behind didn't. There was a head-on crash that took both cars off the road. Lucky the big rig behind could stop in time, too."

"W-was anyone hurt bad?"

"'Fraid so, but don't know any details. I came over to get you out."

"Thanks."

"No problem. Glad that you seem basically okay. Your car just ran off the road—I doubt it's got any serious damage."

Tony groaned. "I hope not. It's my sister's; she's not had it long."

"Well, once the police have done their checking, I guess one of the tow-trucks'll give you a hand to get it back on the road and check it out."

"Yeah."

Another man came over to join them. "You okay?"

"Yeah, I think so, thanks."

"Good."

"Any word on the others?" Serge enquired.

"Not good. Passenger in one of the cars killed. Cops have arrested the driver—drunk—seems he was way over the limit."

"That's bad."

"Yeah. Why do they do it?"

It had been ages. Tony was wrapped in a couple of blankets now, sitting on the grass near his vehicle, away from the main action with so many flashing red, blue, yellow, and white lights: two fire-trucks, two ambulances, scads of police, and shadowy people all moving around.

A cop had been over to him and taken his licence and the vehicle papers (luckily Gina kept them in the glove box). He'd been told to stay put until someone came to get a statement.

He began to go over the accident again, as best he could remember. The brilliant lights coming straight at him, the split-second decision to swerve ...

Suddenly, he froze—an icy chill came over him, an intense awareness of everything around him, and yet, he was not part of it. Events, scenes crowded into his mind—Dana—Gina—Vince. It all became crystal clear.

That idiot driver was drunk; he could have killed me—he did kill someone. He shivered and shook. He heard Jim Broderick's voice, and he knew. He knew that he had overcome the demons. From that moment on.

Tony sat in the passenger seat of the tow-truck as it cruised along, Gina's car in tow. His eyes were seeing the multitudes of lights speeding by, but his mind was not registering them. His thoughts were ranging over the events of the past few hours, culminating in what was ahead of him—having to break the news to Gina that her precious car was damaged, major front suspension work required.

"You okay, man?"

Tony jumped as he heard the driver speak. "Uh? Oh, er, yeah, no problem."

"Take it easy, man. After an accident, you often get the shudders."

"Yeah."

Tony sat back in his seat. He felt good. The coldness had gone, replaced by a warm feeling, deep inside. Now he could see the road ahead, *his* road ahead, and it would be good.

- 35 -

Jane smiled as the Munro front door opened.

"Oh, hi Jane," Caroline greeted. "Come on in. I've just finished spreading things out."

"That's good. We can get started right away. How are you?"

"Good. How's young Trishy?"

"She's fine. Graham is in charge tonight—she let him do everything; not once was there a call for 'Mo-om!'"

"Hah—I can see you've got them both trained."

They both laughed as they moved into the Munro living room. Jane felt comfortable and at ease. Tonight, she and Caroline were into a newly discovered common interest: family history, or genealogy.

"Wow, you've been busy indeed," exclaimed Jane, seeing the spread of material Caroline had put out. "Some of this looks original."

"Yep. Bob collected some of these papers from his grandparents in Scotland. They're pretty faded, but still readable—only just, in a few cases."

They sat down as Jane leafed through a few pages on the table close to her.

"Had an email from Dana a week or so ago," Caroline noted.

"Great, how's she doing?"

"Good. She says she's settling in well now; a group of them were able to go off-base one weekend and sample some Balkan-style food. Oh yes—and she's been appointed in-charge of one of the patrol units. Every few days, they go out and patrol a designated area of responsibility."

"That's really good—quite an added feather in her cap."

"Yes. I still worry about her, though."

"Naturally, what mother wouldn't?" Jane smiled and patted Caroline's arm.

"I'll go put the kettle on. Have a look through—"

The doorbell rang. Caroline looked surprised; Jane watched as she went to the door and opened it, seeing Caroline's gasp and look of horror.

Two men and one woman, all in army uniform, stood there. Jane couldn't hear the initial words spoken, but she stood as Caroline ushered the three into the room.

The first officer, a captain and clearly ill-at-ease, spoke. "Mrs Munro, we are deeply sorry to intrude on you at this time, but we have some very serious information to convey. May I suggest that you be seated?"

Jane could see that the colour had drained from Caroline's face. Jane already sensed what might be coming, and felt awful. Caroline sat down, and motioned to the three visitors to do so also.

The captain looked straight at Jane, as if to ask 'And who are you?' Jane felt she should respond. "I'm a close friend of Caroline's, Jane Stennings. I may be of help here."

"Thank you," began the captain. "I'm Captain Legendre, this is Major the Reverend Olney, and Master Warrant Smith." His arm swept to the others. "We've received word from our unit at CFB

Betsevac that there has been an incident. The area is now insecure. Based on the information we have, Lieutenant Munro, Dana, your daughter, and her crew are listed as 'Missing in Action'.

"Ma'am, we are extremely sad and sorry to have to bring you this news. We can only offer you our sympathy and support."

Jane, as soon as the captain had begun to speak, knew what was coming—she was too close to the Army, through Graham. She had watched Caroline as the words came out; Caroline's hands had gripped the chair arms, her face was white, her body tense, but her eyes were blazing.

"I knew it could come to this, I knew it; but it was her choice, it was h-her choi-ce …" and Caroline sank back, sobbing.

Jane moved to comfort her, helped by the lady Master Warrant, who came to Caroline's other side. Jane found the box of tissues quickly. After a few moments, Caroline was able to compose herself again.

"This is tragic news," Jane started. "This must have happened today?"

"Two days ago, in the morning, European time," said the chaplain. "Mrs Munro, please accept my sympathies, too. I know this has come as a tremendous shock to you. As yet, we don't know the full details, and we can only pray that your daughter is safe. If it will be any comfort to you, I am willing to stay with you this evening as long as you wish."

"Thank you," Caroline's voice was weak and trembling. "My husband will be home in a couple of hours. He's going to be devastated." And the tears began to flood again.

"Would you like me to stay until he returns?"

Caroline nodded as she pulled more tissues from the box.

"I also have some training in this area. I'm a former policewoman," put in Jane. "Are they likely to know more about the incident soon?"

The master warrant spoke. "I'm the immediate direct contact

for CFB Betsevac, so I will be in touch with Mrs Munro as soon as further information becomes available. Here are my contact details." She laid a sheet of paper on the table.

The chaplain spoke. "We also offer continuing counselling support for you and your family; please know you can call me at any time, if you feel the need. Before I leave tonight, I'll give you my contact information and a couple of leaflets that may be of help."

The captain stood, and the master warrant followed suit. The chaplain remained seated.

"Mrs Munro," the captain nodded to Jane also, "once again, we are truly sorry to bring this news. Please don't hesitate to contact us; we are here to give what support we can at this most difficult time."

The two moved toward the front door. Caroline hung back, so Jane took the lead. "We'll look after her, sir," she said to the captain as they reached the door. "Her husband will be home in a couple of hours. I'll stay with her as well."

"Thank you. You've done this sort of thing before?"

"Yes."

The captain and the master warrant left.

Jane turned, tears in her eyes, and hugged Caroline tightly. They sobbed together.

Jane pulled away, and guided Caroline to a chair. "We have to have hope. We have to be positive; we have to hope that Dana has survived this incident." Jane was trying to be reassuring.

Caroline sniffed and wiped her eyes. "Yes," she sobbed. "Yes, I know he said 'Missing in Action', I know. But I feel so cold inside."

"Here, wrap this throw around you," Jane said. "I'm going to make you some camomile tea. Just stay there. Would you care for some too, sir?"

"Thank you, no."

Jane went quickly to the kitchen, put water in the kettle, and turned it on. She knew where Caroline kept her herbal teas, and pulled out a bag for each of them, taking down two mugs from their hooks. She then pulled out her cell-phone and dialled home.

"Hello," came the response.

"Hi Gra, it's me. Look, awful news. There's been an incident on Dana's mission—Dana is MIA. Caroline has just had a visit from a captain, a chaplain, and a master warrant. Chaplain's still here."

"Oh my god, no?"

"Caroline is obviously shaken, so I'm going to stay with her, at least until Bob gets home—then I'll probably have to help support him. Chaplain is staying, too. Look, can you get on the phone and let people know the situation so far? We have to have as much support for this poor family as we can muster."

"Wilco. On it right away. Give Caroline my sympathy and hope for the best."

Jane took the tea back to the living room. The chaplain was speaking.

"… So, one of the ways to help ease the stress could be to hold a vigil, a watch, hoping and praying that she is alive and safe and can return to us. This could provide a way for your family and friends to show their concern and support."

Caroline sipped her tea and nodded, her eyes downcast.

"If you would like to do that, I would be willing to help organize and lead a vigil. Is there some place around here that could be used?"

"I know," said Jane. "The Centre, it would be ideal. Sorry, sir, I mean the Hennigan Centre; it's close by in the community, and it was the brainchild of Dana when she was still a teenager here. It would be very fitting. I can help you with that, too. What do you think, Caroline? We owe it to Dana."

Tears were flowing again. Caroline nodded. "Yes, yes, a vigil; that would be nice."

"Sir, my husband is Captain Graham Stennings, in Logistics. He will help with the vigil, too. I just phoned to give him the news as I made the tea. Caroline, he asked me to give you his sympathy and support."

Caroline gave a smile back.

"That's very good. I look forward to meeting him. I suggest we hold the vigil as soon as possible," said the chaplain, "while still giving people enough time to adjust their schedules. Would the day after tomorrow work, say, early evening? It's quite possible we may have further information by then, but with an insecure situation, it's hard to foretell."

"I can start making the arrangements at the Centre, and give you the administrator's coordinates. Here, I'll write them for you now," offered Jane, as she reached for a notepad on the table.

"Thanks. The important thing now is for us to be hopeful and positive, to be supportive of you, Caroline, and your family. No matter what, it is a stressful time. You will have assistance from your community, and I will coordinate the military side."

- 36 -

Slowly, sound seeped into Dana's mind. She became aware of light, diffuse light, light that commanded. Gradually, the light converged, focussed, took form. And the form was green.

She began to feel, soft against her face. Her eyes were open. Grass, she was lying on grass, wet grass, face down. *Drip, drip,* that sound, *drip, drip.* Water was dripping past her face, through the grass.

Where am I? Her mind began to race. *Where am I?*

And then the pain struck. She winced and gasped as the pain wracked her chest. She lay still—don't move. *Where am I?*

Her head was throbbing. She began to move her hand up to her head, but the pain in her chest was too much. Moving her head slightly, she began to see beyond the blades of grass before her eyes: a tree trunk, and broken twigs.

Where the hell am I? She tried her legs. They worked. She tried her arms, her hands. They worked, but that pain in her chest was agony when she moved her right arm.

Wet. She was wet, cold wet, uncomfortable. *I gotta move.*

Carefully, easing the pain as best she could, she lifted herself up and onto her back. She lay there, eyes closed, in agony. She brought her left hand to the pain, at the bottom of her ribcage on the right.

How long she had lain there on her back she didn't know, but when her eyes opened again, the light was dimmer. Her eyes focussed on the sight above her: branches, branches, and more branches, with tree trunks disappearing upward into a mass of green and speckled light. *Where am I? What has happened?*

Slowly, carefully, she brought herself to a sitting position, rolling out of the little trickle of water that had been running under her. The pain in her chest was bad, but it seemed to have lessened. Her head still throbbed.

Bringing up her left hand, she ran it across her forehead. As she took it away, she saw the blood, and quickly touched her forehead again. *Yes, I must have been hurt there, too. Why? How?*

As she took stock, she realized she was in her combats. *Why?* She racked her brain, trying to remember what she was doing last. *Yes, coming up the mountain road, round the bend near the top of the hill.*

She remembered raising herself up in the hatch of the Coyote to look back at Johnny following fifty metres behind, and Cracker and Paul a more distant third in the old Bison.

But what next …? Nothing. Nothing at all, until this. Something big must have happened, but what? Jeez, what happened to the others, where are they?

As she tried to think back, her head began to clear. Her mind came into gear.

"Okay, Munro," she spoke out loud, "you're in a fix. Don't know what happened. Don't know where you are. What's your status?

"Wet, at least on my front—back seems okay.

"Good.

"Cold. Hurting. Legs okay. Arms okay.

"Good. Then you're mobile. Stand up."

Gingerly she tried to stand, but her head was swimming, and she fell back.

"Not good. Not so fast, Dana."

She had collapsed to a sitting position, knees up. She rested her head sideways on her knees, with her arms around her legs.

This ground's got a hell of a slope, she thought. She looked at the trees more closely. Yes, if they were vertical, she was on a steep hillside.

Light was fading fast now. She realized she had no option but to stay put for the night. In the twilight, she looked around and moved uphill a metre or so to a drier and softer area, with less grass but deep pine needles. Moulding them, she crafted a more comfortable spot to bed down on.

The dawn light brought a familiarity to the small scene around her. She had slept fitfully during the moonless night, aware of the cold, aware of her rib-cage, aware of her plight, but still reacting to the concussion she had obviously suffered.

She had remembered the chocolate bar in her side pocket and had rationed herself to one square during the night. Now she took out the package and broke off another square. Slowly, she placed it in her mouth, and let the sweet chocolate sensation wash through her.

Carefully, she returned the package to her pocket. As she did, she remembered the second chocolate bar in the other pocket—her driver, Randy, knew her love of chocolate, and he had generously tossed his bar over to her as they were setting off from base.

Suddenly, she heard a familiar sound.

Yes, it is: a helo, getting louder, louder, louder. How close is that guy coming? Following the sound, she looked up and out from the hillside, through the trees. She saw the helicopter, white. She could see the UN decal on the side. Relief.

But he can't see me here. She sagged. The helicopter dropped down out of sight, down, down. She could hear him still. He must be hovering, looking.

She struggled to stand, she was on her feet; she grabbed a branch to steady herself, waving frantically with her other arm, wincing at the pain from her ribs.

"Here," she shouted at the top of her voice. "Here. I'm here."

But the helicopter was too low down below the hillside, and the noise would drown her cries.

Gradually, she could hear another sound, above the helicopter, different. A whine, like a jet. Yes, yes, a jet. The scream was intense now, above. *Look up, look up.*

Through the branches, she saw it. *What a sight—high up there—a hover-jet.* Just gently cruising in a tight circle, almost hovering there, poised, for action. *What's he doing? Probably covering the helo,* she realized.

"I'm here," she shouted, "down here." She waved her arm wildly.

Suddenly she heard another sound: gunshots—like rifle shots, almost drowned by the jet's whine, but definitely shots.

Hoo-boy, not good, not safe. And she knew, as the jet veered off and she saw the helicopter rise from below and depart, that her cries were in vain. Whatever, whoever, they had been looking for, she wasn't the lucky one to be found.

Whatever has happened, it must be big—there aren't any fighter-jets in our region. It must have come in to protect the helo. We only have transport and search helos here.

She sank to the ground, and buried her head in her hands. Her plight began to sink in. Something terrible had happened; she was part of it, whatever it was.

They've put out a search, but couldn't see me. Who else is missing? My guys? Jacob? Randy? Schooner? Or everyone—Johnny and his lot, Cracker, Paul ...? Her thoughts trailed off into despair. What the hell has happened? And those rifle shots worried her.

So? What now? In spite of all the discomfort of the night, she felt rested and ready to tackle the day. *Status?*

Head? Seems okay, bit tender there on the forehead, but not serious.

Ribs? Mmm. She felt her side. *Not so bad.* She unbuttoned, and slipped her left hand in under her sweater and tee shirt to find the spot. *Yes, there it is: sharp pain, just below the bra-line on the right ribcage. Guess I've cracked a rib. If that's all it is, I'll have to suffer, I guess. Probably looks ugly, though; doesn't feel to be any broken skin.* She fastened up her clothing.

Okay. Well, Dana, you've gotta get yourself outta here, you're on your own. She stood up. This time, her head was clear. Gingerly, because of the steep slope, she guided herself past the branches and trunks to explore the region to her left, across the slope.

Ten or so metres along, she could go no further. The shelf she was on shrank into a near-vertical rock face. Carefully, she moved back to her original spot. She looked up the slope. About five metres up-slope, the trees stopped at the base of a cliff that rose nearly vertically, so that she could not see its top.

Hoo-boy. She continued on across the slope—but a few metres later, she was confronted with the same problem as before. Her shelf had shrunk to nothing. Nothing left but a rock-face. Gingerly, she turned and returned to her 'home' base.

Very carefully, she let herself downslope against the tree trunks, which became thinner and weaker as she approached the edge of a precipice.

She gasped. She had not realized this until now. Earlier, when the helicopter had been here, she knew it had gone below her level, but she had had no concept of where she was in space. Now, it all became clearer.

She was on a small ledge, a sloping shelf, on a cliff-face going down into a deep gorge. Now that the trees were not obscuring the view, she could see the other side of the gorge—a rugged, craggy hillside, with cliff-faces such as the one she must be on, with pockets of trees clinging precariously to any root-holds they might find.

Far below, she could hear water flowing. *Must be a river. Of course; the Anja, that's what it is. Yeah, this is the gorge we were all following up on the road. Yeah. So where am I? And how the hell did I get here?*

She sat there, safely locked in the trees near the edge of the precipice, staring at the scene. Slowly but surely, the magnitude of her problem dawned on her. *There is no obvious way to get off this ledge by myself. Nobody knows I'm here. Apart from a minor injury, I'm okay.*

She mentally counted the squares on the chocolate bars—*I'm okay for food for a few days. There's a trickle of water coming off the top cliff. Okay, I can stay put for a while—no need to panic, yet.*

But her mind would not let her relax. Now that she knew basically where she was, but not how she got there, she knew that she was in real danger. This gorge region was basically in the hands of the Anjastas, a breakaway rebel group that would not accept UN demands and the cease-fire agreements. That was why her patrol had been moving cautiously up the gorge road—

Oh no, No! Her eyes closed tight. Noise, explosive sound, indescribably loud, shock, moving through space ... She struggled with sensations crowding into her mind, disconnected, fragmented sensations, screams ... *What's happening?*

Shaking, shivering, she opened her eyes again to the scene before her, still the cliffs opposite, the river far below. *Were we attacked? Were we blown up? Is that how I got here? What about the others?*

Shaking, she tried desperately to coax more from her memory, but all she could find were haunting, frightening fragments of sounds and sensations. Nothing, but nothing, rational could she find, beyond that mental image of looking back from her hatch on the Coyote at the other two vehicles following hers up the road.

I'm in deep shit. If we were attacked, that helo and the jet were probably looking for survivors. Given the rebel danger, they'll likely not come in again looking soon. Maybe they've figured everybody was killed.

As she sat there, pondering her fate, another problem came into her consciousness: her fear of heights. It had been with her since childhood, never a real issue for years because she never put herself into such situations. But it had come up seriously in basic training, and could have perhaps cost her her career before it had really begun.

Her mind went back to that day, a hot, dry day out on the range, with those ropes suspended out across the ravine and the river below—the abrasive instructor barking at everyone's heels as they prepared to cross, with an equally barbaric instructor waiting to finish you off over at the other side.

In her mind's eye, she watched as the recruit two ahead of her slipped halfway across. He was left sitting astride the lower rope, hanging frantically onto the two guide ropes, petrified with fear. The two instructors bawled directions at the poor guy, only making him worse. She remembered how, at long last, he recovered and was able to drag himself inelegantly to the far side.

She recalled how she had steeled herself at the outset of her crossing, and had made good progress to about the midpoint, following all the instructions, not looking down, when all at once, she had felt the ropes start to sway sideways, and bounce up and down. The wind had risen.

In a moment of panic, she had glanced down—disaster. She had lost control, her steeling was gone, she was shaking, the ropes were swaying, her stomach was in her mouth, then in her boots. She was frozen.

In the background, she could hear the barked directions, but they made no difference; she alone had to regain control. Slowly, she had mustered up all her parts and, fixing her gaze on the far side, had begun to move again, step by step, hands gripping and sliding alternately.

It took forever, or so it had seemed. But what a relief, and surprise, when, at the end, the instructor put out his hand to guide her onto firm land, saying, "Well done, Dana."

She knew she had come through that time, but that was in training; there were others around to help, and there was a safety rope. Now it was different—a real matter of life or death. She was alone, and there were no convenient ropes or guides, just trees and rocks, and far below, water.

If only Rory or Caleb could be here. She had spent many happy hours, days even, with those two from RMC, hiking and scrambling over rocky hills back home, where nothing as steep and precipitous as this would be attempted—at least not when Dana was with them. She knew Rory and Caleb were expert rock-climbers, but they did that when Dana was not around.

It wasn't that height itself was the problem for her. She didn't mind it when she had the feeling of something solid and extensive beneath her. The CN Tower in Toronto was okay. Even standing at the edge of Niagara Falls, on the firm viewpoints, was not a problem, although, if she watched the water too closely, she did begin to lose control. It was when she didn't have a firm base supporting her that her fear really came to the fore.

But here she was, trapped. Slowly, she turned and dragged herself up away from the precipice. Her ribcage was hurting again—too much stretching was not doing it any good.

She reached her original spot. It was becoming home to her; it had acquired a ring of familiarity. She lay back on the slope and closed her eyes. She shuddered. Fear was not far away, but he had not taken over yet.

The rain was heavier, now. The frail shelter she had managed to build with a few leafy branches was already leaking, and water was dripping through to her at various spots.

The darkness was closing in. She could no longer make out the shapes of the tree trunks downslope at the edge of the precipice. With the complete cloud cover and rain, there was no light at all, now. She was totally trapped, trapped by her surroundings, trapped within her mind—trapped by her mind, constrained to go wherever her mind would go. All she could see was that which was in her mind.

Her mind began to hunt, to hunt for images, old images, childhood images, home, good images, bad images, scary images, Tony, black images that grew to frightening ones.

Get a hold of yourself, Dana—the thought verbalized in her mind. She switched back to the present. Cold and wet, she shifted to another position; she moved a twig to make the water drip in a better spot.

For a while, she focussed on the near world, her mind under control. She leaned back against the sloping ground. Eyes open, eyes closed, it made no difference—there was nothing to see. Time had no meaning—she had no idea how long she had been trapped. Gradually, the darkness bore down on her; her eyes closed by default, and her mind began to wander …

She awoke suddenly. Her face was hard against something rough and wet—her arms flailed out, but were held down by chains. She was shaking, gasping, shrieking, tensing as a reflex into fight mode. Wildly she fought, flinging off the chains and clearing her face.

Sobbing, shivering, shaking, she came to full consciousness, dripping, cold, and wet. Gradually, in the pitch-blackness, she realized again where she was. Her shelter had collapsed on top of her. Now, in her frantic escape from the dream, she had broken it apart completely.

The full rain was now coming down at her through the trees. She could not possibly be any wetter than this.

She shivered in the pre-dawn, faint glimmerings of light, watching, seeking, hearing, listening: sounds of dripping and creaking—images, dark images, gradual forms emerging in the cold, wet greyness of dawn. Endless rain, and now the wind came, moving the trees, groaning, creaking, shuddering in the dripping, growing light of day.

Beyond the trees, shades of light and grey surged by, moving on the wind in endless motion. And stronger wind; now the trees shook and twisted, leaning and groaning, the rain lashing through to sting on her face; gusts that shook and tore, this way, that way.

A brilliant light. She cringed. Crashing rolls of thunder rattled through the gorge.

She cowered down, low to the ground. Water was pouring down the cliff behind her, down the slope, around and through her very being.

She struggled to move to a safer spot, wedged between trees, to ride out the storm. Lightning and thunder filled the air for an endless time, backed by the fury of the wind and the rain …

Numb with cold and drenched to her skin, she gradually realized that the storm was abating; the worst may be over, for now. But what next? The whole cliff, the ledge she was on, everything was saturated, dripping with water. She was trapped, totally trapped.

She began to tremble, partly from the cold, but partly from fear—fear that she may never escape this trap. Condemned by whatever fate brought her here to die. *I cannot escape, and no one will find me. How long? How long will it be?*

She focussed on the reality. She had seven squares of chocolate left. She ate one, and at once felt some warmth. She calculated: *how long can I last with six more? What then? What will it feel like?*

Get a hold of yourself, Dana, be real. You'll find a way.

But there is no way. I cannot get off this ledge; I'm trapped, fucking trapped. Shit! What a fucking waste of a life. All that effort, all that training, all that crap I put up with—just to end up like this? No way.

"No way!" She was shouting. The anger, the frustration, the fear, every emotion was breaking loose. "No fucking way!"

Shattered, she fell back against a tree trunk. *No fucking way, no fucking way ...*

The rain was still falling as the light faded, and the forms of the trees and the cliffs merged into blackness yet again.

The fight had gone from her again. She was cold, and trembling. *What is it like to die? To starve to death? Slowly, agonizingly slowly? What will I do? What will I think about? Will I know what is happening when it happens?*

She shuddered. Her mind filled with panicking images, trembling images, faces, dark faces, tortured faces, screaming faces, shuddering, cold.

Bryce, oh no, Bryce, so cold, he didn't know.

Her mother's face now, sad, a faraway look, inscrutable—*what was she thinking, why didn't she say? What is she doing now?*

Tony. An emptiness engulfed her, and she shuddered again. *Tony, Tony, dear Tony ...*

- 37 -

Dwayne and Elizabeth Hampden approached the outer doors of the Hennigan Centre as a crowd of silent people edged forward; they joined at the rear of the line. Gradually, they moved inside.

"Bob, I am so sorry, this is such a tragedy, such a loss." Dwayne shook Bob Munro's hand.

"Thanks, Dwayne, Ah'm glad ye've come," responded Bob.

"I'm so sorry, dear Bob."

"Guid of you tae come, Elizabeth, thanks," said Bob.

"Caroline, my dear, I am so sorry for you all." Elizabeth embraced Caroline.

"Thank you so much, it's kind of you to come." Caroline tried to smile, but it was clearly difficult.

Dwayne and Elizabeth moved along the line.

"Iain, I've not seen you for quite a while. I'm sorry it's on such a sad occasion."

"Thanks for coming, Mr Hampden. This is my wife, Tracey."

Dwayne shook Iain's and Tracey's hands. Elizabeth hugged them both.

"Thank you, it's kind of you to come," Tracey responded.

Dwayne and Elizabeth found seats near the back, as the hall was almost full already. A small portable organ was playing softly.

Elizabeth looked about her. "There's Dave Adkins, over there in the grey suit."

"Uh-huh."

A quietness descended on the people. Time seemed to hang suspended, as the family members took their seats at the front, near the stage.

A sound of quiet footsteps mingling together came from behind, and a general rustle of sound spread as the people rose to their feet. Dwayne turned slightly to look.

Slowly and surely, led by a chaplain, a group of soldiers moved steadily forward up the aisle. First, a soldier carried a tablet on which rested a cap, belt, and gloves. Following him came two female soldiers. Two male officers brought up the rear. Dwayne recognized one of them to be Graham Stennings.

As the procession reached the front of the hall, the chaplain stepped to the right. The first soldier moved forward with the cap, belt, and gloves to the table set at the front. He placed them carefully in front of a small cross, flanked with flowers. By the flowers were two photographs.

The soldier stepped back two paces, bowed his head, and stepped aside. In turn, the other soldiers stepped forward, bowed heads, and stepped aside. Finally, all five stepped back to form a line, and then returned to places in the front row, furthest from the centre aisle.

"Welcome to this Hennigan Centre," the chaplain began. "At first, this ceremony for our dear Dana was intended as a vigil, in the hope and prayer that she was not lost. However, word was received yesterday …"

The chaplain himself hesitated, clearly moved. "Today, we come not only to mourn her, but to celebrate her life …"

The organ sounded, at the start of a psalm, number twenty-three.

"Crimond," whispered Dwayne, as the familiar tune brought back memories.

As the psalm ended, all sat down. David Adkins stood and walked to a lectern, set to the side of the small table.

"The reading is taken from St. Paul's second letter to the Corinthians, Chapter Four …"

People were attentive, watching and listening to David, whose voice wavered at times. The reading ended. Everyone stood, and the chaplain recited a short prayer.

Rich tones of the organ now filled the hall, carrying up voices in the hymn "Abide With Me". By the end of the hymn, emotion gripped everyone. The people remained standing as the chaplain led them in prayer.

"… glory, for ever and ever. Amen. Please be seated."

People sat down, as the sounds of rustling clothes, and of noses and throats being cleared, wafted through the hall.

The chaplain took up a position at the side of the ceremonial table. "It is hard for us to grasp, to try to understand the loss of a daughter, a sister, a friend, a companion, a comrade, a leader. And it is harder still for us, when she is young and in her prime, with much to offer.

"Dana came to us as a gift from God, and now she returns to her Maker. While she was with us, she did many things for us; many things that will live on with us in our lives. She gave us her love, her concern. She has been an inspiration for us, and she will continue to inspire, for she will remain strong in our memories …"

The chaplain continued; Elizabeth pulled out a tissue. Dwayne reached over to lay his hand on her hand.

"… and let us remember Dana as we knew her. Amen."

There were rustling sounds as people adjusted their positions.

The chaplain continued, "If anyone wishes to share with us their thoughts about Dana, you are welcome to come forward."

A very tall, elderly man with a shock of white hair rose and walked forward to a position by the stage, to the right of the chaplain. Dwayne recognized a friend.

"I'm George Simpson. I have had the privilege of knowing Dana for several years. I came to know her through her brilliant initiative that has resulted in a lasting physical monument to her life, this fine Hennigan Centre.

"I admired her from the moment I met her. I admired her quiet, carefully managed confidence. Her efforts to bring the Centre to the successful venture it now is have benefited us all.

"As many of you know, Kurt Hennigan, the Centre's benefactor, died last year at the age of a hundred and one. During his last days, he said to me, 'Young Dana has been a blessing to me. She has given me five extra years to my life. She has helped to fill the void.'

"Mr Hennigan lost both his son and his daughter in the Korean war, and his wife not long after. During her years at the military college in Kingston, Dana visited Kurt almost every week when she was in the city, to talk with him, to walk with him, to read to him. After she was commissioned and away with the Army, she wrote to him regularly ... And now we mourn her passing. We will remember her always."

George Simpson wiped his eyes as he returned to his seat. The chaplain scanned the congregation.

A young woman walked to the front and turned. "I'm Fiona Stacey. I just want to say, 'Thank you, Dana.' You brought me out into the world. You gave me an example to follow. I know I can't do what you have accomplished, but you gave me the confidence to do well what I can do. I'll never forget you." Red-eyed, Fiona returned to her seat.

An older woman walked to the front of the side aisle, and turned to face the congregation. "My name is Jane Stennings. I would just like to pay tribute to Dana. I first knew her at another tragic moment for her family, the loss of her brother Bryce, and our hearts go out to Caroline, Bob, and Iain at this time. I am proud to have known Dana, and to have worked with her. She was made of the right stuff. She knew what was needed, and did her utmost to see that it was done right. God bless you, Dana."

Dwayne leaned over toward Elizabeth and whispered, "That lady has become a real asset to the community."

The chaplain scanned again. A young man approached the front. He turned. "I'm Jason, Jason Johnson. Dana was fun to be with. She always brightened up the party. She could be serious one moment, and cracking jokes the next. But she always cared. If someone was feeling down, Dana would talk with them and try to cheer them up. We all admire her for what she has done for us, and we're all going to miss her, a lot."

A pause as Jason returned to his place. The chaplain nodded to one of the army officers, who walked to the front by the table and turned to the people.

"Graham. That's appropriate," whispered Dwayne. "He looks very smart in his uniform."

"Lieutenant Munro—Dana—was a respected and capable officer, well-liked by all. During her service in the Armed Forces, she has received several commendations. She was not afraid of hard work, she was full of initiative, and she was a good leader. I have admired Dana since I first came to know her in this community, and I had the privilege of working with her and guiding her as she made her decision to join the Army. My wife Jane and I are deeply saddened by this tragedy."

Graham paused for a moment, clearing his throat and wiping one eye. He continued, "In any theatre of armed conflict, there are great risks. We all know that. But it is particularly difficult for those who are in a peacekeeping role in an unstable environment. Boundaries and rules are ephemeral, and peacekeepers are constrained to be impartial.

"As many of you already know, Lieutenant Munro and her patrol were conducting a routine survey of boundary lines when an explosion under her vehicle blasted it off the road and down a precipitous cliff, into the river below. The vehicle then exploded, and burned fiercely. A search and rescue team examined the site thoroughly, once it was deemed safe to do so, and concluded that none of the vehicle's occupants could have survived; no recoverable or identifiable remains were found …

"I am here today to share in our grief, and to offer condolences to Dana's family, to Caroline, Bob, Iain, and Tracey."

An intense silence followed, as everyone reflected on what had been said. The chaplain looked toward the Munro family.

Bob Munro stood and slowly walked forward. He picked up the cap and, holding it, turned to the people. "Ah'm not used tae talking t'a lot o' people, so please bear with me."

He cleared his throat, and looked downward for a moment. "Ah want tae say that we're proud of our daughter; proud of what she's done for us; proud of what she's taught us; proud of what she's done for our community; er … proud o' what she's achieved in her chosen career.

"Er … Dana volunteered as a peacekeeper because she believed in it … because she believed in the need for an armed force tae be used tae restore or maintain peace … sae long as there's armed conflict in this world."

Bob's voice broke as he choked back emotion. "But tae be in the armed forces means tae be prepared tae take risks, tae take the ultimate risk, tae pay the ultimate price." He glanced down at the cap. "Dana, we love you. God bless you, ma sweet, rest in peace."

Helping hands of friends gently guided Bob, now shaking visibly, back to his seat.

The chaplain, who had receded into the background, came to the front and said quietly, "Let us stand and pray."

A rustling filled the hall as people adjusted to their new positions.

"Almighty God, with whom do live the spirits of them that depart …" As the chaplain reached the end of the prayer, a loud murmured "Amen" filled the hall.

The chaplain paused, and the soldiers took up their positions in formation. A lone piper at the back of the hall began to play a lament. The sad, haunting sound of the pipes took emotion to the breaking point as people openly shed tears.

Dwayne whispered, "That'll be her Uncle Alex. She told me about him one day."

"Rest eternal grant unto her, O Lord, and let light perpetual shine upon her."

"Amen."

Dwayne suddenly realized he was indeed also shedding tears. The enormity of this loss hit him hard. He had never been so close; he had never really given much thought to the lives lost during past wars and conflicts—there was no direct connection for him.

But here, it was personal. He had grown to know, to like, to admire this young woman, and now he understood what she stood for—now he knew what the ultimate sacrifice means—he had heard the words before, but they had been empty, until now. He shuddered; his world was not the same anymore.

Outside the hall, Jane struggled to contain her tears as she held her daughter Trish's hand. Graham was over by two army vehicles, shaking hands with the soldiers.

They exchanged salutes, and Graham turned back toward his family. He put his arm round Jane as she buried her head against his chest, sobbing. The others joined them, Kelly Carson taking hold of Trish's hand, comforting her.

Mike Carson, his ashen face strained, spoke first. "Do they really know what happened yet?"

"'Fraid not. The explosion didn't follow the pattern for a typical IED in that region, and they'd only just swept for mines, anyway. And no one has come up with an alternate explanation that could account for such an explosion from within the vehicle itself. The area is now occupied by one of the breakaway splinter groups, but it's hard to see how they might have some new weaponry."

"Did they find anything in the river?" asked Kelly.

"They sent a search helicopter in as soon as they could safely do so. Because of the new fragility in the situation, they had to wait for separate air-cover. They found the burnt-out hulk, but no survivors."

"No remains?"

"Not that the guys could identify or recover—the fire and explosion had been so intense."

"How does this all affect the peace process?" asked Mike.

"Very difficult to say, right now. No one has claimed any responsibility—and we cannot possibly make any accusations. We have no real evidence to go on right now—though we do have our suspicions. Canadian involvement in this particular UN mission is approaching its end, and this incident might very well have an impact on how long we actually stay in there."

"I thought Bob spoke well," Kelly offered.

"Yes, that poor family has had so much tragedy," acknowledged Jane. "Gra, look after Trish, please. There's someone over there I must talk to right now."

Jane left them abruptly, walking quickly over to a man standing alone, quite apart from the small groups that still hung around outside the Centre. As she approached, Jane called out his name.

Tony sat disconsolate, nursing his coffee, a half-eaten doughnut on the table before him. Jane had called to him as he stood outside after the ceremony. They had come back into the hall to the kitchen, where some refreshments had been laid out.

They had talked—about Dana—about himself, how he felt. Talking with Jane had helped; he liked Jane, she understood. But she had to leave; now he still felt cold, empty.

He stared out of the window, past the parking lot, seeing nothing. Nothing, that is, outside his mind. And his mind's eye could see only one thing—that image of Dana—that last image he had of her.

No tears now. No; now, cold reality was setting in. She was gone—his angel was gone. The only girl he had ever really loved was gone. He knew long ago that he could never hold her again—he knew, after that first visit to old Mr Hennigan, that he could never keep up with her.

And yet, when he had needed help the most, at the bottom of his pit, she had been there. She had held out her hands and led him upward. The rest had followed. He would never let himself go back to that sickening state again—or would he? Could he be sure he was cured?

Yes, he was, he knew he was. Lookit, he'd been dry for over three years, now. But what was he to do now? Even though he knew she could never be his girl again, she would have been his dearest friend, his secret love, his angel in blue jeans, forever. Now she was gone.

He had struggled to contain his despair at the ceremony. It had been so painful. But Gina had helped him. *Dear Gina,* he thought, *she seems to be the only one left who really cares about me now. And Jane—she has helped too.* He knew Jane was deeply hurt.

He looked down at the coffee cup; the dregs were separating at the bottom. *Dregs,* he thought, *dregs, I'm nothing but dregs.*

Absently, he stood up and walked outside. A cool wind was blowing, scudding low clouds across the sky. He looked at his watch.

Seven-twenty-five. Yeah, he thought, I can get there in time.

He reached the church hall at ten to eight. He went in and down the stairs to the basement. A few people were already there. Tom and Jeff were over by the kitchen counter. Steve and somebody he didn't know were chatting over by the chair stacks, taking out some chairs for sitting on. Gerry was wandering about in the kitchen, fussing over a teapot.

As he caught sight of Tony, Tom left Jeff and came briskly over to Tony. "Tony, I'm sorry to hear the news, I really am. Are you all right?"

"I think so," Tony offered hesitantly.

"I'm glad you've come tonight. We're all deeply saddened, and we want to help you pull through."

"Thanks." Tony forced a smile. He knew he was among friends. These guys had all been through the same sort of pit that he'd been through; they'd all had the same kinds of demons to fight, the same temptations to fall backward into the pit.

But they helped one another, they looked out for one another, they cared for one another. They were conscious of each other's weaknesses, and were there with support—not with criticism. Positive, not negative.

As Tom walked Tony over to the counter, to the coffee urn, others joined them, each offering Tony sympathy and condolences. Several had entered after Tony.

"Hi Tony, I'm Jake," said the stranger Tony had seen on first entering. "I joined the group last week. I'm very sorry to hear your sad news. I do sympathize with you. I lost my wife six months ago."

"Thanks, Jake, I'm sorry for you, too."

"Thanks."

"Shall we grab our cups and take our seats, gentlemen?" Tom

was chivvying them just a little.

The group was soon seated, and Tom was about to start the meeting when a redhead rushed through the doorway, a bundle of papers under one arm, a briefcase in his other hand.

"Sorry I'm late—emergency call came through just as I was about leave."

"That's okay, John, so long as you got here safely, that's what counts," responded Tom calmly.

John found himself a seat, and plonked his papers and case on the adjacent seat. He turned to look around at the company.

Tony was watching him; John's gaze met his. John was on his feet in a flash, bounding back two rows to Tony. John was Tony's sponsor. He had been a tremendous help in Tony's early days with AA. Tony liked him. John was about five years older, and worked at a hospital, a very stressful job.

"Tony, glad to see you tonight. I was devastated when I heard the news—I'm sorry I didn't call you sooner, but I've been down in T.O. for the past few days—got back late last night ..."

Tom was fidgeting. He was one of those guys that worked to a schedule. It was time to start.

"... Let's talk some more after, okay?" said John, quietly.

Tony nodded and gave John a brief smile.

Tom was introducing the first speaker, Evan. Evan had been coming to the meetings for about two months. He had been a manager of a credit union, until his problems with alcohol became too bad, sometime last year.

Tony usually found it very helpful to hear about the problems of others and how they were overcoming them, but tonight he just could not concentrate. All the images of Dana were crowding in, alternating with great surges of emptiness.

Evan was followed by Jack, from another group across town somewhere. Tony had shaken his hand at the beginning, and now he perked up at the new face. But soon his mind was again assailed with hurt and loneliness.

"You okay?" The formal part of the meeting was over. John was speaking.

"Uh? Oh, yeah, I guess."

"Come on, let's get a coffee. I've not had a drink since three this aft."

Tony followed John to the kitchen counter, where Gerry was pouring.

"Two coffees, please, G."

"Coming right up. I've brought some raisin cookies too, if you want to try them." Gerry proffered the plate.

"Thanks," said John, taking two. "This is my supper."

Tony took one. "Thanks, G."

"Don't mention it. Say, John," Gerry lowered his voice, "hope you're getting plenty of food."

John laughed. "Don't worry, G. Yes, I am. Today has been exceptional. Thanks, though."

Gerry smiled and nodded.

"Let's go over to the side there." John directed Tony to a couple of chairs over at the side of the hall.

"I hear there was a memorial service today. Did you go?"

Tony nodded.

"Did it help?"

"Yes and no."

"How yes?"

"Everybody was talking about her—they were all saying good things about her—everything was so emotional."

"How no?"

"It couldn't fill the emptiness. I feel so cold, empty, lost ... God, John, I nearly lost it last night. The old craving started ..."

"What did you do?"

"I called Gina."
"Could she help?"
"Yeah, she was great. We talked for two hours."
"It passed?"
"Yeah."
"Hang in there, my friend."
"Yeah, I know, John, I know. I owe it to Dana."
"Good man."

- 38 -

At last, a break in the clouds; a hint of sunlight was filtering through the trees. The branches were still dripping from the incessant rain of the past several days.

Dana was cold, wet, hungry, and feeling very much alone. But the welcome sunlight gave her a new spirit. During the days of rain, her spirits had ranged from deep despair and near panic to anger and frustration. There had been absolutely nothing she could do. The rain made everywhere so slick and slippery. Even if she were a skilled rock-climber, she couldn't have tackled those cliff faces in that rain.

The rough shelter, while it lasted, had shielded her from some of the rain, but after a couple of days, nothing remained dry. At least the little trickle of water that she was lying beside when she first regained consciousness was now a veritable stream, and she didn't go thirsty. But the downside was she just had to get out of her spot to go pee—not easy on a steep slope in the rain.

She had two small squares of chocolate left. She knew her strength was slipping. But she was physically fit; she put in a lot of time at the gym. Maybe it'll all pay off this time. She popped one of the squares into her mouth and chewed on it.

The sunlight was growing stronger. She felt an inner surge of warmth, of hope. *Yes,* she thought, *yes. I'm not going to shrivel up and die here—I wasn't made to end my days here. I can climb off this ledge, I've got to.*

That image of her mother came into her mind's eye again, that evening when she had first told her parents about her wish to join the Army—the sadness in her mother's eyes, that look she had not understood back then.

And there was Tony, again. He'd occupied much of her thoughts these past days. Images of him blended, merging one with another; fond images, sad images; the alcoholic drop-out, that sickening sight; the joys of their early days together; the rocky times; his road to recovery; the pain and the anguish.

Oh God, what will happen to Tony if I don't get out of this? I can't let him down. I can't drive him back to drink. Oh God, no. I've gotta get out of here. Tony, do I ever need you now. Tony—I love you.

She shuddered, and felt the cold seeping into her again. Stretching her legs out, she realized again just how wet she was. *Maybe, if the sun does come out, I can dry out a bit. It'll let the rocks dry off too.*

She moved over to a different spot for a slight change of scene, and began to reconsider her options again, for the umpteenth time. Itemize each option, then shoot it down—that had been her process so far. But this time she took a different tack.

Lookit, Munro, you've gotta get yourself off this ledge and back in the mainstream—you've got these options, and no more. Choose one, and let's get the hell outta here. If it fails, it's curtains for you, but no worse than staying here.

Okay, ma'am. One—upward—near vertical, no notion of what is up there, nor how far up, seems to have an overhang further up—that would kind of rule it out, for now.

Two—downward—down to the precipice and try to climb down— no way of knowing how to get off the shelf onto the rock face—can't see any footholds or handholds from the shelf—could just drop and pray. No, not first choice.

Three—go left on to the cliff-face—yeah, well maybe, but I don't see how yet.

Four—go right. Jeez. I don't know. But something stirred her to rise, and make her way to the right. The trees thinned as the ledge narrowed.

She hung onto the last but one tree and surveyed the scene yet again—the cliff-face stretching away before her; below were more craggy rocks and clumps of trees, and the river. Yes, the sky was clearing. There was blue sky, and sunshine.

She crouched down, wedging herself against the tree, and waited for things to dry out. She gazed across the rocks, looking for a strategy. Some crags beyond the cliff-face looked more reasonable. They were partly covered in trees, but the rock faces were not vertical.

Maybe if I can get across to those crags, I can clamber down.

At last, the moment came. A burst of sunlight triggered her move. She felt her pulse thumping as she reached for the last tree on the ledge, steadied herself, moved her foot over to a narrow foothold, tested it, and moved her weight.

One at a time, came the soft, coaxing voices of Rory and Caleb in her mind. *Test each one.*

She moved her hand to a crevice. *Good. Now the other foot, fine.* Her face was only a hand span from the rock, looking for another handhold. *There, now, let go of the tree.* She was on her way.

Hand by foot, hand by foot, she slowly moved over the rock-face, edging slowly downward, but mainly to her left. Her confidence grew with each move. Her concentration was intense. Never had she examined rocks at such close quarters. Her rib was okay, so long as she didn't hang too long on her right hand.

Take the weight on the left and use the legs. Agh! Her reflexes kicked in as she hung on tightly, her left foot swinging, searching wildly for a hold, as the rock under it crumbled away. Her pulse rate shot up, pounding in her ears, her heart thumping. She levered herself up with both arms, to allow her foot to reach a new hold.

Luckily, new holds appeared. She began to relax a little and rest, putting her weight back onto her feet, steadying with her hands. Her rib was hurting again now—that panicked heave must have overstressed it.

She took stock. Carefully, she looked across and down the rock-face. About six metres down, there was a good ledge about ten centimetres wide that ran across the face.

If I can get to that, I can really move, she thought. But her muscles were starting to protest; they kept going into that quivering state of overstress.

Slowly, she moved each limb. Holds were not hard to find, but after that one panic, she was leery of every one, and tested it thoroughly.

At last she reached the ledge, and was able to traverse quickly. At the other end, the rocks were much less vertical, and she soon reached a safe, almost level, area. She collapsed in a heap, totally exhausted, physically and mentally.

It was nearly dark when she awoke. It took a few moments for her to realize where she was—that she was free. She looked back up the cliff and shuddered. She burst into tears. She sobbed and sobbed and sobbed. That had been the greatest ordeal in her life, and she had overcome, she had won. They were tears of relief, but they did not stop easily.

At last, she wiped her face with her sleeve and took in her new surroundings as the light dimmed. The rocks fell away gradually, down to the river about a hundred metres below. Trees were gathered in clumps. The last light in the sky glinted on the river a little way upstream, silhouetting something angular in the water.

Dana found a hollow in the rocks with some moss and small bushes, and nestled down for the night—free once again.

Having slept for so long after her climb down the cliff, she did not need sleep now that it was dark. But she knew she could not move. She listened to the wind in the trees, a gentle wind now, rustling the leaves. Occasionally, she heard the call of a night-bird, an eerie call, unnerving at first.

In the darkness, her mind began to race. Now that she was free from the prison of the ledge, she had her life ahead to plan. How should she set about finding her way back to real safety, to the Base?

She knew the general geography of the region—the river was flowing basically south-westward. So if she could follow this gorge downstream, she would eventually reach the plain, and so-called friendly territory. But that was too far—she couldn't last that long—not without some relief, some food and shelter.

No, there has to be some point to break off and make for Betsevac Base, overland, and just hope that none of the rebels are around. She remembered her map, feeling inside her pockets for it. Not there. She puzzled for a moment, but could not remember why it was missing.

Daybreak came. Dana roused, and was soon down at the water's edge. She remembered that dark silhouette from the night before, and eased her way upstream along the shoreline, sometimes rocky, sometimes pebbly. She stumbled over boulders, slipping on greasy vegetation, until there she was, gazing in horror at the source of the silhouette.

There at the edge of the river lay a mangled, blackened mass of tortured metal, blasted open by explosion and fire. Trees on the riverbank were burnt and scorched—there was an overpowering smell of damp ashes and burnt oil. Emotion overwhelmed her, tore at her heart—it was her vehicle, the Coyote. There was the number, scorched, but just readable.

Her legs weakened, and she fell to her knees. *Oh God, no—No!*

Jacob, Randy, Schooner, you poor guys! Tears were streaming down her face as she stood up, trembling, and edged a few steps along the shore, along the broken rock at this place.

Suddenly, her attention was drawn to something lying in the shallow water. As she approached, her stomach retched at the sight—the remains of an arm, badly burnt, with bits of blackened cloth.

In horror, she turned away, not wanting, yet wanting, to find more. Despairing, she slumped down on a rock.

My guys, are they all gone? What did happen? How did I escape? Why can't I remember?

❊❊❊

She stumbled through bushes into a clearing. Ahead was a trail, and beyond that, an old gate. At last, at last; signs of people at last. She collapsed on the soft grass.

Dana was close to her limit. How far she had walked and stumbled, first along the river, then cross-country—how many days since her escape from the cliff-face—she did not know. Apart from a few berries here and there that she had dared to eat, and the few squares of chocolate, she had not eaten for many days, now. She was very weak, bruised, scratched, and sore. Her feet were blistered from being continually wet inside her boots. Her hair was matted and tangled. Her combats were torn, and plastered in mud.

She did not know how long she lay there, nor did she care. At last she had found some sign of people. *Please God, let them be friendly,* she thought. Slowly she raised herself up, and painfully limped along the trail toward the gate …

Dana opened her eyes—and tensed in surprise. Her body went into reflex fight mode, and her right arm came up quickly. She tried to sit up, but her strength was not there.

A face, an old face, was close to her left side. It smiled. A hand came over her forehead and gently stroked her hair.

Where was she? What was going on? She tried to lift her head and body. Another hand came up to the face and put its forefinger on the lips, as if to say 'be still'. The lips were smiling.

Dana relaxed back down. The face turned and spoke—a woman's voice, old and wavering, the sounds unintelligible. A deeper voice responded. Dana sensed a shadow come over her.

Her eyes moved as she began to take in her surroundings. The face took form as part of a body. Behind stood another body, its face old and furrowed, its eyes smiling. Gradually, a corner of a wall, of a room, took form. A crucifix hung on the wall. She turned her head to see the couple more clearly. The woman took her hand and squeezed it gently, all the while stroking her hair.

The man offered her a mug. Dana raised herself slightly and took it gratefully. The warm, sweet liquid was like nectar as it trickled down her throat. She smiled a thank-you.

The man and the woman smiled and nodded their heads. Dana felt reassured, in spite of having no idea where she was. *Am I in safe hands, or is this a trap? Whatever, I need the food and drink.*

Gradually, she felt strength returning as she drank the welcome drink. She tried to sit up. The woman helped her turn to sit on the side of the simple low bed.

They were an old couple, both backs were stooped, the woman with white hair, the man's still dark. Their clothes were sombre brown and black. It was a simple room, with a stove and table and chairs, a low ceiling, and small window, typical of some of the small farmers' homes she had seen while on patrol.

The woman spoke to her in words she did not recognize. Dana smiled and shook her head. The woman grinned and repeated the words, making signs of eating with her hands. Dana realized at once and nodded her head vigorously.

Gently, the man helped her stand, and led her to a chair at the table. The woman placed a bowl of soup in front of her. The man placed some bread at her side. Only then did Dana really appreciate just how hungry she was.

"Thank-you," she mouthed as she began to eat. The couple nodded their heads again, all the while smiling at her.

When she had finished the bowl of soup laced with vegetables, the man placed some thin slices of meat before her, and some vegetables she did not recognize. No matter. She ate them all—and then more of the sweet nectar.

As they sat watching her, she signed that she was full, and again mouthed a thank-you. The woman smiled and clapped her hands. The man nodded his head in agreement and stood up.

He moved to Dana's side and touched her Canada flag patch. Surprised—and rather concerned—she turned her head, watching him cautiously.

He walked over to a small shelf on the wall, and took down a picture in a frame. He brought it back to the table. The main picture was a faded photograph of a man, probably in his twenties, she thought, and stuck into the bottom left corner was a small cameo photo of a little girl, maybe ten or so.

In the bottom right corner was a small decal, showing the CN tower in Toronto backed by the maple leaf emblem.

Dana pointed to the decal and up to her Canada flag emblem, then back to the man and girl and then to the couple. She looked quizzically at the couple as they nodded vigorously. She understood—they had a Canada connection.

The man brought out a piece of paper and an old-fashioned pen and laid them on the table. He produced a small bottle of dark liquid.

Ink, realized Dana, *how quaint.* He flattened the paper, dipped the pen into the ink, and began to draw a map. Dana watched intently.

First, he drew a rough rectangle near the centre of the left side. Nearby, he drew a long sinuous line down the page, passing the rectangle to the left, and then doubled it.

Dana looked at him quizzically. He leaned back in his chair, pointed to the rectangle, and signed with his arms, pointing to the walls. *This house,* realized Dana.

She pointed to the double line, and looked at him. He made billowing wave motions with his hands. *Of course, the river.* Dana nodded her head.

The man continued, drawing a long, winding line from the house across the page. Then he began another line from near the top, crossing the first line, continuing on down. At the crossing, he drew a rough, small circle, and wrote a word. Dana did not understand it.

He drew another line from near the river at the top, slanting across the other lines and ending near the bottom left corner. There, he drew another rough circle. Dana saw that these lines must be roads.

Carefully, the man was drawing something in the last circle. Dana was puzzled. She was, in reality, drained, mentally, physically, emotionally. Her mind was not at its best; she couldn't catch his point.

He smiled, pointed to his last drawing, and pointed to her flag patch. *Of course, of course,* he'd drawn a maple leaf, difficult at the best of times. Dana laughed. The man and the woman laughed, too.

The man picked up the pen again, and by the side of the maple leaf, he wrote something. Dana looked at it carefully. It was difficult, but then it clicked. *Betsevac.* That's what it said. *Our base!*

She pointed to it and then to herself. The woman clapped her hands, and the man nodded his head. Then he drew another line, sweeping across from the top left of the map, curving under the first crossroads, between them and Betsevac, and across to the river. Right across the map, above that line, he wrote. Dana watched closely.

A-n-j-a-s-t-a-s. Anjastas. *Oh, no. The rebels.* She looked at the couple. Their faces were downcast as the man swept his hand slowly over the map indicating the sweep of the Anjastas. Dana's heart sank.

Her face obviously showed her feeling, for the woman took her hand and led her to the small window, pointing. It was dark outside. The woman made the sleeping sign with her hands, and pointed to herself, the man, and Dana. She raised six fingers, one by one, and repeated the sleep sign, followed by a wide sweeping action with her arms over her head.

Dana nodded vigorously. *Yes, we sleep for six hours and then morning.* The man motioned her back to the map. He pointed to all three of them and then passed his finger on the map from the house along the road through the first crossroads with the circle—*maybe that's a town,* thought Dana—onward to the next crossroads, and down to the Betsevac base. Dana understood.

The woman took Dana's arm and motioned her to come with her. She gently led Dana outside into the darkness. Dana felt a soft breeze against her face. Across a small courtyard was a little cabin. The woman smiled and offered Dana to proceed.

Of course, the privy. It was dark, smelly, and awkward. The woman was waiting, and led Dana back. Inside, the man had spread out some bedding in one corner. The woman led Dana to the bed where she had first wakened.

Dana made motions of protest, querying what the man and woman would do for sleeping. The woman reassured her that they would use the bedding in the corner. Dana was their guest, and she would have the bed. Soon the light was out, and very quickly Dana was asleep.

It was light when Dana awoke. She sat up at once. The man was sitting at the table. Smiling, he turned toward her and, holding out his hand, beckoned her to the table to eat. She obliged, and sat down.

The door opened and in came the woman, carrying a pail of water. On the table were bread, cheese, milk, and some hard-boiled eggs.

Dana broke off a piece of the crusty bread, took an egg, and a piece of cheese. They tasted so good. The woman came over to the table with another mug, giving it to Dana. Dana nodded her thanks and poured some milk. She sipped it. So different—so smooth, and warm, creamy—it must be very fresh.

After the meal was over, the woman went to a big closet in the far corner and brought out a black garment, a cloak. She put it over Dana's shoulders, wrapping it around and pulling it straight. Then she brought a dark headscarf and, signing for Dana to kneel down, bound up the scarf around Dana's head, covering her hair, with the scarf ends hanging down over her neck.

The man brought over an old, chipped mirror for Dana to see herself. Dana nodded in agreement and smiled—she looked like a peasant girl. Fortunately, the cloak was so long it covered her legs and hid her booted feet.

The woman then began what Dana thought was close to a charade. First, she touched Dana's arm to gain her attention, and pointed first at Dana and then at herself. She began to rub her stomach and groan, her knees sinking, as she slowly lowered herself to the ground, where she lay curled, groaning. The man joined in, pointing first at his wife and then at Dana.

At first, Dana was at a loss, but at last it dawned on her. They wanted her to act as if she were ill. *Okay.* She groaned, sighed, rubbed her stomach, fell to the ground, the works.

The woman clapped her hands, nodding her head and smiling. Dana relaxed and sat up. The man helped her to stand but, continuing the act, put Dana's arm up around his neck. The woman came to her other side, as if to help bear her weight.

As a trio, they moved to the door. Outside, the act continued. They led her across the courtyard, which Dana could now see was part of a small farmyard. A few chickens scratched over by a low stone building, and a pile of straw lay by a low, crumbling wall.

They were making their way toward an old, battered car. There were only two doors, so it was a struggle for Dana to clamber into the backseat. The man indicated for her to lie down across the seat.

The car pulled out onto a bumpy road—at least, Dana assumed that was so. All she could do was try to interpret the sounds of the engine, the grinding gearbox, the bumps on the road that seemed to be transmitted directly to her bones, and the swaying as the car rounded an endless sequence of bends. She recalled how winding the man had made that road on the map last night.

The journey seemed endless, but at last she sensed by the frequent stopping, turning, and starting, that they were meeting other roads. But then the car stopped, and the man turned off the engine.

Dana tensed. What was going on? A door opened, and the woman got out. Dana peered up to try to see. The man was turning to her, his finger on his lips, the other hand telling her to stay low.

Dana could hear voices outside—some seemed excited. Carefully, she peeked out from under her scarf. She could see the stone wall of a building, a window, and the edge of a red tile roof ...

Then, the back of someone darkened her view, someone with a gun slung on his shoulder. She retreated under the scarf. She could hear agitated voices.

Suddenly, the door opened, and the woman climbed in. The engine started, and they were moving. Carefully, Dana moved aside the scarf.

The woman was watching her, and burst into a grin, waving a large, corked bottle in her hand. She made signs of pouring some of the dark liquid inside onto a spoon and offering it to Dana, pointing to her stomach. Dana relaxed and smiled. This couple really were putting a lot at stake for her.

Abruptly, the car stopped again, and the engine turned off. *What now?* she thought. There was shouting from outside and responses shouted from inside; the windows were open. The driver, the old man, got out, shutting the door.

Suddenly, the door was wrenched open and something hard thrust into the backseat, into her; she stifled a sound. She could feel it—the business end of a rifle.

The old woman was now yelling, clearly cursing, though Dana understood not a word. The gun was retracted. A driver, the old man Dana prayed, got in, the engine started, and they were on their way again. She felt the old woman reach back and pat her leg. Dana moved aside the scarf, and her eyes met the kindly gaze of the old woman.

The journey continued. The road was better now, and the drone of the engine made Dana feel sleepy, but she knew she must stay alert—who knew what might happen next.

She felt something poking her and looked up. The woman was offering her some bread. She took it gratefully. She sensed that the car was going more slowly, and became aware of an unpleasant odour.

The car stopped, its engine still running. And then she heard the cows. She smiled to herself. Even in a war-ravaged country like this, some basics can still go on. Soon, they were on their way again.

At last, the car came to a halt, and the engine stopped. Dana tensed. What next? The doors opened, and the man and the woman both got out. The woman moved her seat, and beckoned Dana to get out.

Uncertain of what would come next, Dana clambered out. The man and the woman were standing right in front of her as she straightened up her body. Gently, they turned her round and pointed.

To her surprise and joy, a hundred metres away was the gate and guard post of CFB Betsevac. She turned back to the couple. They were all smiles. She embraced them both, long and hard. This was almost too much. Tears fell from her eyes as she realized the man and the woman were weeping, too.

They had to part. The man indicated to her to go to the base. She embraced them both again, waved farewell, turned, and walked, as a peasant girl, toward the gate. Halfway there, she turned to wave. The couple and the car were gone.

- 39 -

Caroline Munro turned her head at the sound of the doorbell. So many times in the past days had that sound been the beginning of yet another difficult visit with friends and family, and strangers too, all coming with the best of intentions to offer their sympathy to Bob and herself.

Of course she appreciated their coming, their concern, their sadness and horror at the loss of Dana. But it was so hard to cope. She had felt so empty, so cold—as if there was no purpose anymore.

But she and Bob had come closer to one another, closer than they had been for a very long time. She knew he was taking it badly too, but differently. The shock, the tragedy, seemed to have brought him out of himself, out of the quiet, almost shadowy person he had been since Bryce's death. Maybe it was by way of helping her, helping to shield her from the social niceties that seemed to be necessary at times like these. She was proud of what he had said at the memorial service—she knew he spoke from the heart.

Bob came into the room. "Hem—Caroline, dear, we have visitors."

Caroline looked up. These visitors were very welcome. They really had been supportive. "Hello, Kelly, Mike. Come on in."

"Thanks, Caroline," Kelly sat on the sofa with Caroline. "I hope you and Bob don't mind, but Mike and I were just sitting there feeling lost, and we knew your family visitors were out tonight, so we thought we would come over to see if there was anything we could do to help. If you two want to have the time to yourselves, just say. You know we'll understand."

"I'm glad you've come, both of you. I must say, I did wonder, when the doorbell rang—there've been so many people. And it's been so hard to talk with some of them—I guess they've wanted to show their concern, but after they've said that, they've seemed lost for words—which puts the onus back on Bob and me. Don't get me wrong—we do appreciate what people have said and done—but it's been a real drain on us. But you two, we know we can talk easily with you."

"I know what you mean, that's what happened to me, when I lost Mum and Dad and Ted so quickly. And at that time, I really didn't have anyone to turn to for help. I really was alone."

"Can Ah get you anything?" Bob was hovering by the doorway through to the kitchen.

"No thanks, Bob. Come and sit down, relax, don't feel you have to do anything special at all for us."

"Okay." Bob came over to the group and sat on the edge of his easy chair. "Mike, if ye have jist a moment, Ah've got a wee problem downstairs you might take a look at for me. It's the electronic dust-trap thingamajig."

"Sure, lead on. You mind?" Mike was asking Kelly and Caroline. They waved him on. Mike and Bob disappeared downstairs.

"Kelly, dear, I just have to tell you something. I don't know what it means, and I don't understand. But last night we were in bed. Everything was dark and quiet. Bob had finally dropped off to sleep, and was on his side, so he was quiet. I couldn't go to sleep. It's been awful these past nights—thank goodness I've not had to go into school each day.

"Anyway, I don't think I had dropped off, but it was like a dream—but then, it couldn't have been, because I remember distinctly hearing the furnace motor cut in as it was happening—anyway, I suddenly had this strange feeling of relief about Dana, a feeling of uplift. It really was uncanny. Kelly, I don't know what to make of it, I really don't."

Kelly put her hand out and rested it on Caroline's arm. "Our feelings and our emotions do lots of strange things to us at a time like this. I had all kinds of strange thoughts, some quite frightening, others warm and reassuring, after Ted was drowned. I don't know, some of them I'm sure were dreams, but I think others came from constantly thinking about him and the life we'd had together. It was a long time before they started to fade. Even now, sometimes, a subtle feeling comes back—maybe when I see something, or do something we used to do together. But you know, Caroline, Mike is wonderful, he's so understanding, and he knows I love him."

"I can see you two were meant for each other." Caroline laughed. She felt so much better now, it amazed her. Whatever it was, the stress was falling away; she felt light-hearted—and yet, still, she felt guilty for feeling that way.

"Well," said Mike, shaking his head, still holding the guts of the electronic air-filter in his hands, "it doesn't look good, Bob."

"No, Ah guess not." Bob was glum. "Just something else tae go wrong."

"But not too serious. Look, let me take it into work tomorrow, and I'll get Gilles to have a good look at this capacitor here—it looks to me as if it might have blown. We might be able to replace it, if that's all it is."

"Go ahead, it's nae use as it is. What's a new unit cost?"

"Oh, about two hundred or so, I think. Not too sure, as I don't deal too much with the cost side of things—I just fix 'em or replace 'em."

"That's the way it was in the Air Force."

"I didn't know you were in the Air Force, Bob."

"Aye, a long time ago now." Bob sighed.

"What did you do, if you don't mind me asking?"

"Ground crew, CF104s—Starfighters—they were challenging birds."

"Wasn't that the one that …"

"Aye, the newspapers called it the 'widow-maker'. That's the one, all right."

"Was it really that bad?"

"No, but we lost a few real good guys."

Mike waited. He sensed there was more to come.

Bob was wrestling to say something. "A—Ah lost a real good friend, a real good officer …"

Mike waited patiently.

"Ma plane was one of the ones we lost."

"I'm sorry, Bob; I didn't know, or I wouldn't have pressed the topic."

Bob grimaced a smile. "Dinnae worry, Mike. It's a thing Ah should've got over years ago, but Ah guess Ah never have. He was a great guy, was Flight Lieutenant Crowther—Roy."

Bob fell into a wistful silence. Mike waited.

"Y'know, Mike, when Dana first told me she wanted to join the Army, she started off by asking me about ma time in the Air Force—y'know, what was it like. But Ah jist couldna tell her the real story. Ah made some half-assed comment about there being some good times and some god-awful times and left it at that …"

The sound of the phone ringing broke Bob's sentence. "Ah guess Ah'd best go see who's callin' now."

Bob and Mike made their way back upstairs.

Caroline picked up the phone. "Hello?"

"Is this Mrs Munro?" a female voice asked.

"Yes, who's calling, please?"

"This is Master Warrant Smith; we met the other day, ma'am. I have some very good news for you. Please hold the line; I need to patch you through …"

Caroline held on, her pulse racing. *What on earth is happening now?*

"Mrs Munro?" It was a male voice now, a bit fainter.

"Yes, may I ask what is happening?"

"Of course. I have someone who would very much like to speak with you. Just a sec."

Caroline's heart was really racing now.

"Hi, Mom! It's me, Dana, I'm alive."

"Oh my god …" Caroline's legs gave way, as she sank back onto the sofa. She waved the phone toward her husband. "It's … Dana."

"Put it on speaker."

Caroline fumbled for the button, but Mike reached out and pushed it for her.

"Are you there, Mom? I know it's a big shock, but I really am here, and I'm okay. Is Dad there?"

"Aye, Ah'm here, my love. This is wonderful. Where are you, pet?"

"I'm at the base here, Betsevac. I'm in the hospital being checked out."

"This is amazing, dear." Caroline was regaining her composure. "It's a miracle. What happened to you?"

"Mom, it's a long story, and I don't really know all that happened. I'm a bit fuzzy on it. Can we talk about it later, please?"

"Kelly and Mike are here too, dear."

"Yeah, this is fantastic news, Dana, great to hear you," Mike added.

"Kelly here. So relieved to hear your voice."

"And it's great to hear all of you. I thought I would never see you again. Er ... my doctor is saying I need to close off now. I'll be able to come home soon. Love to everybody."

"This really is a miracle. Bye, my dear, we look forward to you coming," said Caroline.

"Bye then, my sweet, we love you," added Bob.

❋❋❋

Dave Adkins was pleased, very pleased. Once again, the Brewster community had shown its stuff and put on a party, this time to celebrate Dana's return. As soon as he had suggested the idea, it had spread quickly through the Gardens and the Mews, and the response had been immediate. People were overjoyed, and wanted to show it.

The contrast to the preceding days of sadness, emptiness, darkness, and gloom was complete. If the community had shown the full extent of its sympathy and caring at the Memorial Service, then it had outdone itself in joy and thanksgiving this day.

Even newcomer families, who knew little of the role of Dana in the Gardens community years ago, had contributed. The Hennigan Centre had never seen a celebration so spontaneous, so heartfelt, not even at the gala opening back at the beginning.

Dana was overwhelmed, and so was her family. Poor Caroline, her mother, had burst into tears as she entered the hall. Dana was speechless at the ovation she received. During the course of the afternoon, she had managed to talk with just about everyone there.

Dave felt especially thankful for her safe return. He was forever grateful to Dana. Without her inspired initiative in the first place, he wouldn't have this job of Administrator of the Centre. He could honestly say that these years at the Centre had been the most contented years of his life. The Centre had gone from strength to strength. Dana had come back to visit whenever she could, though in these last years her visits had been fewer, as her army career took her far away.

Whenever she had dropped in at a Youth Council meeting, a spark was ignited, and something new and good came out of it. But then, he recalled the last council meeting, after the tragic news had come through. The spark, the fire, had gone—nothing new could be done that night; they could only remember.

But now, life had returned. All was well.

"This is a great sight, Dave."

Dave turned toward the voice, at his left. Graham Stennings had joined him. "Oh, hi there, Graham. Yep, it's real good to see her back. She's really something, eh?"

"You bet. You know, it's marvellous how even the young kids seem to take to her, considering that she hasn't really been around much during their lifetimes."

"Yeah, goes to show how much charisma she has, and how the older people have passed on her image to the little ones."

"Oh—hello there, Caroline—and Dwayne, too." Caroline Munro and Dwayne Hampden had quietly joined them.

Caroline laughed. "David, I really do want to thank you for organizing this party. It's been wonderful. Bob and I are so grateful to everyone, and I know Dana is too."

"It was the least we could do, Caroline," said Dave. "It's just so great to have her back."

"It's a miracle—it really is. You can't ever appreciate what this has done for Bob and me. Sorry." She turned away to dab tears in her eyes. "It's just overwhelming. I feel so happy and relieved."

Jane had just joined the group; she took Caroline's arm. "Don't worry about a few tears. We know how you must feel, even though we can't fully appreciate it."

"Thanks."

Dwayne spoke. "Caroline, if you don't mind me asking, have they figured out how Dana survived?"

Caroline took a deep breath. "We-ell, so far as they've been able to piece bits together from reports from the other vehicles behind hers and what Dana has remembered—you know she has a mental blank, and doesn't know what happened right at the time of the explosion. And please, please don't press her on that when you're talking with her, it's probably for her own good that she can't remember.

"Anyway, it seems that as they were approaching the top of a hill, Dana was in the lead vehicle, standing half-out of the hatch, glancing back at the following ones. Suddenly, there was a great explosion, and her vehicle was blown upward and over the cliff edge to the side.

"From one of the other vehicles behind, someone saw Dana's overturning as it fell, and then it crashed against a crag, careened off, and down into the gorge. There was another explosion, and black smoke rose up from below. They can only surmise that Dana was thrown from the vehicle as it hit that crag on the way down."

"Wow." Dwayne sucked in his breath.

"But then it seems she was trapped on a ledge on the cliff-face, and it took her many days to get off and be found by some locals, who drove her to the base. She seems all very woolly about it, and not eager to talk."

"Quite an ordeal," Dwayne said quietly, quite moved.

"Yes, it has been, for all of us." Caroline smiled wistfully.

"But this is so fantastic, after what we've all gone through these past days," said Jane. "We're so happy for you."

"Thank you again, you've all been so kind and supporting throughout. And Graham, we really did appreciate Reverend Olney organizing the ceremony, and Captain Legendre and the other soldiers coming to us. Were they going to the other families?"

"Actually, the captain was visiting each of the other families, but who went with him depended on where. Two of the crew came from Nova Scotia, and one from Saskatchewan. Chaplains in those regions would go with him."

"And those poor families have no joy." Caroline wiped her eyes.

Tony and Gina slipped into the hall, into a wall of sound—of voices and laughter and music.

"There she is." Gina motioned with her arm.

"Okay, but I don't want to butt in when she's with people."

"But Tone, if you want to talk with her, you'll have to. Everybody wants to talk with her today."

"Yeah, I know." Tony knew this was not going to be the right time—there were too many people vying for Dana's attention. But he desperately wanted to talk with her. When he and Gina had gone to the Munro house the day Dana arrived home, she had given him such a warm embrace. But they couldn't talk, not then. Her parents were there of course, and some relatives too, and other people kept coming to the door to welcome Dana home.

No, he knew he would have to wait. And he wasn't at all sure what her reaction would be. After all, he'd made a disgusting mess of his life—but she had been his angel, she had pulled him up, she had saved him.

A sudden stir and drop in the sound level caught his attention. Dana was rushing from the group she had been with into the washrooms. Gina put her hand in front of Tony.

"Wait there!" Gina followed Dana.

Tony stood there, puzzled. *Is something wrong?* What had Gina seen that he hadn't?

After a few minutes, Dana appeared, looking decidedly unhappy, and walked quickly toward the exit doors. Gina had followed her out of the washrooms, and rejoined Tony.

"Go with her," whispered Gina. Tony's eyes were following Dana as she left the hall. He hesitated. Gina nudged him. "Go on, Tone, go to her—she needs help."

Tony squeezed his sister's arm and made toward the door.

Outside, Dana was sitting on one of the park benches along the sidewalk to the parking lot. She was staring vacantly into the distance.

"Mind if I join you, Dan?" Tony was apologetic.

Dana looked up and smiled tearfully. She patted the bench beside her. Tony sat down. They sat in silence for several minutes. He could sense that something was troubling her, but hesitated to pry. He felt the urge to offer help, but could not bring himself to speak.

At last, she turned her face. He could see the tears in her eyes. "Tone, I just had to come outside. It was such a wonderful party, with everyone so happy to see me. And I was happy to see them too—but ..."

She lowered her head. "I just can't forget my guys that didn't survive. How can I be happy when their families are so devastated? It's just not right. I should be helping their families, their parents, their brothers and sisters, not here celebrating like this. If only we'd not been on that damn road ..."

"Dan, you can't take any blame, you're not at fault. Look, we're all happy that you survived—"

The sounds of people coming out of the Centre interrupted Tony. They were joking and laughing.

"Bye, Dana. Glad you're home safe!"

"Bye, Dan. Bye."

"Great party, Dan. You take it easy now."

"Bye, Dana, see you soon."

"Bye, everyone, thanks," Dana responded, weakly.

The group passed on toward the Gardens.

"Look, Dan," Tony continued. "We're all sorry for the other guys and their families, it's real sad. But that can't stop us all being happy that you're here with us, an' it shouldn't stop you being happy to be alive."

Dana forced a smile, and rubbed her eyes with a tissue. More sounds distracted her. A group of children was being shepherded out of the Centre. They all waved to Dana and Tony as they passed.

"Bye, everybody. Thanks for coming."

Dana turned back to Tony. "Can we go for a walk, please? Away from here?"

Tony, surprised at her request, agreed.

Slowly, they strolled across the grass toward the line of the old track-bed. The bushes and trees had thickened out considerably over the years. Tony's thoughts went back to those days, years ago now, he realized, when they had first walked together down this path. How he wished that they could be as they were then.

They turned onto the trail and ambled along in silence, Tony brushing aside light branches from time to time.

Suddenly, he felt Dana's hand grasp his, at his side. He gave it a squeeze. She responded.

They continued on in silence, reaching the old bridge pier. There, Dana released his hand and sat down, her legs folding under her. Tony sat, too. Together, they watched the water swirling around the rocks that protruded up from the stream-bed.

Birds were flitting around the trees on the opposite bank. Leaves rustled in the light wind. Once again, he felt that longing deep inside. He looked at Dana as she continued to gaze into the waters—the light playing on wisps of her hair, gently moving in the breeze, her now-soft breathing moving her body so slightly, the shapes he had known so well, the cute angle of her nose ... and yet, he sensed the anguish she must be going through.

But deep down, he knew the time had come, this was it.

"Dan, if it wasn't for you, I wouldn't be alive now." He'd said it, at last. It sounded so stilted, the way it had come out; it had broken a beautiful silence, but he had been wanting to say it for so long. Now, having said it, he worried that he had destroyed the moment. Dana didn't move. She continued to gaze at the waters below.

"Tony," she said softly, not turning her gaze. "If you only knew how it was that you saved my life, too."

He was puzzled, but knew he could not ask now. He watched as the light played on her hair and cheek. She was the same girl, even though the years had passed for both of them.

"Dana, I love you."

Slowly, she turned to face him. Her eyes were sparkling as they met his. She leaned forward to embrace him. "And I love you too."

Tony had no idea how long they embraced, and it didn't matter. It felt so great to be holding her.

At last, she grasped his hand, and together they stood up. As she looked up to his face, he reached down and kissed her. She returned the kiss, pressing hard.

Slowly, they turned and started back along the trail, holding hands. After a few steps, Dana stopped. She was looking downward. Tony watched her. Slowly, she lifted her face to his. Looking into her eyes, he could see the tears forming again. He squeezed her hand.

"Tony, there is something I must do, but I cannot do it alone. I must go to the families of my guys, I really must. Will you come with me, please?"

Tony felt the urge to hold her, to support her. He sensed the tension in her. "Yes, I will."

Her eyes sparkled, the teardrops glistening. She grasped both his hands. "Tony, can we be together for always?"

His heart skipped a beat.

"Yes."

ENVOI

- 40 -

Dwayne Hampden pulled his coat collar up around his neck as he walked up the slope toward the barricades set up for crowd control at the side of the roadway in Confederation Square. It was a cool morning, just above freezing, but a brilliant sun shone in a clear blue sky, with the promise of warmth by midday—early November in Ottawa.

He had come early so he could select a front-row spot by a barricade, from which he would have a good view of the ceremony. He knew he would not see all the details of the wreath-laying at the foot of the National War Memorial, but that was not his main reason for being there.

Not totally unexpected, he was nonetheless surprised by how many people were already there. He soon selected his spot. From there, he would have good views of the parades, and would see the arrivals of the dignitaries; yet he would not have the sun in his eyes. He could see the Cenotaph through the lower branches of a large tree across the street.

This was not going to be a normal day. Just three weeks ago, the city—indeed, the country—had been shocked by the actions of a lone gunman who had shot and killed a soldier on ceremonial guard duty at the Tomb of the Unknown Soldier beside the War Memorial, with subsequent shootings in the Parliament buildings nearby.

A few days later, Dwayne had stood with hundreds of others on a highway overpass to pay tribute to the young soldier as his funeral motorcade passed by on its way to the soldier's hometown. And in Quebec, a soldier had been deliberately run down and killed by a car driven by a radicalized crazy.

These tragic events had stimulated an outpouring of grief, of support, of patriotic fervor across the country. There was sure to be a bigger crowd than usual here this year at the Remembrance Day ceremony.

Dwayne looked around. Public Works men were busy adjusting some barricades. Paramedics were setting up their stations. Sound technicians were working up near the Tomb of the Unknown Soldier. Military personnel were moving about purposefully. Legion members were assisting and ushering frail veterans and other special guests to positions close to the Cenotaph. Photographers and media people were prominent. He could see the booms of television cameras sweeping across the scene. There was a sense of business, of action, of purpose.

But unlike previous years, armed security personnel were very evident. Dwayne's quick scan over the scene showed yellow jackets everywhere: police, auxiliaries, and military police, all visibly armed. And then, also, he could see the plain-clothes security, strategically placed, greatcoats unbuttoned, eyes watching everyone and everywhere.

He gazed up at the buildings behind and above him, overlooking the square. *They must have been searched and secured*, he thought. He settled down for the long wait, satisfied that all appeared to be in order, but feeling a tad apprehensive nonetheless.

Angel in Blue Jeans

Dwayne was confident he would be okay; Elizabeth, his wife, had not been so sure. He was seventy-eight now, and in good health. She was two years younger, but not in good shape, not able to cope with such a challenge, and she was naturally concerned that Dwayne would find the long period of standing too much for him. But she would not hold him back—it meant so much to him.

"Make sure you have a hot drink after, and use your cell phone if you have a problem," she had insisted.

The Peace Tower Carillon was playing familiar tunes, relayed throughout the square on the sound system speakers. He was listening to the bells when he sensed a presence near him—more than a presence, in fact. He glanced slightly to the right. A couple of paces away stood a man wearing a grubby greatcoat, a small haversack on a strap over one shoulder and across his chest, and on his head a tattered beret with a badge, with grizzled unkempt greying hair and ragged beard. He wore fingerless, woollen gloves.

Dwayne quickly turned his head back to the front. The smell was sickening. Uncomfortable, Dwayne pondered his next action.

Then suddenly the man spoke, not to Dwayne, but to the air. "I told you I would come, Hal, like I always do."

Dwayne froze. The silence seemed eternal.

Then the man pulled a small flask out of a pocket, took a swig from it. His next words sent a chill down Dwayne's spine: "I'll never forget, Hal. Be here next year." The man turned and moved away, as Dwayne watched him hobble unsteadily on worn, down-at-the-heel boots. A yellow-jacketed security cop was watching him, too.

Dwayne shuddered. His feelings were torn between disgust and sympathy. He was appalled by the stench he had experienced and by the appearance of the guy, but he was moved by the expression of an apparently deep emotion and memory of someone, maybe a relative or fellow soldier—Dwayne guessed that the beret with cap badge meant that the man had been in the army.

The crowd was growing rapidly now, and Dwayne had to concentrate on maintaining his spot at the barricade. He was impressed by the range of ages—lots of grey heads like himself, but many younger adults, and a goodly number of children. He noticed many military folk, in uniform, in the crowd. After the shootings three weeks ago, military personnel had been ordered not to wear uniform in public—but today was different.

Dwayne's daughter Andrea had said that she would be there, but they had not planned to meet, as she would come straight from her office. Andrea's son Trevor, his grandson, had been deployed to the Middle East conflict zone just four weeks ago, and he knew it would mean a lot to her to be at the ceremony.

Dwayne was proud of his grandson. Trevor had not had an easy childhood, with his single mother trying hard to raise him and hold down a job, too. Dwayne and Elizabeth had helped and supported where they could, but they had tried to hold back as much as possible.

Trevor was not very interested in pure academic studies, but was heavily into mechanical and electronic devices. He had found his element as an avionics tech in the Air Force. When Trevor had first told them about his plans to join up, Dwayne had had misgivings, but he had soon come to realize that it was a good career choice.

Dwayne caught the sound of a distant drumbeat; the parade was on its way. He shook his body inside his coat, stamped his feet, and prepared himself.

He had not always come to this annual remembrance ceremony at the National War Memorial; it was only in recent years that he had felt a strong obligation to do so. Dwayne's own immediate family had had no connection with the military; earlier generations had all been associated with the farming business in the upper Ottawa River valley.

Dwayne was the first breakaway, having come to Ottawa on a whim, joining the Public Service as an accountant. There were some distant cousins in Britain who had served in World War Two, but that was all, until his grandson joined the Royal Canadian Air Force two years ago.

But as Dwayne stood there on this November morning, his mind went back, as it did every year, to that remarkable sequence of events that had changed his view of the world forever, to the miraculous survival of Dana Munro, and the tragic loss of her comrades.

Dwayne watched intently as the parade approached the National War Memorial and the waiting crowds. The band led, followed by the Military College Cadets, regular and reserve Armed Forces, the RCMP, and finally, platoons of youth in the Cadet programs. It took some considerable time to assemble all these units into position around the square.

Dwayne realized that his left foot was tingling. He stamped it on the ground and alternated pressure on both feet, bending his legs; this had the desired effect of getting the circulation going again.

The skirl of the pipes caught his attention. The veterans' parade was on its way. As they passed by, some two or three hundred of them, he was taken by the stoic expressions on their faces, so many of them determined to march tall and upright; but it pained him to note that some of them were so frail. And what stories might they tell.

The memory of that vagrant fellow who had stood by him earlier came back to him—what was his story, what had brought him to that sorry, filthy, alcoholic state? Dwayne shuddered involuntarily.

The dignitaries were arriving. Today's special guest, the Princess Royal, Princess Anne, accompanied by the Governor-General, after receiving the salute, chatted briefly with disabled veterans near the Cenotaph. There was an expectant atmosphere in the crowd. The flags that had been hanging limp earlier in the morning were now flying free in a light breeze. Dwayne stamped his feet again and checked his coat collar. He was surrounded by a respectful, friendly crowd.

Dwayne's thoughts drifted back to his youth; he was fourteen when the Korean War started—yes, he remembered how he and his pals were impressed when that tough Johnny Heidegger from the farm up along the old forced road in the Valley had joined the Army. But he was never the same when he came back from Korea—he had had a pretty rough time. His life was destroyed, he was a wreck.

Why do ethnic quarrels devolve into such vicious conflicts? pondered Dwayne, as his gaze wandered over the assembled crowd. *I suppose it isn't fundamentally different from much smaller conflicts back at home,* he rationalized, *like when those townhouses were built near the Gardens.*

Some of the comments made by normally sedate neighbours had been extremely vicious, inflammatory, and accusatory, he remembered. *Just let the situation escalate many times, throw in money, politics, wealth, and poverty, and what have you got?* he thought. *War.*

The band's opening notes of the National Anthem were picked up by the people around him as they all joined in to sing. Then the trumpet call, the Last Post, sent shivers down his spine as the crowd fell silent.

The Peace Tower clock began to strike eleven, and in the distance, he heard the first gun salute.

―――

The haunting sounds from the lone piper, as he played the Lament, carried Dwayne's thoughts back to that solemn and sad memorial ceremony for Dana, believed at the time to have been killed. It was truly when his understanding and appreciation of what is meant by 'sacrifice' deepened, and when he resolved never to miss this Remembrance Parade, so long as his body allowed him.

Another shiver ran through him as the words of the Act of Remembrance were spoken: *"They shall grow not old, as we that are left grow old …"*

―――

Dwayne wiped away the tears that had formed at the corners of his eyes as the rabbi had pronounced a stirring and uplifting benediction at the end of the ceremony. He had stood firm during the Royal Anthem, but now he had to give in. Emotion took hold of him. He thought of his grandson Trevor, far away, in potential danger; he thought of those men and women who had, in fact, lost their lives in that far-away conflict in Afghanistan; he thought of the fallen in wars long ago; he wondered about Hal, named by that vagrant earlier that morning …

He turned, not sure for a moment where he was going. The crowds were too thick for him to go up to see the new additions at the War Memorial; that would have to wait for another day.

He had been standing for almost three hours; he suddenly realized that he was cold, stiff, his back was aching, and he needed a hot drink. His mind was focussing now on immediate bodily needs, and his stride picked up.

Suddenly he felt a vibration and heard his cell-phone ringing. He fumbled to find it deep in an inside pocket.

"Hello?"

"Dad, it's me. Where are you?" The voice was trembling—it was his daughter.

"Hi, Andrea. I'm just leaving the Cenotaph. Are you okay? Where are you?"

"I'm not okay, Dad—it's Trevor—he's been wounded. I just got word. I can't get hold of Mom—she's not answering the phone …"

Dwayne's pulse had suddenly sky-rocketed—he felt unwell. But his daughter was crying—she needed help.

"Love, where are you now? There's nothing you can do for Trevor right now, so try to be calm. Can you go to our house and see if your Mom is there and okay? I'll meet you there as soon as I can."

"Yes, Dad, I'm still at the office, but I'll go to your place. Oh Dad, I'm so worried."

"Go carefully, dear. I'll see you there."

He closed the phone and put it in his pocket. The world about him was spinning, it was going grey ... black ...

Dwayne could hear the sounds of voices. He opened his eyes to find faces in front of him—above him, he quickly realized.

"You're okay, sir. I'm Jonathan; I'm a paramedic. You've just had a faint, here on the sidewalk. You're going to be fine. There's an ambulance on its way. We'll check you out. Does anything hurt? There is someone here who knows you."

Dwayne was still puzzling over what had happened.

"Hi, Mr Hampden, it's Dana Munro. I hadn't expected to see you—and definitely not in this way. But I'm glad I am here. You're in good hands."

Dwayne tried to ease himself into a sitting position. The paramedic helped him, cautiously. Dana lowered herself to a squatting position.

"Dana—Dana, this is a surprise." He looked up at her, in uniform, trim and smart. He smiled. "I'm not sure I would have recognized you."

"No, you've rarely seen me dressed like this." She grinned. She turned. "Tony is here too."

Dwayne looked up. There stood Tony in a smart overcoat. He smiled.

Suddenly, Dwayne remembered what he had been doing, and tried to get up. The paramedic gently dissuaded him. "Steady on, Mr Hampden, you've had a fall. Just wait till the ambulance gets here in a moment."

"But I've just had a call from my daughter. She needs me. My grandson has been wounded, somewhere in the Middle East."

"Oh! May I call her back, Mr Hampden?" Dana asked. "Tony and I will do whatever we can to help."

"But …" Dwayne realized that he was not feeling as well as he should be. He fumbled for his cell-phone. "It's the last number that just called me," he said.

Dana took the phone, stood up, and moved a slight distance away. Dwayne could vaguely hear her voice.

As Dana, Tony, and Dwayne approached the door of the Hampden residence, it opened and Elizabeth came out toward them. "Look at you, Dwayne, you're all of a mess. Come on in, all of you; come and get warmed up. My word, Dana—you are an angel to bring him home—oh, hi, and Tony, too. Come on through, never mind about shoes.

"Let's get your coat off, Dwayne … Here, give it to me. Sit down in your chair. Oh, Dana, Tony, make yourselves at home. What can I get you? Dwayne, you'll want a hot drink. You must all be starved. I knew I couldn't stand that long, but Father here insisted he could. Tea, coffee, Dana, Tony, or something stronger?

"Oh, here's someone else coming to the door—oh, it's Andrea. Did you not see her at the ceremony, Dwayne? Hi, dear, come on in, we've got a houseful. Your dad had a bit of a turn, and luckily Dana and Tony here were nearby and have brought him home. They called me—lucky, 'cause I'd just come back from visiting next door." She finally paused, enough for Andrea to put in a few words.

"Mom, I've been trying to call you—Trevor has been wounded—I got word this morning—I got hold of Dad on his cell, but I couldn't get you."

"What—oh no—the poor boy. Is he going to be okay? Is it bad? Oh, I have to sit down. Oh my, all this at once." She sat awkwardly on an upright chair. Andrea was in tears again, but she moved over to reassure her mother. Dwayne was still sitting, a blank look on his face.

Dana looked at Tony. "Help me in the kitchen. We need to get them some drinks. They need a few moments together."

Quietly, Dana and Tony moved into the kitchen. Dana found some coffee to put in the basket while Tony put water into the coffee pot that sat on the counter. Dana was relieved that the controls were simple.

"It'll just take a few minutes. Do you see any mugs or cups?"

"Over here." Tony brought back five mugs.

The coffee pot was brewing. Dana put her arms round Tony and laid her head on his shoulder. His hand came up to caress her hair.

"It never gets any easier," she said softly, as tears welled up.

Tony held Dana tight. He knew that she needed reassurance herself at this point; she felt deeply about all the casualties in the Afghan and Middle East conflicts, and especially those caused by IEDs. There were times even now when she woke at night, shaking and sobbing—fighting down images from the tragedy that she alone had miraculously survived.

She still grieved the loss of her comrades, her crew in that exploded vehicle. She and Tony had visited all their families; each visit was different, each difficult in its own way, but appreciated by the families.

But, as Tony knew, the terrors, the fractured images and sounds, the memories of her own ordeal, did not go away. She still suffered from that trauma. She had sought help, but the little help there was at the time had not been enough. Consequently, her career had suffered, and even now she was not reaching her full potential.

The recent shooting at the War Memorial had reawakened her terrors, and she and Tony had spent several difficult, unsettling nights in recent weeks. She was not alone. Tony had heard that others too were struggling.

"Thanks so much for being an angel, Dana; I don't know what would have happened with Dad if you and Tony had not been close by to help him." At this point, Andrea was at last able to compose herself.

Dana knew Andrea was about fifteen years older than she was, but the stress of the morning made it seem like she was much older. They were all crowded into the Hampdens' living room. Tony was sitting near the fireplace, chatting with Dwayne and Elizabeth. Andrea and Dana were standing near the doorway to the kitchen, sipping from their mugs of coffee.

"Yes, it was lucky; we saw the sudden cluster of people and the paramedics running over—it was just a little way in front of us. I think it was probably the combination of cold, hunger, thirst, weariness, and the shock of hearing about your son. He seems okay now. I am so sorry about your son, though. What have you heard?"

"That he has been wounded, is comfortable, and is going to be okay. I don't know anything more at this stage. Don't even know where."

"I know it'll be hard for you, but be positive, and patient. Those words are encouraging. They wouldn't have said that if it were not so. At this stage, they may still be assessing the full situation. Do you know when it happened?"

"No, they didn't say."

"Hmm. They probably don't want to give out info potentially useful to the enemy. Do you have more family?"

"No, Trevor is my only child. His father left us not long after Trevor was born, and has never contacted us since. I've no idea where he might be. And no interest."

"I'm so sorry, I …"

"Dana, Andrea, come and join us here by the fire." Dwayne was clearly feeling brighter as he waved them over.

"It's so nice to see you both, even though it is in such an unexpected way," said Elizabeth, looking toward Dana and Tony. "You must have such busy lives, you young couples."

"You're darn right." Dana laughed. "Too busy at times. I'm at NDHQ right now; job's reasonably interesting, but demanding."

"What about you, Tony?" asked Dwayne.

"I'm a technician at the Rehab Centre at the General Hospital on Smyth. I find it really interesting and worthwhile. We get quite a lot of wounded soldiers come through, as well as industrial accident victims."

"And Tony volunteers at one of the shelters," added Dana.

"You mean, where the street people and homeless go?" asked Andrea.

"Yeah, it's quite a challenge, but I feel good about it."

"Had a strange fellow come up beside me this morning, before the crowds came," put in Dwayne. "He stank to high heaven—it made me feel quite uneasy—but he had come to pay his respects at the Cenotaph. He stood in silence, and then spoke out loud to the memory of someone he called Hal. He had old, decrepit, army-style clothing, and a beret with a badge on."

"Was his hair grizzly and grey? About five foot six, stocky?" asked Tony.

"Yes, I would say so. He had a haversack across his shoulder, and a mickey flask."

"That was Robert. I know Robert; he comes to our shelter once in a while. Sad case. Hal was his best friend in Vietnam, blown up right beside him. Robert has never been right since—PTSD—shell-shock.

"Don't know how he ended up in Ottawa. He's never been able to hold down a job for long, has lived on the street for years; it's amazing how he has survived so long, but he has. When he comes to the shelter, if I'm there, I always sit and talk with him—he reminds me so much of someone I knew long ago."

Dana looked over to Tony—his eyes were watering. She put her hand on his arm; she knew he was thinking of Albert, and his own time on the street.

"Do you help at the 'Mission', where that gunman who shot the sentinel guard had stayed?" asked Dwayne. "That was a terrible goings-on."

"No, it's another one further out from downtown," replied Tony.

"Mom, do you mind? I'm just going into the kitchen to put the radio on for a few minutes, to catch the news." Andrea stood.

"Why, dear—oh, yes, of course, dear."

Dana guessed that Elizabeth had realized Andrea's concern for news of Trevor.

Andrea returned a few minutes later, tears streaming down her face again. They all turned to her.

"There's been another shooting; that must be how Trevor was hurt. It was at the barracks in Kuwait where he is staying. Apparently, a lone gunman infiltrated the area, and managed to shoot four airmen before someone got him. Thank goodness no one was killed. They've got the gunman alive, this time."

"Come sit down again, dear," Elizabeth soothed. "There's nothing more you can do right now. Trevor is going to be all right, don't you worry."

It was late afternoon when Dana and Tony left the Hampdens' house in Brewster Gardens. As they walked to their car, Dana looked up. "It's ages since we were last here; let's just wander over by the Centre."

"Sure." Tony nodded. He realized that he had not been back to the area for a very long time. His last visits to his old home had indeed not been pleasant.

Much had happened since those days of their youth. Dana's parents, not long after Dana and her brother Iain had left home, had moved into a small apartment condo downtown, partly, Tony rationalized, to get away from the scene of the tragedy of Bryce's death. But Tony and Dana often visited her parents, and had kept in touch with Iain and Tracey and their kids, now in Calgary.

Tony's own family had basically disintegrated; the younger ones, Angelo and Roberta, had left home and gone their separate ways—Tony rarely heard from them. Gina did keep in touch a few times a year, but she had a partner, and was living in Toronto, now. His parents had never made Tony and Dana welcome when they had tried to visit.

Dana had been posted across the country a couple of times, to Edmonton and to Gagetown. Tony was still in training during the Alberta stint, and they had found that separation hard. But he was fully qualified during the Gagetown posting, and he'd found a job in Fredericton, not too far away.

As they approached the Hennigan Centre, the door opened and Kelly Carson stepped out.

"Hey Kelly," called Dana. "Long time—no see!"

Kelly, surprised, looked over, instantly recognizing the pair. "You don't say. Great to see you. What brings you here?"

They exchanged hugs. Dana quickly explained the incident with Dwayne.

"Dwayne and Liz—they're such a nice couple," noted Kelly. "Say, I'd love to ask you round for a longer chat, but Mike has the kids over at his mum's, and I promised I'd be there by five. But, you two, you're looking good. Smart uniform, Dana."

"Thanks. Can't complain." Dana grinned. "How is this place doing?" She nodded toward the Centre.

"Doing okay. I suppose you know that Dave Adkins left us a year and a half ago to go to be administrator at a Sportsplex north of Toronto—it was a big step-up for him, so you can't blame him. Mike and I now run the Centre on a part-time basis—we have a Board of Directors that runs the trust. You know that George Simpson passed away …"

"Yes, that was really sad news—and it was at a time when I just could not take leave to come back to Ottawa."

"Look, now that you're back in town, do come and visit with us. I really must dash now. Great to see you both."

"Bye, Kelly." Tony grinned. Dana waved.

"Let's go along the old track," said Dana, reaching for Tony's hand. "I need some peace."

They walked along in silence. Over the years, the underbrush had grown considerably—some of the bushes were now overhanging the trail, such that Tony had to make quite an effort to brush them away.

They reached the old bridge pier, and stood watching the water swirl over the stones below.

Dana turned toward Tony. The late afternoon sun lit up the wisps of her hair that were now escaping her regulation military bun. A feeling of great warmth spread over him. They were together; through trials, through tribulations, through tragedies, through triumphs, they were together.

He marvelled at her beauty, at her class, at her poise—standing there in her uniform. There was no need for words, just their love for each other, as they embraced. He just knew—she was his angel in blue jeans.

ABOUT THE AUTHOR

Richard Coles and his family survived when their home was badly damaged by enemy bomb debris during World War II two weeks after his birth in England. He graduated from the University of Liverpool with a Physics degree, and trained as a teacher at the University of Bristol. He taught at schools in England and, after emigration to Canada with his wife, he taught at a high school in Winnipeg. At the University of Manitoba, he undertook further post-graduate studies.

Coles moved his family to Ottawa to begin a thirty-year career as a research geophysicist and manager with the Federal Government. His volunteer work includes twelve years of youth leadership with Scouts Canada and ten years as a volunteer and Civilian Instructor with a Royal Canadian Army Cadet Corps.

Coles has received the Meritorious Service Medal for his volunteer service with the Royal Canadian Legion. He was honoured to receive the Queen's Diamond Jubilee Medal for service to Canada.

Coles and his wife have recently 'retired' to Victoria, BC, to be closer to their sons and most of their grandchildren.